Krishna

Defender of Dharma

CAMPFIRE®

KALYANI NAVYUG MEDIA PVT LTD

Krishna
Defender of Dharma

SCRIPT **SHWETA TANEJA**

ART **RAJESH NAGULAKONDA**

CONTENT RESEARCH AND DEVELOPMENT **SUKANYA MEHTA**

EDITS **SOURAV DUTTA**

DESKTOP PUBLISHING **BHAVNATH CHAUDHARY**

www.campfire.co.in

Published by Kalyani Navyug Media Pvt Ltd
101 C, Shiv House, Hari Nagar Ashram, New Delhi 110014, India
ISBN: 978-93-80741-12-3

Printed in India

About the author

When I was a child, my grandmother would tell me stories of mighty kings and gods and how they slew one demon after another. Soon, these legends started living in my mind. I would imagine demons coming into my classroom, especially during maths class, and it would be up to me to save my classmates and teacher.

I grew up and became a journalist. I wrote about fashion, health, and other mundane issues, till I got the chance to relive a story from my childhood – the legend of Krishna. While researching for and writing this book, I delved into its fabulous world. I became all the characters I wrote about, and I had all their adventures.

I live in Bangalore where I work as a technology journalist and novelist. When I am not writing, I like to create stories about the people I see around me, with a steaming hot cup of green tea to help me keep imagining.

– **Shweta Taneja**

About the artist

Lines and colours have been a part of my life right from my childhood in my hometown of Chirala, Andhra Pradesh. My grandfather was a goldsmith and my father a printer. Both of them influenced me to take up art as a career.

I believe in instinct rather than education. I mostly spend my time alone trying to explore different forms of art, such as sculpture, nail art on paper, metal engraving, and of course, painting.

I live in Delhi with my wife and two daughters...

...and with dreams of becoming a versatile artist.

– **Rajesh Nagulakonda**

Krishna: The Legend

In Indian thought and philosophy, the notion of avatar has a unique significance. It is believed that when evil becomes irrepressible, god comes to earth in the human form to rid it of evil. And it is Vishnu, the Preserver of all creation in the Hindu Trinity of Godhead, who takes on different avatars to protect mankind and all creation from destruction. One such avatar, it is believed, was Krishna.

The literal meaning of the name Krishna is 'black'. Traditionally, he is thought to have had a 'bluish black' complexion. Krishna also means 'attractive' – one who draws others to himself. In fact, in all visual depiction of Krishna, his bewitching, mesmerising quality is most prominent.

Krishna is a multi-faceted character – in every stage of his life, we see a different persona. While as a child, he was endearingly naughty and playful, in his youth, he became the protector of his village, and later in the battle of Kurukshetra, he emerged as a shrewd strategist. He also acts as Arjuna's philosophical guide in the battle, and his words of wisdom are cited and revered to this day.

In India, Krishna is worshipped in different forms – Orissa worships him as Lord Jagannath, Rajasthan as Shrinaathji, and Maharashtra as Vithoba. In the 16th century, Shri Chaitanya Mahaprabhu started the Bhakti Movement in Bengal centred around devotion and submission

to Krishna. With time, the fervour of the movement spread far and wide, and in 1960, the International Society for Krishna Consciousness (ISKCON) was instituted in New York City. Based on the teachings of the Bhagvad Gita, the popularity and following of this institution is testimony to the universal appeal of Krishna.

Till a few decades back, Dwarka, the city Krishna founded, was thought to be mythical. Since the 1980s, however, archaeological findings off the coast of Gujarat have provided what some claim is proof that a city much like Dwarka did exist. Ancient artefacts, pottery, and ruins of an ancient city were part of the findings.

The qualities of Krishna are inspirational. Following his example is to celebrate life in all its colours – to drown in the gleeful abandon of a child, to seize every moment and live it to the fullest, and to face each challenge with wisdom, verve, and style.

Many festivals in India celebrate events of his life. The colourful rapture of Holi brings us close to the idea of Krishna. In Vrindavan and Brij in Uttar Pradesh, India, the celebration of Holi is the celebration of the love of Krishna and his soulmate Radha. The Govardhan incident is celebrated in the observance of Govardhan Puja. Its significance transcends the merely religious and ritualistic with the message of conserving and protecting the environment. The birth of Krishna is celebrated as Janmashtami. Another important festival, Navratri, is

linked with the story of Krishna in some parts of India, with community dances being organised for nine nights in a row. Quite clearly, the idea of Krishna is deeply embedded in the culture of the country, and in the consciousness of its people.

The devotion, joy, and love for life which Krishna's actions evoke, have inspired poets and writers down the ages. During the Bhakti Movement that swept northern India between the 14th and 16th centuries, poets like Surdas, Raskhan, and Rahim penned beautiful compositions. But whether seen from the devotional perspective or from a prosaic, social standpoint, every facet of Krishna's life not just speaks of universal love and joy, it has a practical message on how to live life as well.

Dharma

The Indian concept of dharma is difficult to translate into English, as its meaning spans the entire range from righteousness to social order. Krishna, in his role as the defender of dharma, eradicates all that is unjust. In the process, he often encourages unfair conduct, but justifies it by saying that such behaviour is sometimes necessary to defeat a greater evil, and that it is in response to deceit that unjust conduct is often resorted to. At one point, Krishna tells the elder Pandava Yudhishthira that sometimes, dharma can only be protected by forgetting it.

Mathura

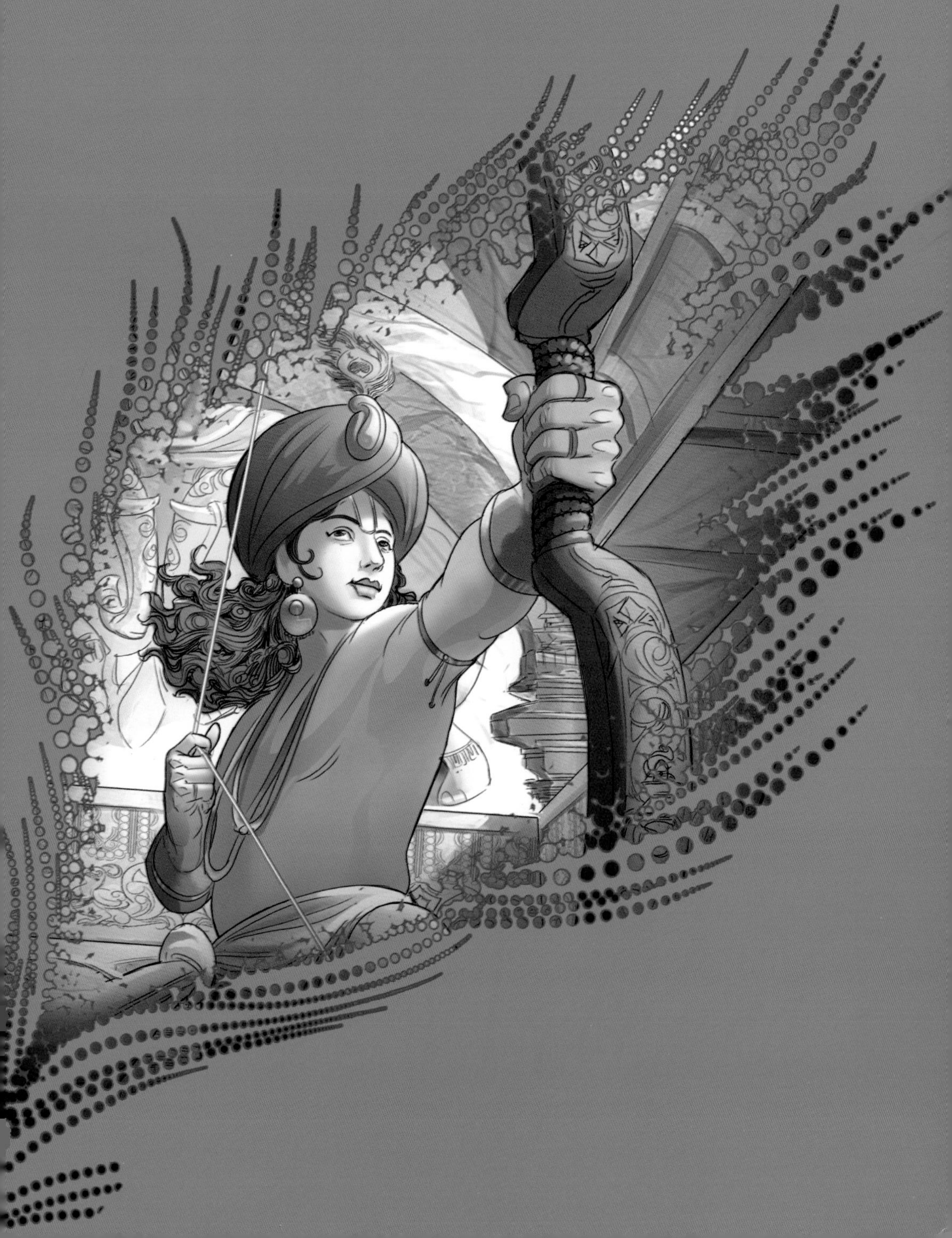

Mathura

The story of Krishna begins in the city of Mathura, the capital of the Surasena kingdom, a stronghold of the Yadava clan. Kansa, who is the reincarnation of the evil demon Kalanemi, has taken over his father King Ugrasena's throne, and has become a tyrant. Filled with arrogance, he has even challenged the mighty Indra, king of heaven. The time has come for Vishnu, the preserver of the universe, to be born and rid the earth of this evil.

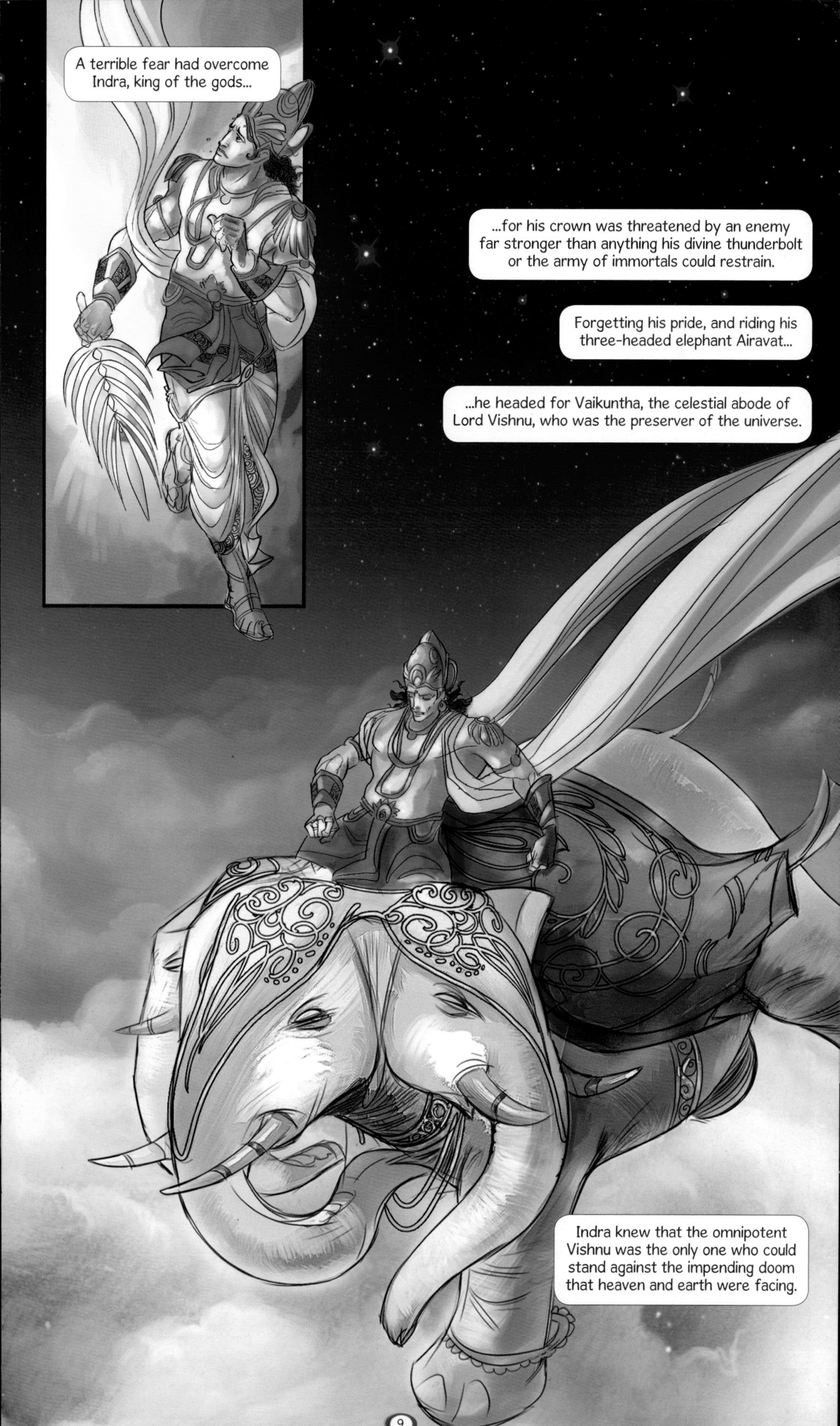
A terrible fear had overcome Indra, king of the gods...
...for his crown was threatened by an enemy far stronger than anything his divine thunderbolt or the army of immortals could restrain.
Forgetting his pride, and riding his three-headed elephant Airavat...
...he headed for Vaikuntha, the celestial abode of Lord Vishnu, who was the preserver of the universe.
Indra knew that the omnipotent Vishnu was the only one who could stand against the impending doom that heaven and earth were facing.

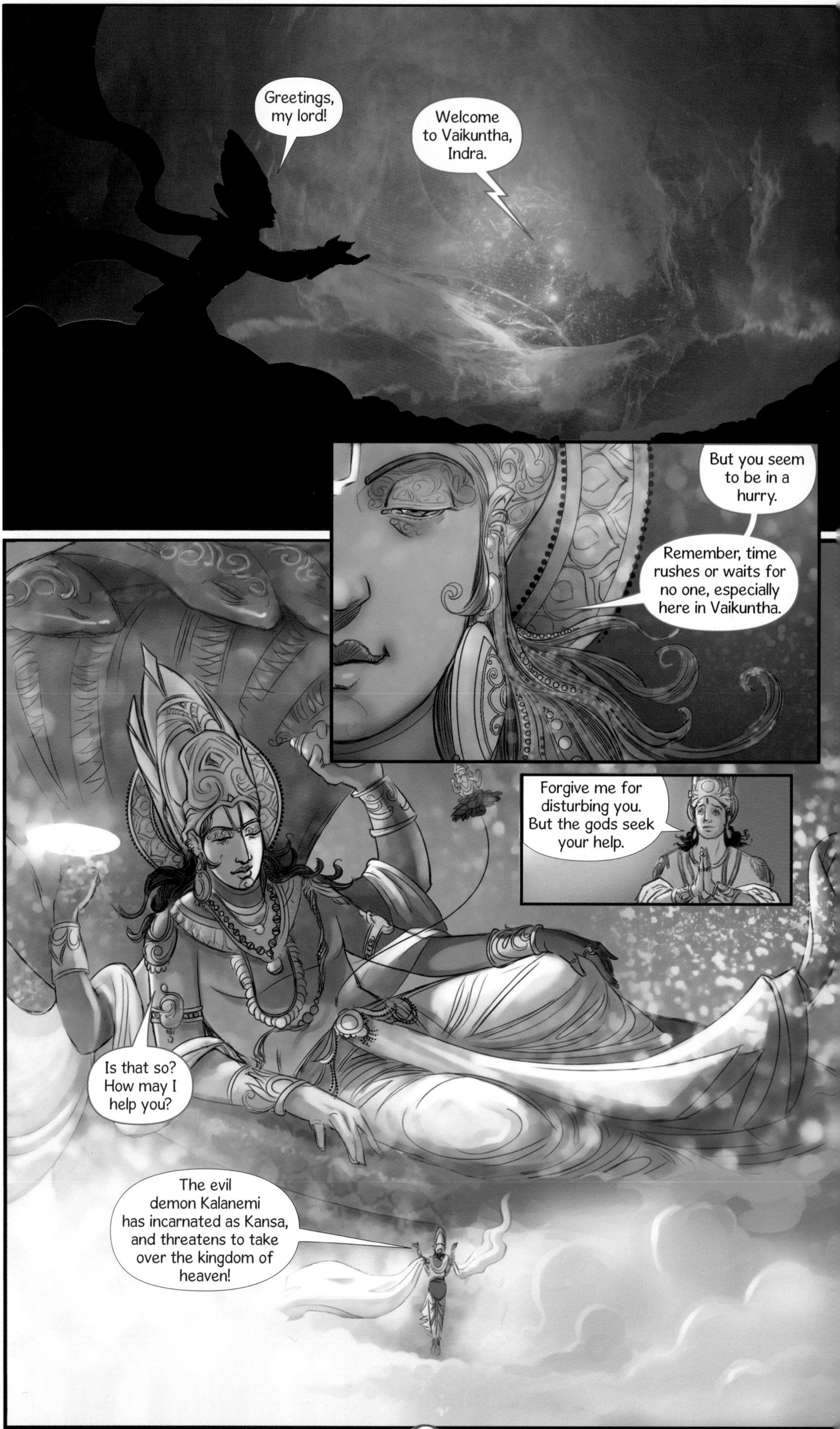

Greetings, my lord!
Welcome to Vaikuntha, Indra.
But you seem to be in a hurry.
Remember, time rushes or waits for no one, especially here in Vaikuntha.
Forgive me for disturbing you. But the gods seek your help.
Is that so? How may I help you?
The evil demon Kalanemi has incarnated as Kansa, and threatens to take over the kingdom of heaven!

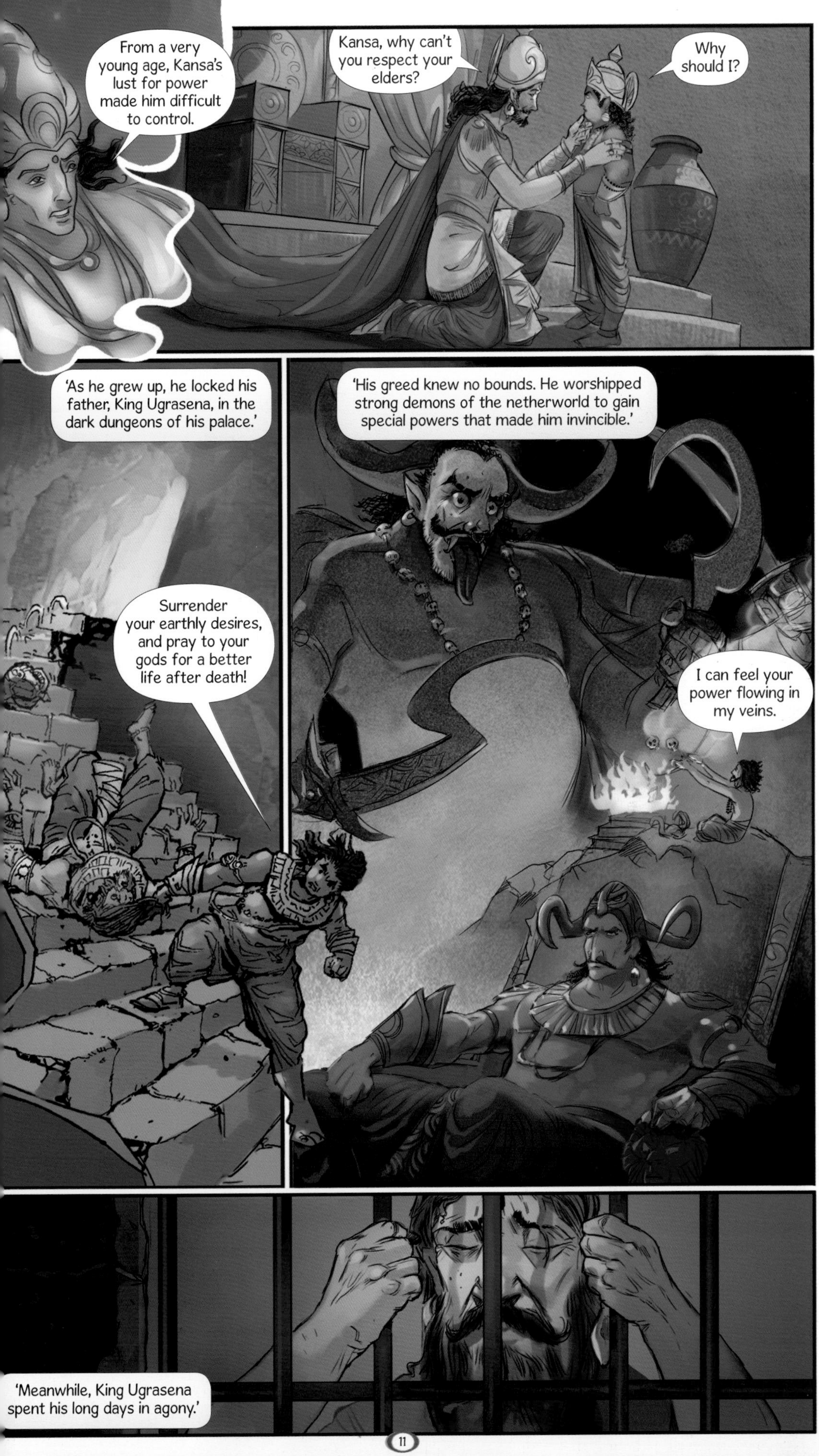
From a very young age, Kansa's lust for power made him difficult to control.
Kansa, why can't you respect your elders?
Why should I?
'As he grew up, he locked his father, King Ugrasena, in the dark dungeons of his palace.'
Surrender your earthly desires, and pray to your gods for a better life after death!
'His greed knew no bounds. He worshipped strong demons of the netherworld to gain special powers that made him invincible.'
I can feel your power flowing in my veins.
'Meanwhile, King Ugrasena spent his long days in agony.'

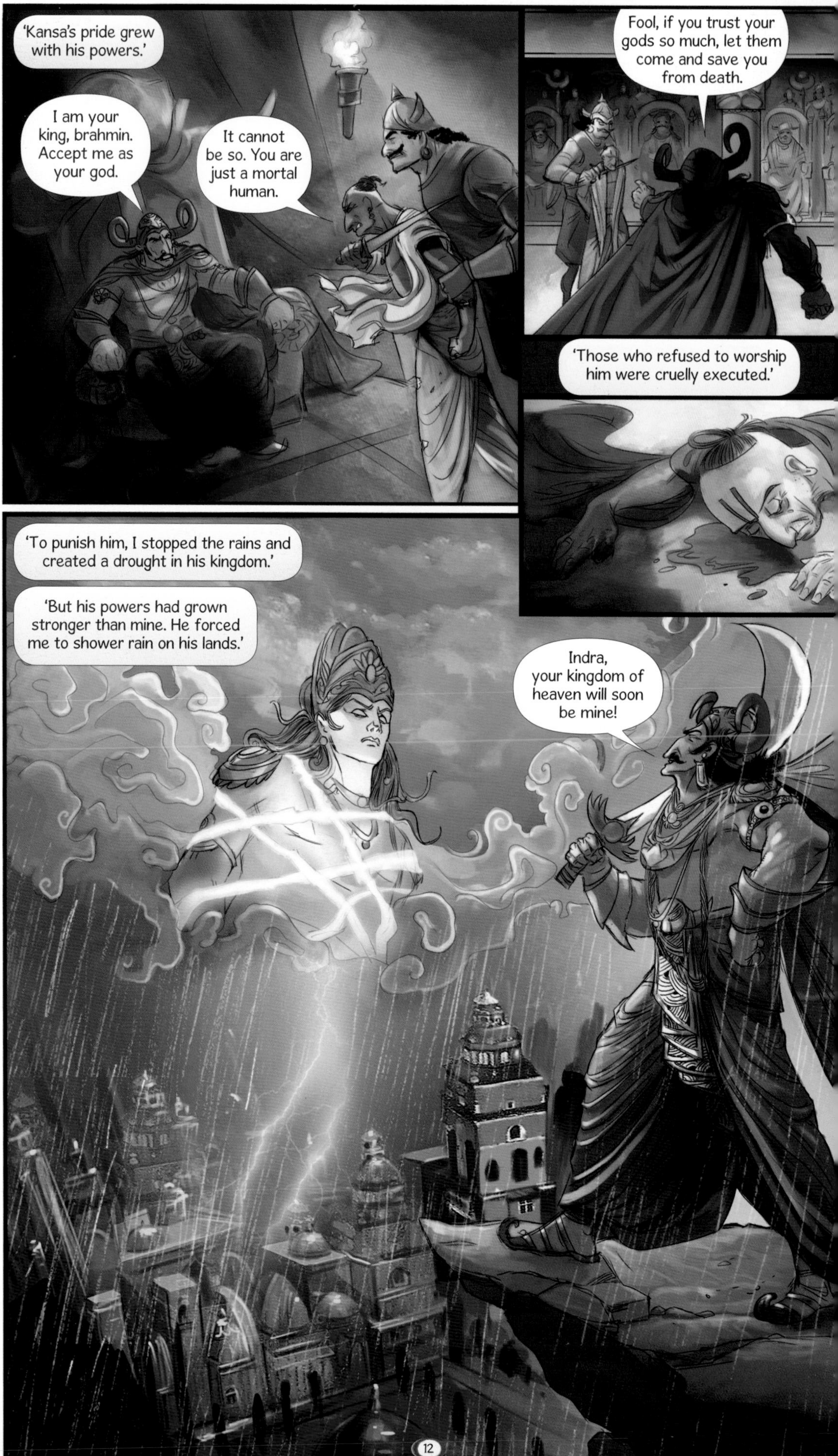
'Kansa's pride grew with his powers.'
I am your king, brahmin. Accept me as your god.
It cannot be so. You are just a mortal human.
Fool, if you trust your gods so much, let them come and save you from death.
'Those who refused to worship him were cruelly executed.'
'To punish him, I stopped the rains and created a drought in his kingdom.'
'But his powers had grown stronger than mine. He forced me to shower rain on his lands.'
Indra, your kingdom of heaven will soon be mine!

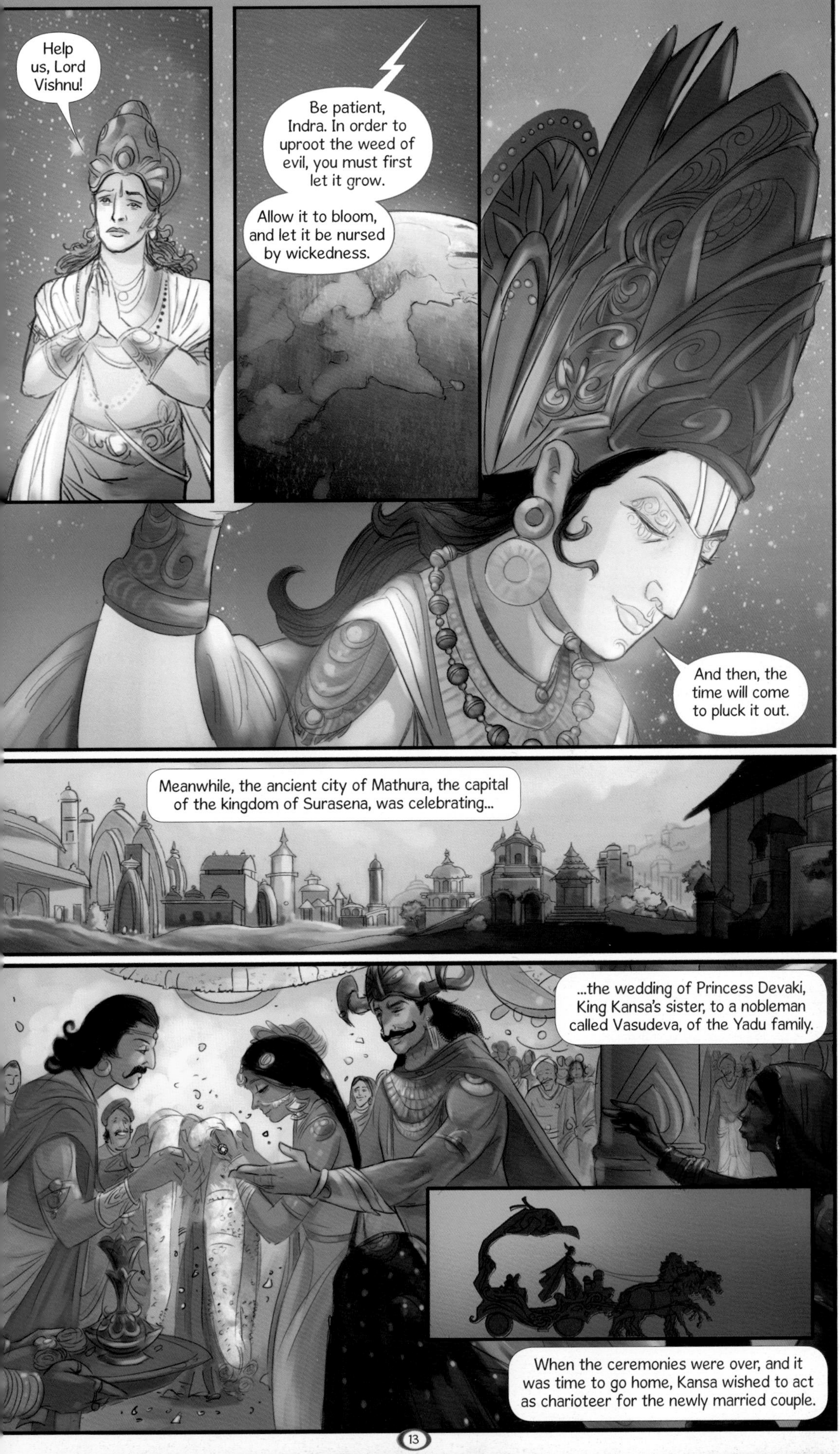
Help us, Lord Vishnu!
Be patient, Indra. In order to uproot the weed of evil, you must first let it grow.
Allow it to bloom, and let it be nursed by wickedness.
And then, the time will come to pluck it out.
Meanwhile, the ancient city of Mathura, the capital of the kingdom of Surasena, was celebrating...
...the wedding of Princess Devaki, King Kansa's sister, to a nobleman called Vasudeva, of the Yadu family.
When the ceremonies were over, and it was time to go home, Kansa wished to act as charioteer for the newly married couple.

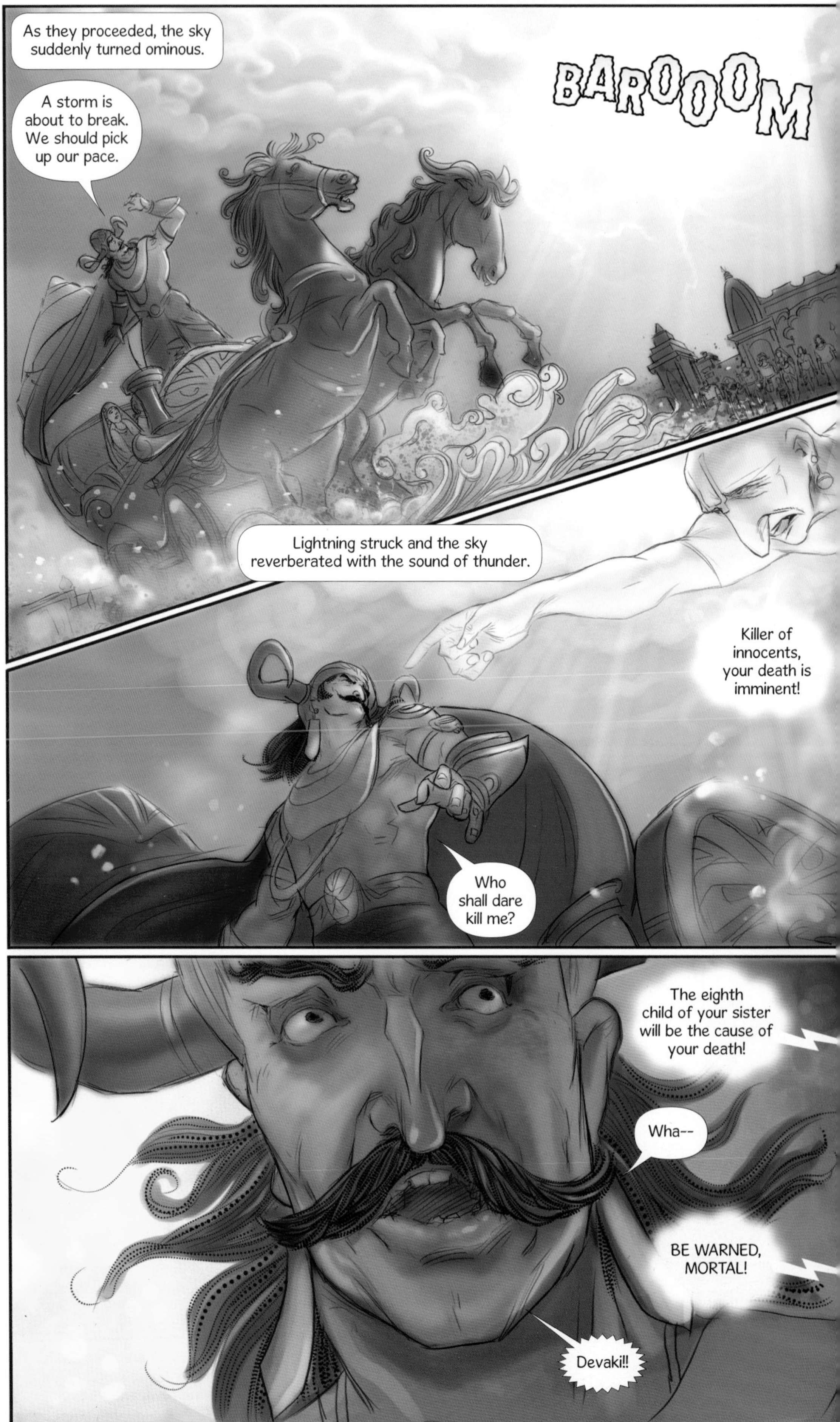
As they proceeded, the sky suddenly turned ominous.
A storm is about to break. We should pick up our pace.
BAROOOM
Lightning struck and the sky reverberated with the sound of thunder.
Killer of innocents, your death is imminent!
Who shall dare kill me?
The eighth child of your sister will be the cause of your death!
Wha--
BE WARNED, MORTAL!
Devaki!!

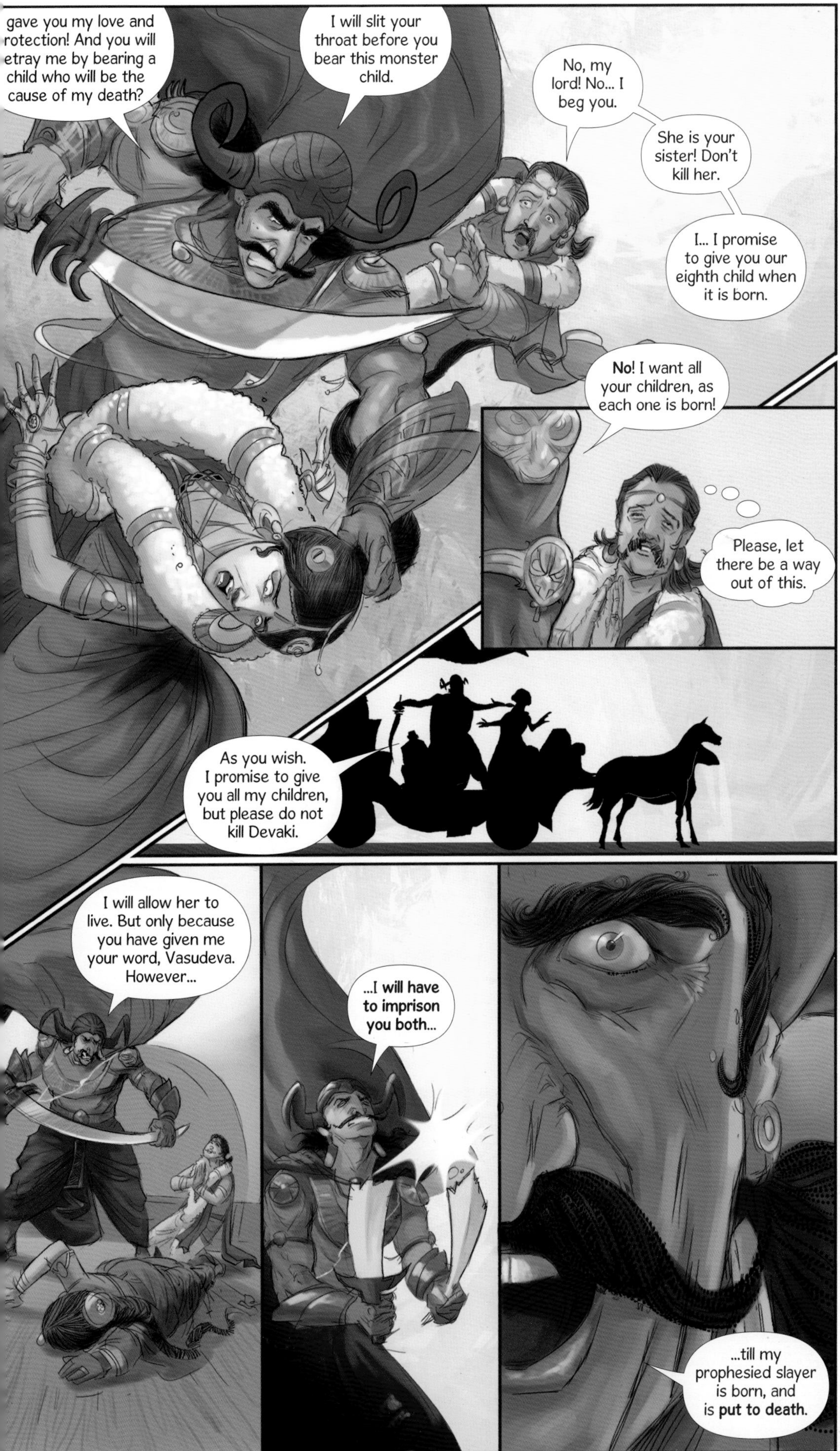
gave you my love and rotection! And you will etray me by bearing a child who will be the cause of my death?
I will slit your throat before you bear this monster child.
No, my lord! No... I beg you.
She is your sister! Don't kill her.
I... I promise to give you our eighth child when it is born.
No! I want all your children, as each one is born!
Please, let there be a way out of this.
As you wish. I promise to give you all my children, but please do not kill Devaki.
I will allow her to live. But only because you have given me your word, Vasudeva. However...
...I will have to imprison you both...
...till my prophesied slayer is born, and is **put to death**.

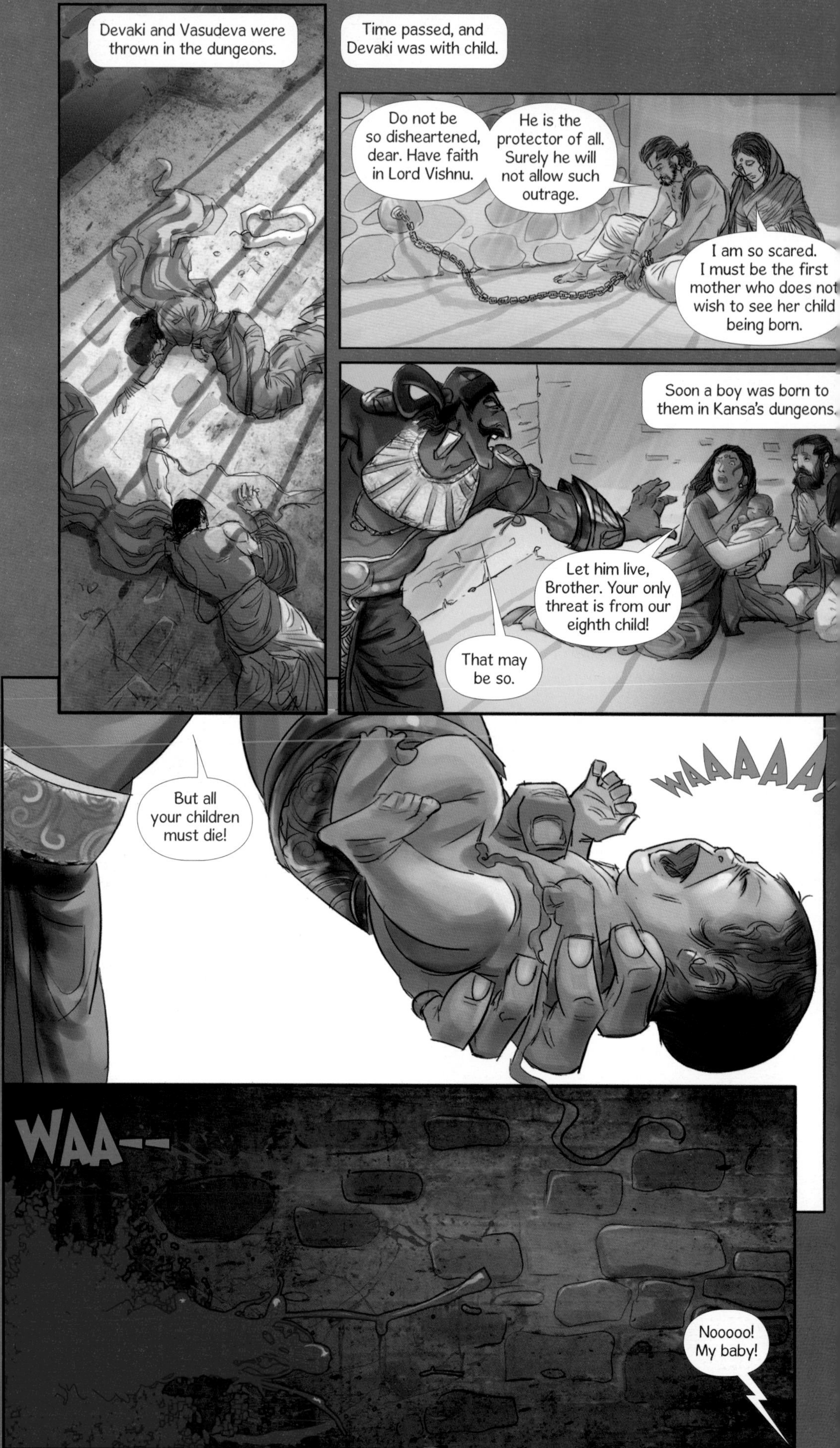
Devaki and Vasudeva were thrown in the dungeons.
Time passed, and Devaki was with child.
Do not be so disheartened, dear. Have faith in Lord Vishnu.
He is the protector of all. Surely he will not allow such outrage.
I am so scared. I must be the first mother who does not wish to see her child being born.
Soon a boy was born to them in Kansa's dungeons.
Let him live, Brother. Your only threat is from our eighth child!
That may be so.
But all your children must die!
WAAAAA!
WAA--
Nooooo! My baby!

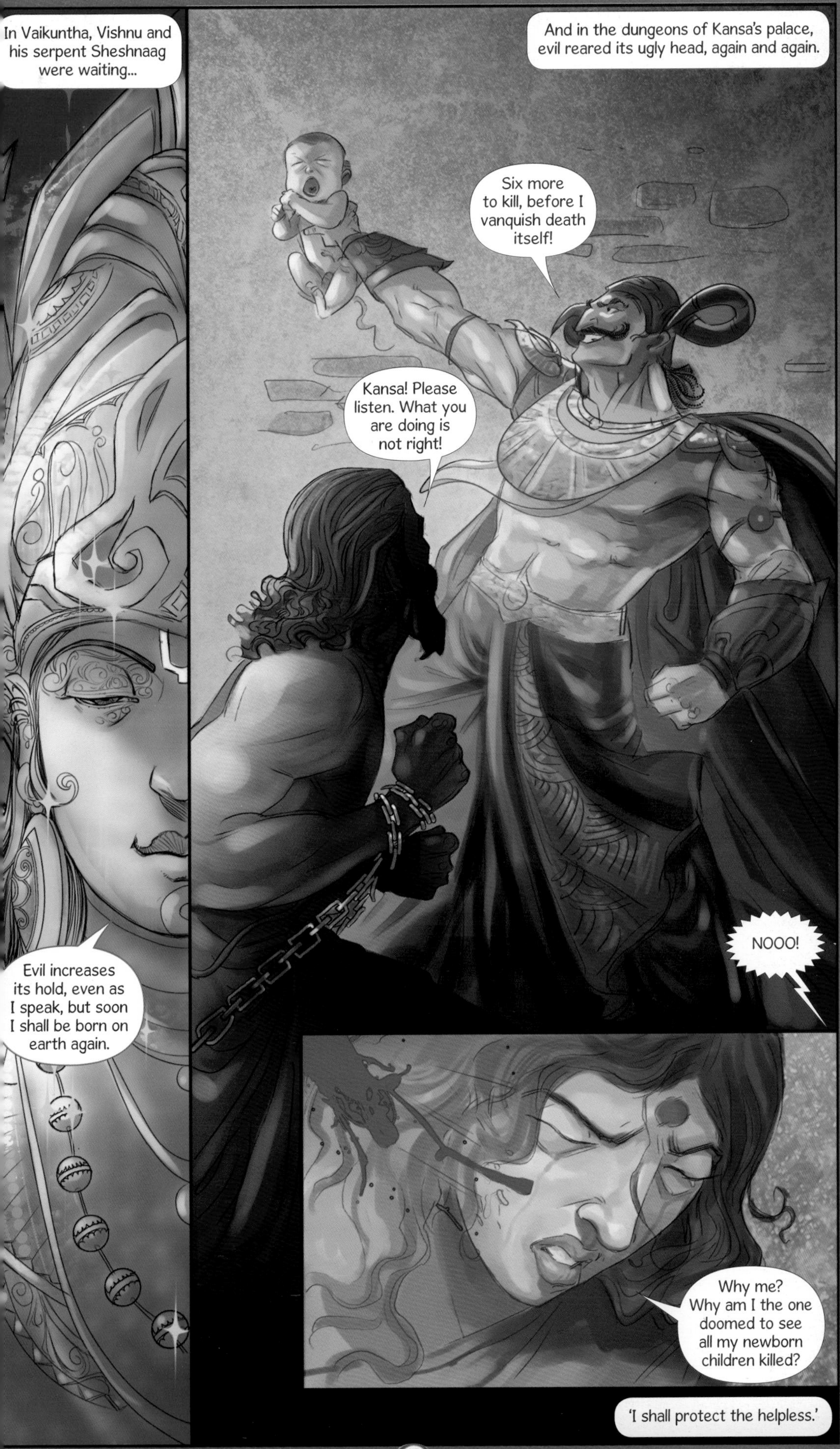

In Vaikuntha, Vishnu and his serpent Sheshnaag were waiting...
Evil increases its hold, even as I speak, but soon I shall be born on earth again.
And in the dungeons of Kansa's palace, evil reared its ugly head, again and again.
Six more to kill, before I vanquish death itself!
Kansa! Please listen. What you are doing is not right!
NOOO!
Why me? Why am I the one doomed to see all my newborn children killed?
'I shall protect the helpless.'

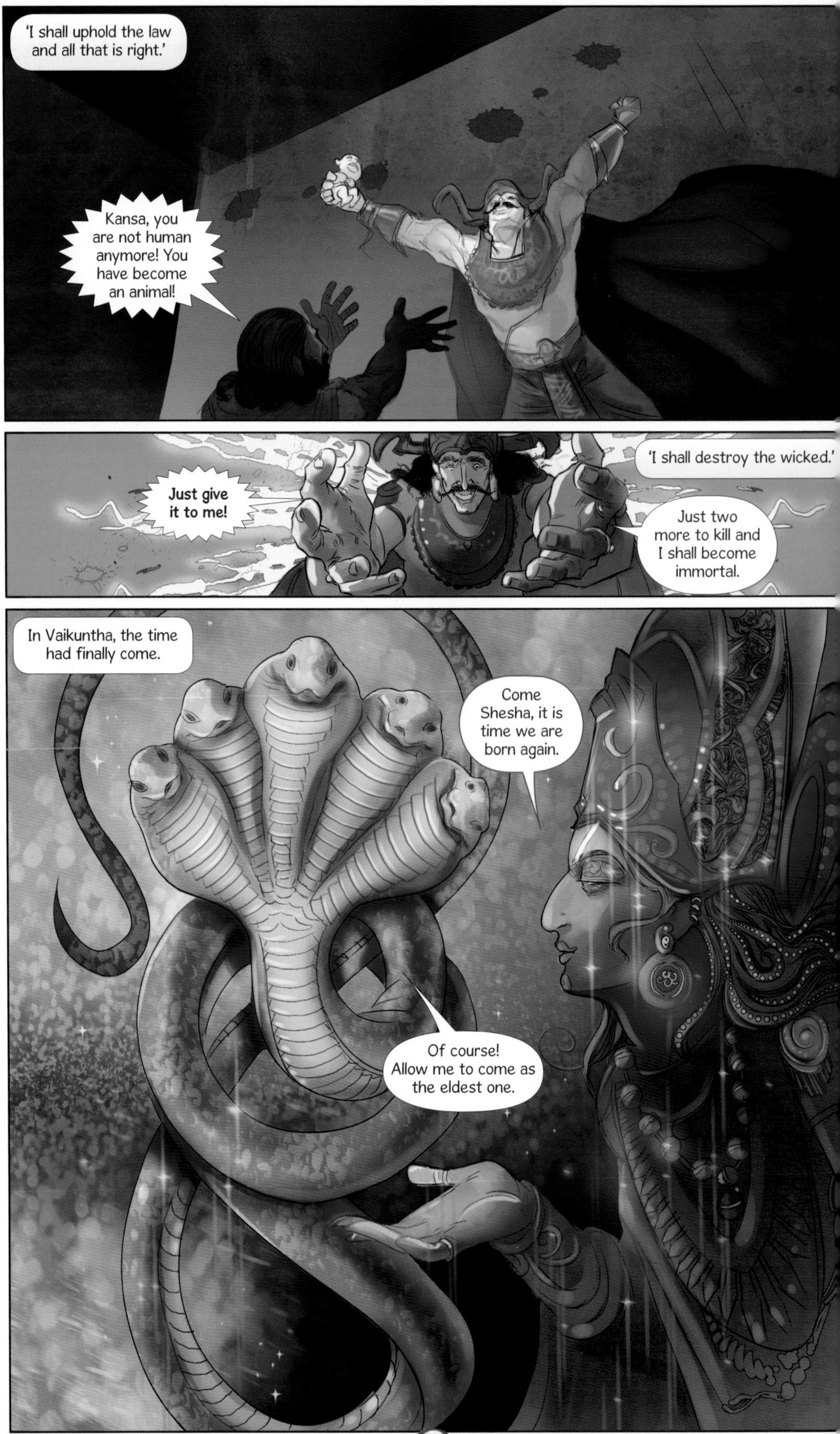
'I shall uphold the law and all that is right.'
Kansa, you are not human anymore! You have become an animal!
Just give it to me!
'I shall destroy the wicked.'
Just two more to kill and I shall become immortal.
In Vaikuntha, the time had finally come.
Come Shesha, it is time we are born again.
Of course! Allow me to come as the eldest one.

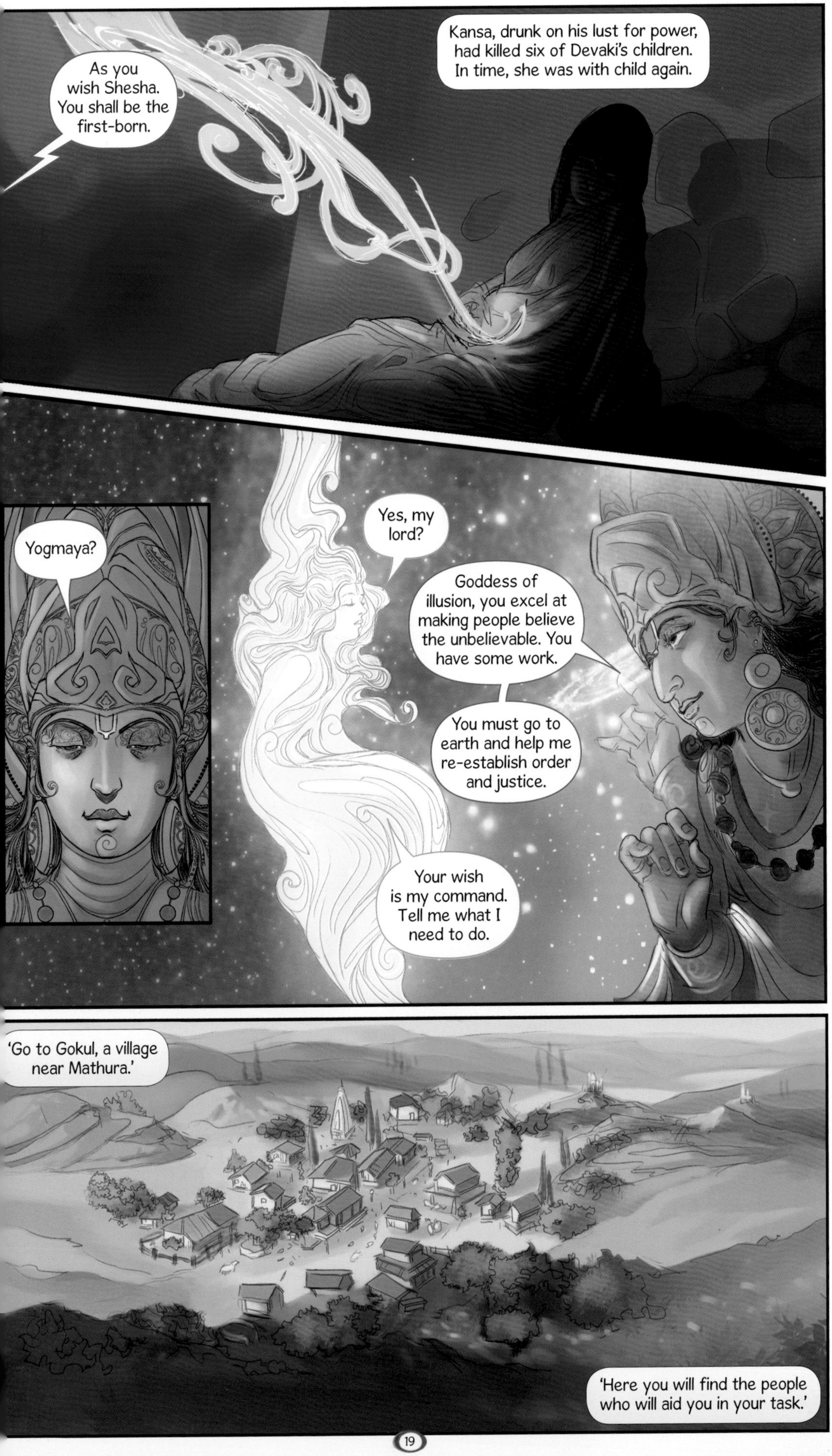
Kansa, drunk on his lust for power, had killed six of Devaki's children. In time, she was with child again.
As you wish Shesha. You shall be the first-born.
Yogmaya?
Yes, my lord?
Goddess of illusion, you excel at making people believe the unbelievable. You have some work.
You must go to earth and help me re-establish order and justice.
Your wish is my command. Tell me what I need to do.
'Go to Gokul, a village near Mathura.'
'Here you will find the people who will aid you in your task.'

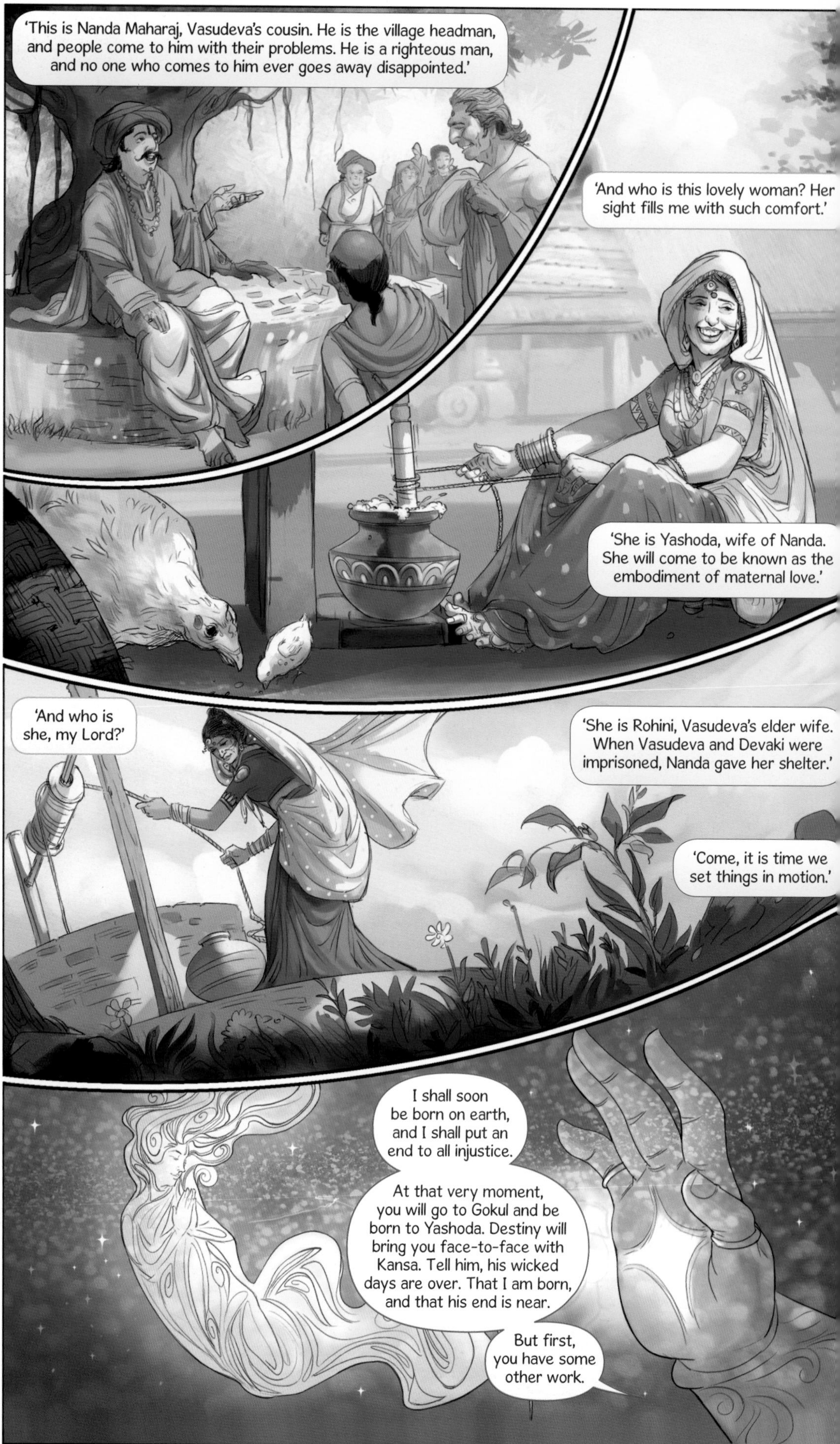
'This is Nanda Maharaj, Vasudeva's cousin. He is the village headman, and people come to him with their problems. He is a righteous man, and no one who comes to him ever goes away disappointed.'
'And who is this lovely woman? Her sight fills me with such comfort.'
'She is Yashoda, wife of Nanda. She will come to be known as the embodiment of maternal love.'
'And who is she, my Lord?'
'She is Rohini, Vasudeva's elder wife. When Vasudeva and Devaki were imprisoned, Nanda gave her shelter.'
'Come, it is time we set things in motion.'
I shall soon be born on earth, and I shall put an end to all injustice.
At that very moment, you will go to Gokul and be born to Yashoda. Destiny will bring you face-to-face with Kansa. Tell him, his wicked days are over. That I am born, and that his end is near.
But first, you have some other work.

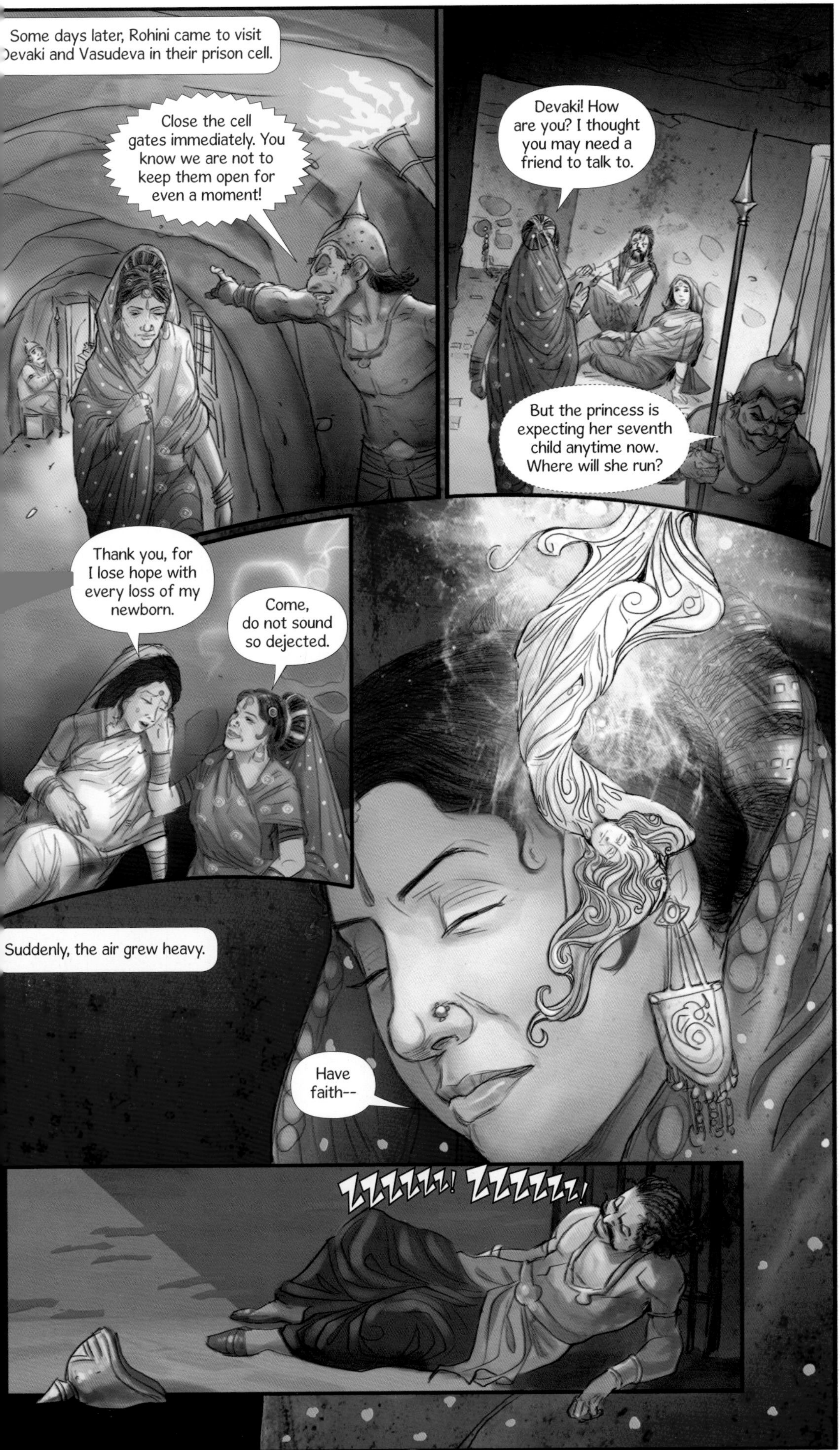
Some days later, Rohini came to visit Devaki and Vasudeva in their prison cell.
Close the cell gates immediately. You know we are not to keep them open for even a moment!
Devaki! How are you? I thought you may need a friend to talk to.
But the princess is expecting her seventh child anytime now. Where will she run?
Thank you, for I lose hope with every loss of my newborn.
Come, do not sound so dejected.
Suddenly, the air grew heavy.
Have faith--
ZZZZZZ! ZZZZZZ!

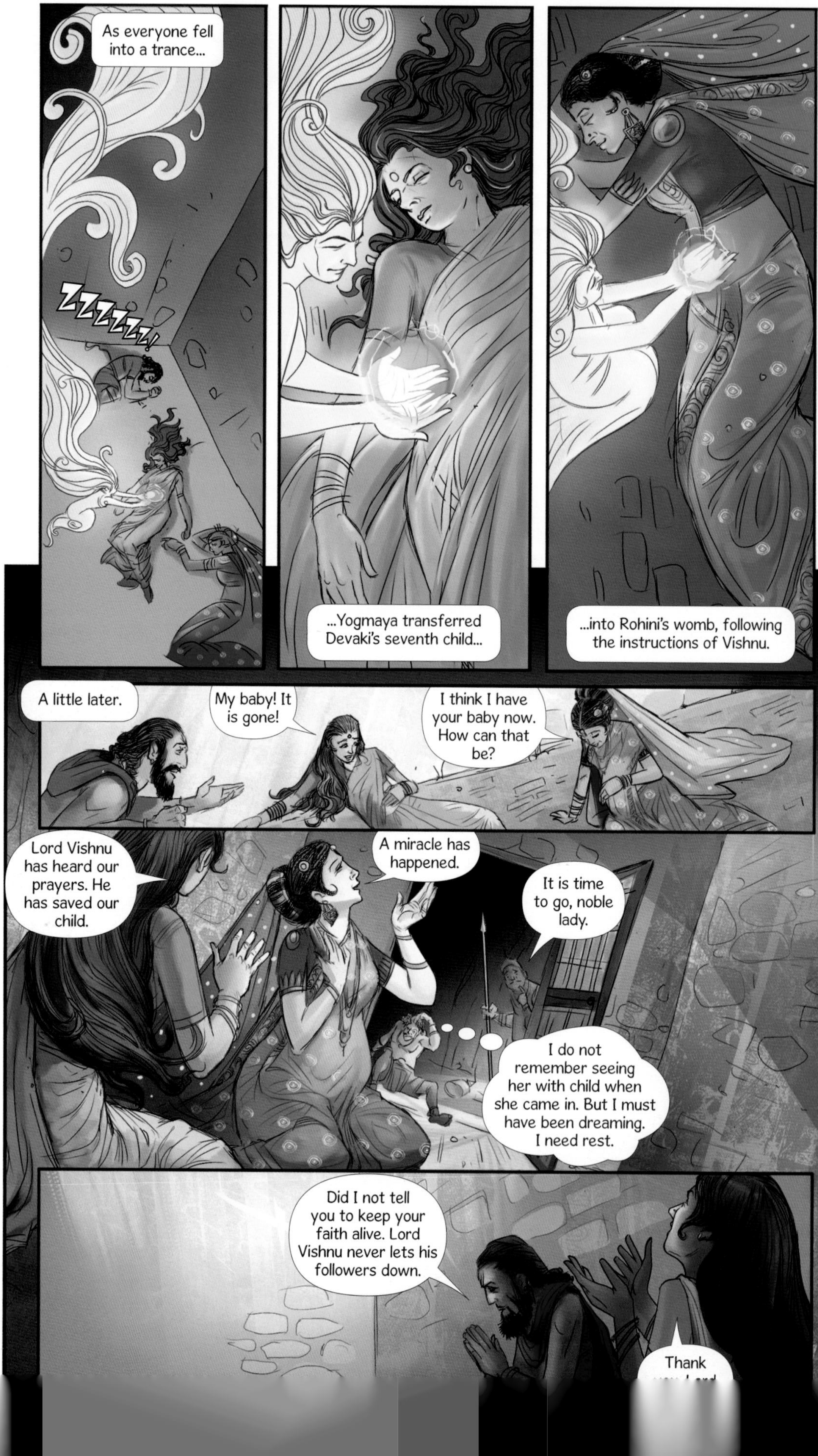
As everyone fell into a trance...
ZZZZZZ!
...Yogmaya transferred Devaki's seventh child...
...into Rohini's womb, following the instructions of Vishnu.
A little later.
My baby! It is gone!
I think I have your baby now. How can that be?
Lord Vishnu has heard our prayers. He has saved our child.
A miracle has happened.
It is time to go, noble lady.
I do not remember seeing her with child when she came in. But I must have been dreaming. I need rest.
Did I not tell you to keep your faith alive. Lord Vishnu never lets his followers down.
Thank

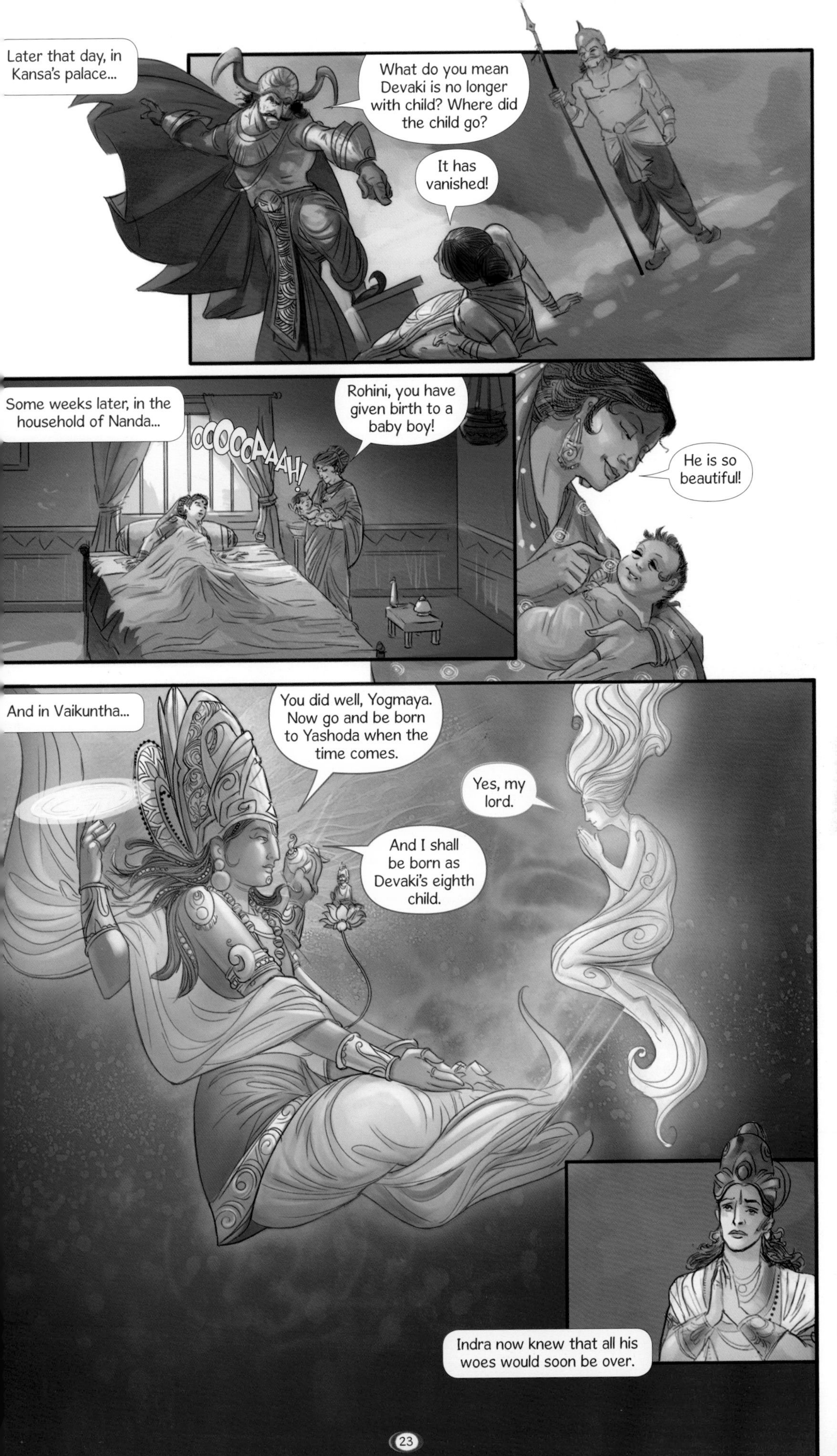
Later that day, in Kansa's palace...
What do you mean Devaki is no longer with child? Where did the child go?
It has vanished!
Some weeks later, in the household of Nanda...
Rohini, you have given birth to a baby boy!
OOOOOAAAH!
He is so beautiful!
And in Vaikuntha...
You did well, Yogmaya. Now go and be born to Yashoda when the time comes.
Yes, my lord.
And I shall be born as Devaki's eighth child.
Indra now knew that all his woes would soon be over.

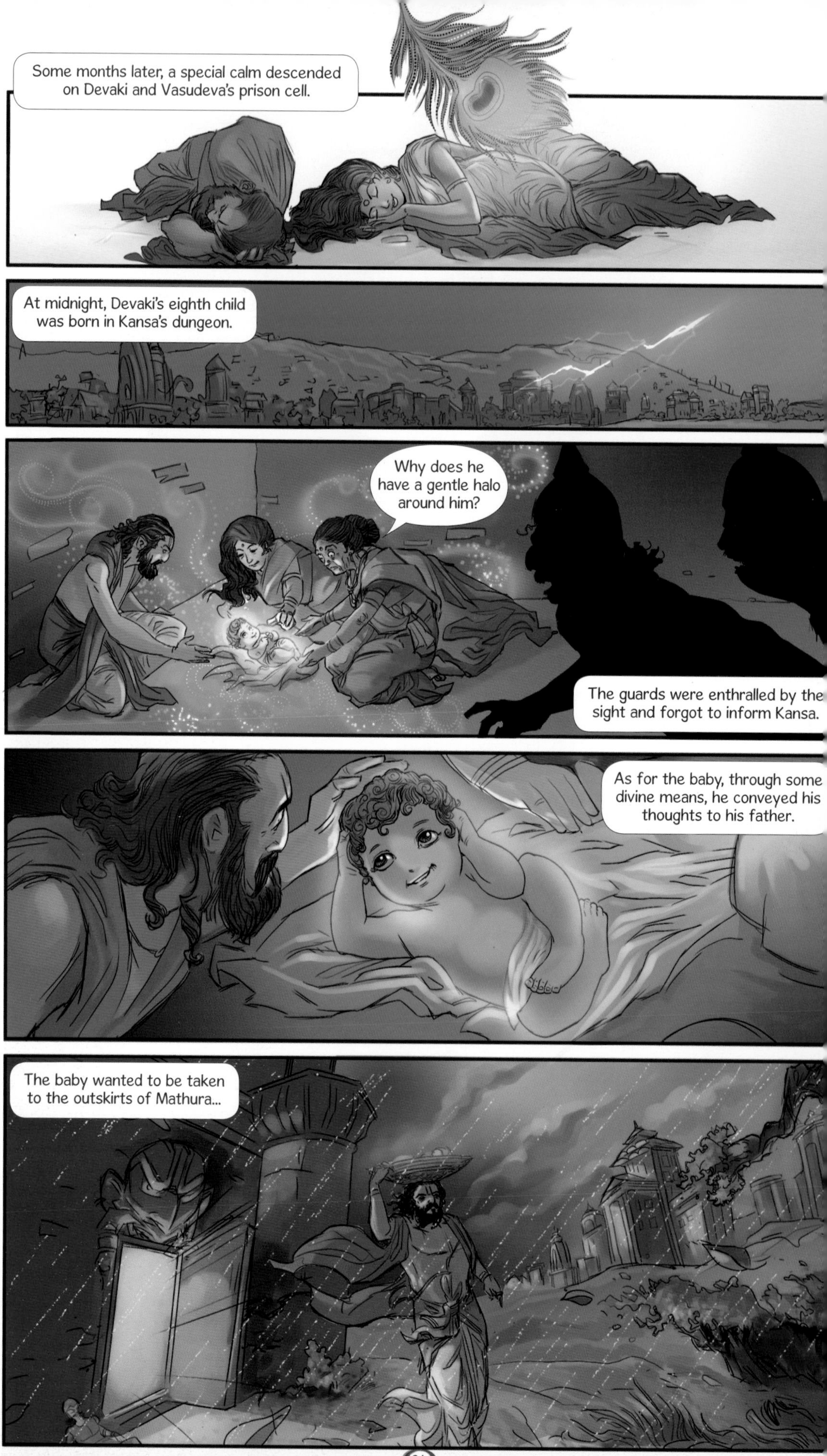
Some months later, a special calm descended on Devaki and Vasudeva's prison cell.
At midnight, Devaki's eighth child was born in Kansa's dungeon.
Why does he have a gentle halo around him?
The guards were enthralled by the sight and forgot to inform Kansa.
As for the baby, through some divine means, he conveyed his thoughts to his father.
The baby wanted to be taken to the outskirts of Mathura...

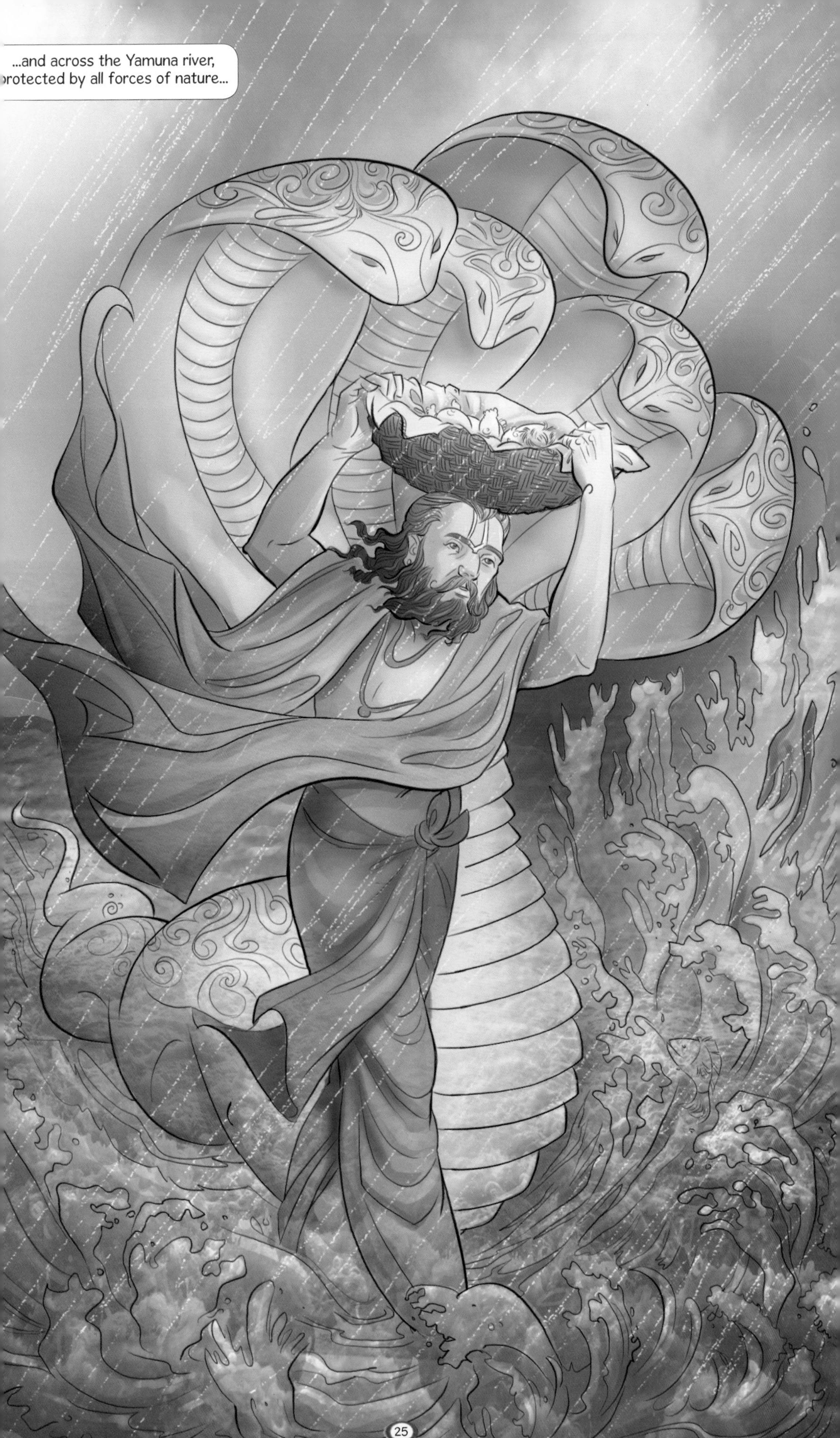
...and across the Yamuna river,
protected by all forces of nature...

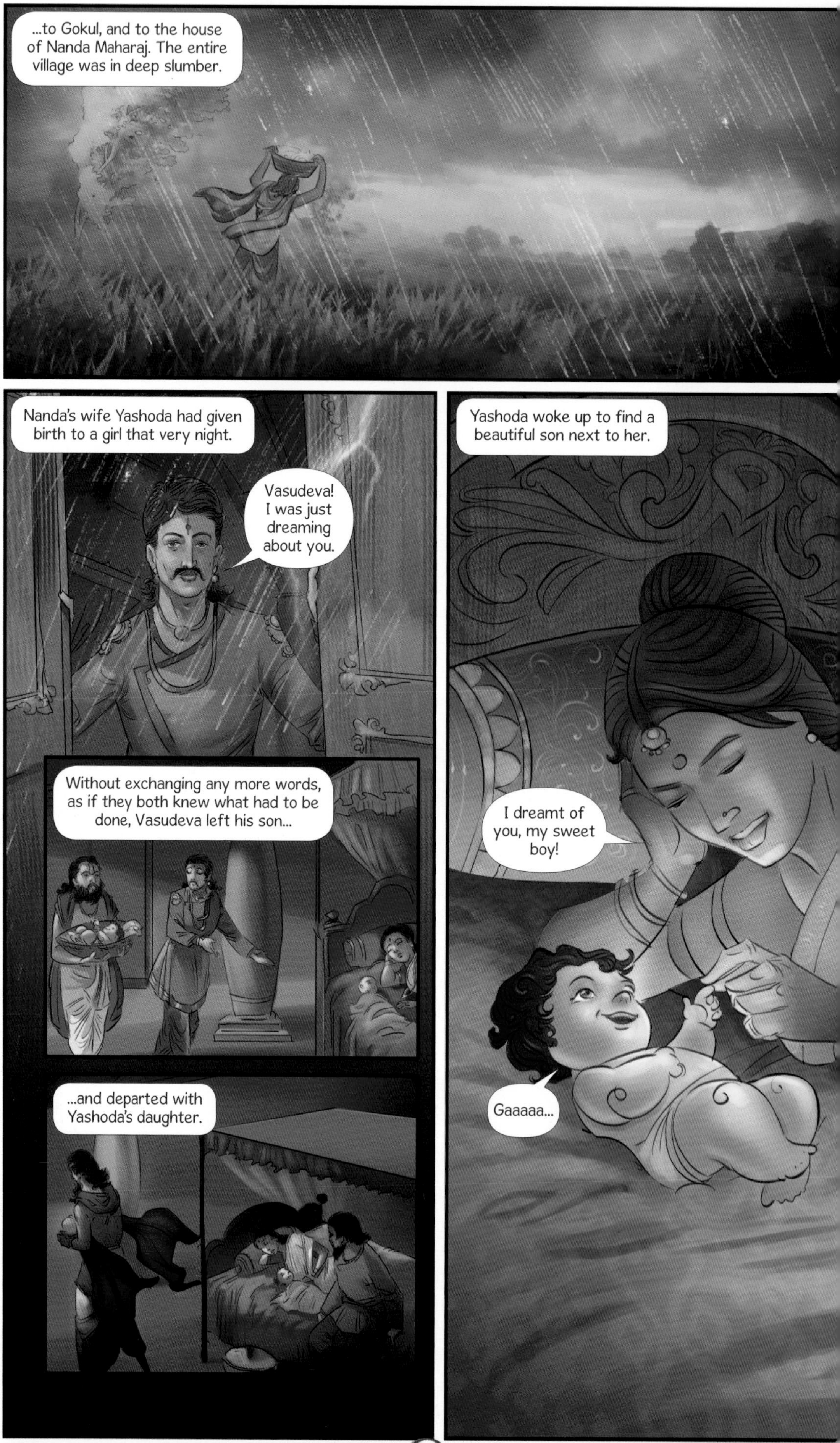
...to Gokul, and to the house of Nanda Maharaj. The entire village was in deep slumber.
Nanda's wife Yashoda had given birth to a girl that very night.
Vasudeva! I was just dreaming about you.
Without exchanging any more words, as if they both knew what had to be done, Vasudeva left his son...
...and departed with Yashoda's daughter.
Yashoda woke up to find a beautiful son next to her.
I dreamt of you, my sweet boy!
Gaaaaa...

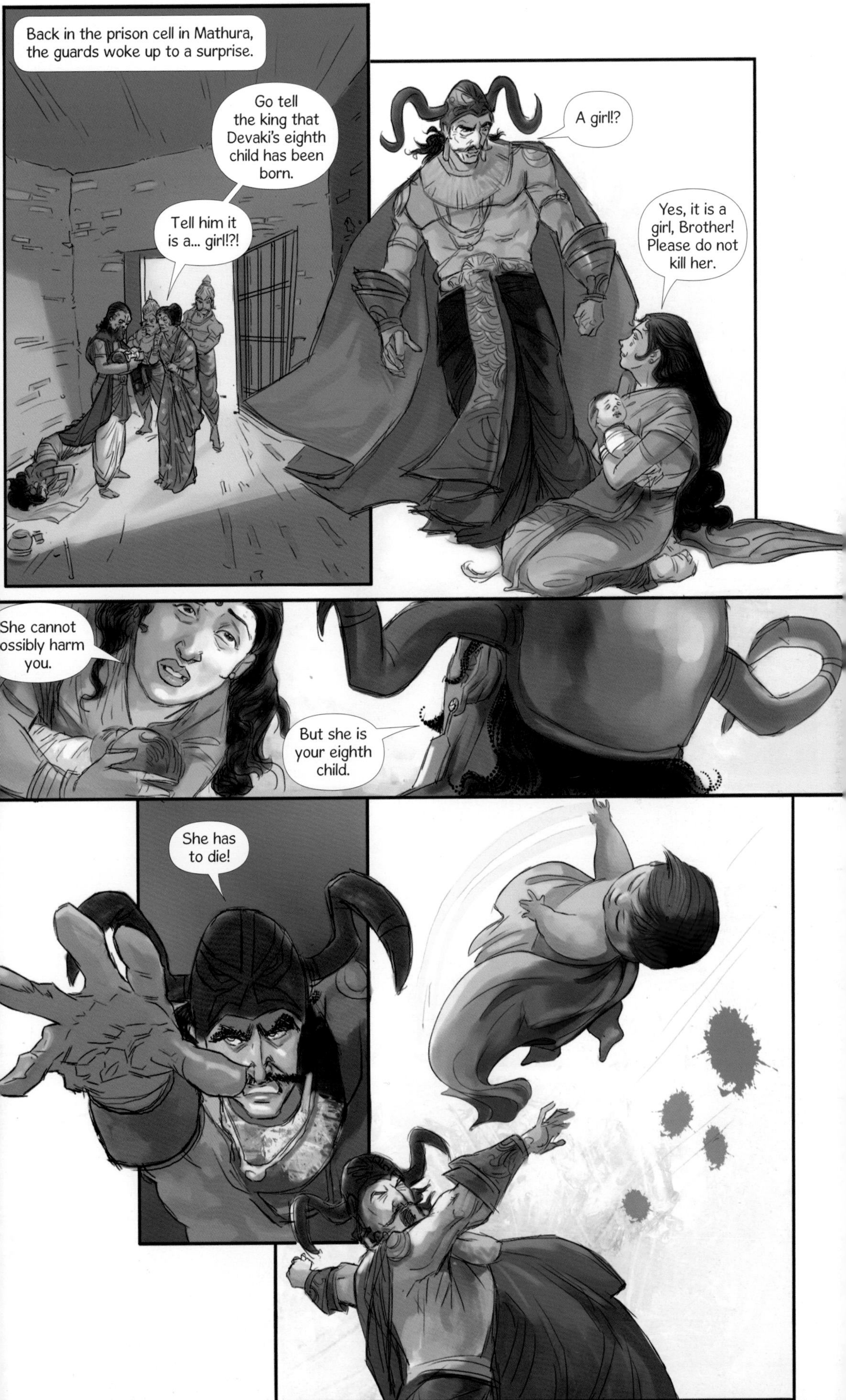

Back in the prison cell in Mathura, the guards woke up to a surprise.
Go tell the king that Devaki's eighth child has been born.
Tell him it is a... girl!?!
A girl!?
Yes, it is a girl, Brother! Please do not kill her.
She cannot ossibly harm you.
But she is your eighth child.
She has to die!

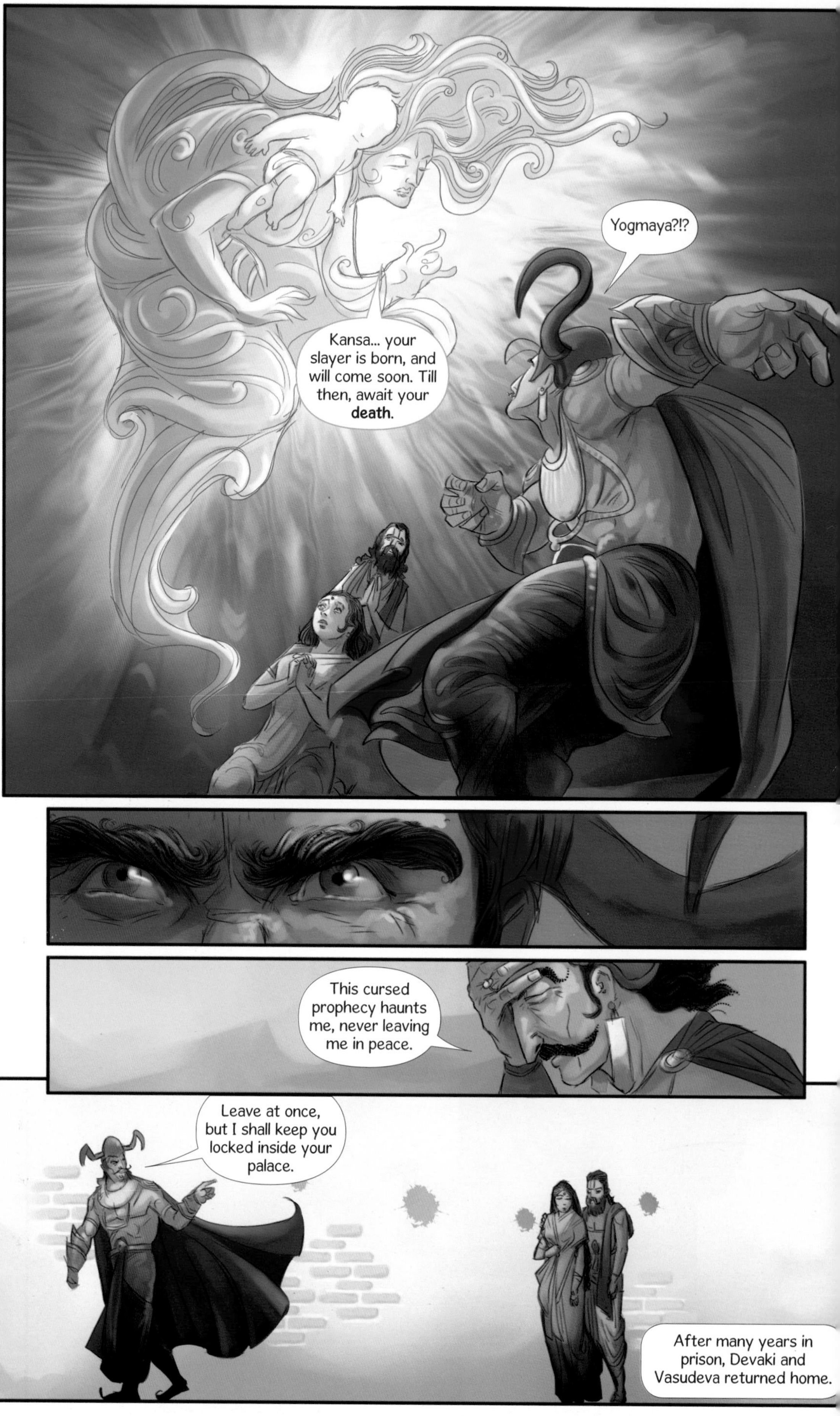
Yogmaya?!?
Kansa... your slayer is born, and will come soon. Till then, await your **death**.
This cursed prophecy haunts me, never leaving me in peace.
Leave at once, but I shall keep you locked inside your palace.
After many years in prison, Devaki and Vasudeva returned home.

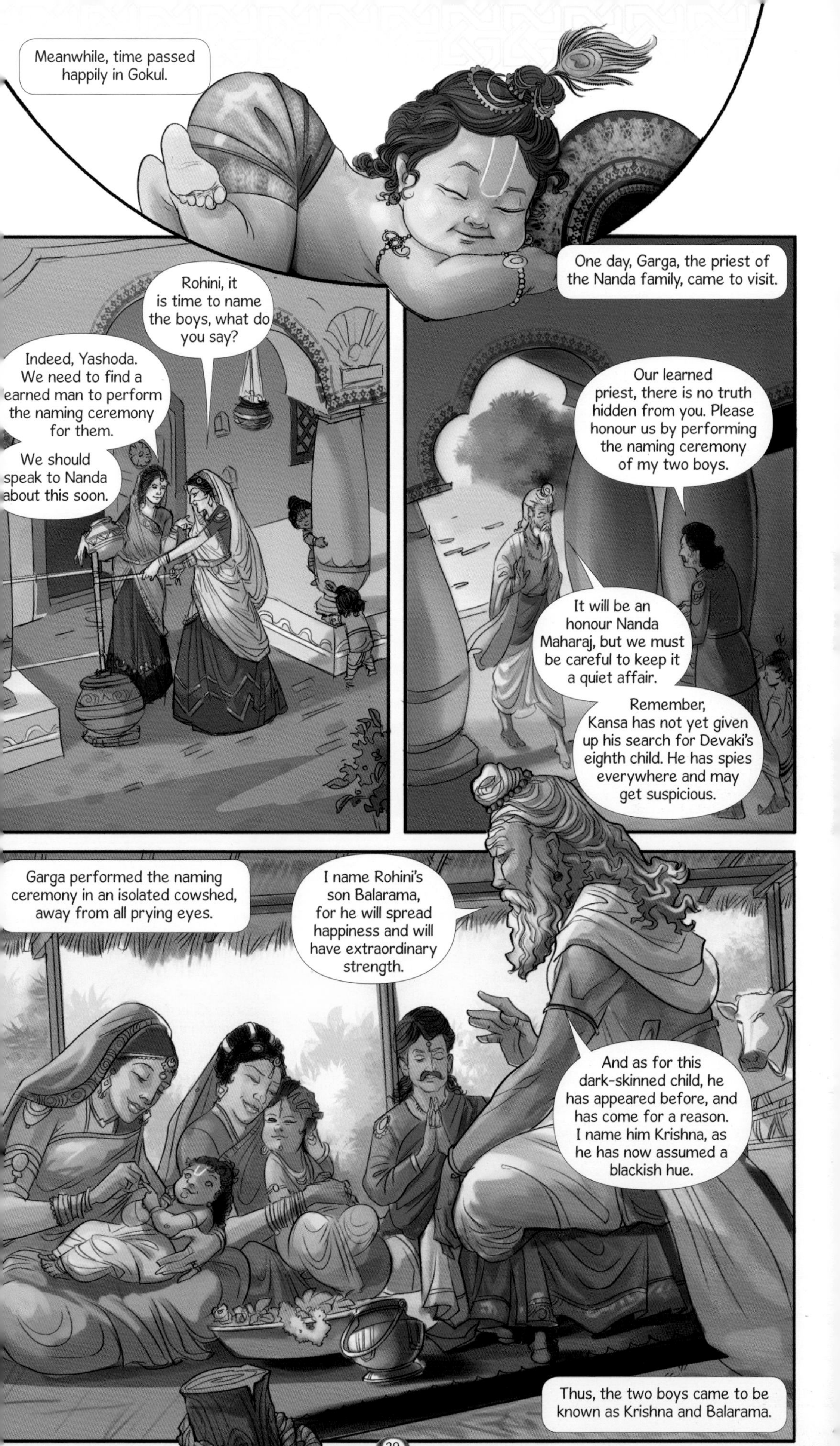

Meanwhile, time passed happily in Gokul.
Rohini, it is time to name the boys, what do you say?
Indeed, Yashoda. We need to find a earned man to perform the naming ceremony for them.
We should speak to Nanda about this soon.
One day, Garga, the priest of the Nanda family, came to visit.
Our learned priest, there is no truth hidden from you. Please honour us by performing the naming ceremony of my two boys.
It will be an honour Nanda Maharaj, but we must be careful to keep it a quiet affair.
Remember, Kansa has not yet given up his search for Devaki's eighth child. He has spies everywhere and may get suspicious.
Garga performed the naming ceremony in an isolated cowshed, away from all prying eyes.
I name Rohini's son Balarama, for he will spread happiness and will have extraordinary strength.
And as for this dark-skinned child, he has appeared before, and has come for a reason. I name him Krishna, as he has now assumed a blackish hue.
Thus, the two boys came to be known as Krishna and Balarama.

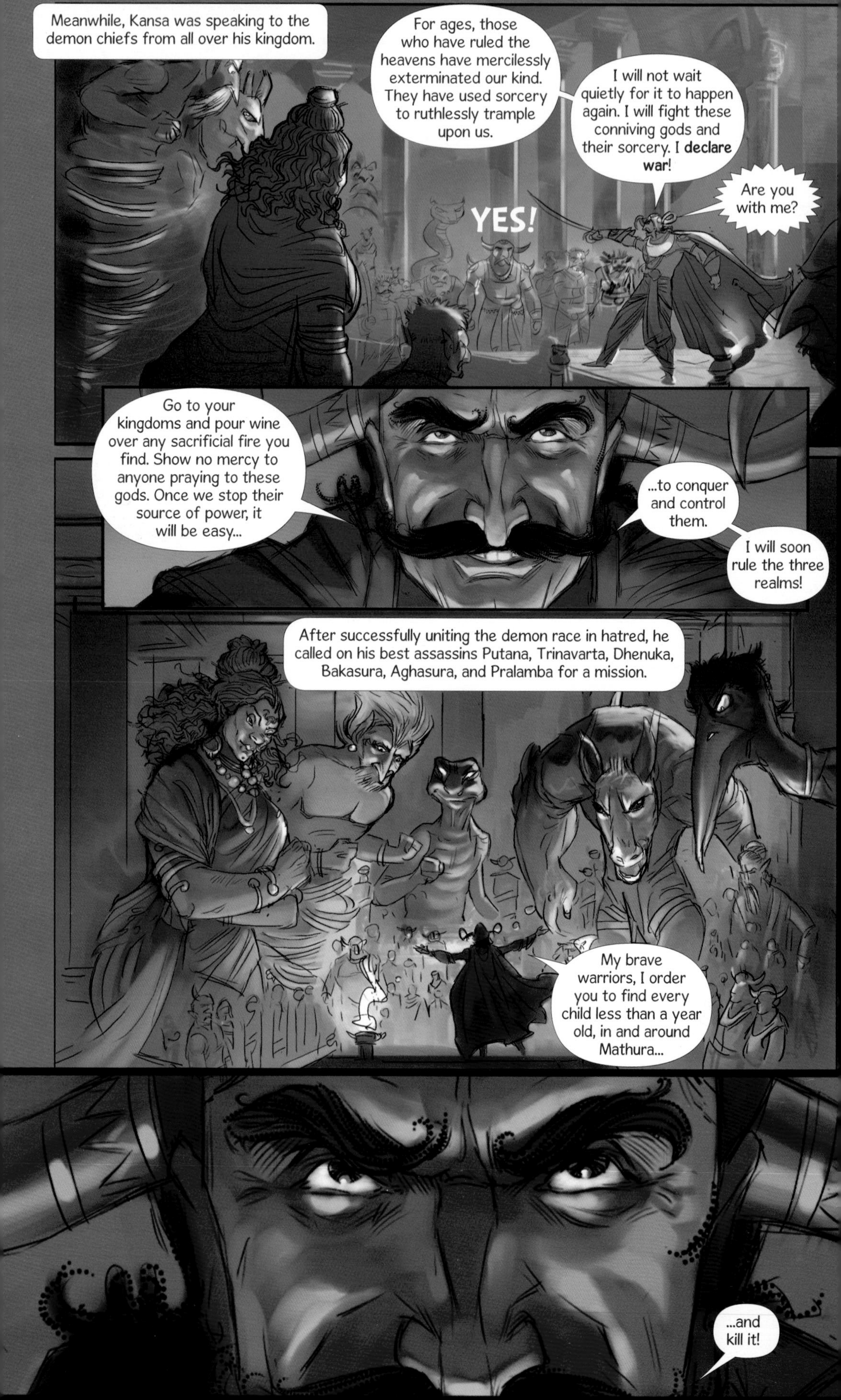
Meanwhile, Kansa was speaking to the demon chiefs from all over his kingdom.
For ages, those who have ruled the heavens have mercilessly exterminated our kind. They have used sorcery to ruthlessly trample upon us.
I will not wait quietly for it to happen again. I will fight these conniving gods and their sorcery. I **declare war**!
Are you with me?
YES!
Go to your kingdoms and pour wine over any sacrificial fire you find. Show no mercy to anyone praying to these gods. Once we stop their source of power, it will be easy...
...to conquer and control them.
I will soon rule the three realms!
After successfully uniting the demon race in hatred, he called on his best assassins Putana, Trinavarta, Dhenuka, Bakasura, Aghasura, and Pralamba for a mission.
My brave warriors, I order you to find every child less than a year old, in and around Mathura...
...and kill it!

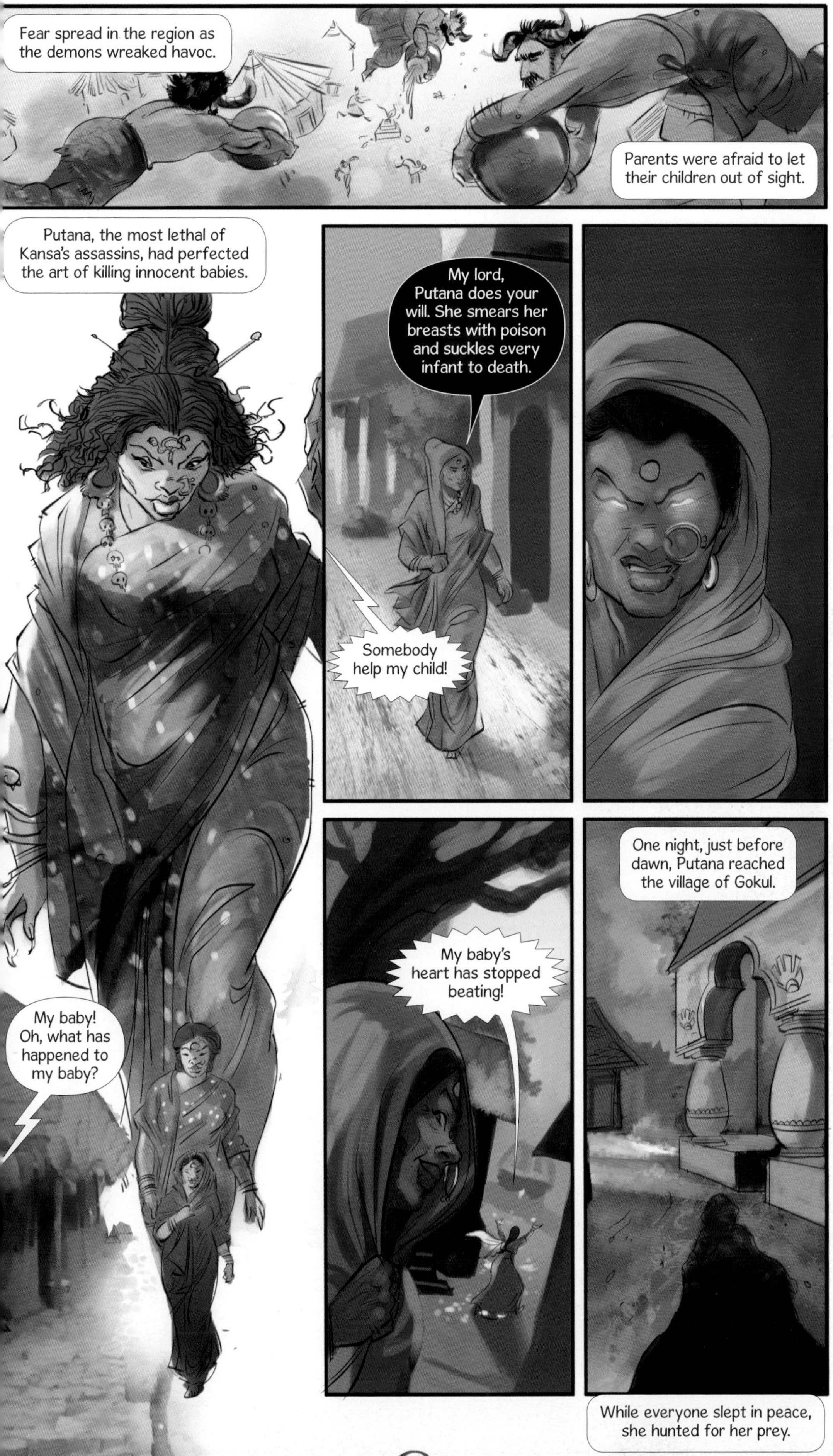

Fear spread in the region as the demons wreaked havoc.
Parents were afraid to let their children out of sight.
Putana, the most lethal of Kansa's assassins, had perfected the art of killing innocent babies.
My baby! Oh, what has happened to my baby?
My lord, Putana does your will. She smears her breasts with poison and suckles every infant to death.
Somebody help my child!
My baby's heart has stopped beating!
One night, just before dawn, Putana reached the village of Gokul.
While everyone slept in peace, she hunted for her prey.

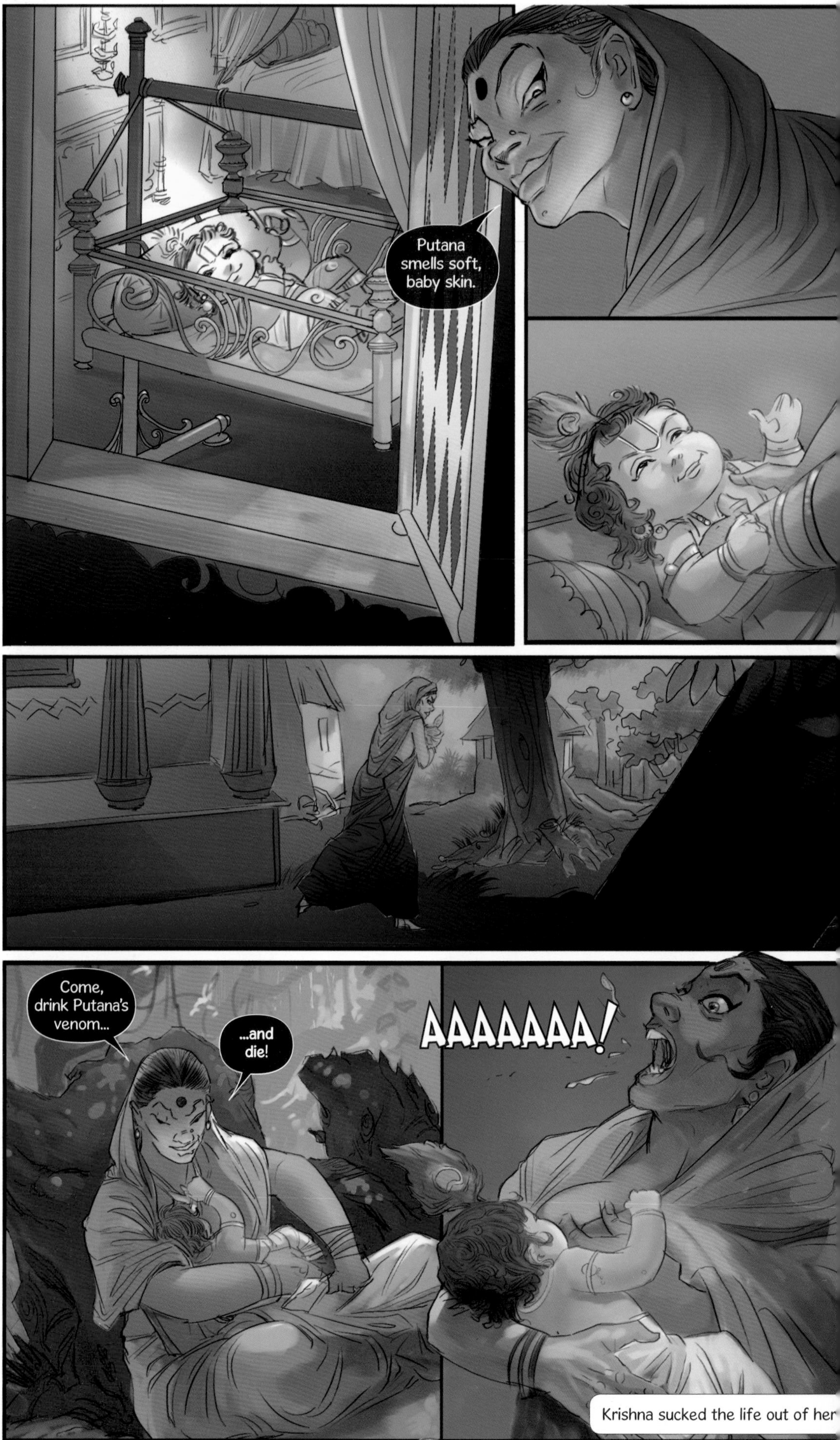
Putana smells soft, baby skin.
Come, drink Putana's venom...
...and die!
AAAAAAA!
Krishna sucked the life out of her

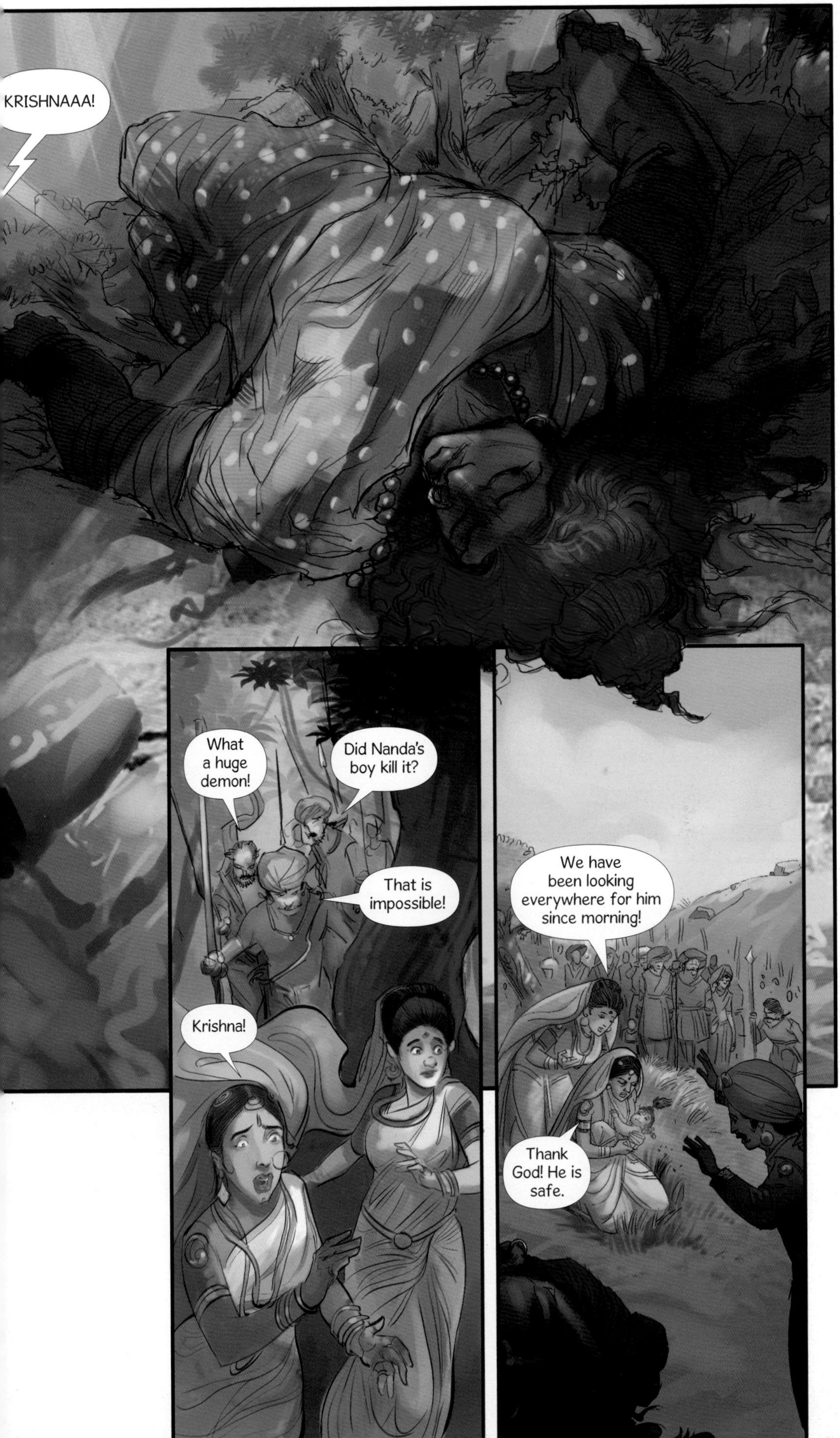
KRISHNAAA!
What a huge demon!
Did Nanda's boy kill it?
That is impossible!
Krishna!
We have been looking everywhere for him since morning!
Thank God! He is safe.

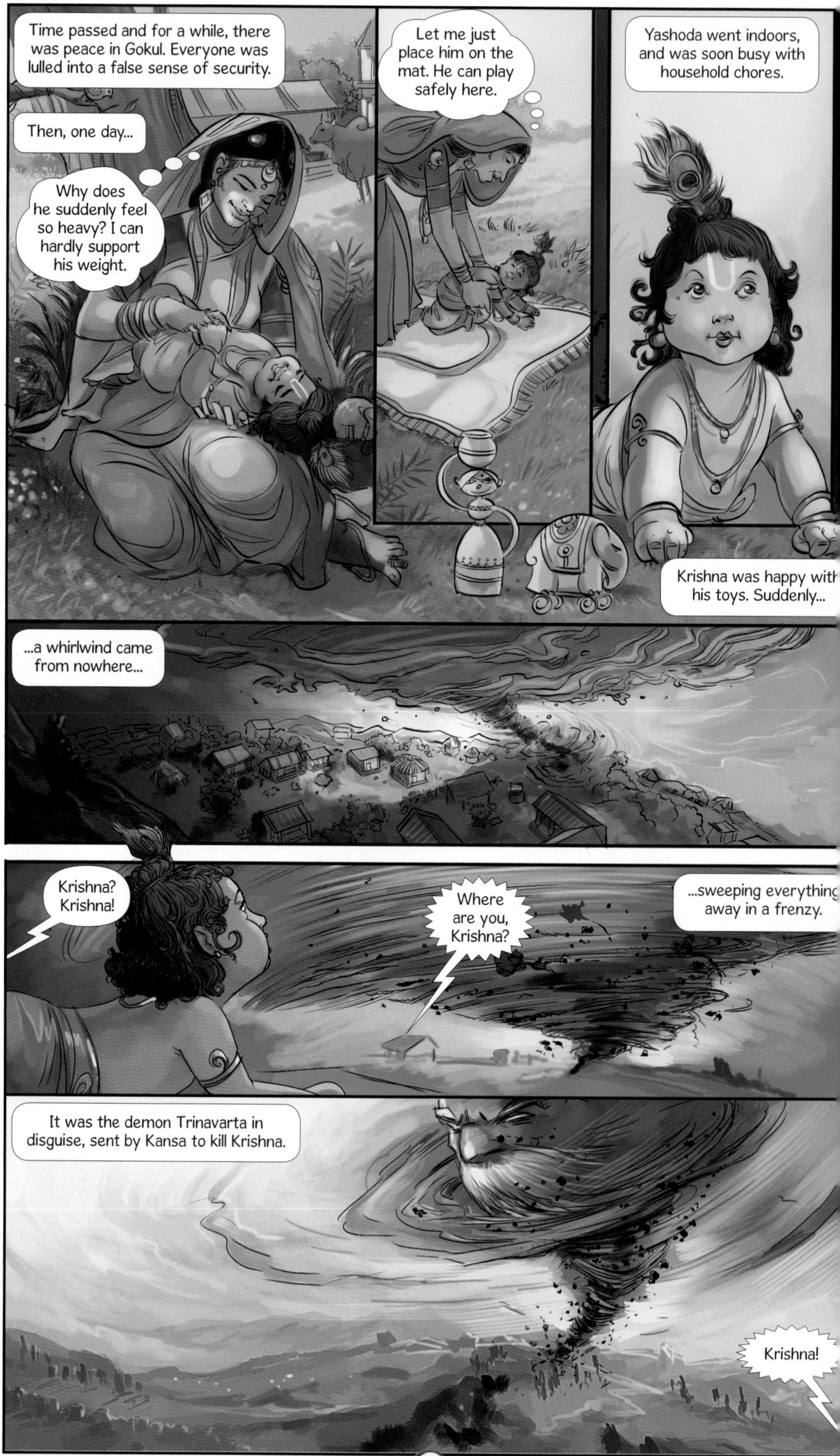

Time passed and for a while, there was peace in Gokul. Everyone was lulled into a false sense of security.
Then, one day...
Why does he suddenly feel so heavy? I can hardly support his weight.
Let me just place him on the mat. He can play safely here.
Yashoda went indoors, and was soon busy with household chores.
Krishna was happy with his toys. Suddenly...
...a whirlwind came from nowhere...
Krishna? Krishna!
Where are you, Krishna?
...sweeping everything away in a frenzy.
It was the demon Trinavarta in disguise, sent by Kansa to kill Krishna.
Krishna!

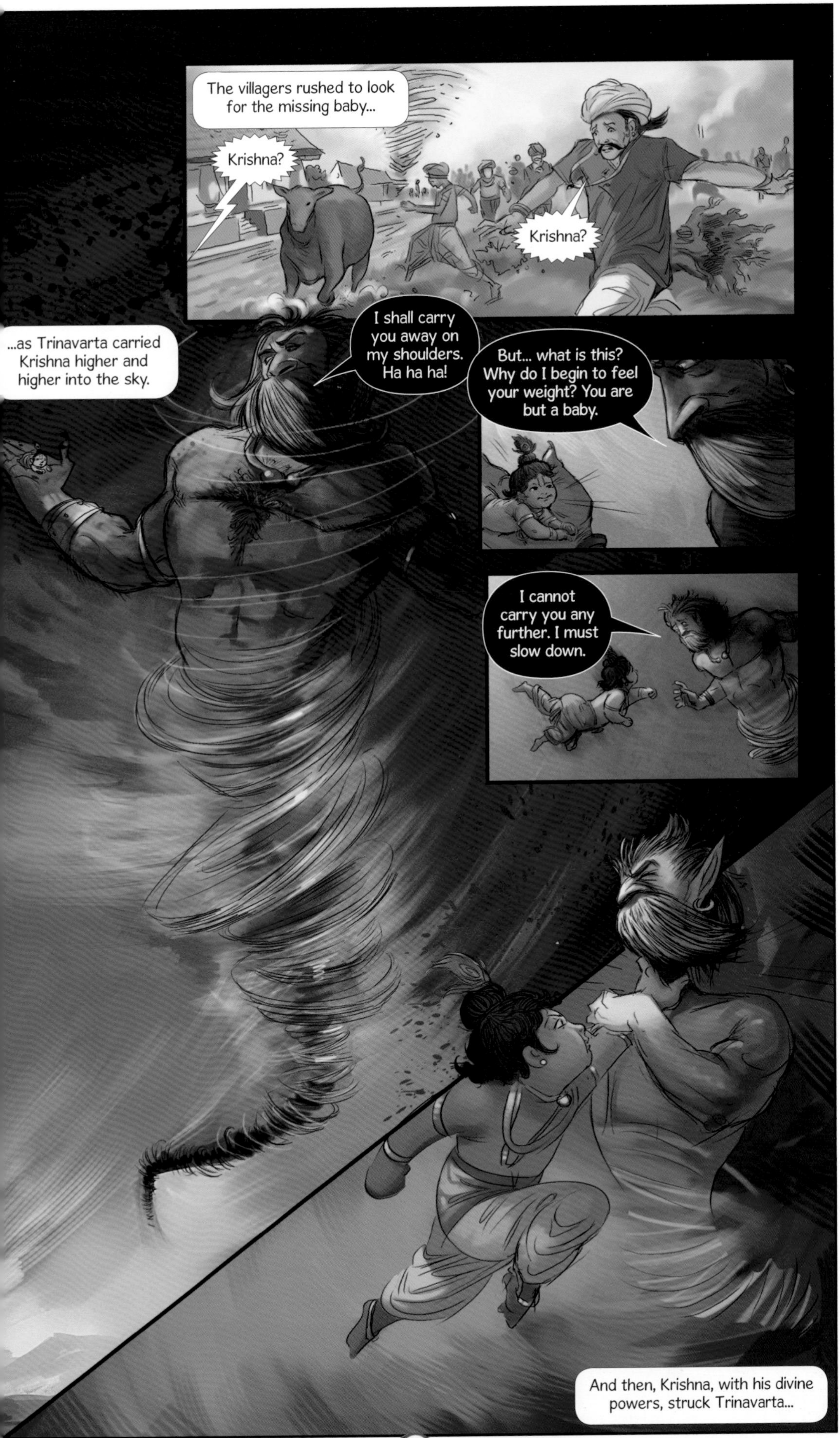

The villagers rushed to look for the missing baby...
Krishna?
Krishna?
...as Trinavarta carried Krishna higher and higher into the sky.
I shall carry you away on my shoulders. Ha ha ha!
But... what is this? Why do I begin to feel your weight? You are but a baby.
I cannot carry you any further. I must slow down.
And then, Krishna, with his divine powers, struck Trinavarta...

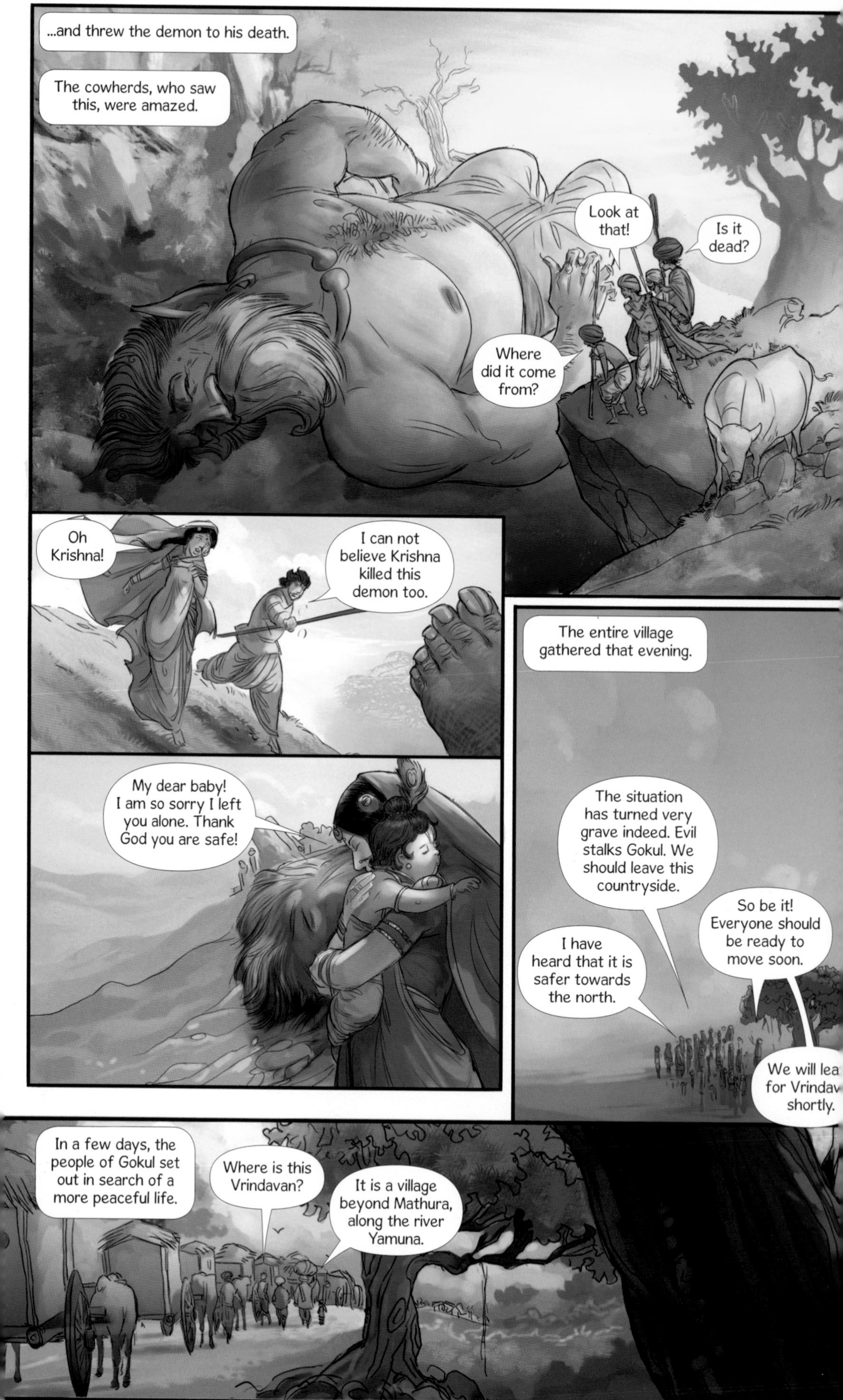
...and threw the demon to his death.
The cowherds, who saw this, were amazed.
Look at that!
Is it dead?
Where did it come from?
Oh Krishna!
I can not believe Krishna killed this demon too.
My dear baby! I am so sorry I left you alone. Thank God you are safe!
The entire village gathered that evening.
The situation has turned very grave indeed. Evil stalks Gokul. We should leave this countryside.
I have heard that it is safer towards the north.
So be it! Everyone should be ready to move soon.
In a few days, the people of Gokul set out in search of a more peaceful life.
Where is this Vrindavan?
It is a village beyond Mathura, along the river Yamuna.

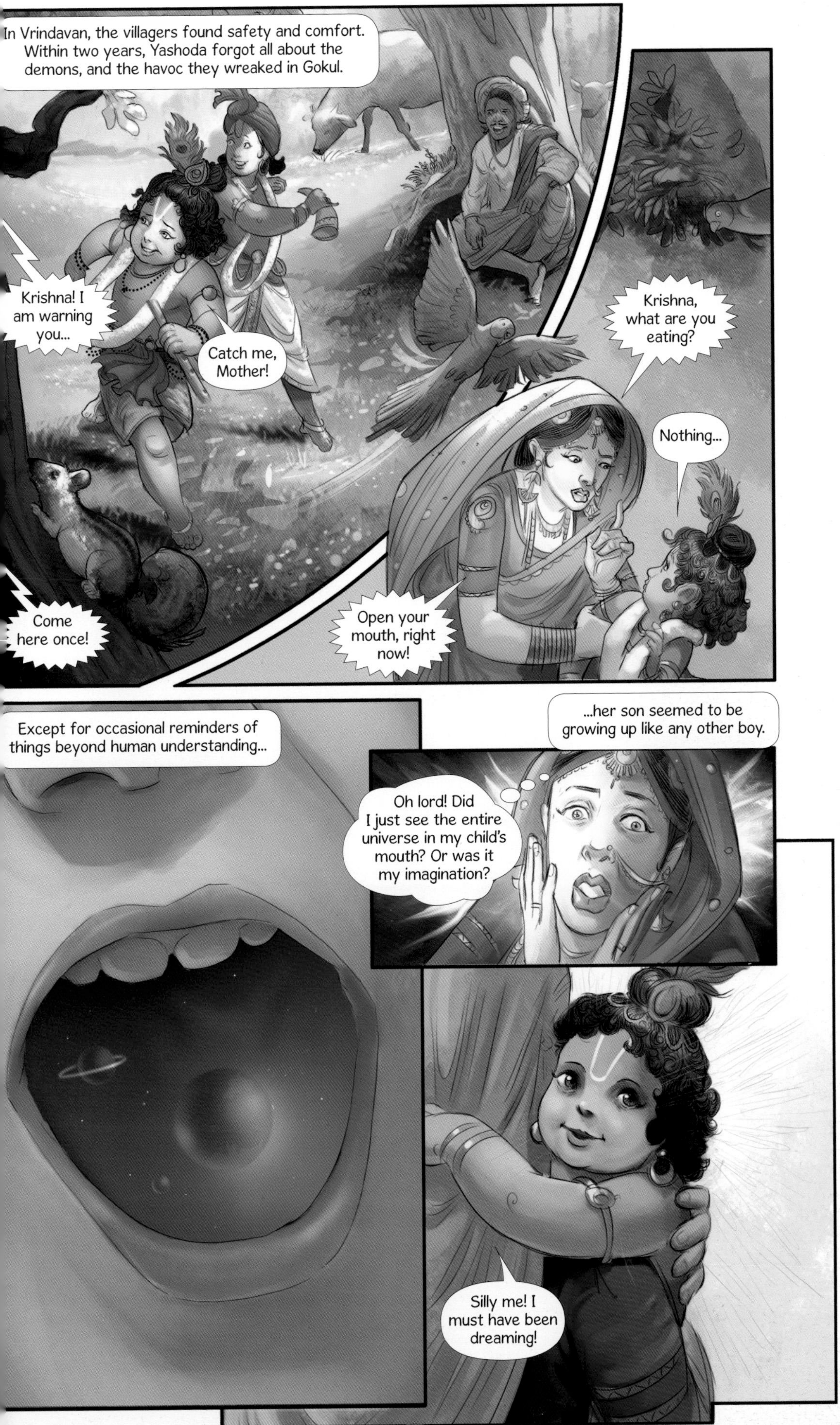

In Vrindavan, the villagers found safety and comfort. Within two years, Yashoda forgot all about the demons, and the havoc they wreaked in Gokul.
Krishna! I am warning you...
Catch me, Mother!
Come here once!
Krishna, what are you eating?
Nothing...
Open your mouth, right now!
Except for occasional reminders of things beyond human understanding...
...her son seemed to be growing up like any other boy.
Oh lord! Did I just see the entire universe in my child's mouth? Or was it my imagination?
Silly me! I must have been dreaming!

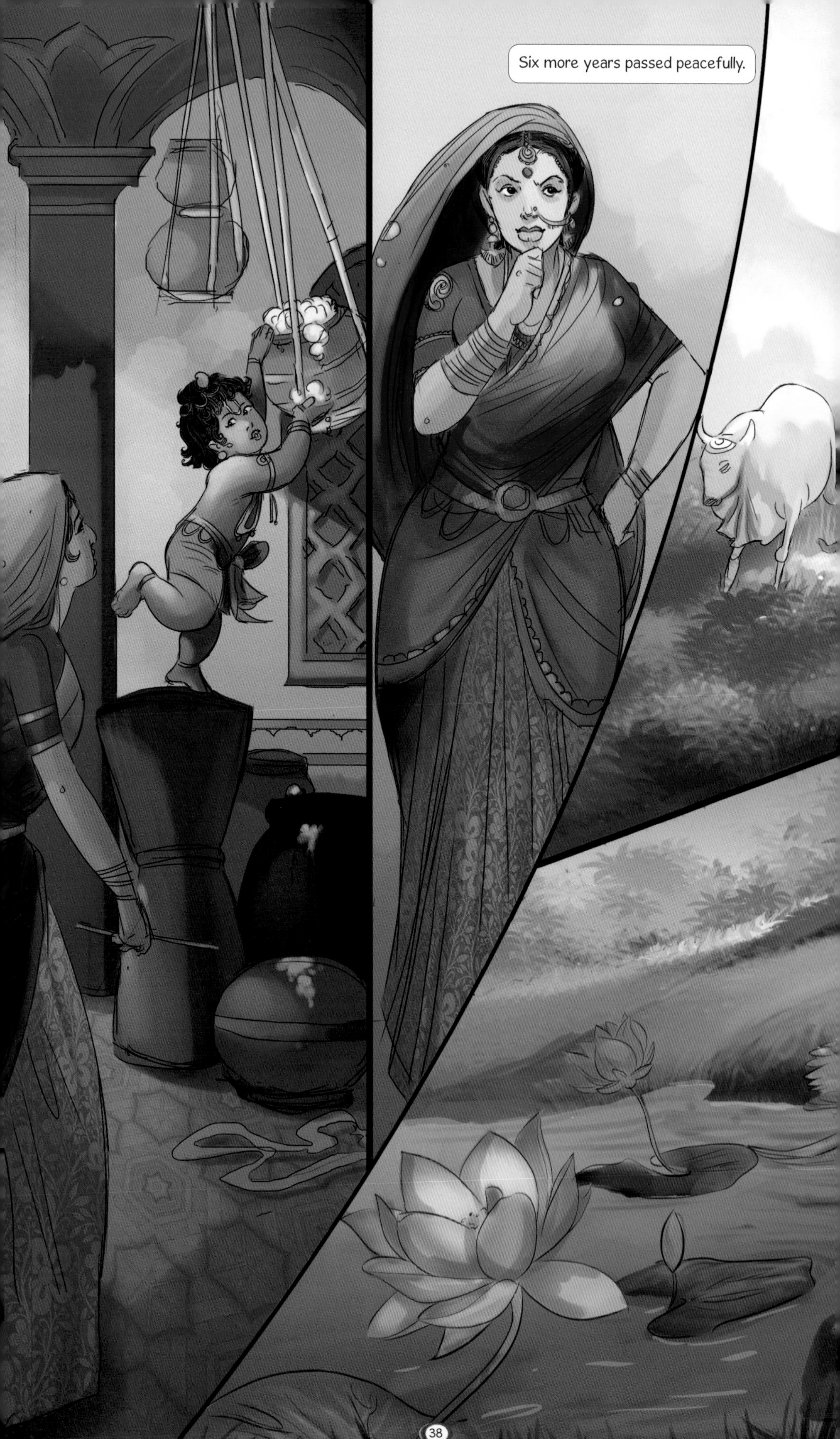
Six more years passed peacefully.

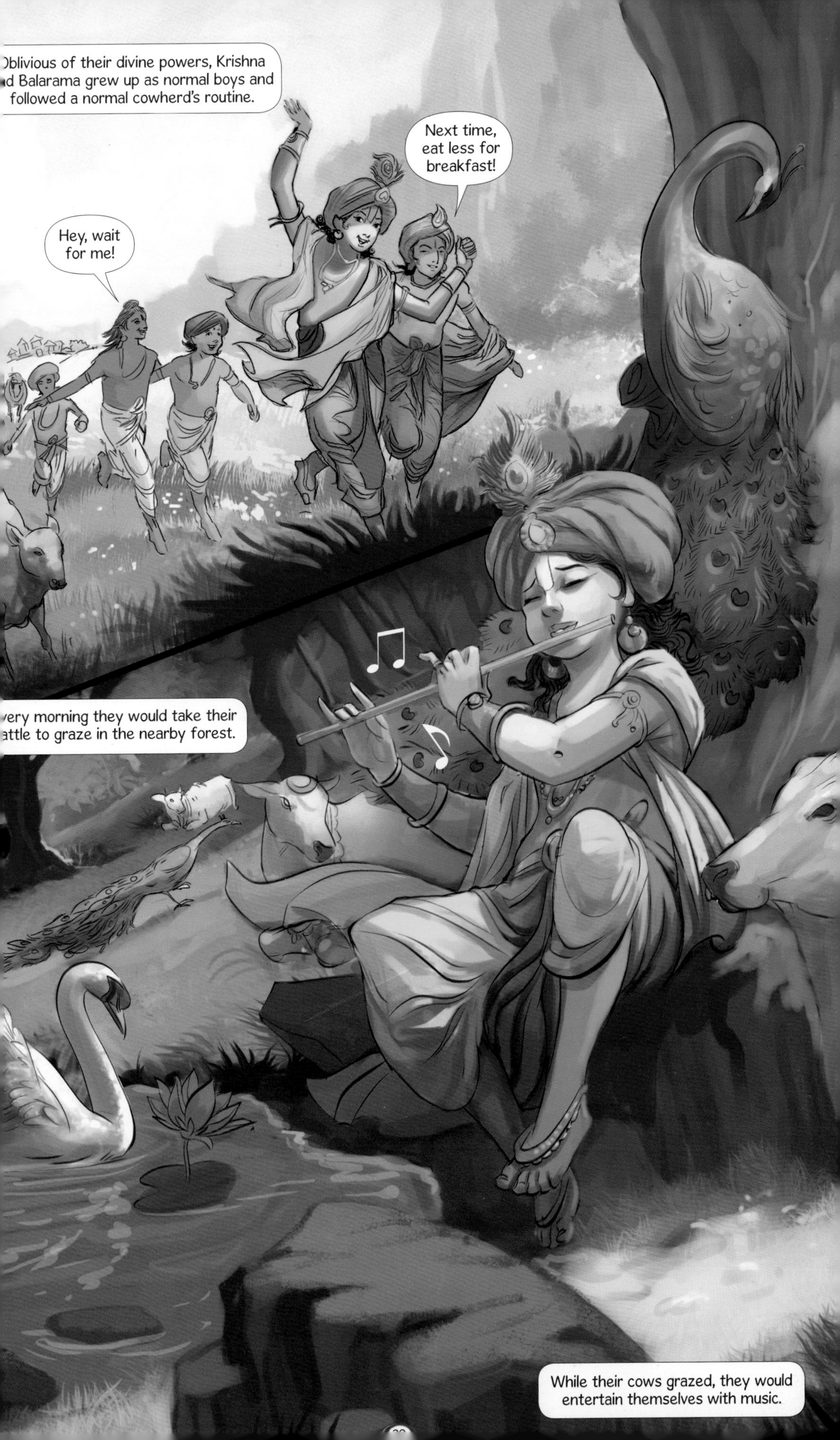
blivious of their divine powers, Krishna
d Balarama grew up as normal boys and
followed a normal cowherd's routine.
Hey, wait for me!
Next time, eat less for breakfast!
very morning they would take their
attle to graze in the nearby forest.
While their cows grazed, they would entertain themselves with music.

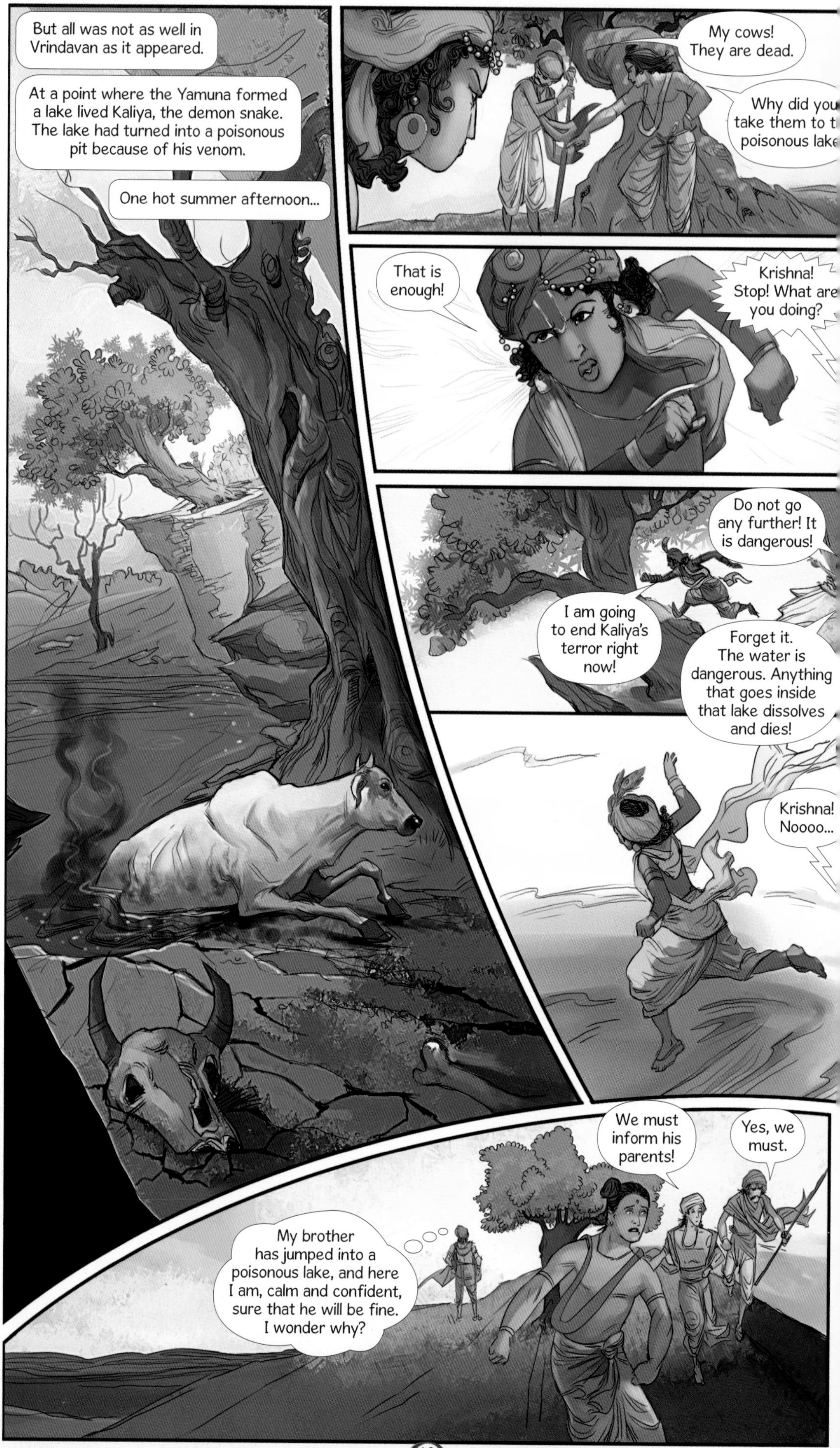
But all was not as well in Vrindavan as it appeared.
At a point where the Yamuna formed a lake lived Kaliya, the demon snake. The lake had turned into a poisonous pit because of his venom.
One hot summer afternoon...
My cows! They are dead.
Why did you take them to t poisonous lake
That is enough!
Krishna! Stop! What are you doing?
Do not go any further! It is dangerous!
I am going to end Kaliya's terror right now!
Forget it. The water is dangerous. Anything that goes inside that lake dissolves and dies!
Krishna! Noooo...
We must inform his parents!
Yes, we must.
My brother has jumped into a poisonous lake, and here I am, calm and confident, sure that he will be fine. I wonder why?

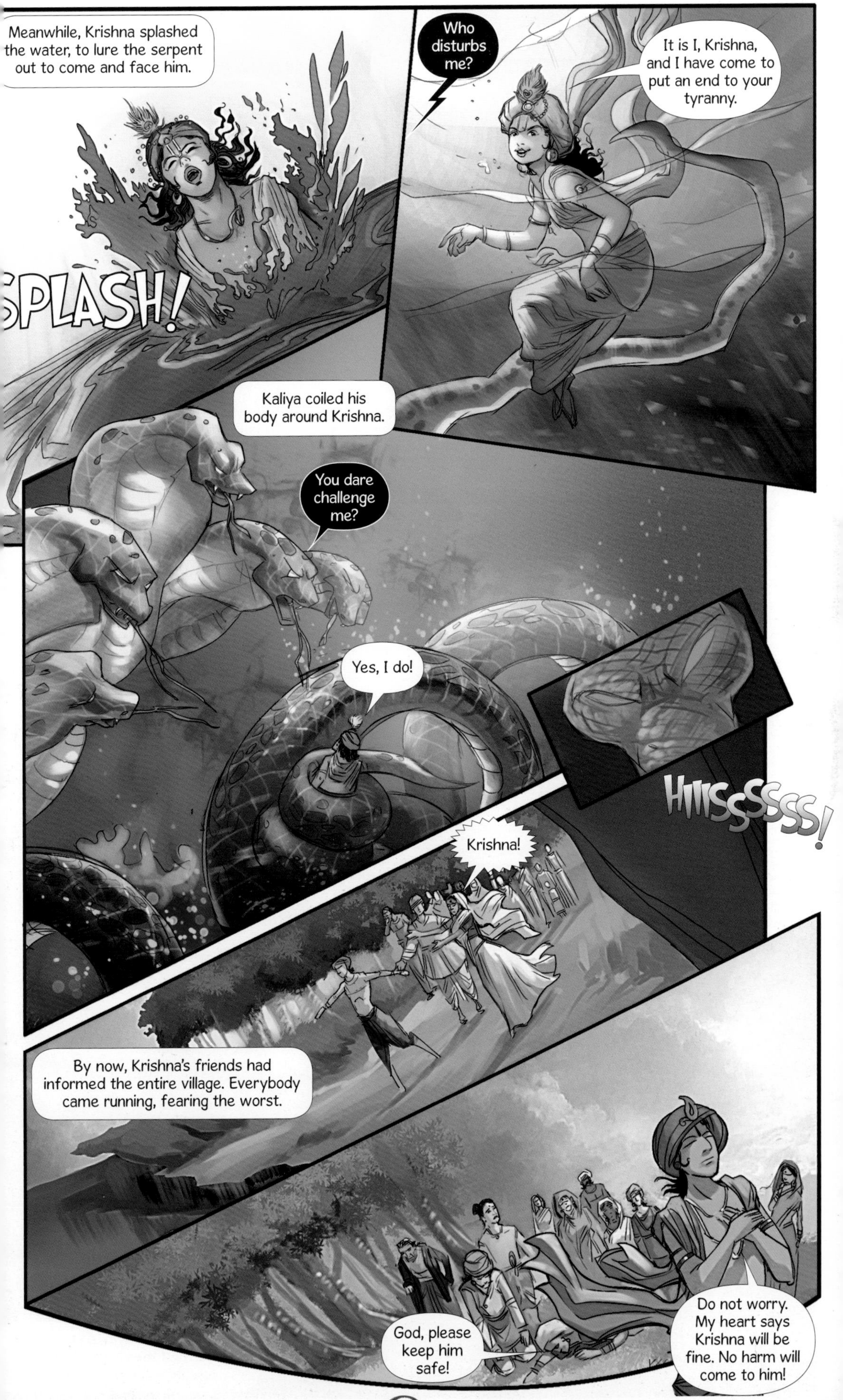
Meanwhile, Krishna splashed the water, to lure the serpent out to come and face him.
SPLASH!
Who disturbs me?
It is I, Krishna, and I have come to put an end to your tyranny.
Kaliya coiled his body around Krishna.
You dare challenge me?
Yes, I do!
HIIISSSSSS!
Krishna!
By now, Krishna's friends had informed the entire village. Everybody came running, fearing the worst.
God, please keep him safe!
Do not worry. My heart says Krishna will be fine. No harm will come to him!

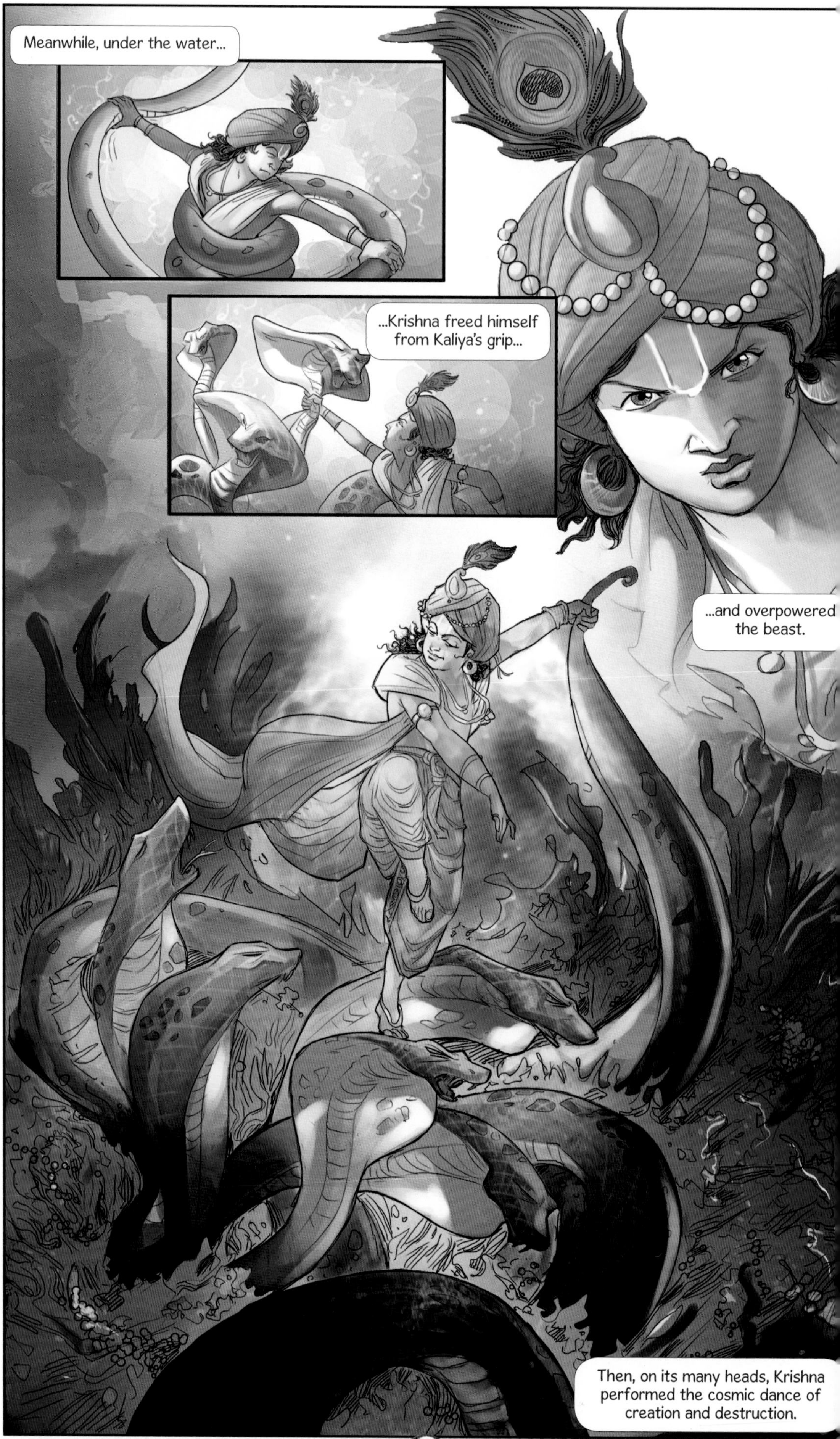
Meanwhile, under the water...
...Krishna freed himself from Kaliya's grip...
...and overpowered the beast.
Then, on its many heads, Krishna performed the cosmic dance of creation and destruction.

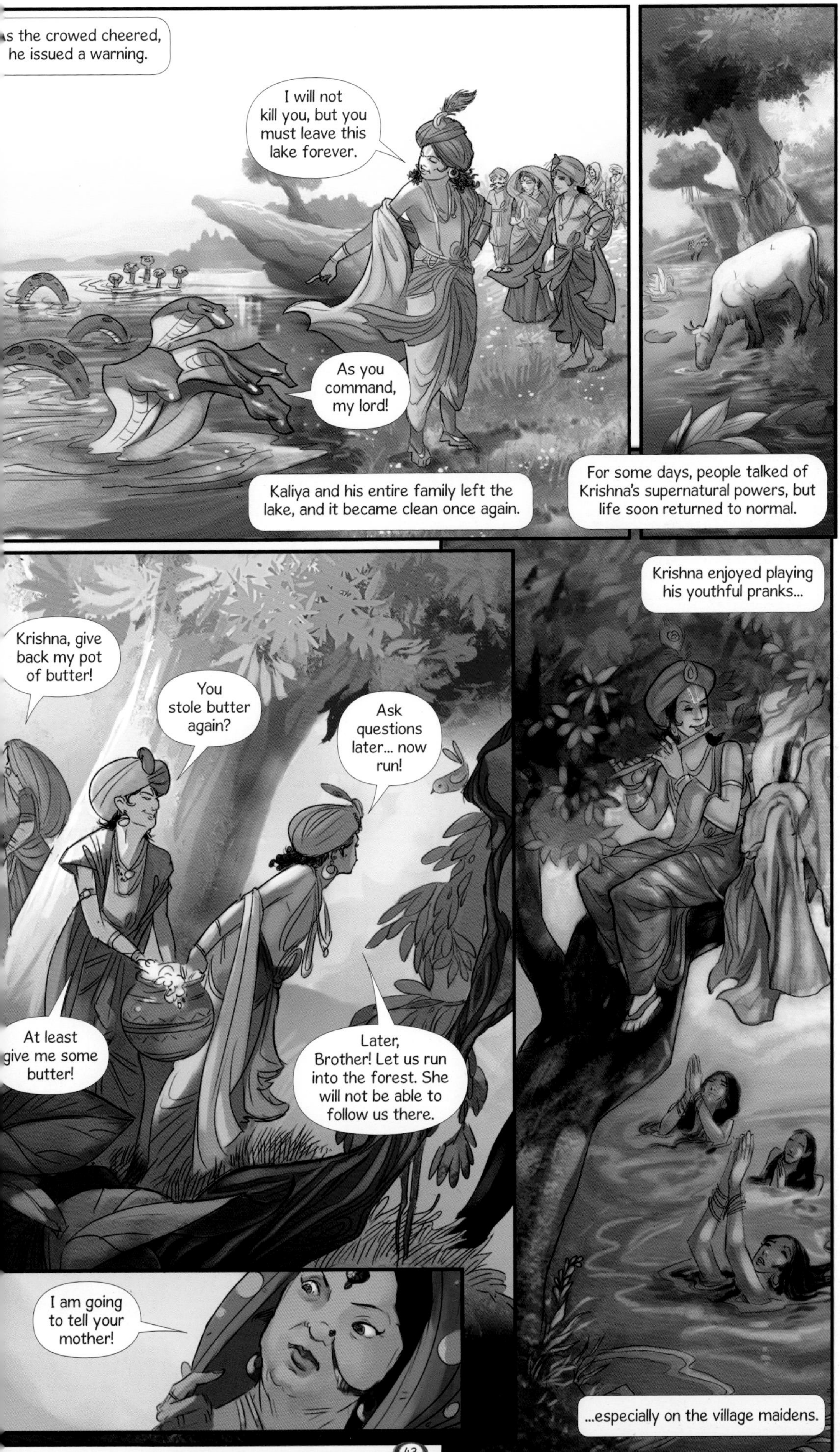

s the crowed cheered, he issued a warning.
I will not kill you, but you must leave this lake forever.
As you command, my lord!
Kaliya and his entire family left the lake, and it became clean once again.
For some days, people talked of Krishna's supernatural powers, but life soon returned to normal.
Krishna, give back my pot of butter!
You stole butter again?
Ask questions later... now run!
At least give me some butter!
Later, Brother! Let us run into the forest. She will not be able to follow us there.
I am going to tell your mother!
Krishna enjoyed playing his youthful pranks...
...especially on the village maidens.

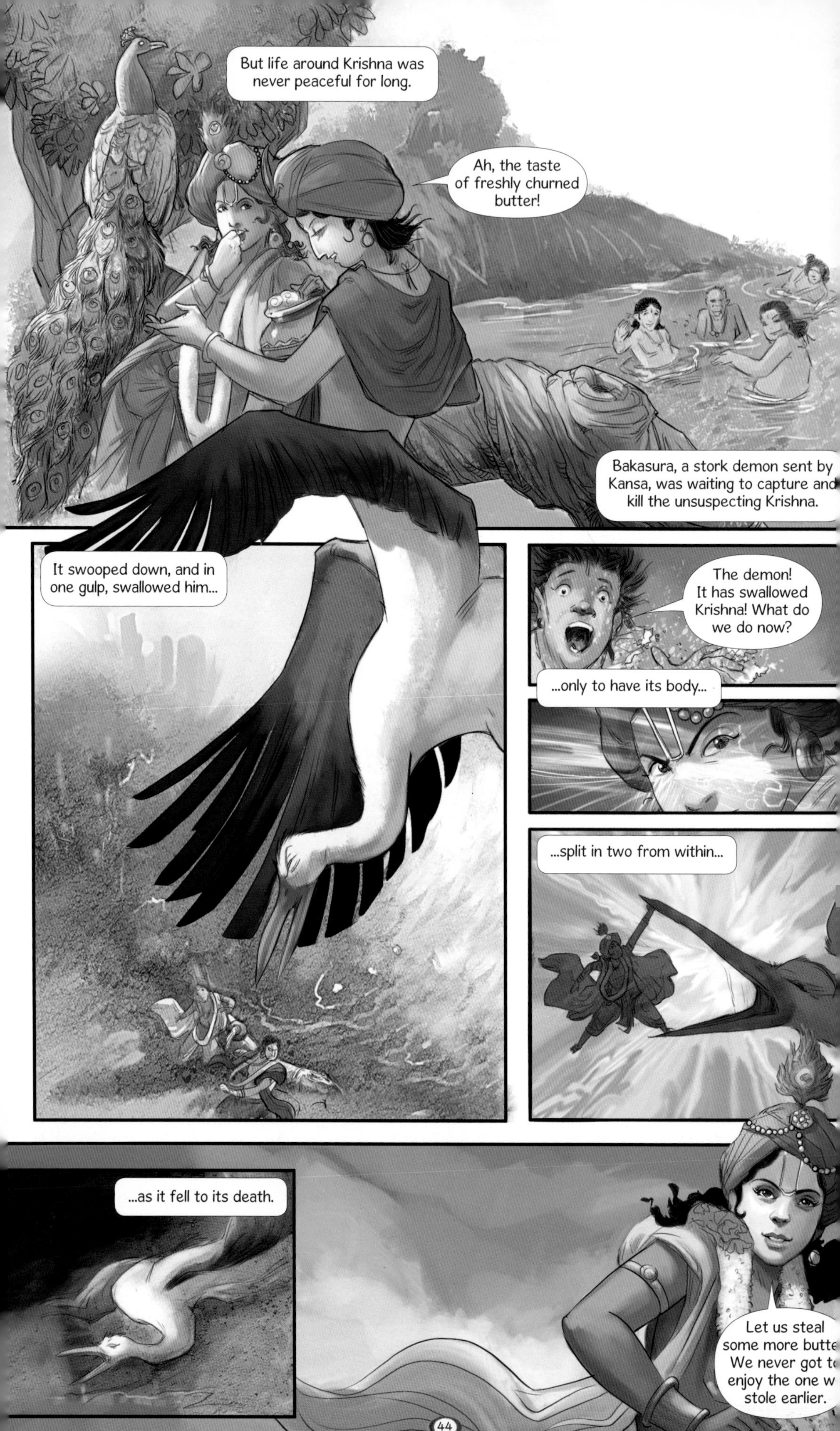
But life around Krishna was never peaceful for long.
Ah, the taste of freshly churned butter!
Bakasura, a stork demon sent by Kansa, was waiting to capture and kill the unsuspecting Krishna.
It swooped down, and in one gulp, swallowed him...
The demon! It has swallowed Krishna! What do we do now?
...only to have its body...
...split in two from within...
...as it fell to its death.
Let us steal some more butte
We never got t
enjoy the one w
stole earlier.

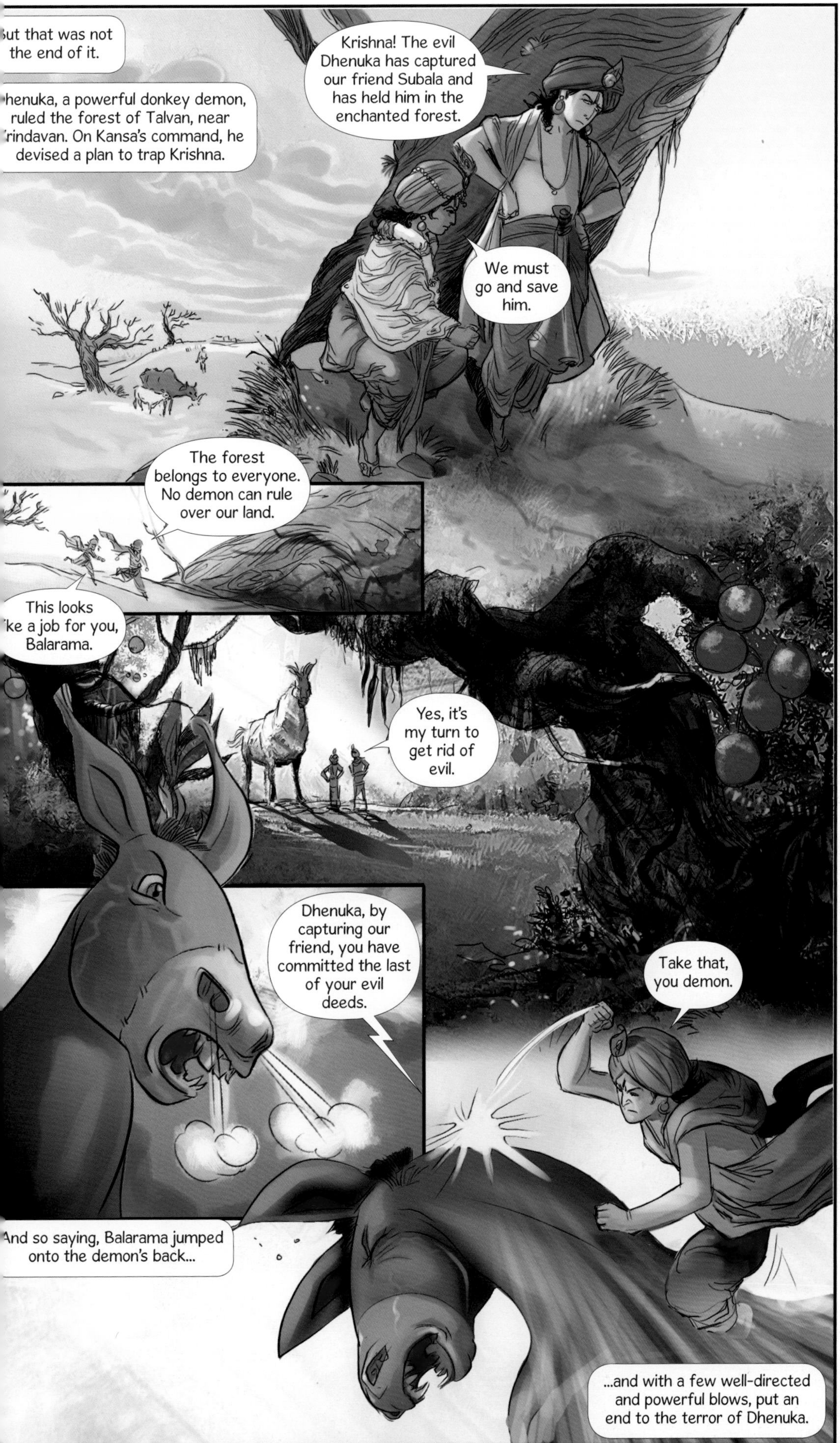
But that was not the end of it.
Dhenuka, a powerful donkey demon, ruled the forest of Talvan, near Vrindavan. On Kansa's command, he devised a plan to trap Krishna.
Krishna! The evil Dhenuka has captured our friend Subala and has held him in the enchanted forest.
We must go and save him.
The forest belongs to everyone. No demon can rule over our land.
This looks like a job for you, Balarama.
Yes, it's my turn to get rid of evil.
Dhenuka, by capturing our friend, you have committed the last of your evil deeds.
Take that, you demon.
And so saying, Balarama jumped onto the demon's back...
...and with a few well-directed and powerful blows, put an end to the terror of Dhenuka.

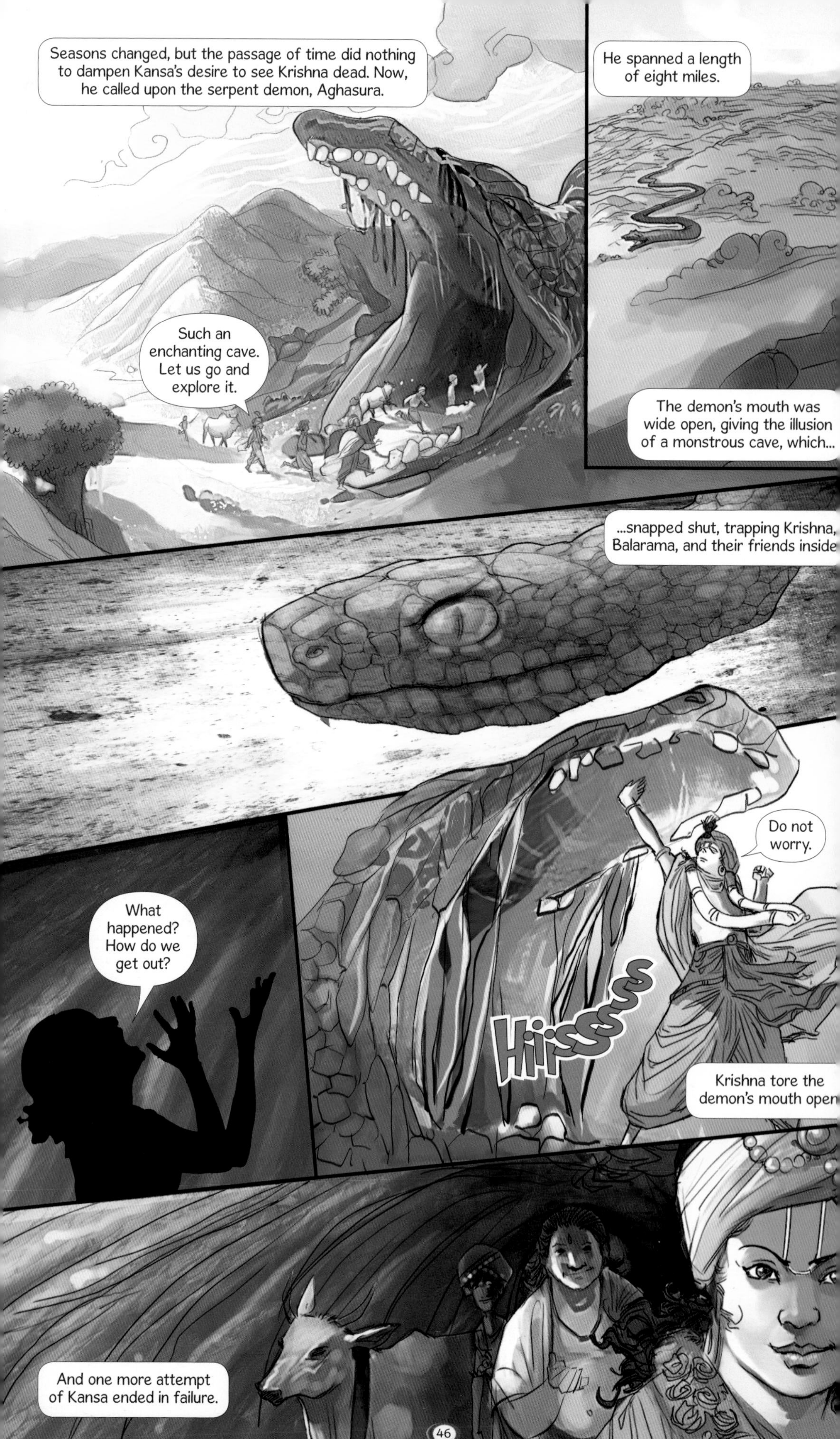

Seasons changed, but the passage of time did nothing to dampen Kansa's desire to see Krishna dead. Now, he called upon the serpent demon, Aghasura.
Such an enchanting cave. Let us go and explore it.
He spanned a length of eight miles.
The demon's mouth was wide open, giving the illusion of a monstrous cave, which...
...snapped shut, trapping Krishna, Balarama, and their friends inside
What happened? How do we get out?
Do not worry.
Hiiissss
Krishna tore the demon's mouth open
And one more attempt of Kansa ended in failure.

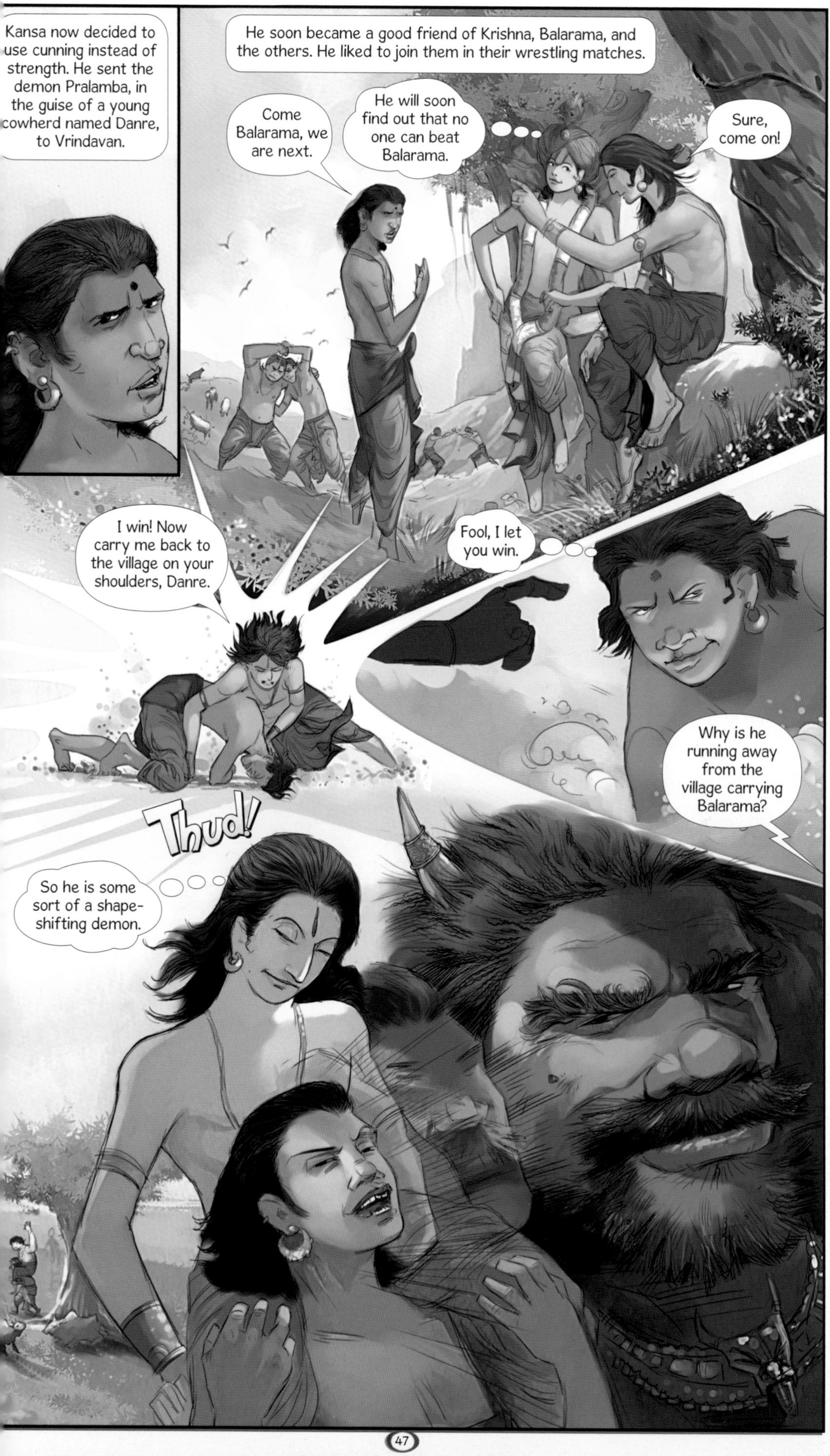

Kansa now decided to use cunning instead of strength. He sent the demon Pralamba, in the guise of a young cowherd named Danre, to Vrindavan.
He soon became a good friend of Krishna, Balarama, and the others. He liked to join them in their wrestling matches.
Come Balarama, we are next.
He will soon find out that no one can beat Balarama.
Sure, come on!
I win! Now carry me back to the village on your shoulders, Danre.
Fool, I let you win.
Why is he running away from the village carrying Balarama?
Thud!
So he is some sort of a shape-shifting demon.

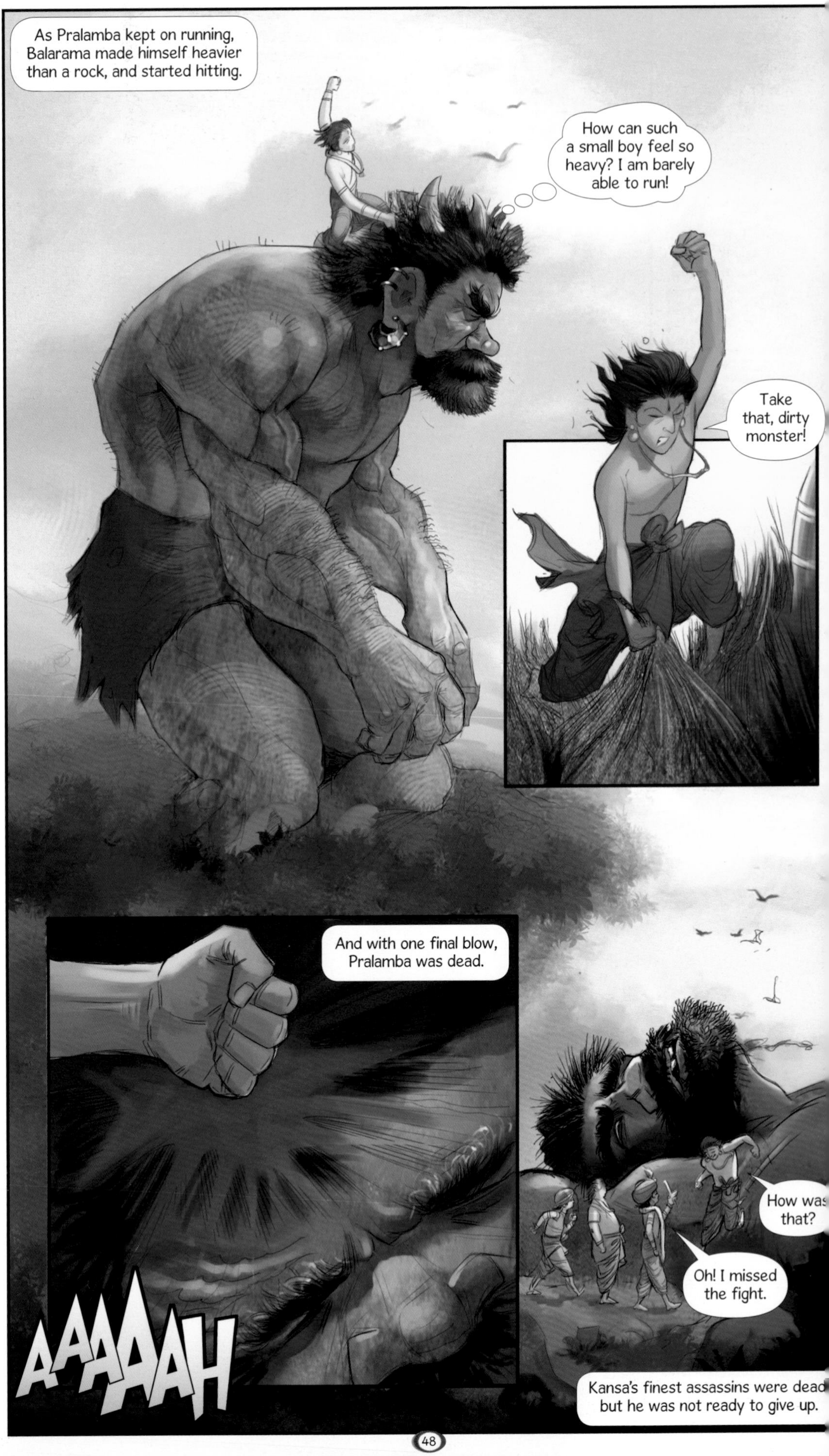
As Pralamba kept on running, Balarama made himself heavier than a rock, and started hitting.
How can such a small boy feel so heavy? I am barely able to run!
Take that, dirty monster!
And with one final blow, Pralamba was dead.
AAAAAH
How was that?
Oh! I missed the fight.
Kansa's finest assassins were dead but he was not ready to give up.

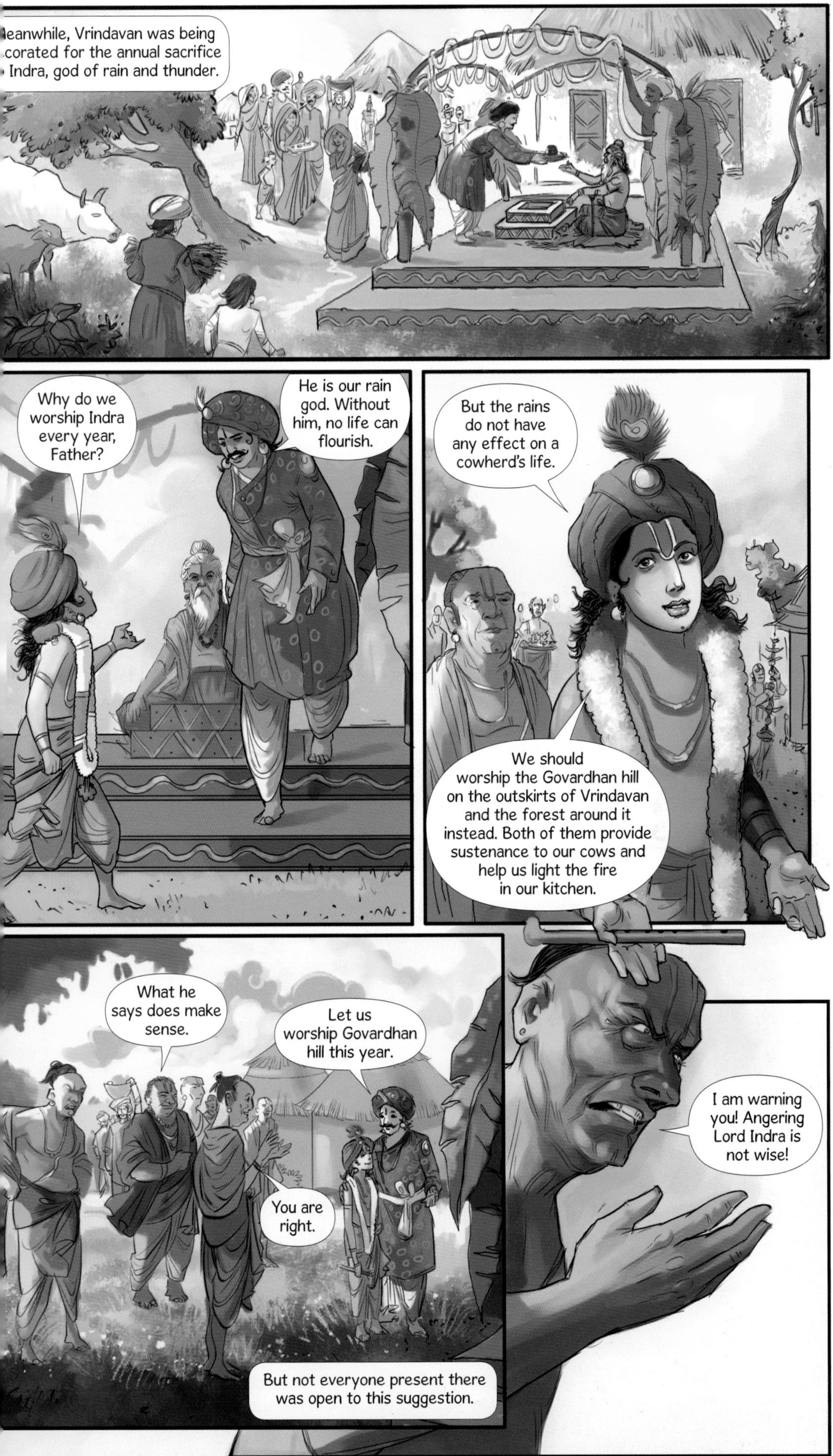
eanwhile, Vrindavan was being corated for the annual sacrifice Indra, god of rain and thunder.
Why do we worship Indra every year, Father?
He is our rain god. Without him, no life can flourish.
But the rains do not have any effect on a cowherd's life.
We should worship the Govardhan hill on the outskirts of Vrindavan and the forest around it instead. Both of them provide sustenance to our cows and help us light the fire in our kitchen.
What he says does make sense.
Let us worship Govardhan hill this year.
You are right.
But not everyone present there was open to this suggestion.
I am warning you! Angering Lord Indra is not wise!

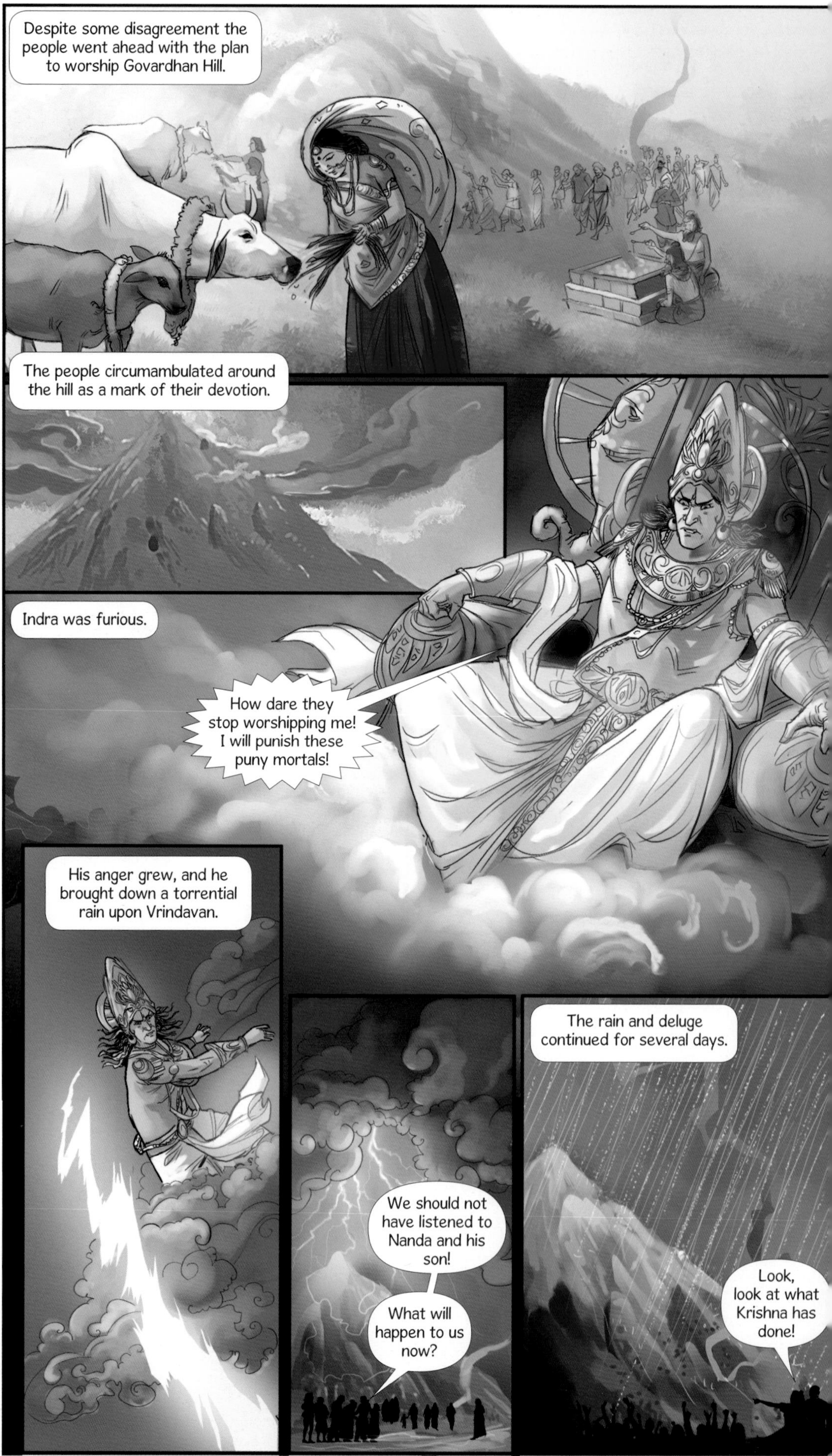
Despite some disagreement the people went ahead with the plan to worship Govardhan Hill.
The people circumambulated around the hill as a mark of their devotion.
Indra was furious.
How dare they stop worshipping me! I will punish these puny mortals!
His anger grew, and he brought down a torrential rain upon Vrindavan.
We should not have listened to Nanda and his son!
What will happen to us now?
The rain and deluge continued for several days.
Look, look at what Krishna has done!

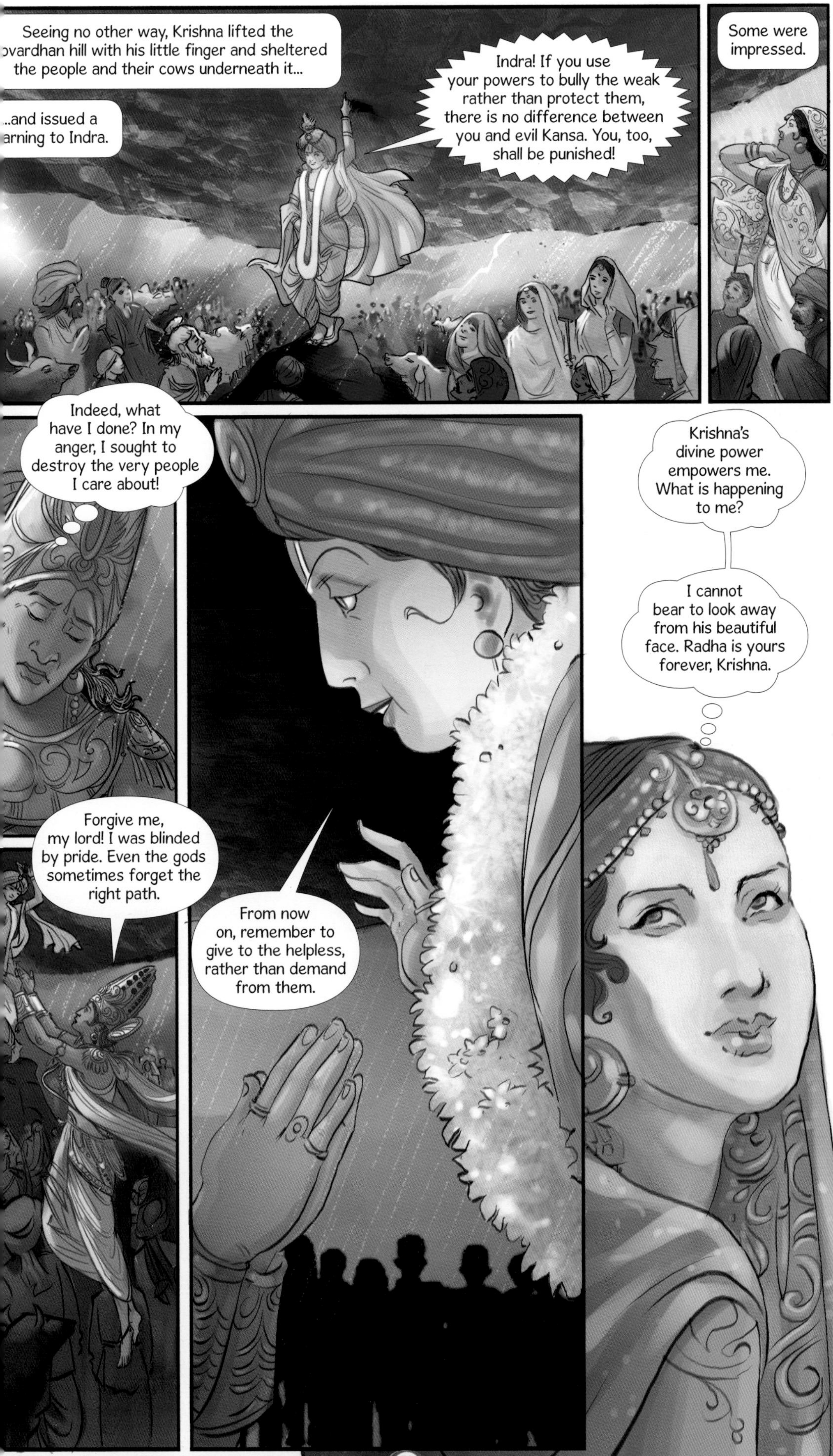

Seeing no other way, Krishna lifted the ovardhan hill with his little finger and sheltered the people and their cows underneath it...
..and issued a arning to Indra.
Indra! If you use your powers to bully the weak rather than protect them, there is no difference between you and evil Kansa. You, too, shall be punished!
Some were impressed.
Indeed, what have I done? In my anger, I sought to destroy the very people I care about!
Forgive me, my lord! I was blinded by pride. Even the gods sometimes forget the right path.
From now on, remember to give to the helpless, rather than demand from them.
Krishna's divine power empowers me. What is happening to me?
I cannot bear to look away from his beautiful face. Radha is yours forever, Krishna.

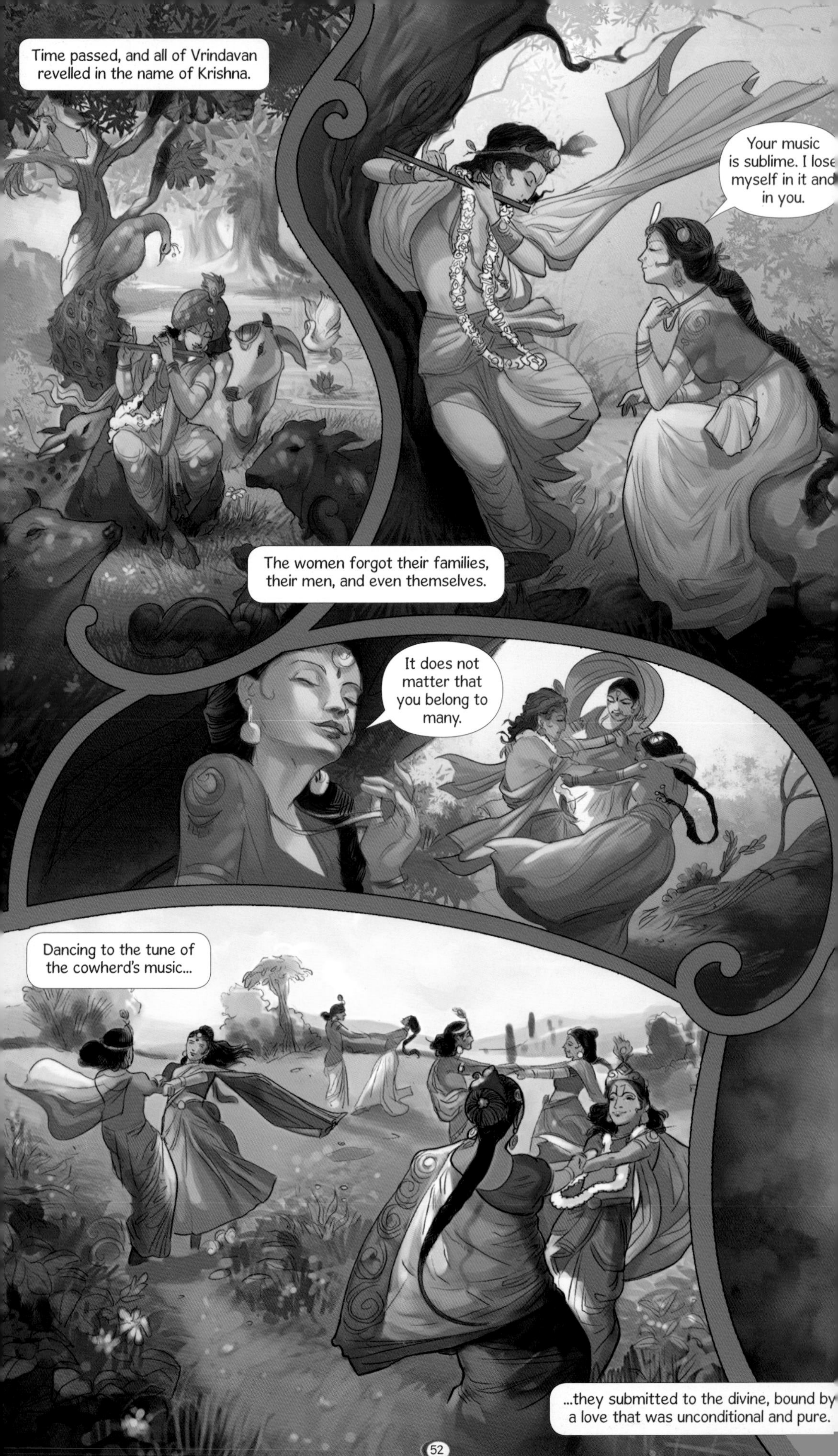
Time passed, and all of Vrindavan revelled in the name of Krishna.
Your music is sublime. I lose myself in it and in you.
The women forgot their families, their men, and even themselves.
It does not matter that you belong to many.
Dancing to the tune of the cowherd's music...
...they submitted to the divine, bound by a love that was unconditional and pure.

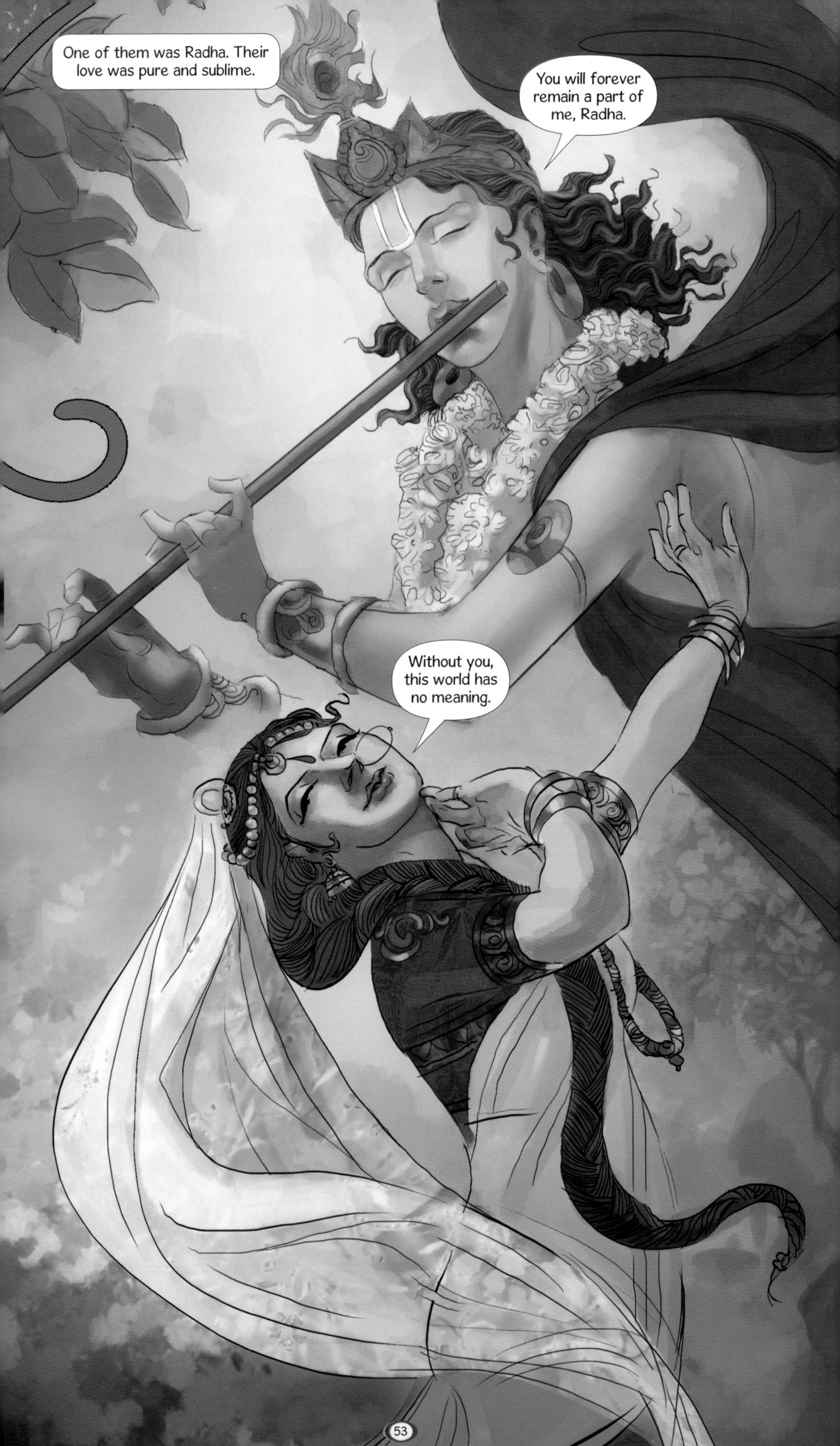
One of them was Radha. Their love was pure and sublime.
You will forever remain a part of me, Radha.
Without you, this world has no meaning.

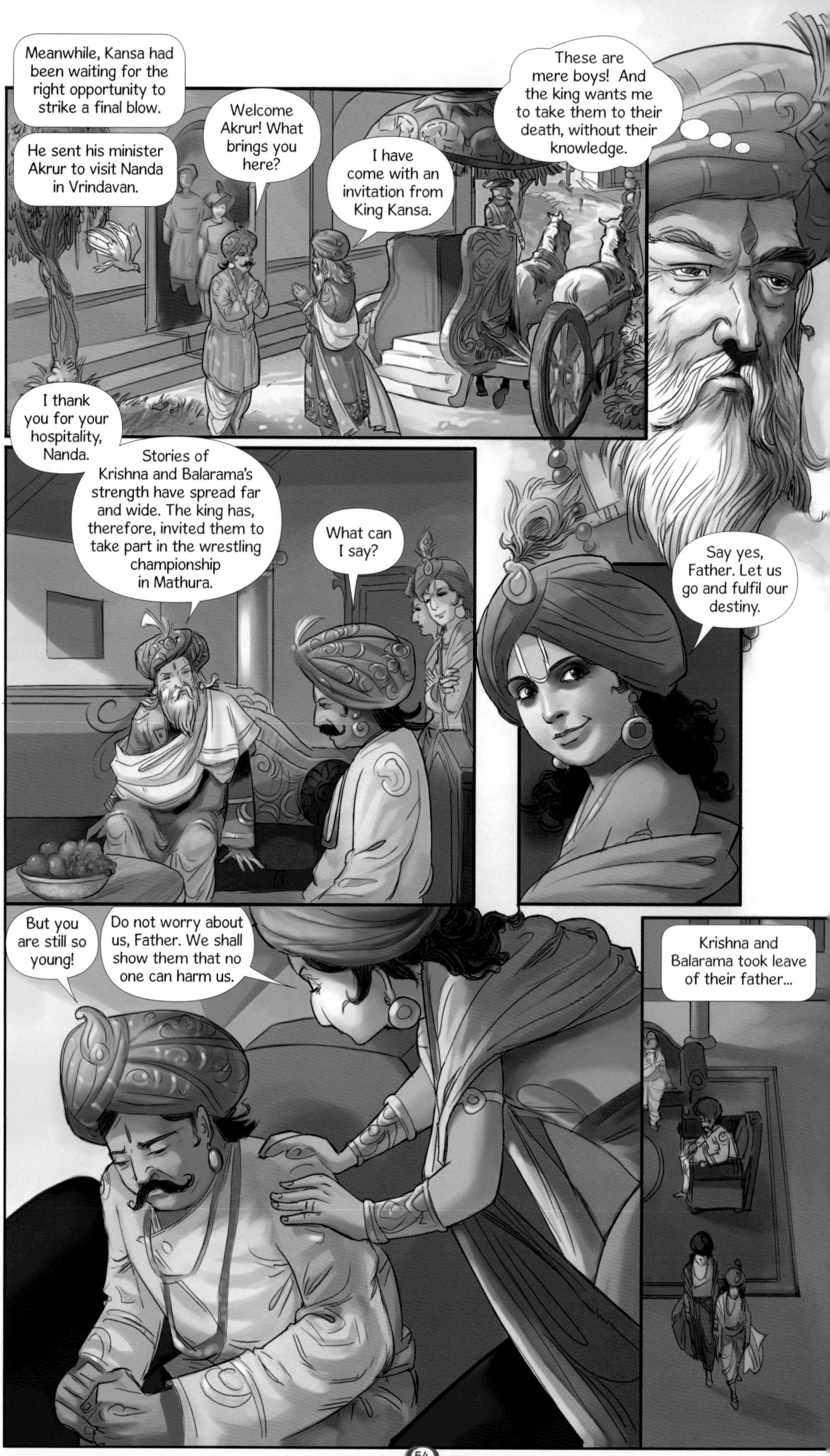
Meanwhile, Kansa had been waiting for the right opportunity to strike a final blow.
He sent his minister Akrur to visit Nanda in Vrindavan.
Welcome Akrur! What brings you here?
I have come with an invitation from King Kansa.
These are mere boys! And the king wants me to take them to their death, without their knowledge.
I thank you for your hospitality, Nanda.
Stories of Krishna and Balarama's strength have spread far and wide. The king has, therefore, invited them to take part in the wrestling championship in Mathura.
What can I say?
Say yes, Father. Let us go and fulfil our destiny.
But you are still so young!
Do not worry about us, Father. We shall show them that no one can harm us.
Krishna and Balarama took leave of their father...

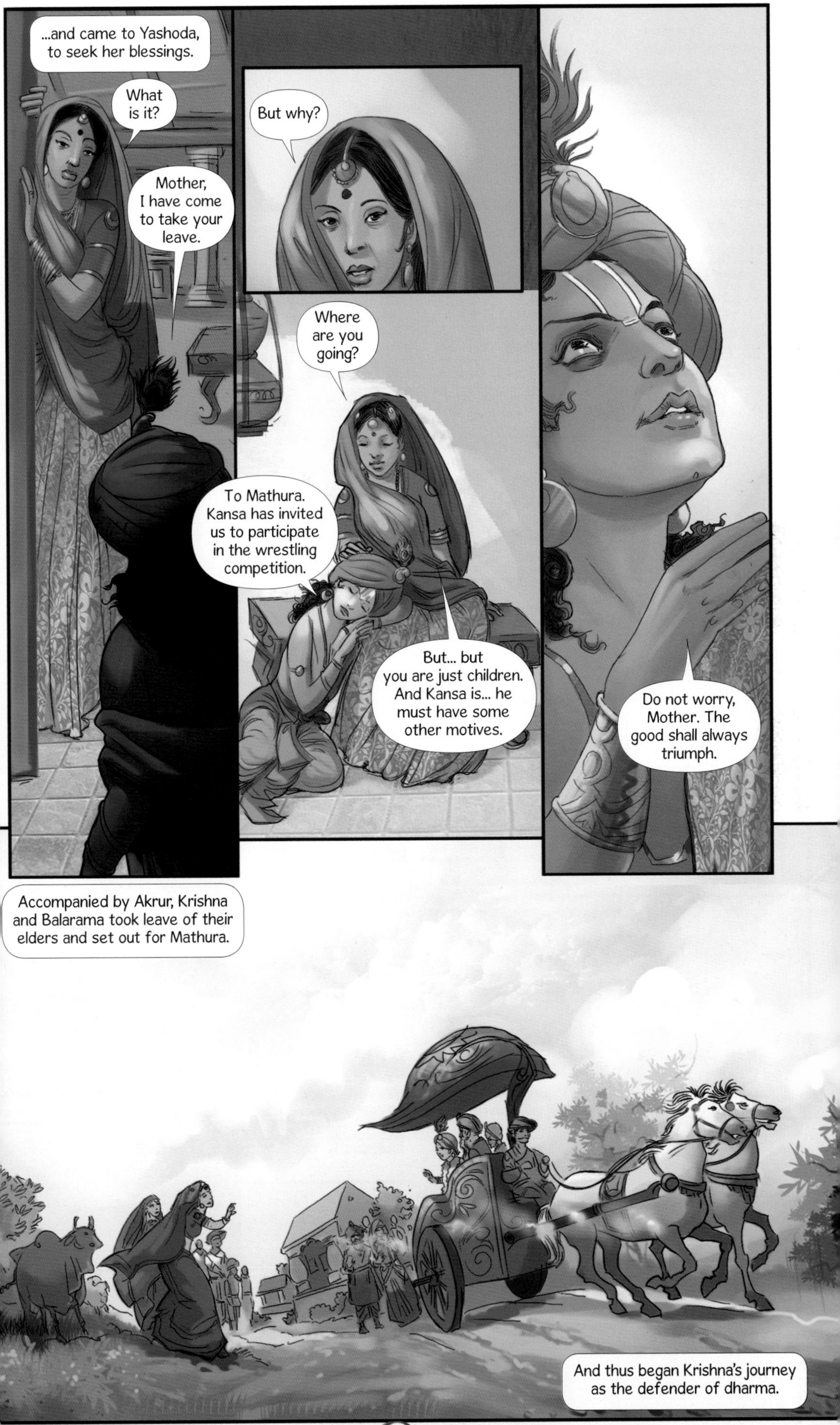
...and came to Yashoda, to seek her blessings.
What is it?
Mother, I have come to take your leave.
But why?
Where are you going?
To Mathura. Kansa has invited us to participate in the wrestling competition.
But... but you are just children. And Kansa is... he must have some other motives.
Do not worry, Mother. The good shall always triumph.
Accompanied by Akrur, Krishna and Balarama took leave of their elders and set out for Mathura.
And thus began Krishna's journey as the defender of dharma.

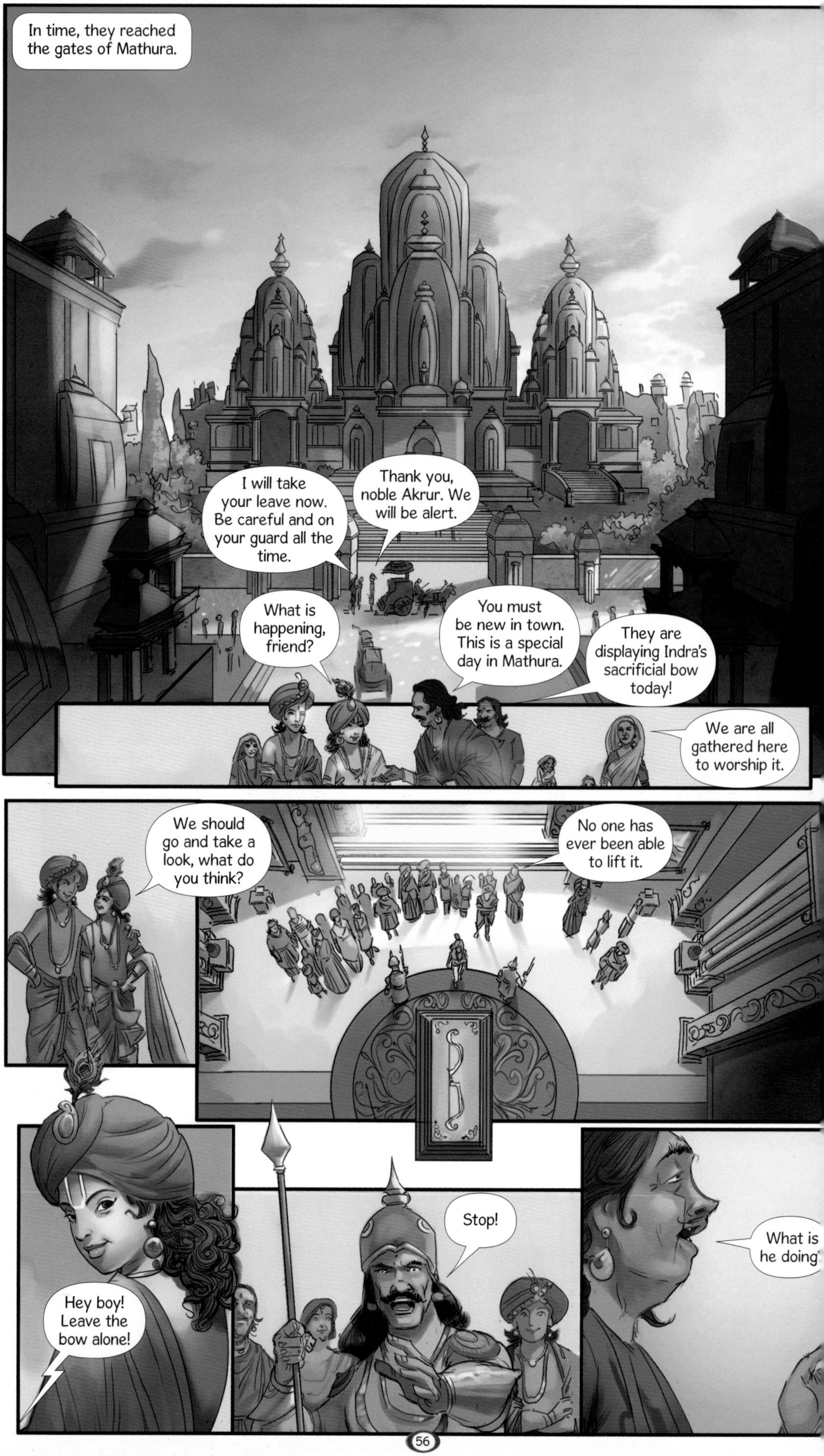
In time, they reached the gates of Mathura.
I will take your leave now. Be careful and on your guard all the time.
Thank you, noble Akrur. We will be alert.
What is happening, friend?
You must be new in town. This is a special day in Mathura.
They are displaying Indra's sacrificial bow today!
We are all gathered here to worship it.
We should go and take a look, what do you think?
No one has ever been able to lift it.
Hey boy! Leave the bow alone!
Stop!
What is he doing

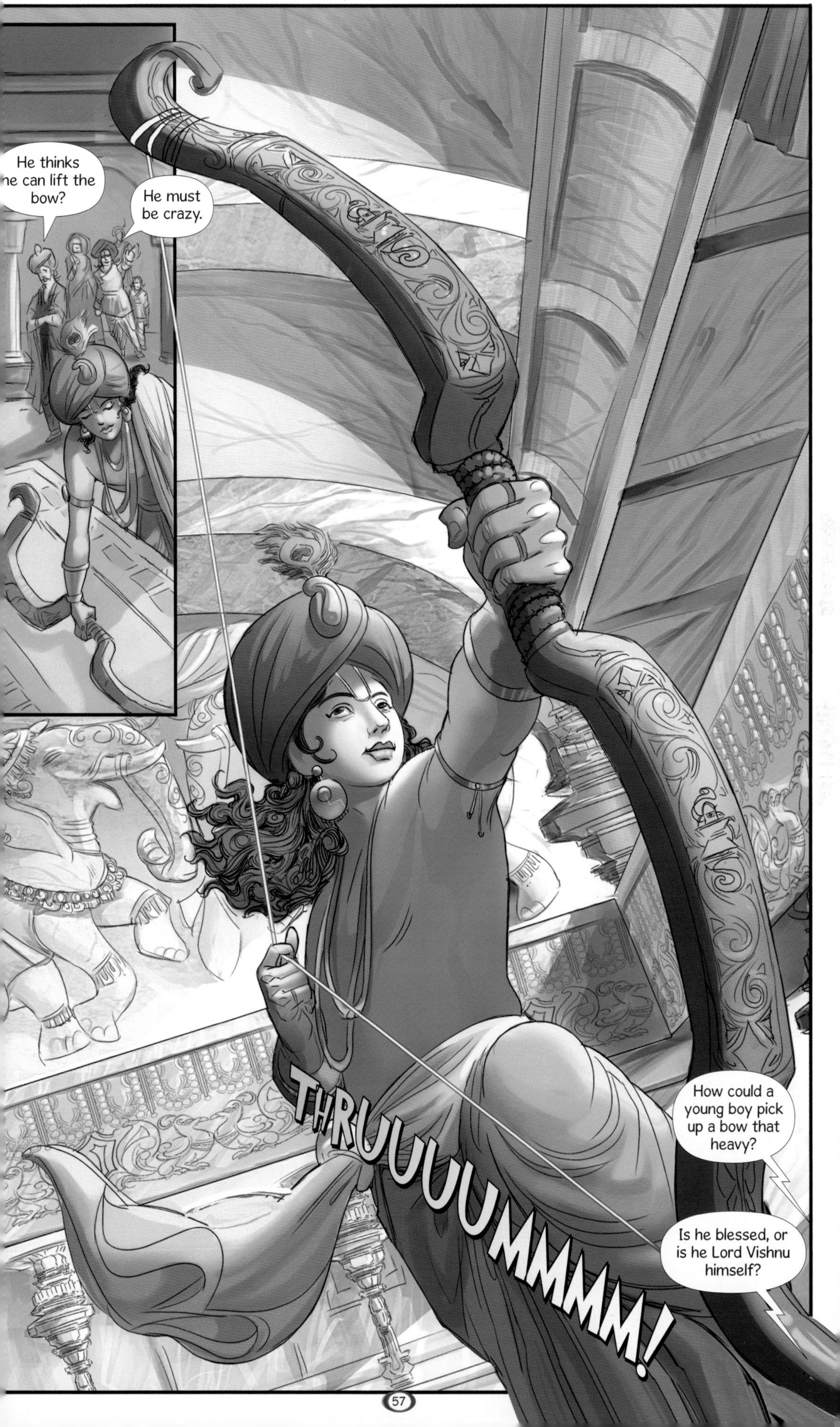
He thinks he can lift the bow?
He must be crazy.
THRUUUUMMMMM!
How could a young boy pick up a bow that heavy?
Is he blessed, or is he Lord Vishnu himself?

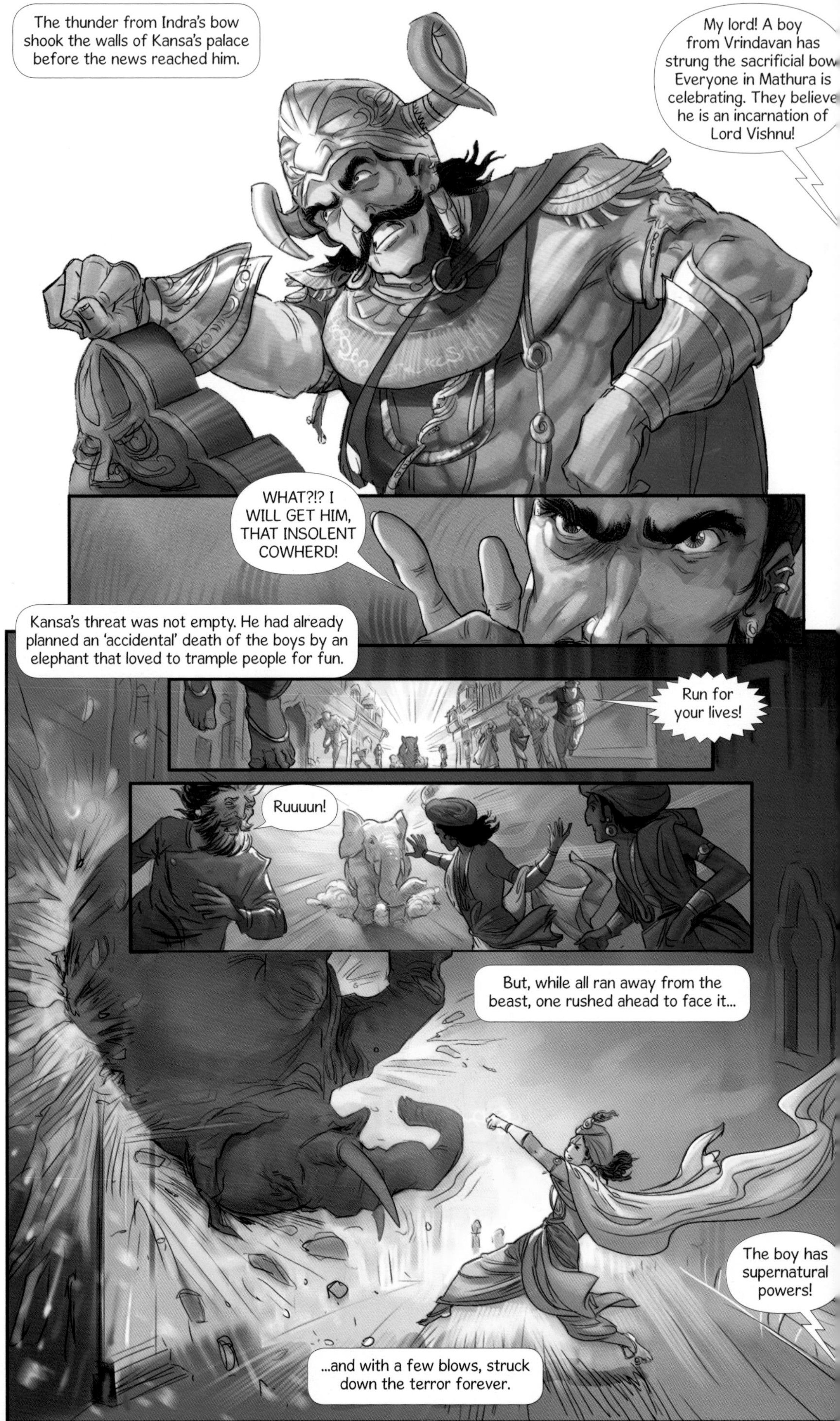

The thunder from Indra's bow shook the walls of Kansa's palace before the news reached him.
My lord! A boy from Vrindavan has strung the sacrificial bow Everyone in Mathura is celebrating. They believe he is an incarnation of Lord Vishnu!
WHAT?!? I WILL GET HIM, THAT INSOLENT COWHERD!
Kansa's threat was not empty. He had already planned an 'accidental' death of the boys by an elephant that loved to trample people for fun.
Run for your lives!
Ruuuun!
But, while all ran away from the beast, one rushed ahead to face it...
The boy has supernatural powers!
...and with a few blows, struck down the terror forever.

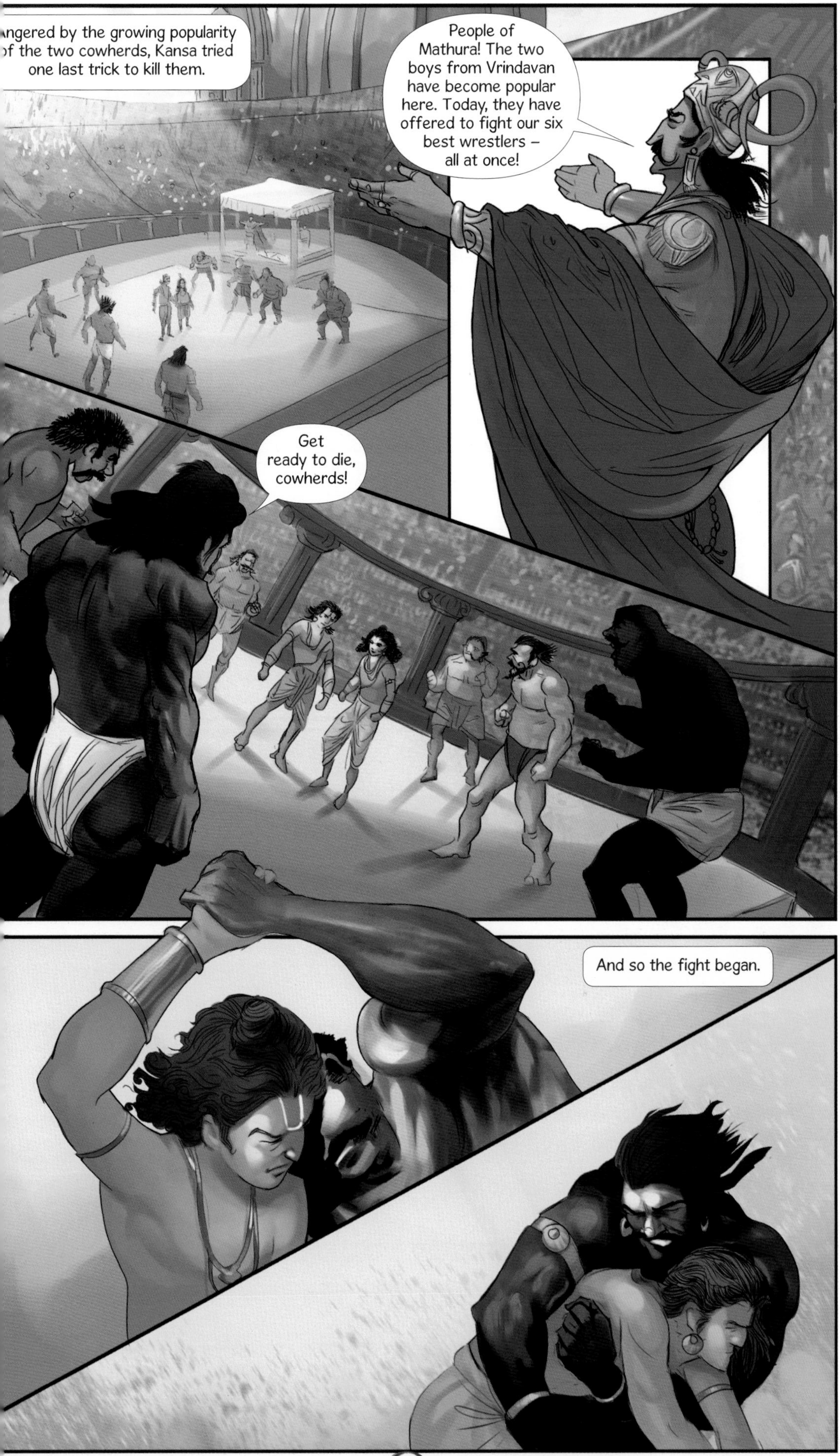

ngered by the growing popularity of the two cowherds, Kansa tried one last trick to kill them.
People of Mathura! The two boys from Vrindavan have become popular here. Today, they have offered to fight our six best wrestlers – all at once!
Get ready to die, cowherds!
And so the fight began.

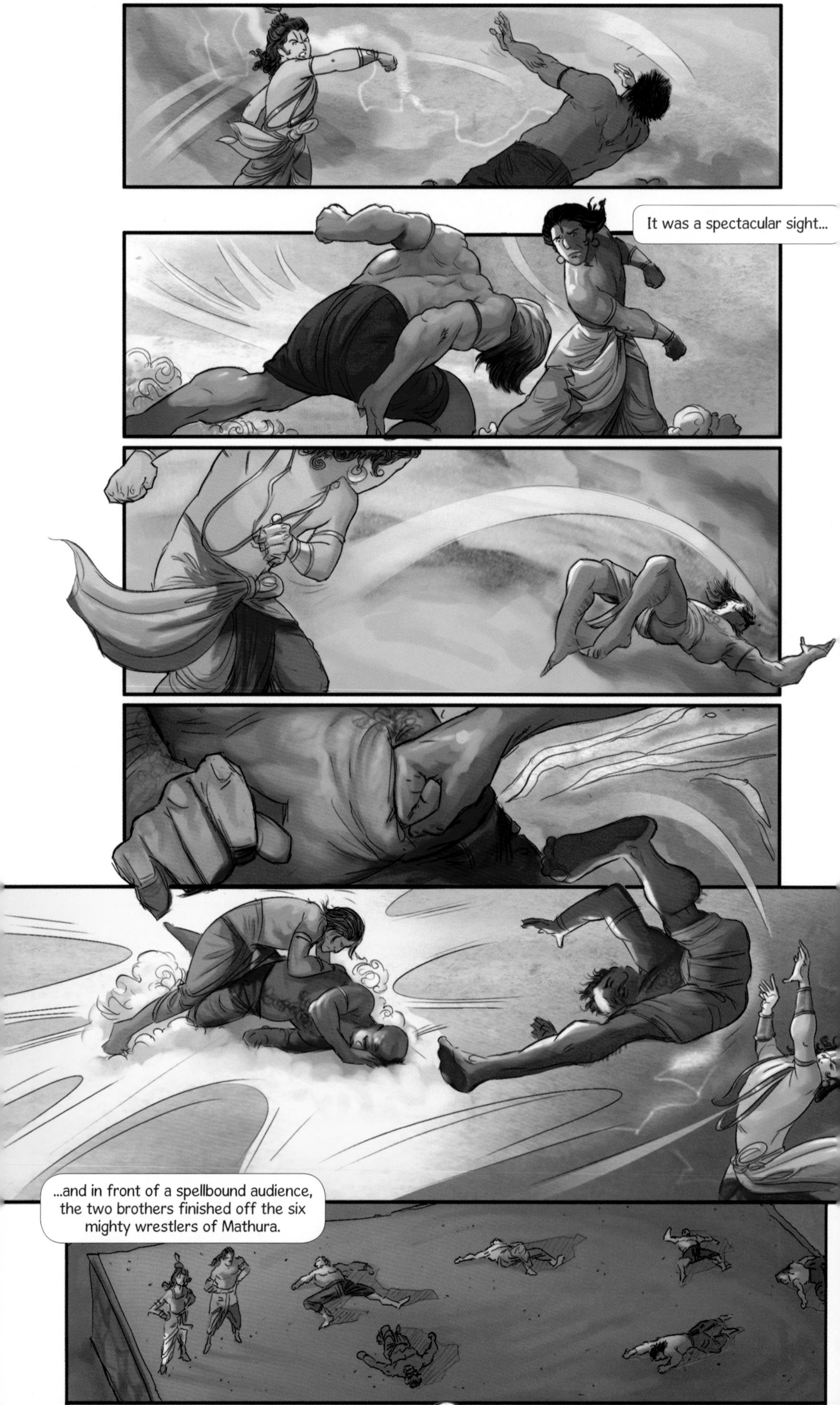

It was a spectacular sight...
...and in front of a spellbound audience, the two brothers finished off the six mighty wrestlers of Mathura.

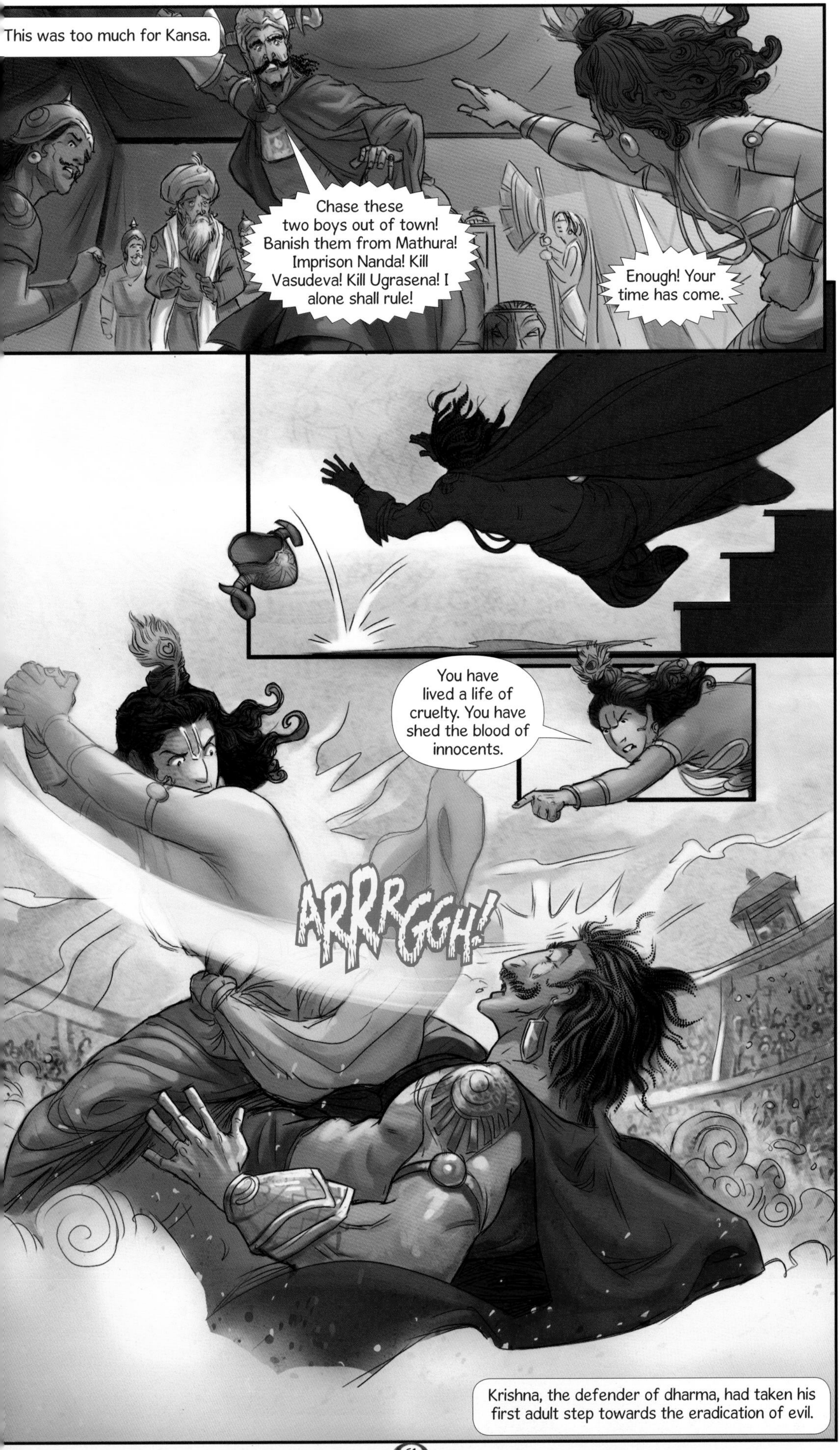

This was too much for Kansa.
Chase these two boys out of town! Banish them from Mathura! Imprison Nanda! Kill Vasudeva! Kill Ugrasena! I alone shall rule!
Enough! Your time has come.
You have lived a life of cruelty. You have shed the blood of innocents.
ARRRGGH!
Krishna, the defender of dharma, had taken his first adult step towards the eradication of evil.

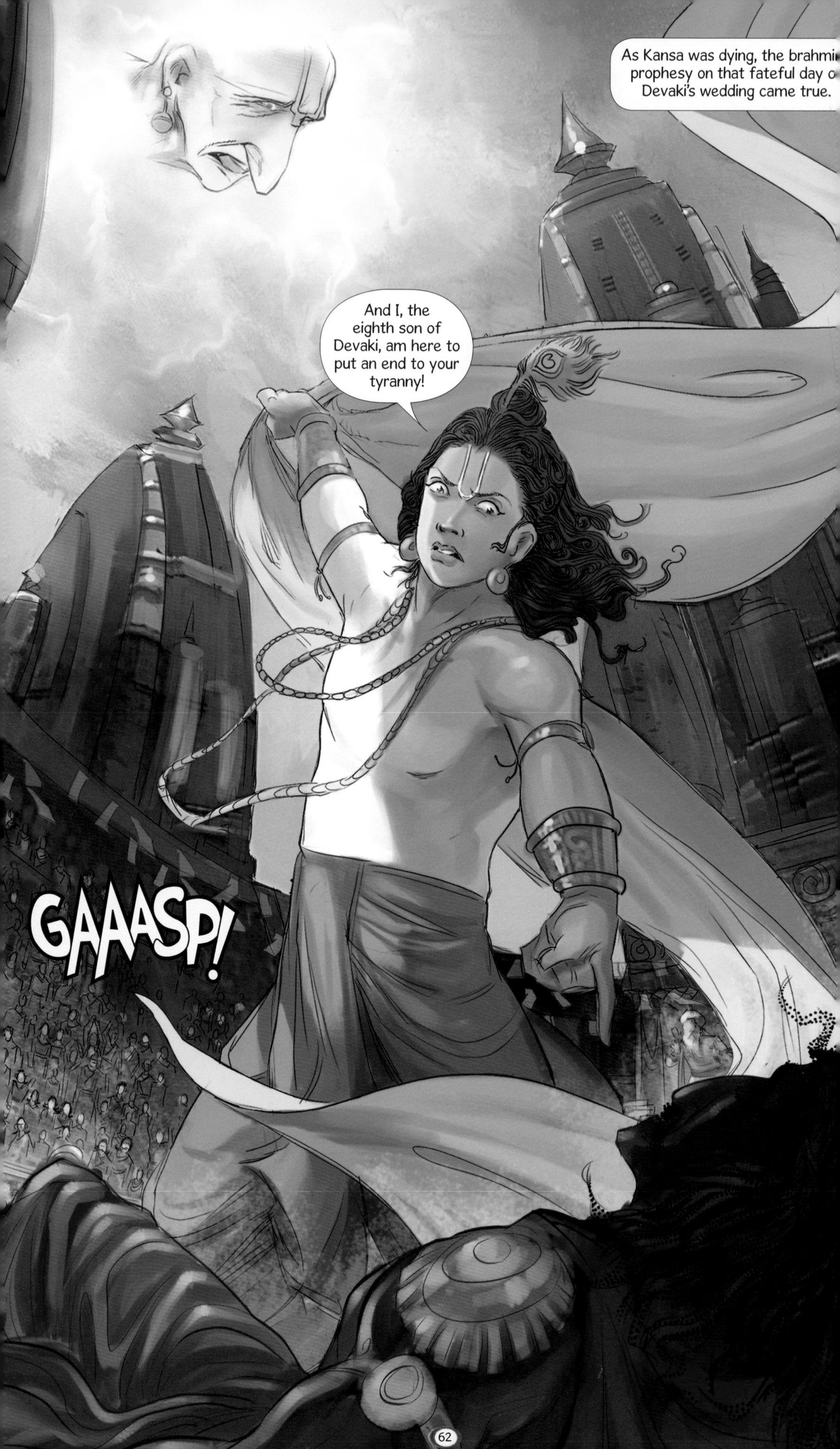
As Kansa was dying, the brahmi
prophesy on that fateful day o
Devaki's wedding came true.
And I, the eighth son of Devaki, am here to put an end to your tyranny!
GAAASP!

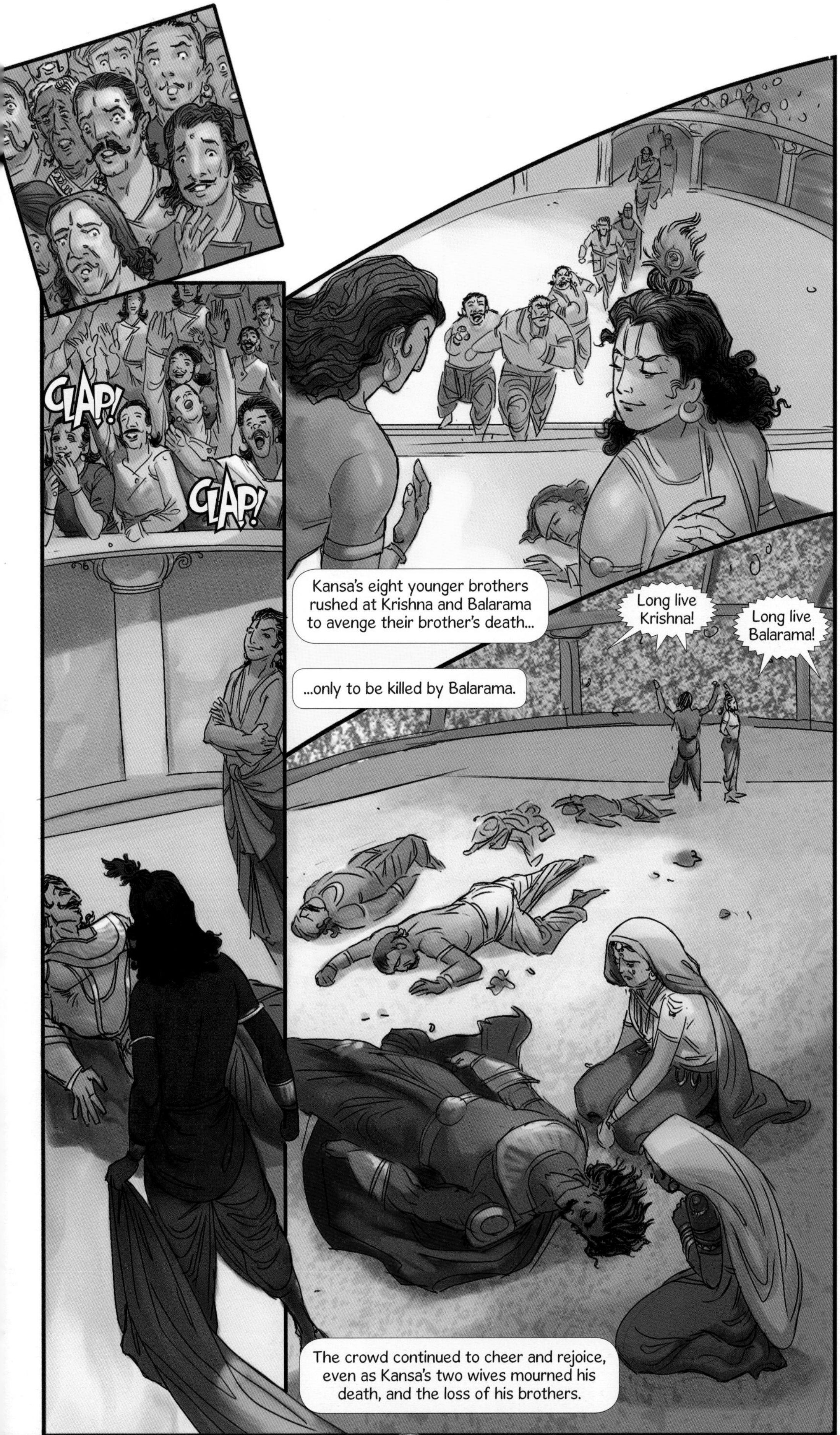
CLAP!
CLAP!
Kansa's eight younger brothers rushed at Krishna and Balarama to avenge their brother's death...
...only to be killed by Balarama.
Long live Krishna!
Long live Balarama!
The crowd continued to cheer and rejoice, even as Kansa's two wives mourned his death, and the loss of his brothers.

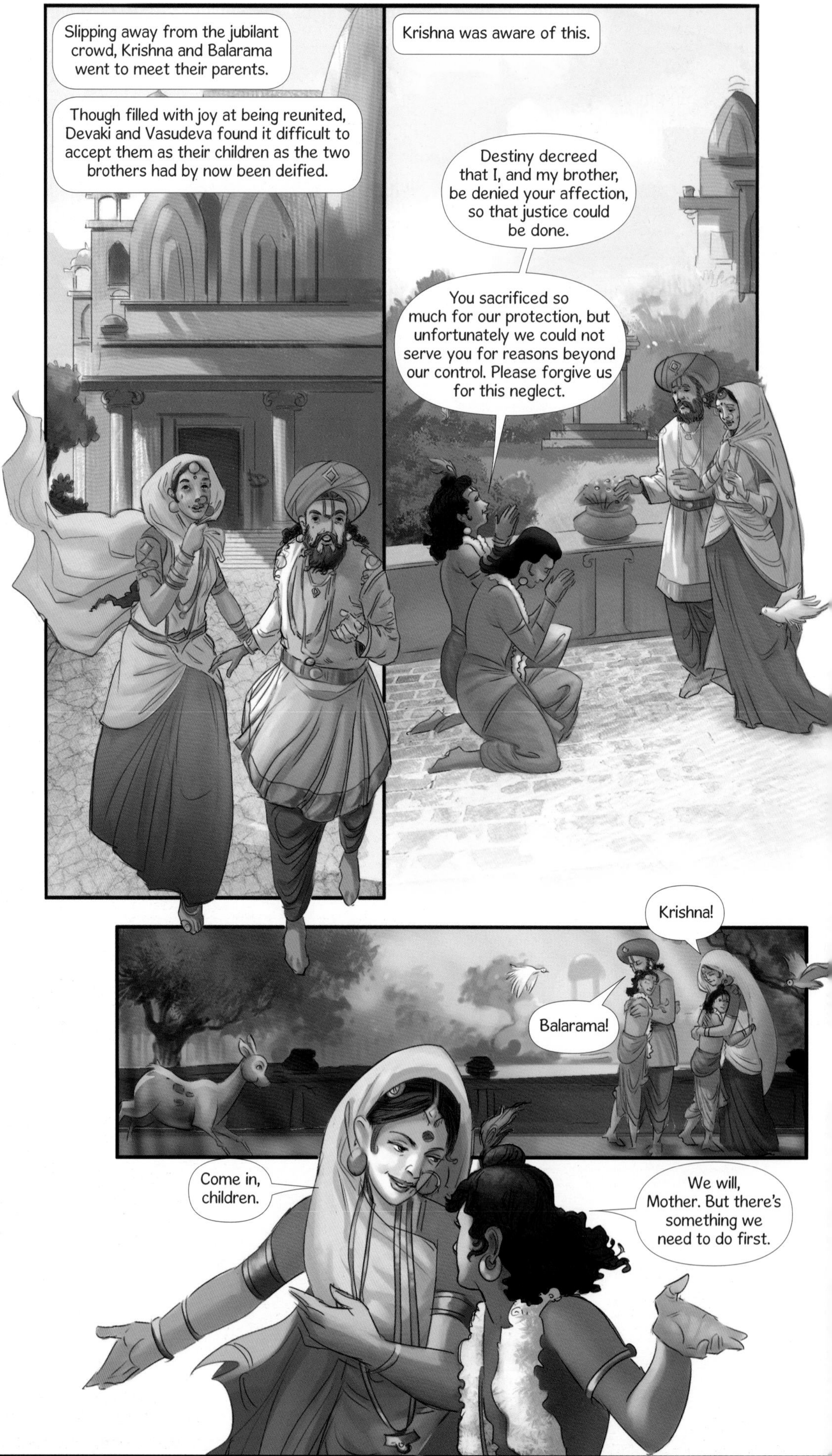
Slipping away from the jubilant crowd, Krishna and Balarama went to meet their parents.
Though filled with joy at being reunited, Devaki and Vasudeva found it difficult to accept them as their children as the two brothers had by now been deified.
Krishna was aware of this.
Destiny decreed that I, and my brother, be denied your affection, so that justice could be done.
You sacrificed so much for our protection, but unfortunately we could not serve you for reasons beyond our control. Please forgive us for this neglect.
Krishna!
Balarama!
Come in, children.
We will, Mother. But there's something we need to do first.

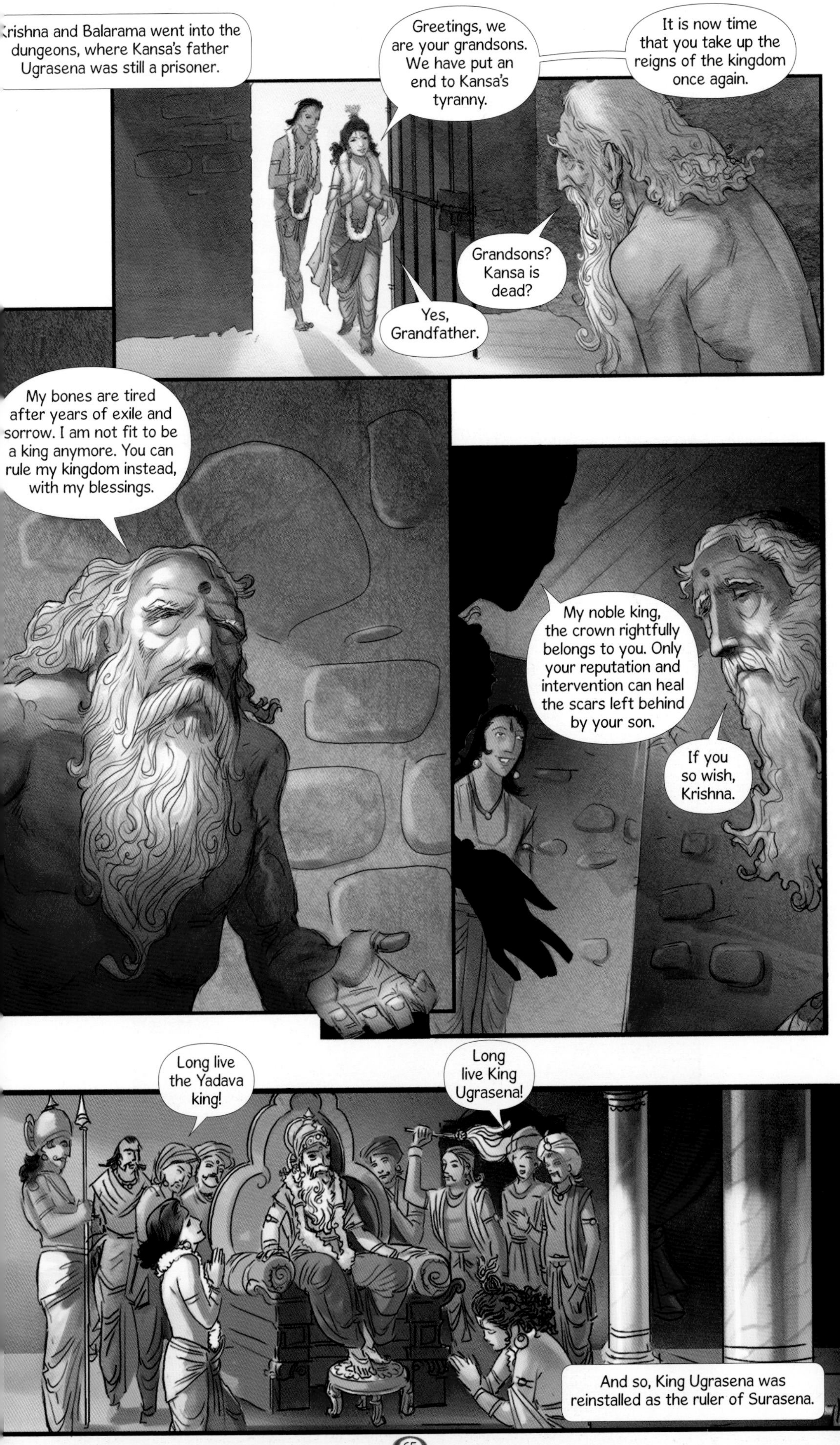
Krishna and Balarama went into the dungeons, where Kansa's father Ugrasena was still a prisoner.
Greetings, we are your grandsons. We have put an end to Kansa's tyranny.
It is now time that you take up the reigns of the kingdom once again.
Grandsons? Kansa is dead?
Yes, Grandfather.
My bones are tired after years of exile and sorrow. I am not fit to be a king anymore. You can rule my kingdom instead, with my blessings.
My noble king, the crown rightfully belongs to you. Only your reputation and intervention can heal the scars left behind by your son.
If you so wish, Krishna.
Long live the Yadava king!
Long live King Ugrasena!
And so, King Ugrasena was reinstalled as the ruler of Surasena.

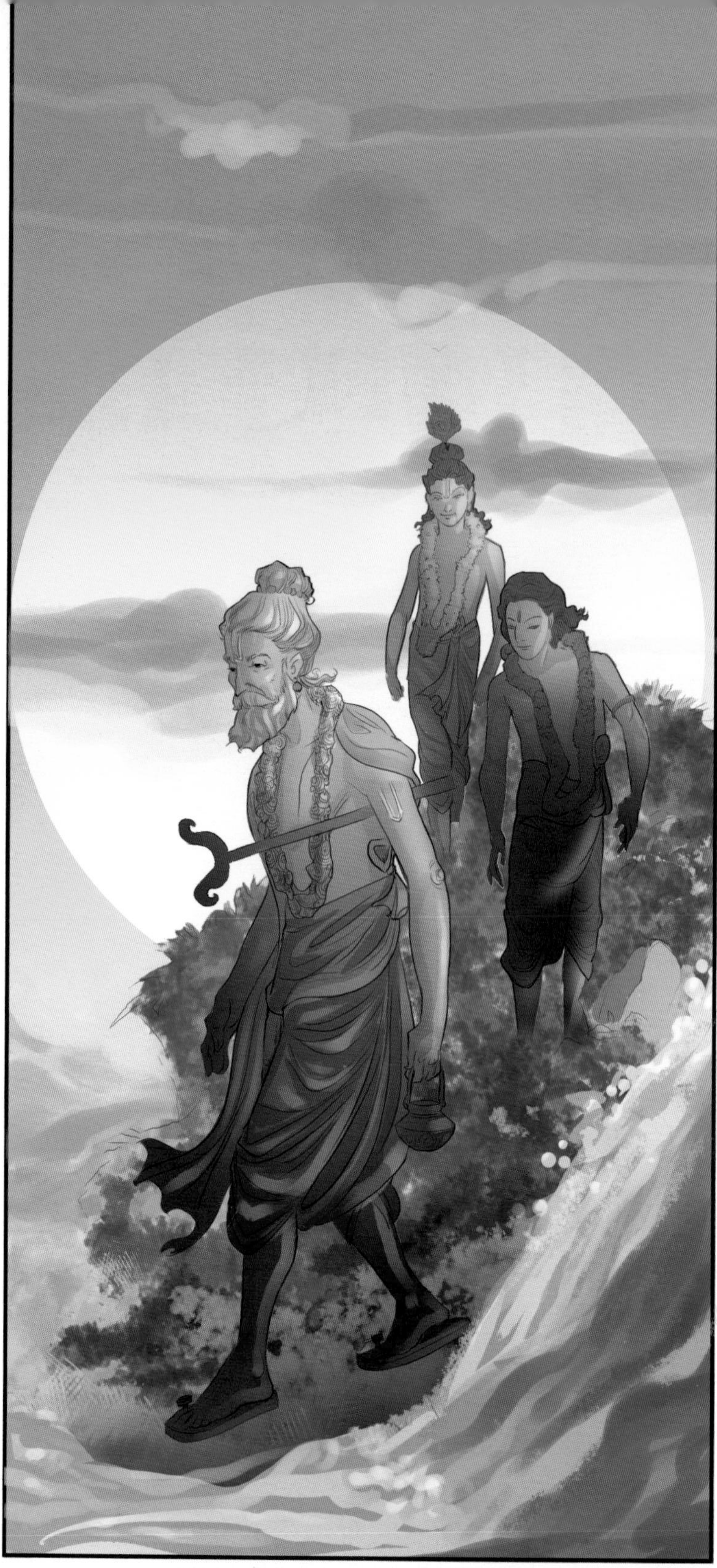

And then, with peace reigning in Mathura, Krishna and Balarama accompanied guru Sandipani to his school in Ujjain to study politics, philosophy, and military science.

Dwarka

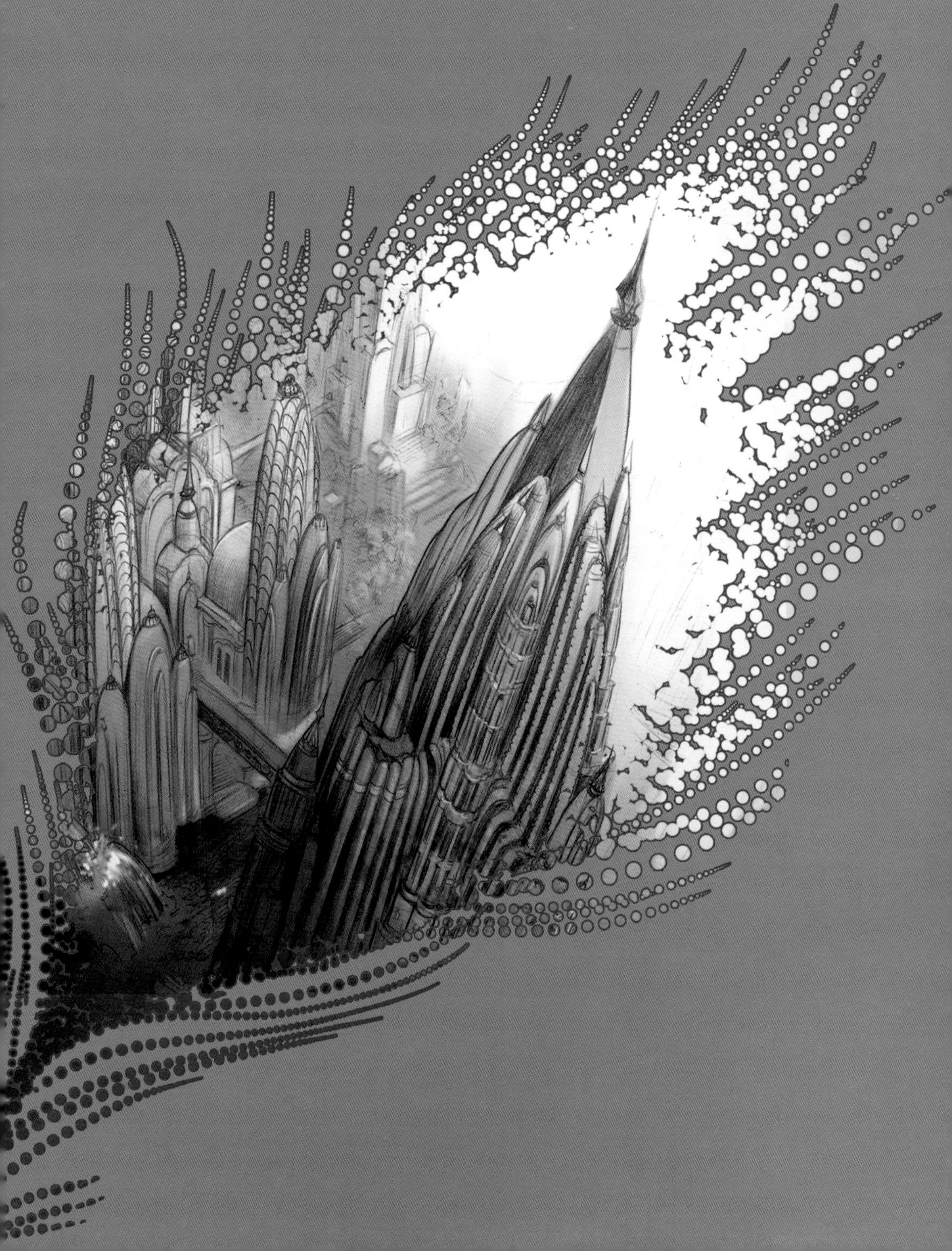

Dwarka

After completing their education and training, Krishna and Balarama return to King Ugrasena's court in Mathura. Well-versed in the arts of statecraft, they take an active interest in court affairs. Many years pass by peacefully. But all is not as quiet as it seems. Krishna has a new enemy, Jarasandha, the mighty king of Magadha. Jarasandha had given his two daughters in marriage to Kansa, whose death had left them widowed and now Jarasandha seeks his revenge. He keeps on attacking Mathura, but fails to breach its defences.

Also unhappy about Kansa's death is Rukmin, son of Bhishmaka, the king of Vidarbha. Kansa and Rukmin were close friends, and in joining hands with Jarasandha, Rukmin thinks he has found the perfect opportunity to defeat Krishna and avenge his friend's death.

Meanwhile, Krishna's fame has started spreading far and wide as tales of his wisdom are told throughout the land. Krishna has now grown and matured as a person. He is not the innocent cowherd any longer. He is now a shrewd strategist and respected statesman. One of his many admirers is Princess Rukmini of Vidarbha, sister of Rukmin. Even without ever having met him, she sets her heart upon marrying Krishna, much to the displeasure of her brother.

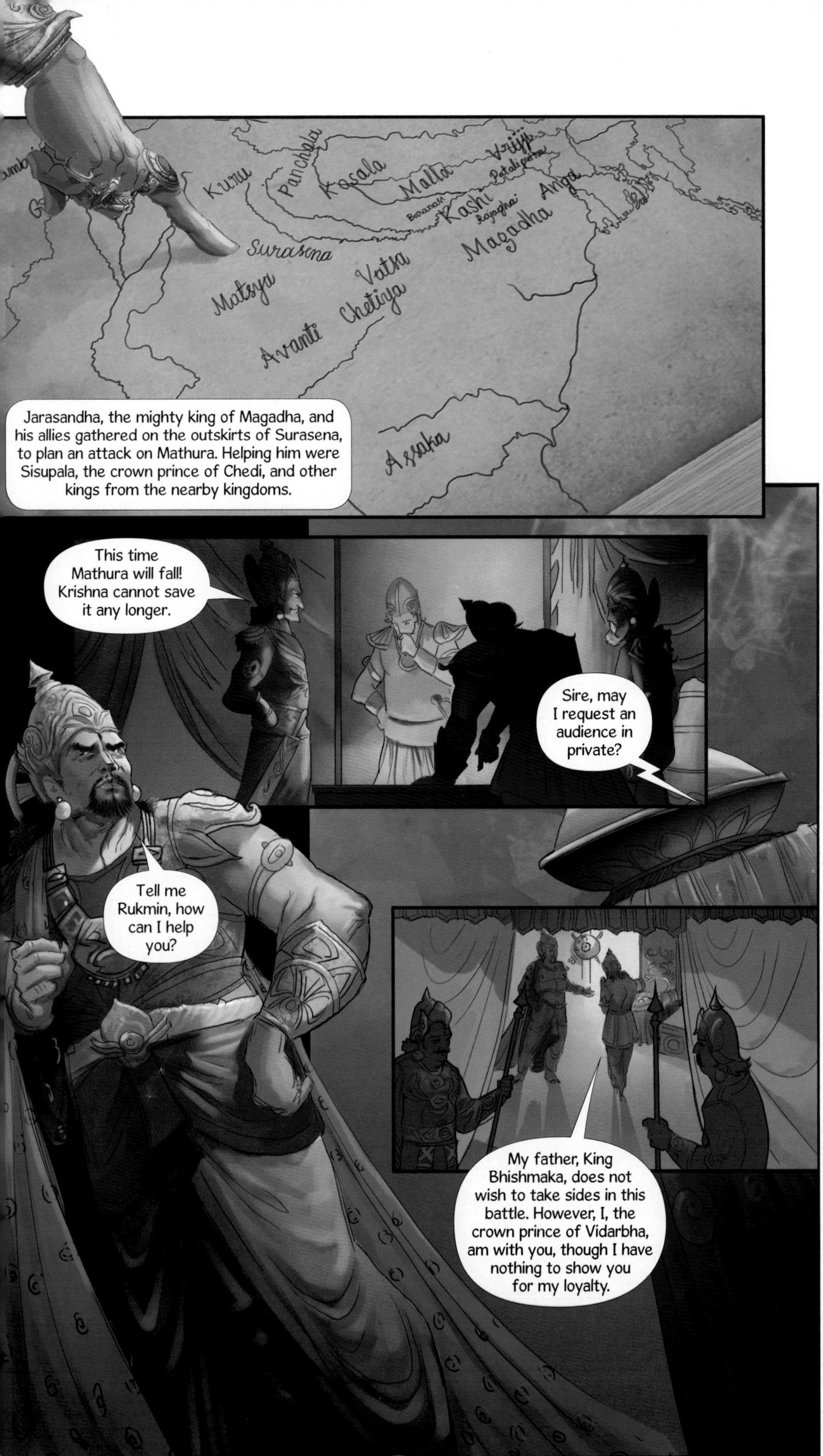
Kuru
Panchala
Kosala
Malla
Vrijji
Pataliputra
Baranasi
Kashi
Rajagriha
Anga
Surasena
Magadha
Vatsa
Matsya
Chetiya
Avanti
Assaka
Jarasandha, the mighty king of Magadha, and his allies gathered on the outskirts of Surasena, to plan an attack on Mathura. Helping him were Sisupala, the crown prince of Chedi, and other kings from the nearby kingdoms.
This time Mathura will fall! Krishna cannot save it any longer.
Sire, may I request an audience in private?
Tell me Rukmin, how can I help you?
My father, King Bhishmaka, does not wish to take sides in this battle. However, I, the crown prince of Vidarbha, am with you, though I have nothing to show you for my loyalty.

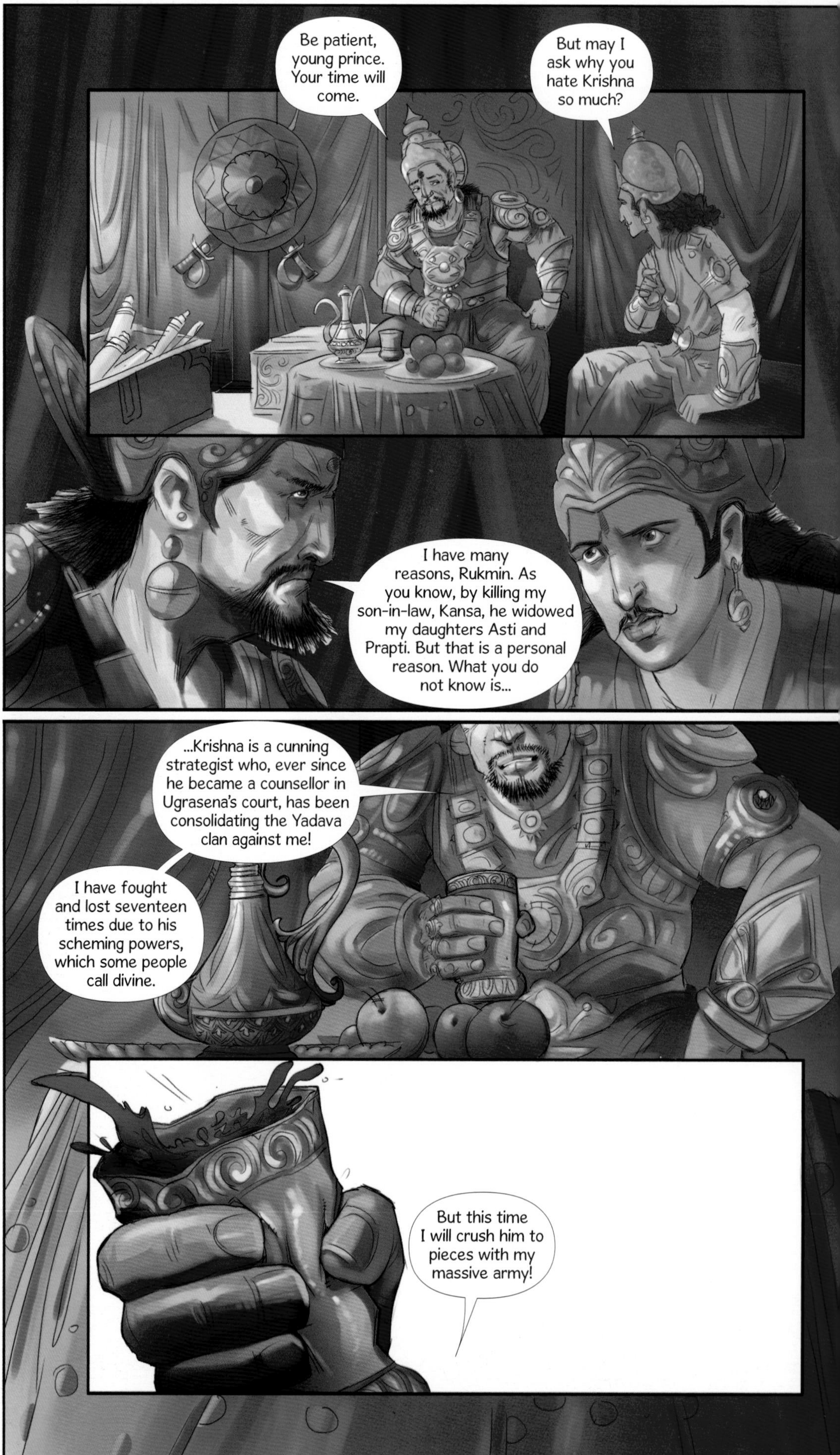

Be patient, young prince. Your time will come.
But may I ask why you hate Krishna so much?
I have many reasons, Rukmin. As you know, by killing my son-in-law, Kansa, he widowed my daughters Asti and Prapti. But that is a personal reason. What you do not know is...
...Krishna is a cunning strategist who, ever since he became a counsellor in Ugrasena's court, has been consolidating the Yadava clan against me!
I have fought and lost seventeen times due to his scheming powers, which some people call divine.
But this time I will crush him to pieces with my massive army!

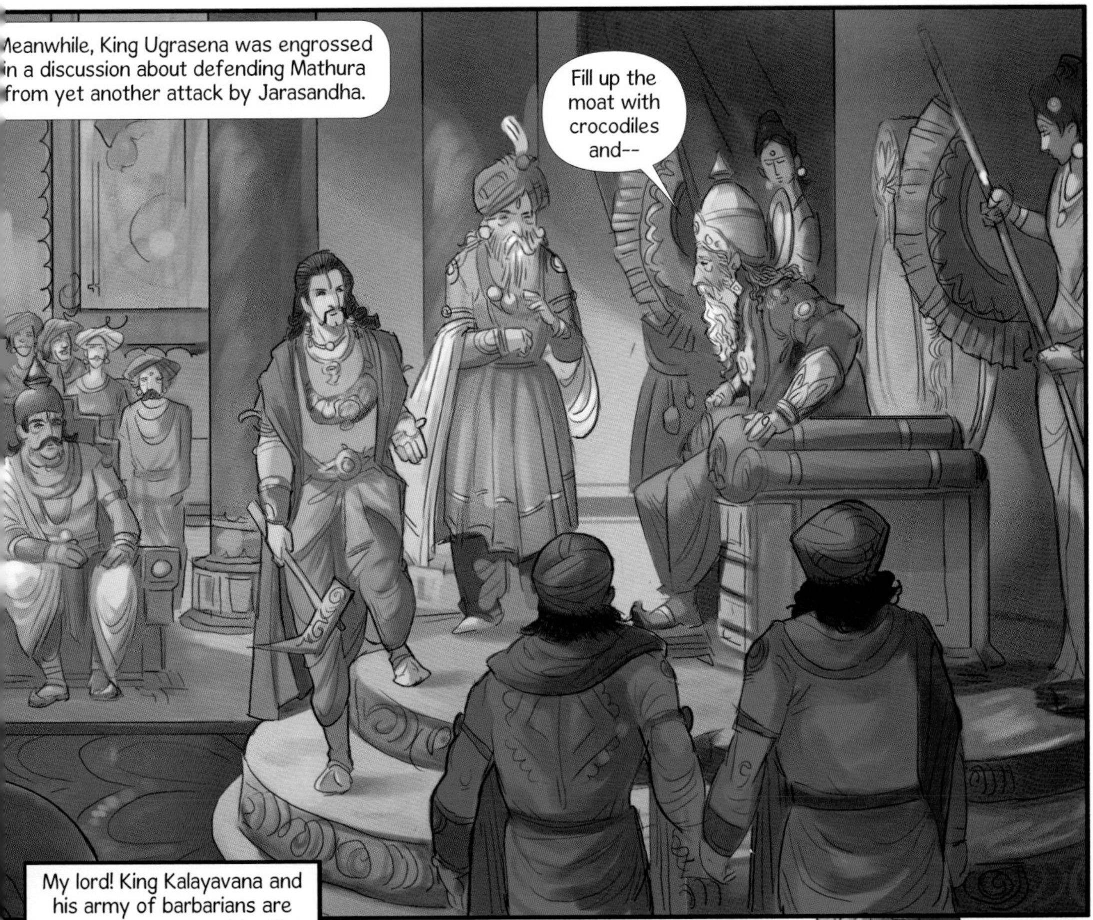
Meanwhile, King Ugrasena was engrossed in a discussion about defending Mathura from yet another attack by Jarasandha.
Fill up the moat with crocodiles and--

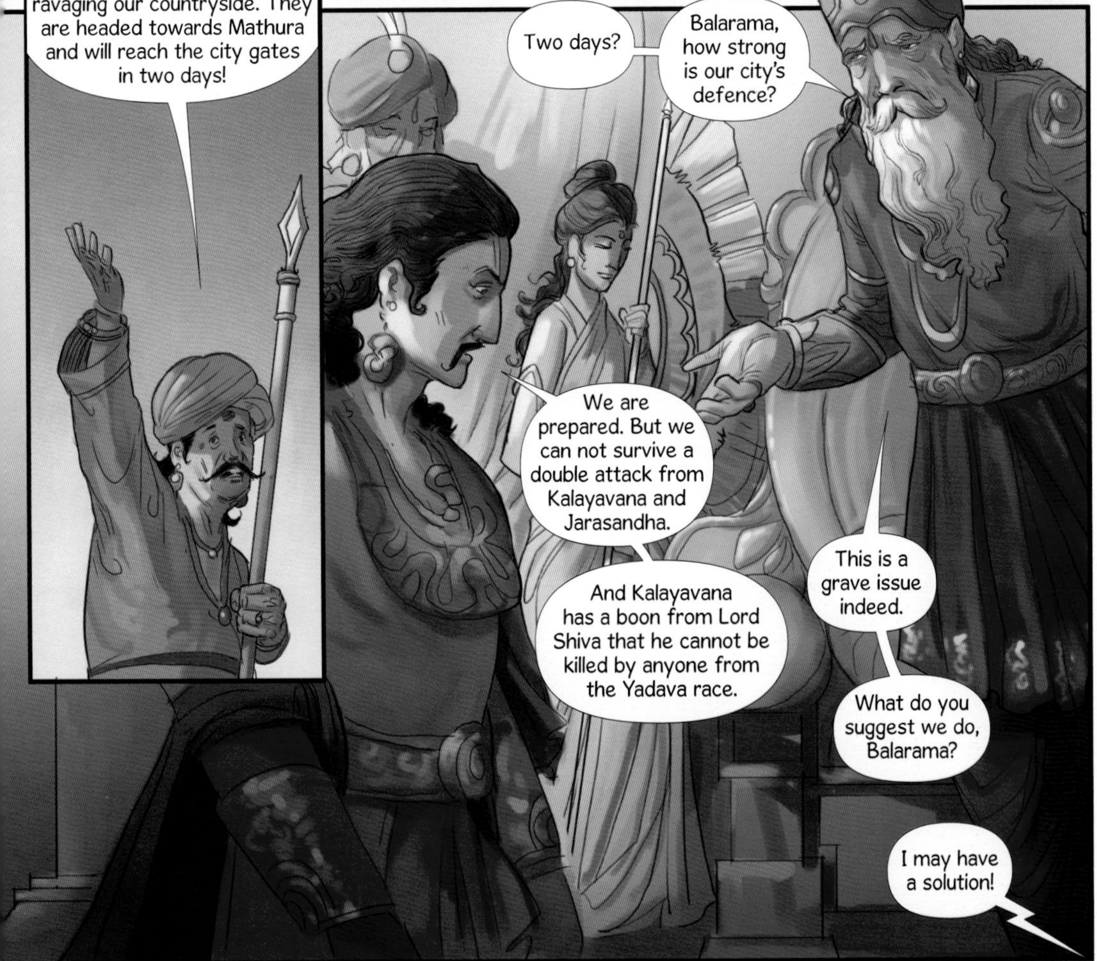
My lord! King Kalayavana and his army of barbarians are ravaging our countryside. They are headed towards Mathura and will reach the city gates in two days!
Two days?
Balarama, how strong is our city's defence?
We are prepared. But we can not survive a double attack from Kalayavana and Jarasandha.
And Kalayavana has a boon from Lord Shiva that he cannot be killed by anyone from the Yadava race.
This is a grave issue indeed.
What do you suggest we do, Balarama?
I may have a solution!

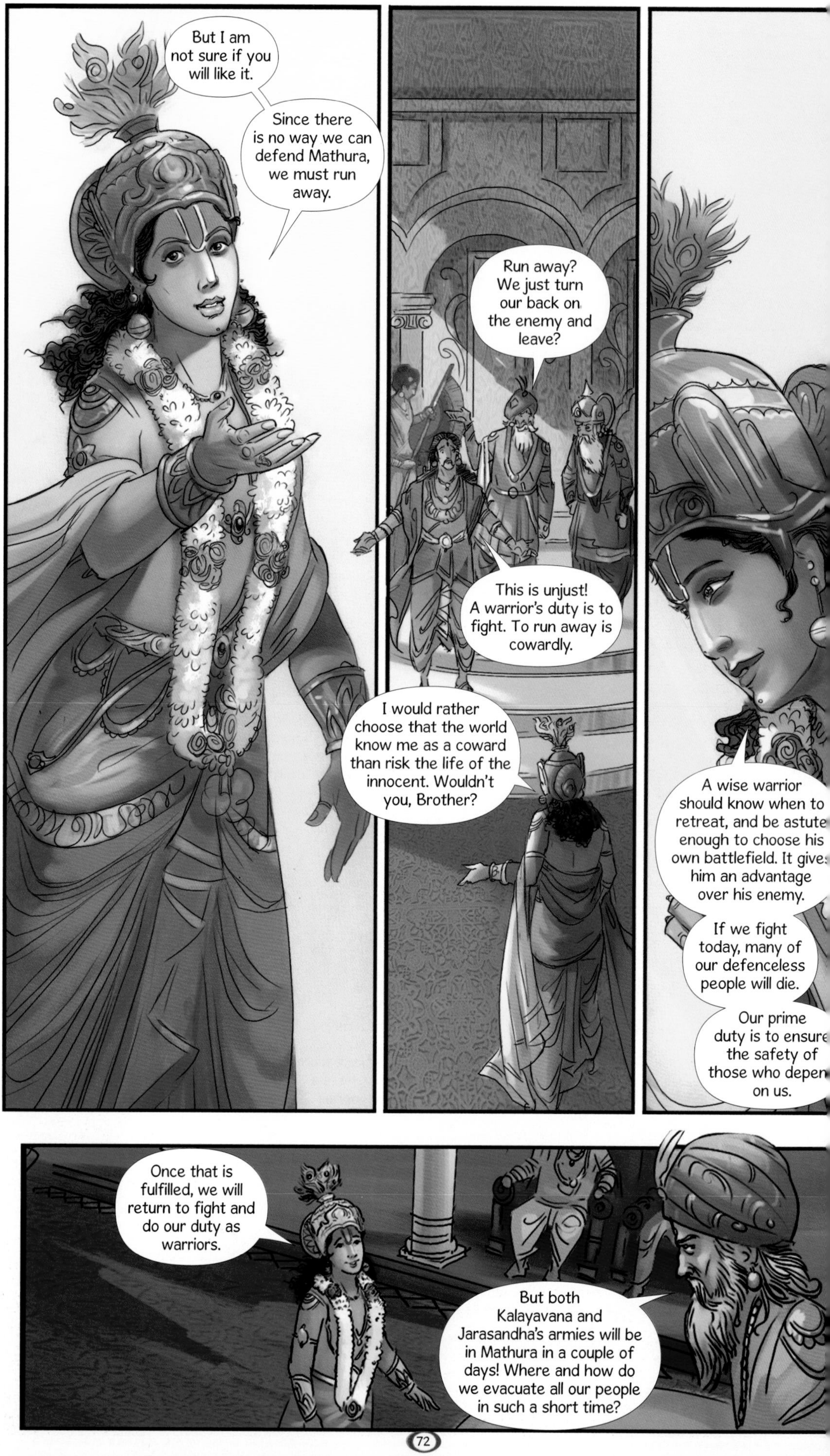
But I am not sure if you will like it.
Since there is no way we can defend Mathura, we must run away.
Run away? We just turn our back on the enemy and leave?
This is unjust! A warrior's duty is to fight. To run away is cowardly.
I would rather choose that the world know me as a coward than risk the life of the innocent. Wouldn't you, Brother?
A wise warrior should know when to retreat, and be astute enough to choose his own battlefield. It gives him an advantage over his enemy.
If we fight today, many of our defenceless people will die.
Our prime duty is to ensure the safety of those who depen on us.
Once that is fulfilled, we will return to fight and do our duty as warriors.
But both Kalayavana and Jarasandha's armies will be in Mathura in a couple of days! Where and how do we evacuate all our people in such a short time?

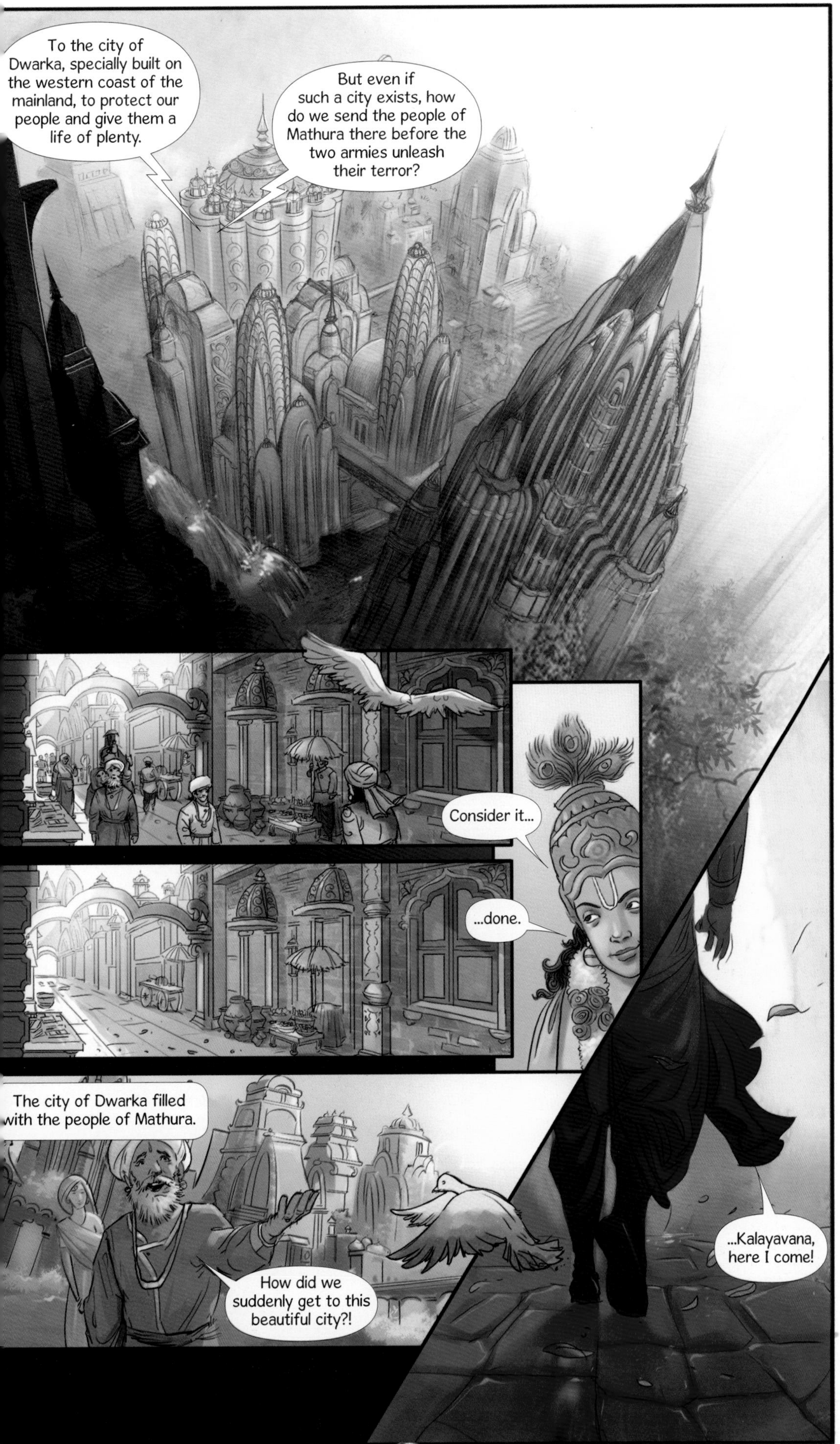
To the city of Dwarka, specially built on the western coast of the mainland, to protect our people and give them a life of plenty.
But even if such a city exists, how do we send the people of Mathura there before the two armies unleash their terror?
Consider it...
...done.
The city of Dwarka filled with the people of Mathura.
How did we suddenly get to this beautiful city?!
...Kalayavana, here I come!

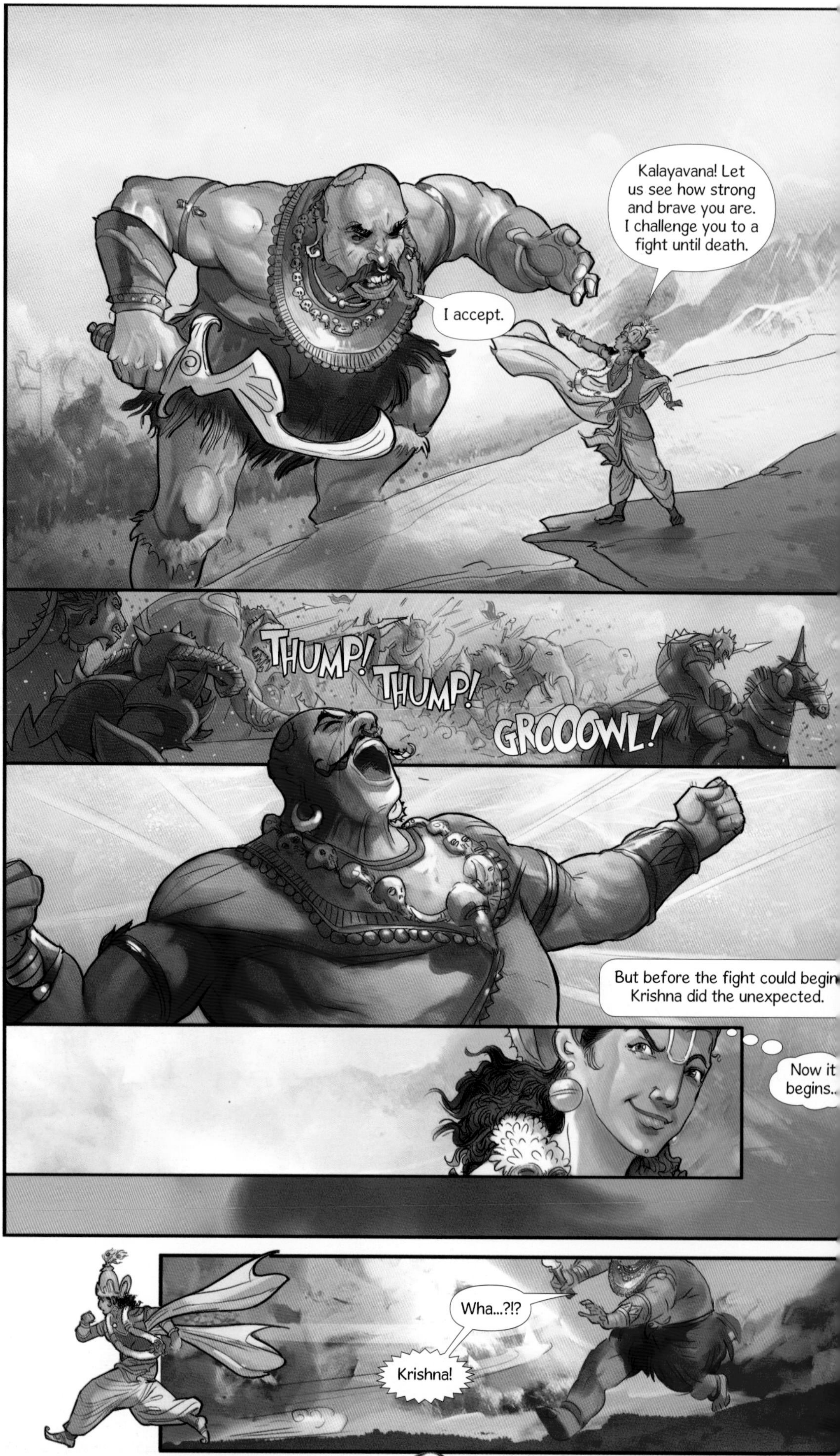
Kalayavana! Let us see how strong and brave you are. I challenge you to a fight until death.
I accept.
THUMP! THUMP!
GROOOWL!
But before the fight could begin Krishna did the unexpected.
Now it begins...
Wha...?!?
Krishna!

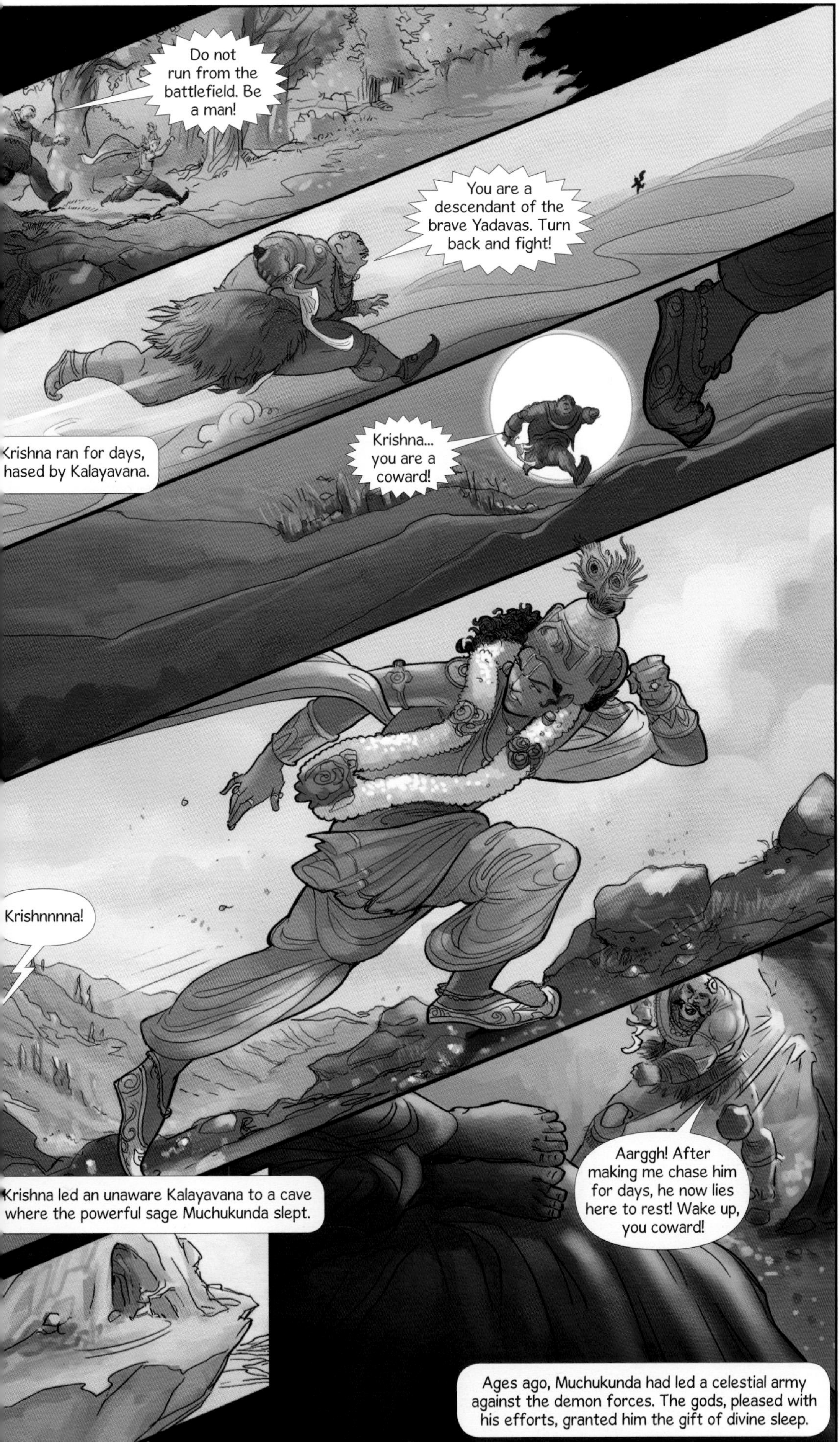

Do not run from the battlefield. Be a man!
You are a descendant of the brave Yadavas. Turn back and fight!
Krishna ran for days, chased by Kalayavana.
Krishna... you are a coward!
Krishnnnna!
Krishna led an unaware Kalayavana to a cave where the powerful sage Muchukunda slept.
Aarggh! After making me chase him for days, he now lies here to rest! Wake up, you coward!
Ages ago, Muchukunda had led a celestial army against the demon forces. The gods, pleased with his efforts, granted him the gift of divine sleep.

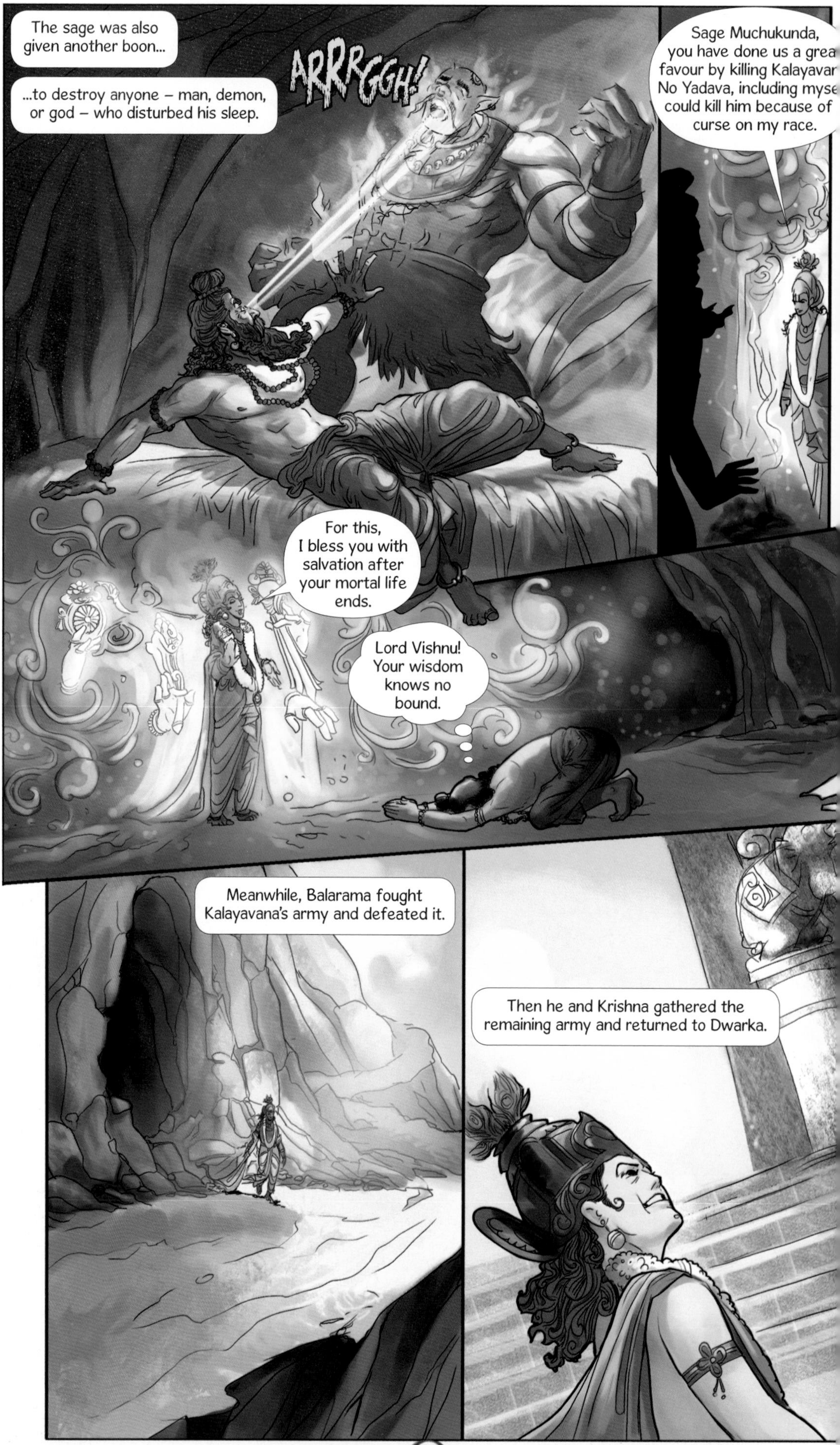
The sage was also given another boon...
...to destroy anyone – man, demon, or god – who disturbed his sleep.
ARRRGGH!
Sage Muchukunda, you have done us a grea favour by killing Kalayavar No Yadava, including myse could kill him because of curse on my race.
For this, I bless you with salvation after your mortal life ends.
Lord Vishnu! Your wisdom knows no bound.
Meanwhile, Balarama fought Kalayavana's army and defeated it.
Then he and Krishna gathered the remaining army and returned to Dwarka.

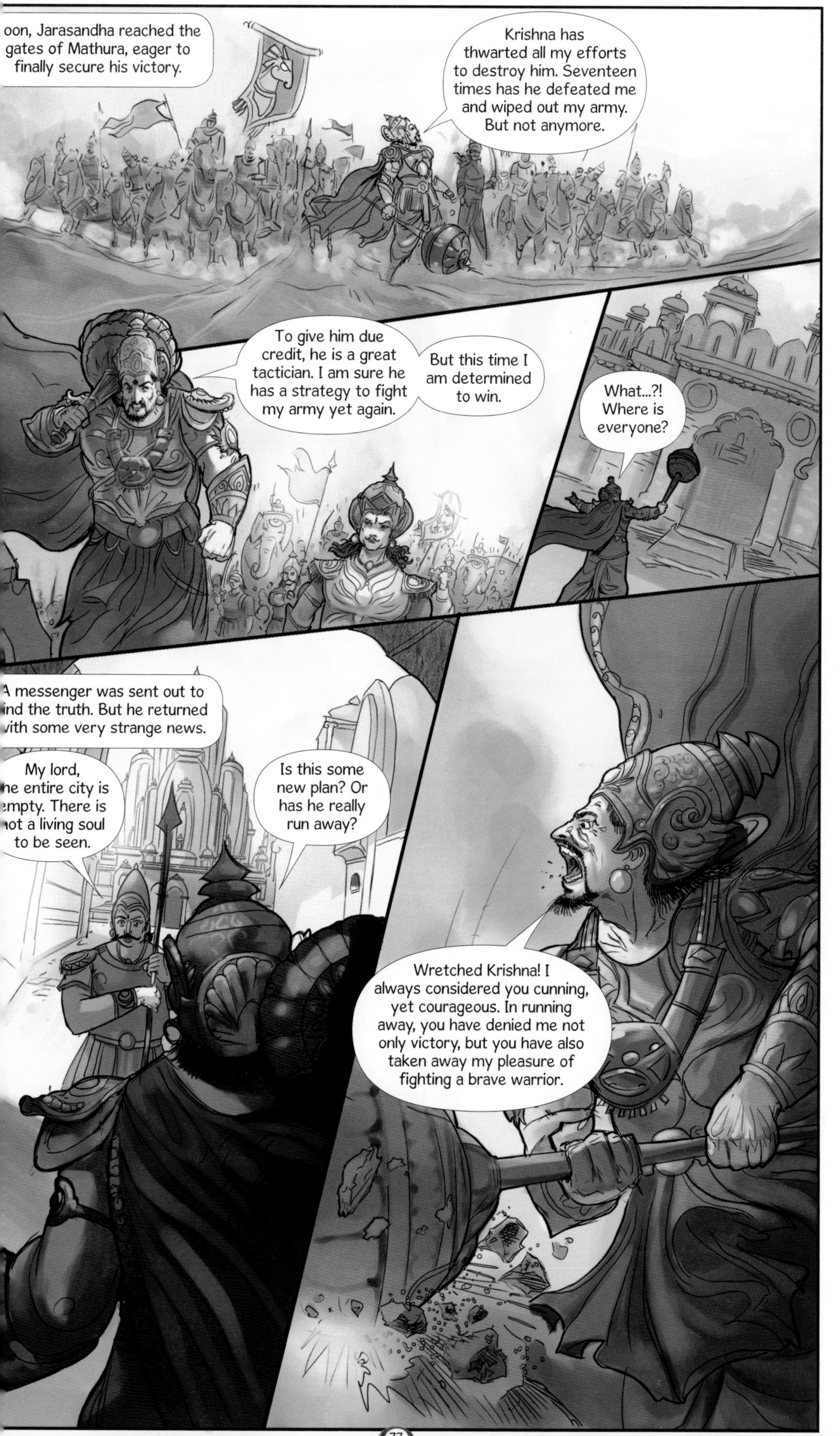
oon, Jarasandha reached the gates of Mathura, eager to finally secure his victory.
Krishna has thwarted all my efforts to destroy him. Seventeen times has he defeated me and wiped out my army. But not anymore.
To give him due credit, he is a great tactician. I am sure he has a strategy to fight my army yet again.
But this time I am determined to win.
What...?! Where is everyone?
A messenger was sent out to ind the truth. But he returned vith some very strange news.
My lord, ne entire city is mpty. There is not a living soul to be seen.
Is this some new plan? Or has he really run away?
Wretched Krishna! I always considered you cunning, yet courageous. In running away, you have denied me not only victory, but you have also taken away my pleasure of fighting a brave warrior.

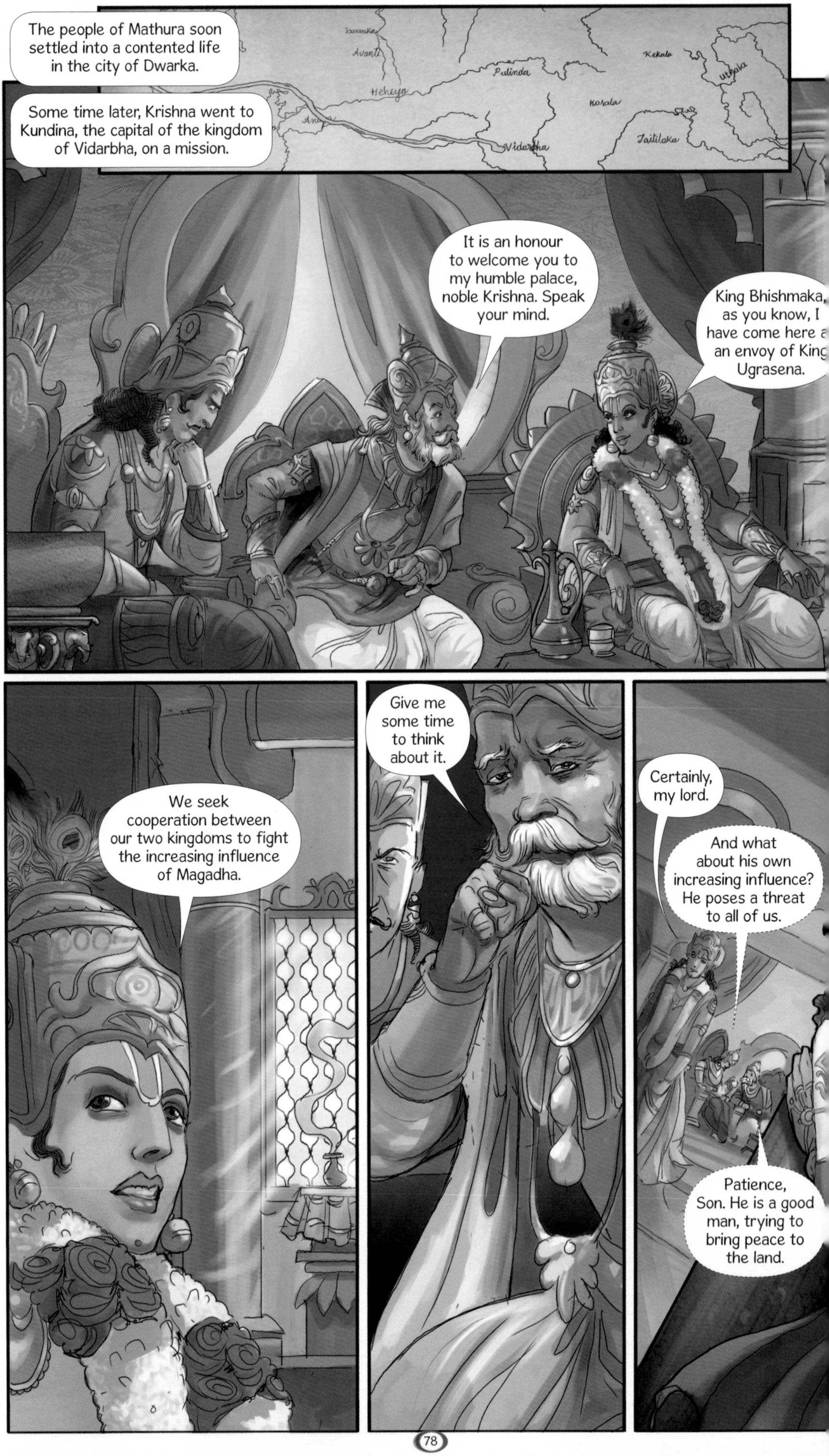

The people of Mathura soon settled into a contented life in the city of Dwarka.
Avanti
Pulinda
Kekala
Heheya
Kosala
Vidarbha
Some time later, Krishna went to Kundina, the capital of the kingdom of Vidarbha, on a mission.
It is an honour to welcome you to my humble palace, noble Krishna. Speak your mind.
King Bhishmaka, as you know, I have come here a an envoy of King Ugrasena.
We seek cooperation between our two kingdoms to fight the increasing influence of Magadha.
Give me some time to think about it.
Certainly, my lord.
And what about his own increasing influence? He poses a threat to all of us.
Patience, Son. He is a good man, trying to bring peace to the land.

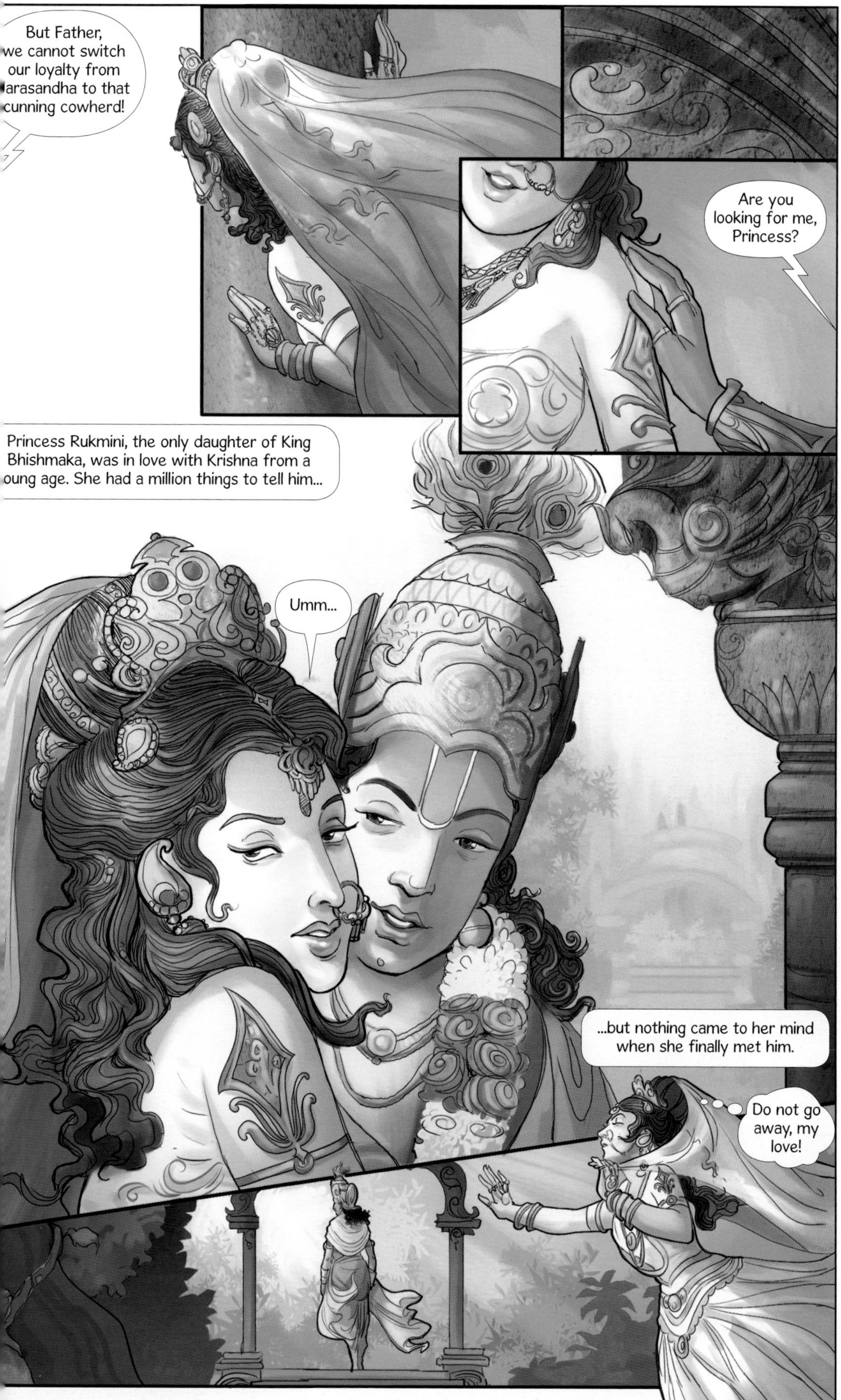
But Father, we cannot switch our loyalty from arasandha to that cunning cowherd!
Are you looking for me, Princess?
Princess Rukmini, the only daughter of King Bhishmaka, was in love with Krishna from a oung age. She had a million things to tell him...
Umm...
...but nothing came to her mind when she finally met him.
Do not go away, my love!

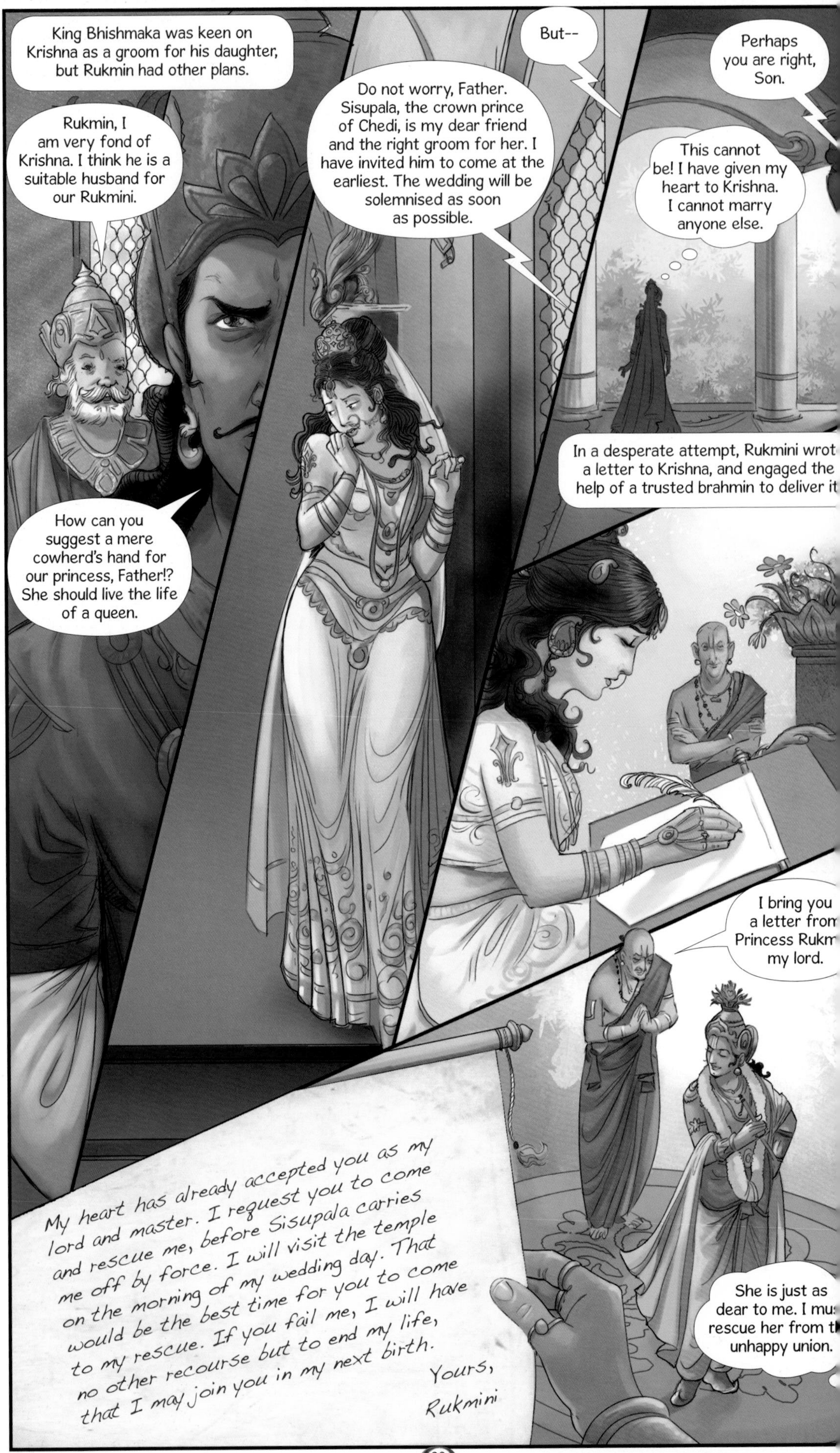

King Bhishmaka was keen on Krishna as a groom for his daughter, but Rukmin had other plans.
Rukmin, I am very fond of Krishna. I think he is a suitable husband for our Rukmini.
How can you suggest a mere cowherd's hand for our princess, Father!? She should live the life of a queen.
Do not worry, Father. Sisupala, the crown prince of Chedi, is my dear friend and the right groom for her. I have invited him to come at the earliest. The wedding will be solemnised as soon as possible.
But--
Perhaps you are right, Son.
This cannot be! I have given my heart to Krishna. I cannot marry anyone else.
In a desperate attempt, Rukmini wrot a letter to Krishna, and engaged the help of a trusted brahmin to deliver it
I bring you a letter from Princess Rukm my lord.
My heart has already accepted you as my lord and master. I request you to come and rescue me, before Sisupala carries me off by force. I will visit the temple on the morning of my wedding day. That would be the best time for you to come to my rescue. If you fail me, I will have no other recourse but to end my life, that I may join you in my next birth.
Yours,
Rukmini
She is just as dear to me. I mu rescue her from t unhappy union.

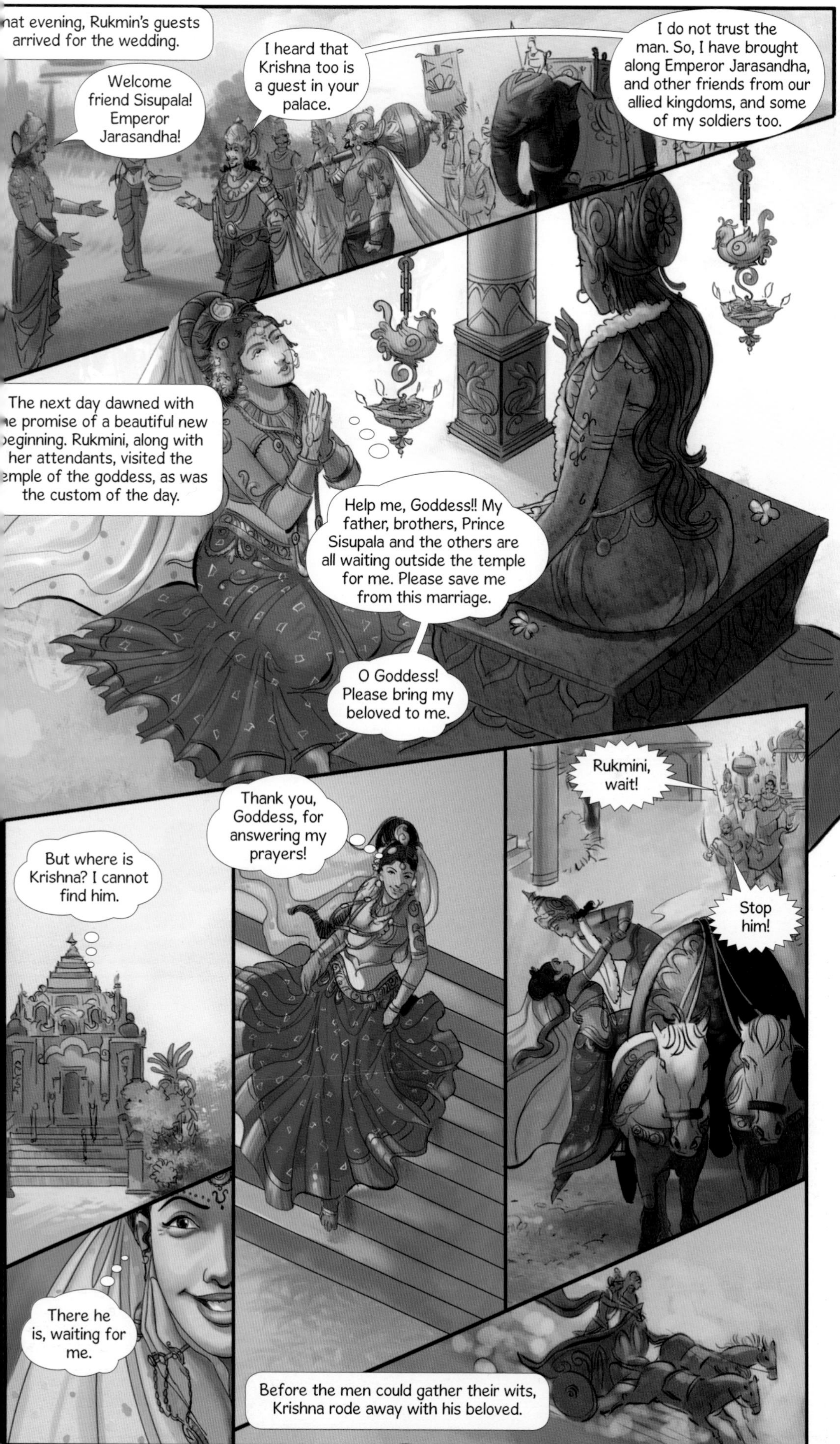

hat evening, Rukmin's guests arrived for the wedding.
Welcome friend Sisupala! Emperor Jarasandha!
I heard that Krishna too is a guest in your palace.
I do not trust the man. So, I have brought along Emperor Jarasandha, and other friends from our allied kingdoms, and some of my soldiers too.
The next day dawned with he promise of a beautiful new beginning. Rukmini, along with her attendants, visited the emple of the goddess, as was the custom of the day.
Help me, Goddess!! My father, brothers, Prince Sisupala and the others are all waiting outside the temple for me. Please save me from this marriage.
O Goddess! Please bring my beloved to me.
But where is Krishna? I cannot find him.
There he is, waiting for me.
Thank you, Goddess, for answering my prayers!
Rukmini, wait!
Stop him!
Before the men could gather their wits, Krishna rode away with his beloved.

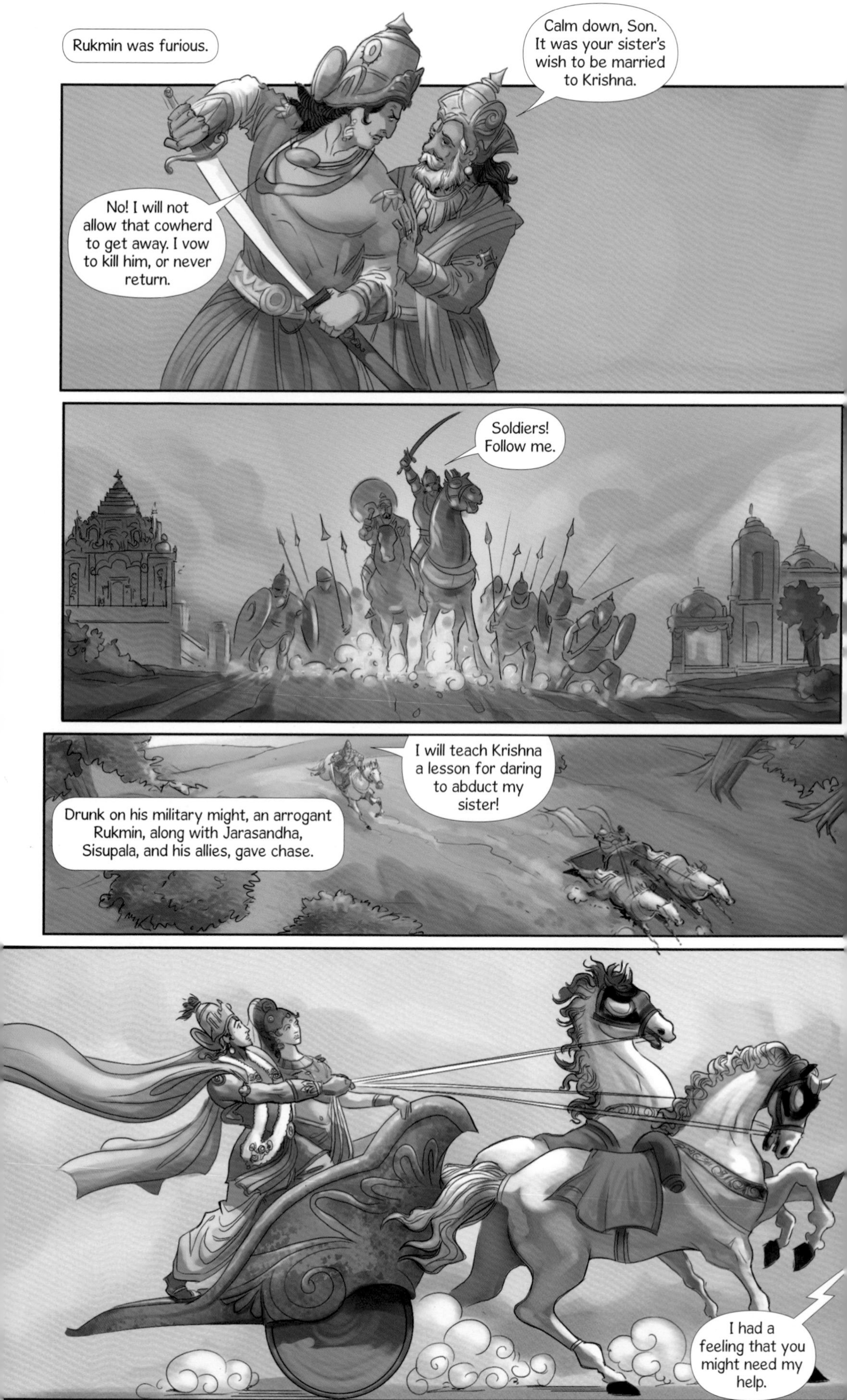

Rukmin was furious.
Calm down, Son. It was your sister's wish to be married to Krishna.
No! I will not allow that cowherd to get away. I vow to kill him, or never return.
Soldiers! Follow me.
Drunk on his military might, an arrogant Rukmin, along with Jarasandha, Sisupala, and his allies, gave chase.
I will teach Krishna a lesson for daring to abduct my sister!
I had a feeling that you might need my help.

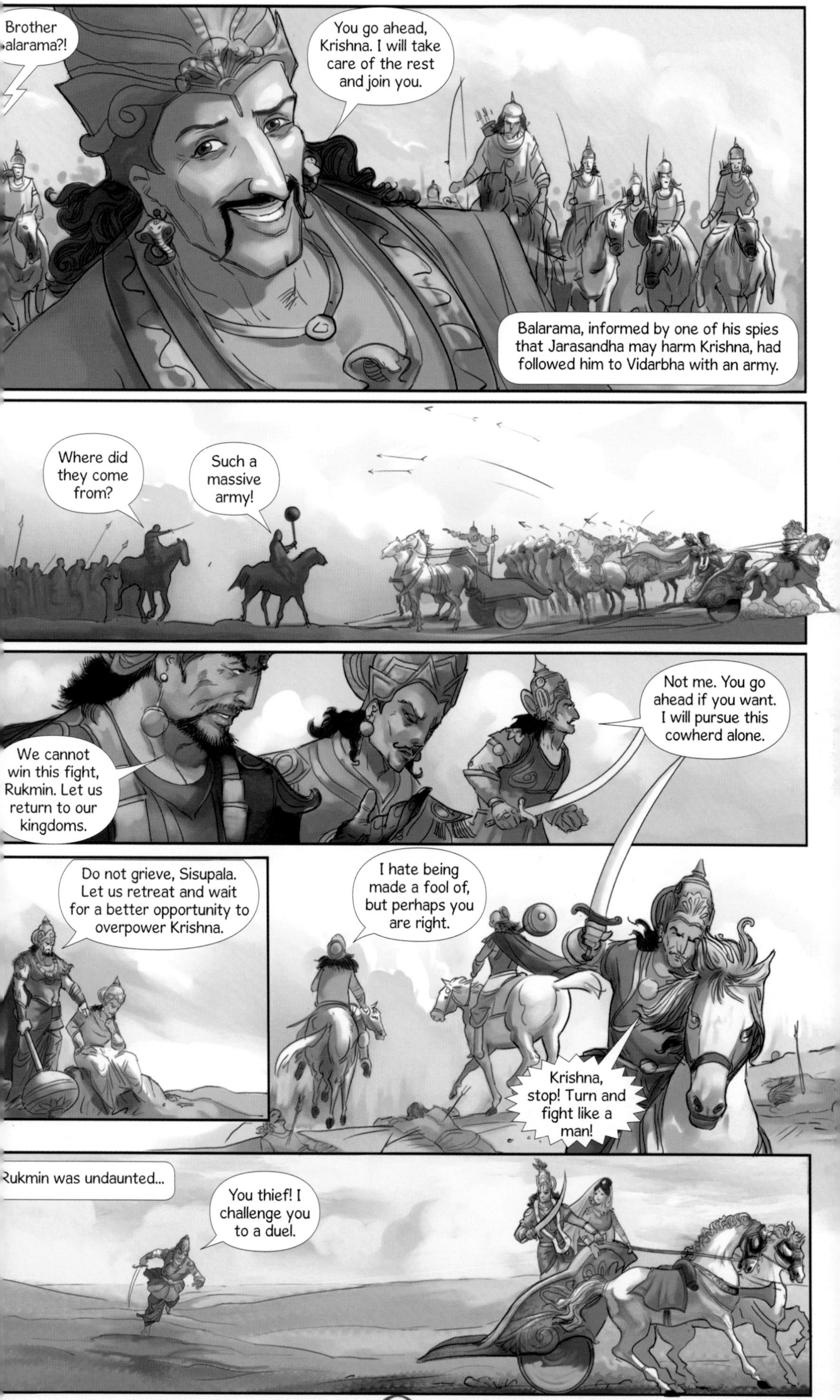

Brother
alarama?!
You go ahead, Krishna. I will take care of the rest and join you.
Balarama, informed by one of his spies that Jarasandha may harm Krishna, had followed him to Vidarbha with an army.
Where did they come from?
Such a massive army!
We cannot win this fight, Rukmin. Let us return to our kingdoms.
Not me. You go ahead if you want. I will pursue this cowherd alone.
Do not grieve, Sisupala. Let us retreat and wait for a better opportunity to overpower Krishna.
I hate being made a fool of, but perhaps you are right.
Krishna, stop! Turn and fight like a man!
Rukmin was undaunted...
You thief! I challenge you to a duel.

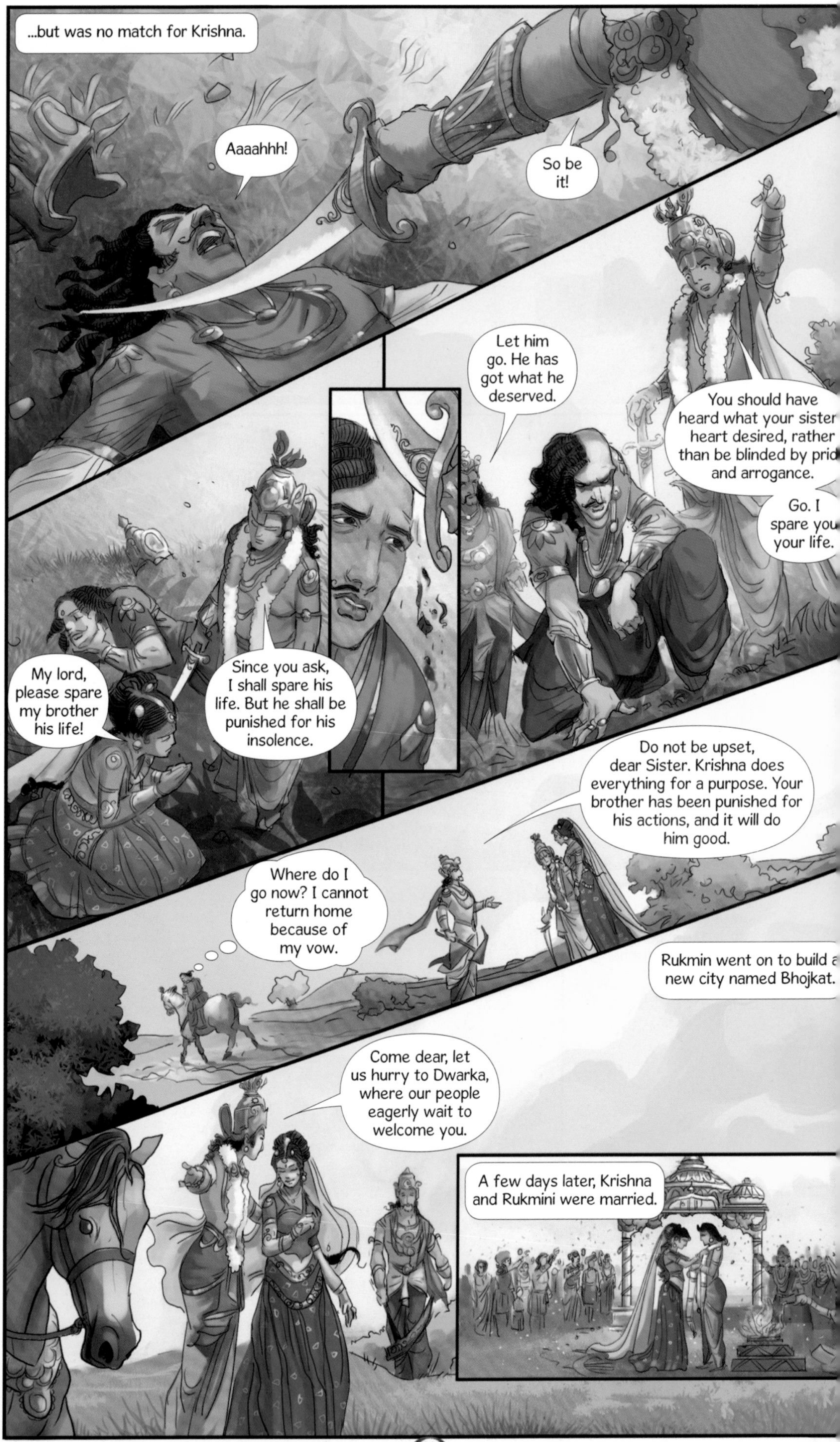
...but was no match for Krishna.
Aaaahhh!
So be it!
Let him go. He has got what he deserved.
You should have heard what your sister heart desired, rather than be blinded by prid and arrogance.
Go. I spare you your life.
My lord, please spare my brother his life!
Since you ask, I shall spare his life. But he shall be punished for his insolence.
Do not be upset, dear Sister. Krishna does everything for a purpose. Your brother has been punished for his actions, and it will do him good.
Where do I go now? I cannot return home because of my vow.
Rukmin went on to build a new city named Bhojkat.
Come dear, let us hurry to Dwarka, where our people eagerly wait to welcome you.
A few days later, Krishna and Rukmini were married.

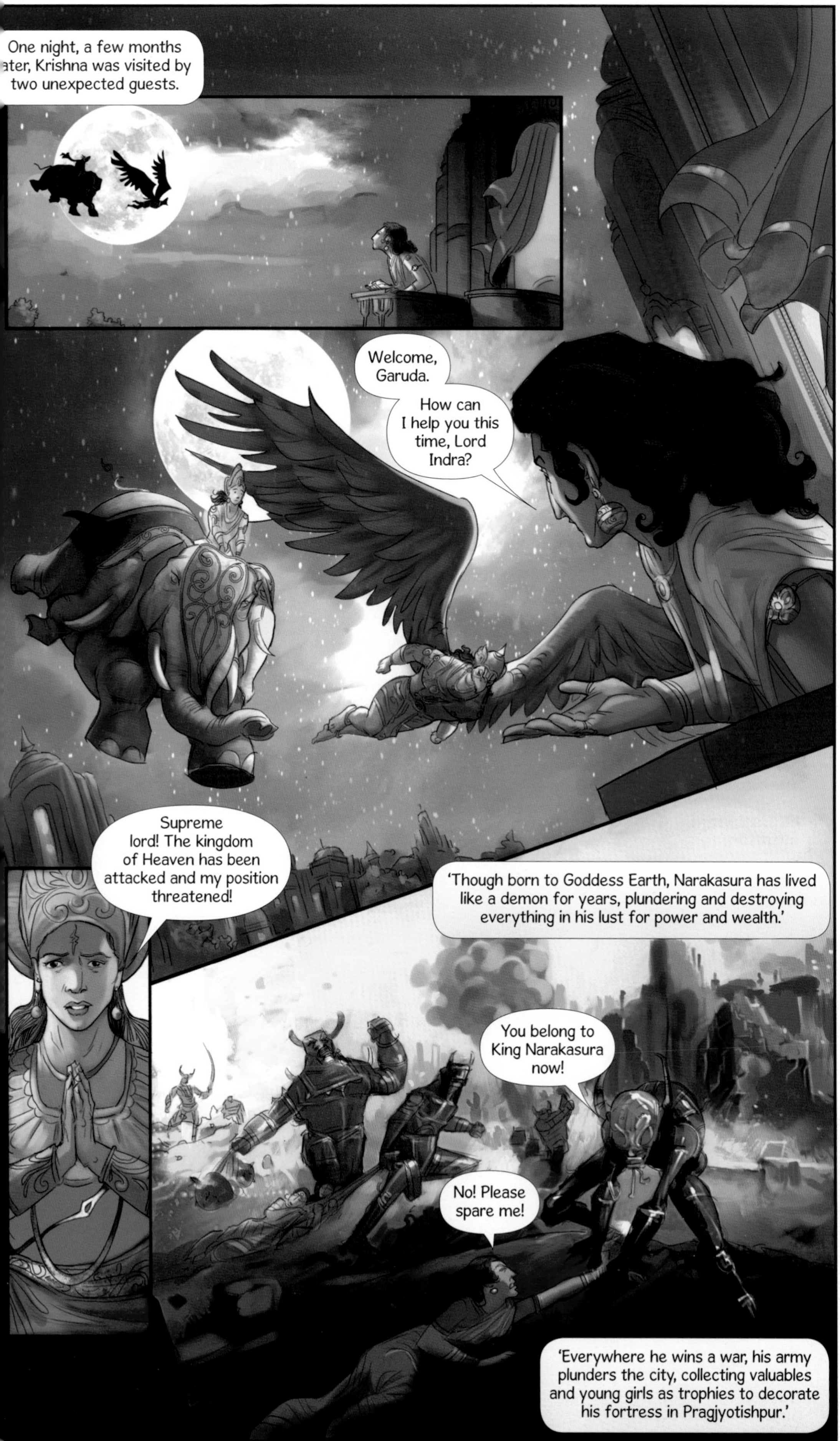
One night, a few months later, Krishna was visited by two unexpected guests.
Welcome, Garuda.
How can I help you this time, Lord Indra?
Supreme lord! The kingdom of Heaven has been attacked and my position threatened!
'Though born to Goddess Earth, Narakasura has lived like a demon for years, plundering and destroying everything in his lust for power and wealth.'
You belong to King Narakasura now!
No! Please spare me!
'Everywhere he wins a war, his army plunders the city, collecting valuables and young girls as trophies to decorate his fortress in Pragjyotishpur.'

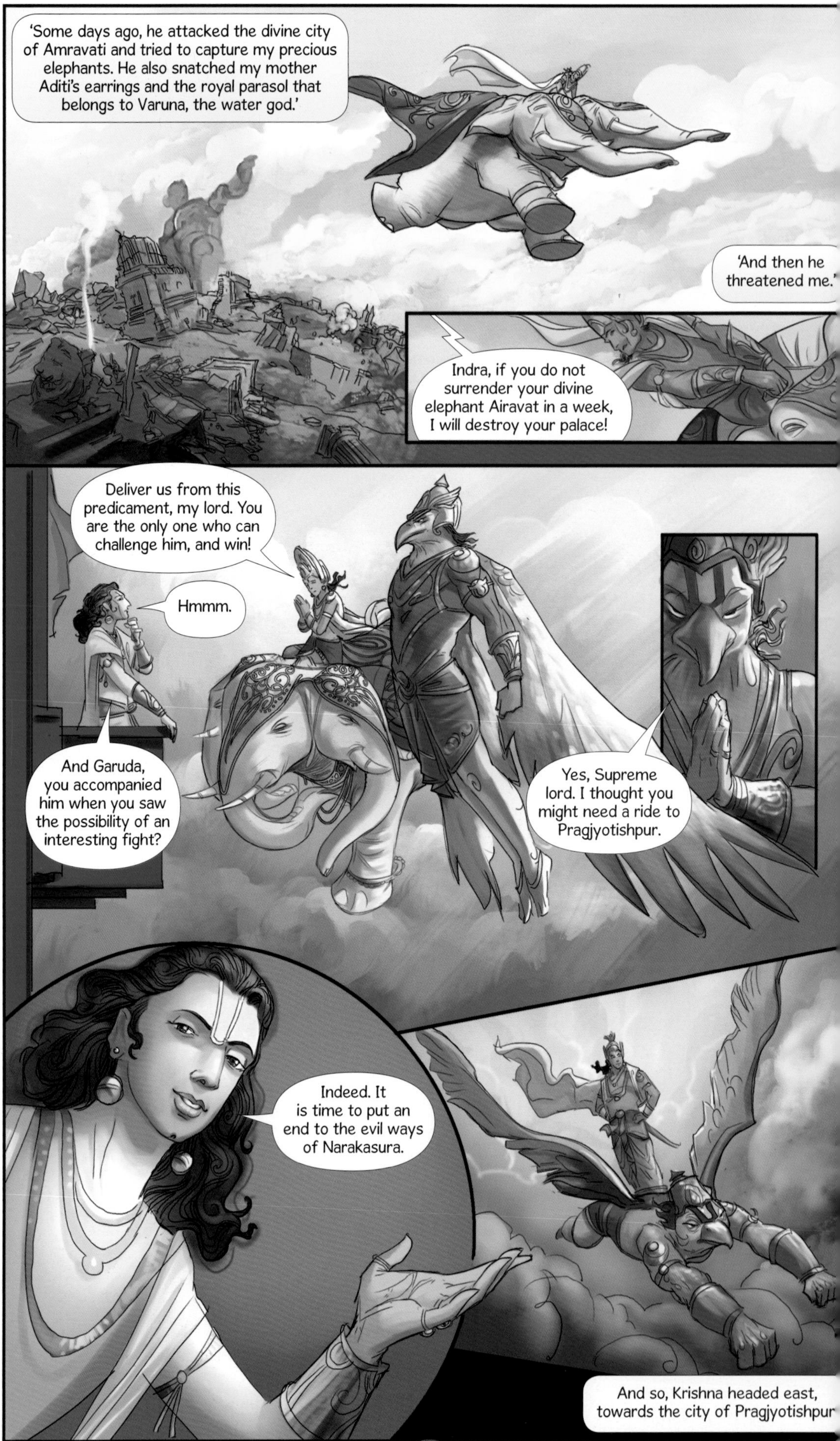
'Some days ago, he attacked the divine city of Amravati and tried to capture my precious elephants. He also snatched my mother Aditi's earrings and the royal parasol that belongs to Varuna, the water god.'
'And then he threatened me.'
Indra, if you do not surrender your divine elephant Airavat in a week, I will destroy your palace!
Deliver us from this predicament, my lord. You are the only one who can challenge him, and win!
Hmmm.
And Garuda, you accompanied him when you saw the possibility of an interesting fight?
Yes, Supreme lord. I thought you might need a ride to Pragjyotishpur.
Indeed. It is time to put an end to the evil ways of Narakasura.
And so, Krishna headed east, towards the city of Pragjyotishpur

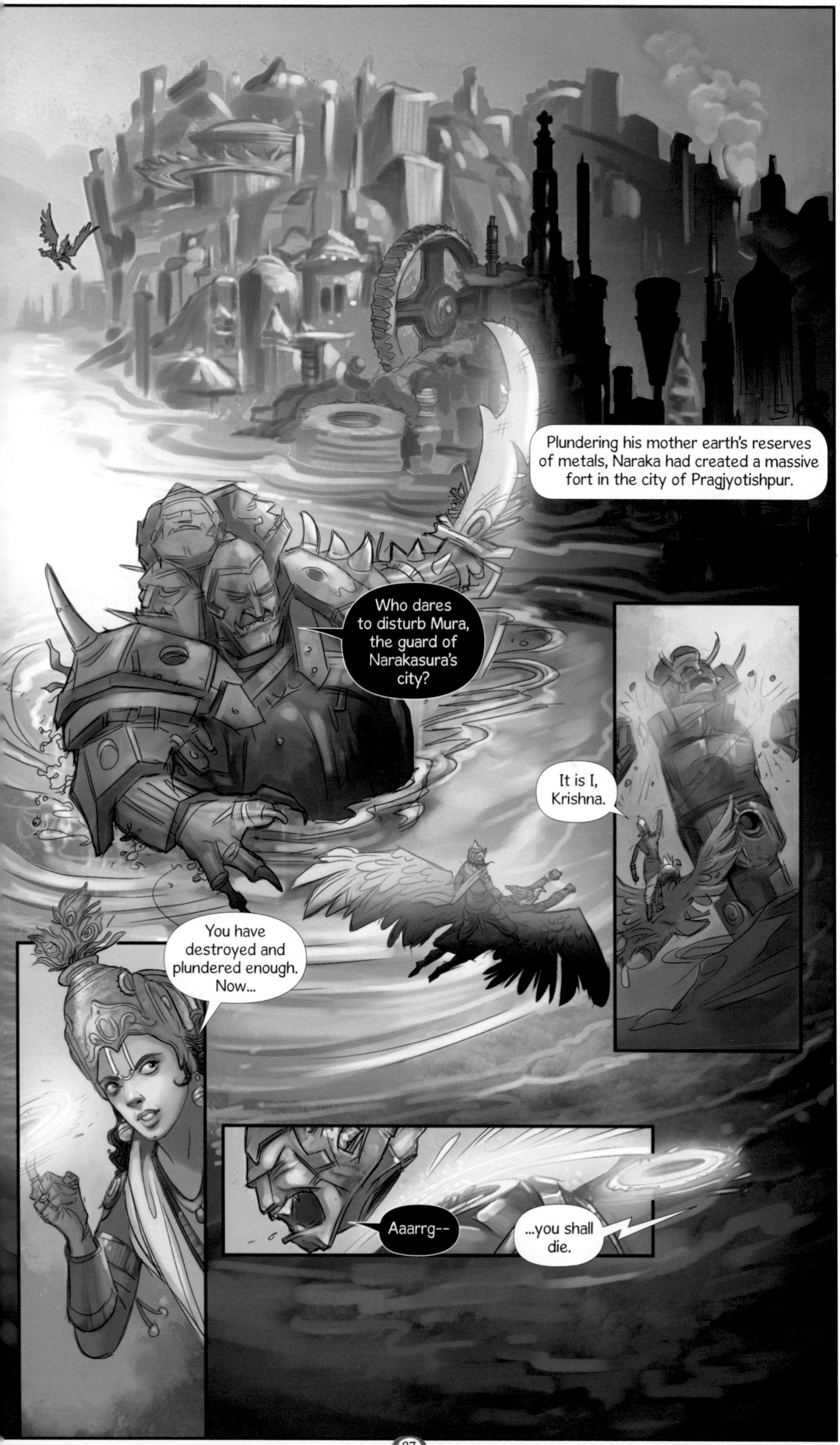

Plundering his mother earth's reserves of metals, Naraka had created a massive fort in the city of Pragjyotishpur.
Who dares to disturb Mura, the guard of Narakasura's city?
It is I, Krishna.
You have destroyed and plundered enough. Now...
Aaarrg--
...you shall die.

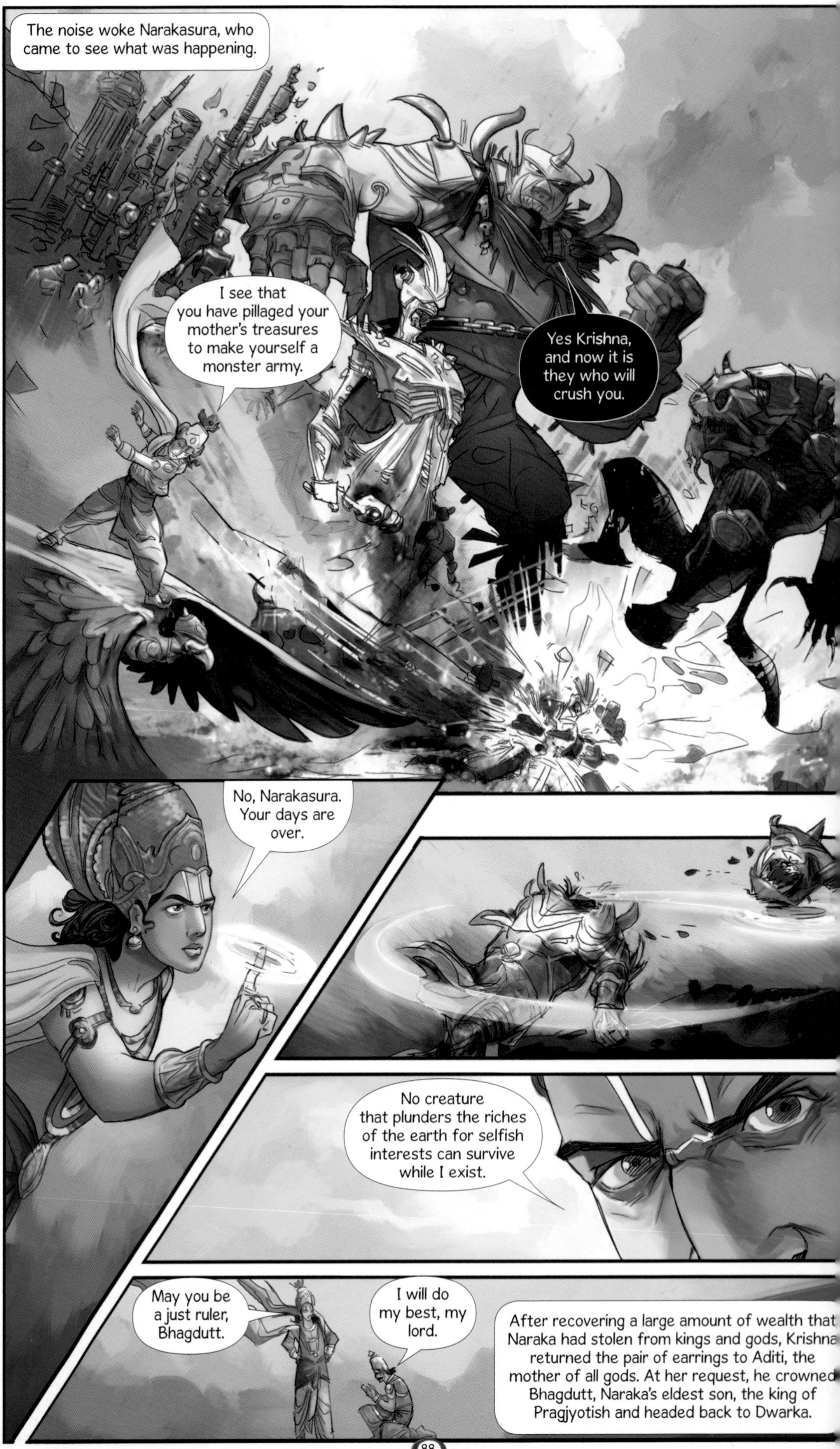

The noise woke Narakasura, who came to see what was happening.
I see that you have pillaged your mother's treasures to make yourself a monster army.
Yes Krishna, and now it is they who will crush you.
No, Narakasura. Your days are over.
No creature that plunders the riches of the earth for selfish interests can survive while I exist.
May you be a just ruler, Bhagdutt.
I will do my best, my lord.
After recovering a large amount of wealth that Naraka had stolen from kings and gods, Krishna returned the pair of earrings to Aditi, the mother of all gods. At her request, he crowned Bhagdutt, Naraka's eldest son, the king of Pragjyotish and headed back to Dwarka.

Indraprastha

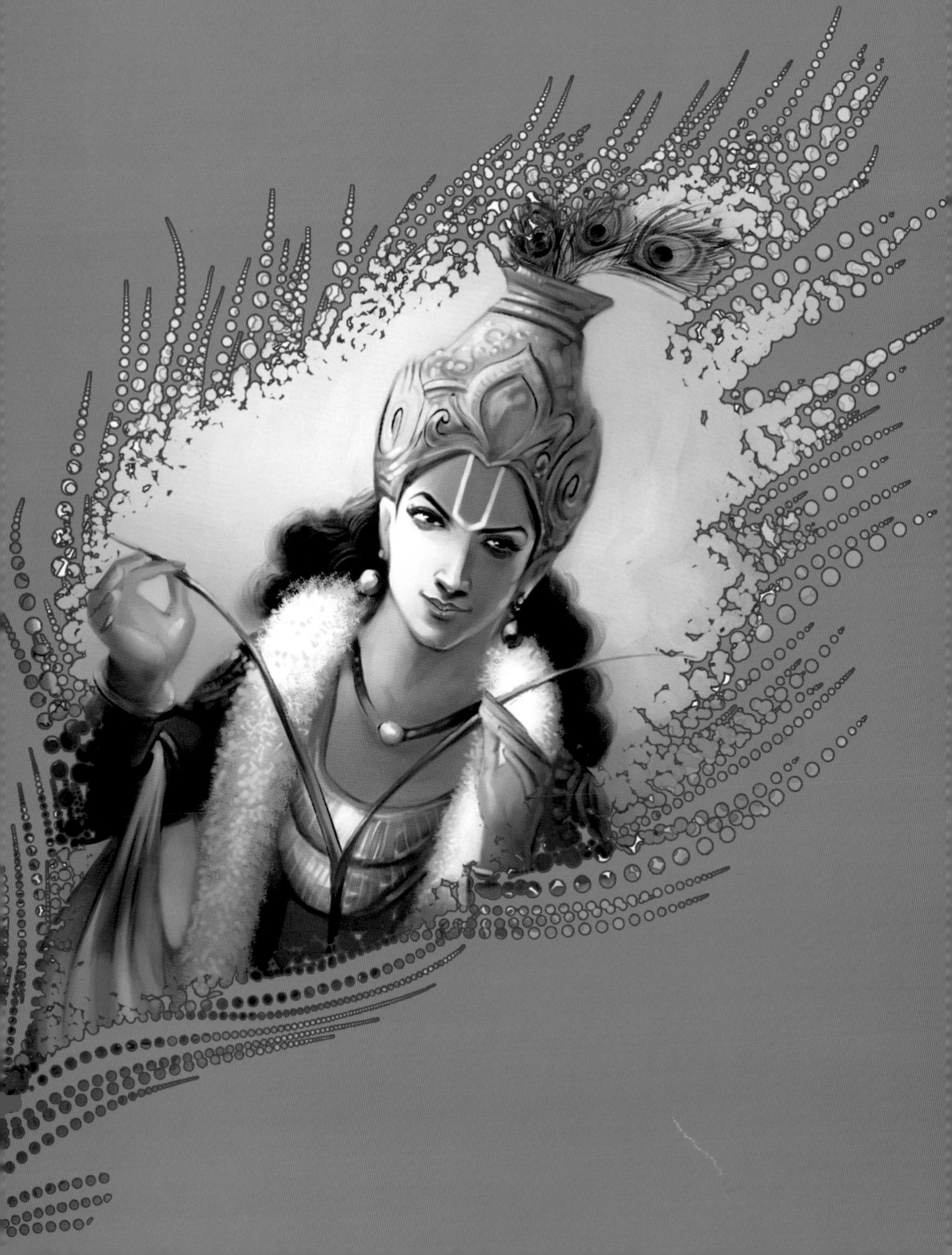

Indraprastha

Meanwhile, the Pandavas of the Kuru dynasty have set up their capital in Indraprastha. The Pandavas are Krishna's cousins. Yudhishthira, the eldest of the Pandava brothers, is heir to the throne of the Kuru kingdom. However, the Pandavas' dispute with their cousins and rival claimants to the throne, the Kauravas, forces King Dhritarashtra to divide the Kuru kingdom into two parts. Yudhishthira becomes ruler of one half. He builds a magnificent palace in the capital city of Indraprastha, and plans to conduct a *rajsuya yagya*, a ceremony to proclaim himself emperor. Only Jarasandha stands in his way.

Krishna now assumes the role of a teacher, as the Pandavas learn that sometimes, in order to maintain righteousness, it is necessary to take up arms.

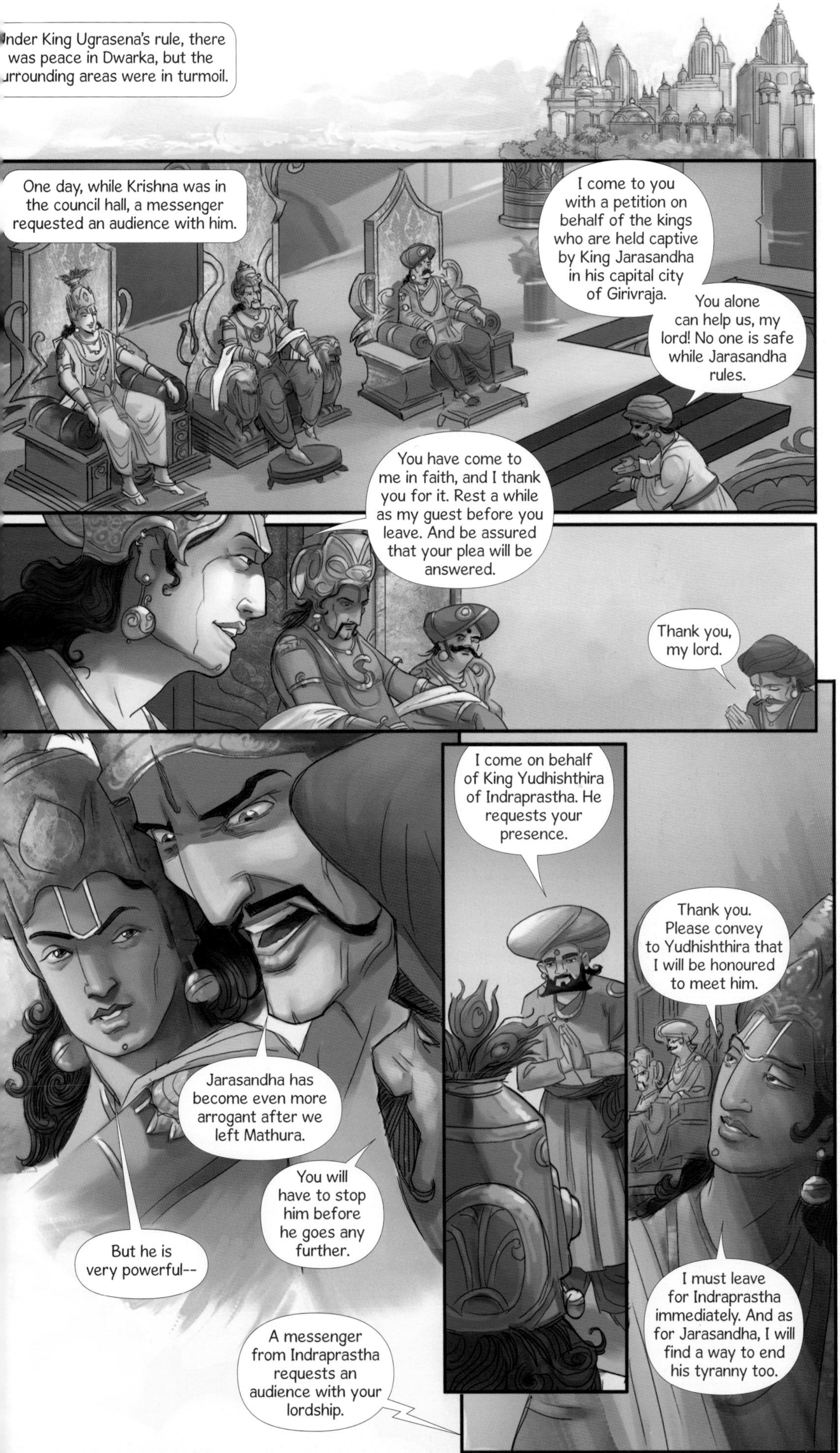
Under King Ugrasena's rule, there was peace in Dwarka, but the surrounding areas were in turmoil.
One day, while Krishna was in the council hall, a messenger requested an audience with him.
I come to you with a petition on behalf of the kings who are held captive by King Jarasandha in his capital city of Girivraja.
You alone can help us, my lord! No one is safe while Jarasandha rules.
You have come to me in faith, and I thank you for it. Rest a while as my guest before you leave. And be assured that your plea will be answered.
Thank you, my lord.
Jarasandha has become even more arrogant after we left Mathura.
You will have to stop him before he goes any further.
But he is very powerful--
A messenger from Indraprastha requests an audience with your lordship.
I come on behalf of King Yudhishthira of Indraprastha. He requests your presence.
Thank you. Please convey to Yudhishthira that I will be honoured to meet him.
I must leave for Indraprastha immediately. And as for Jarasandha, I will find a way to end his tyranny too.

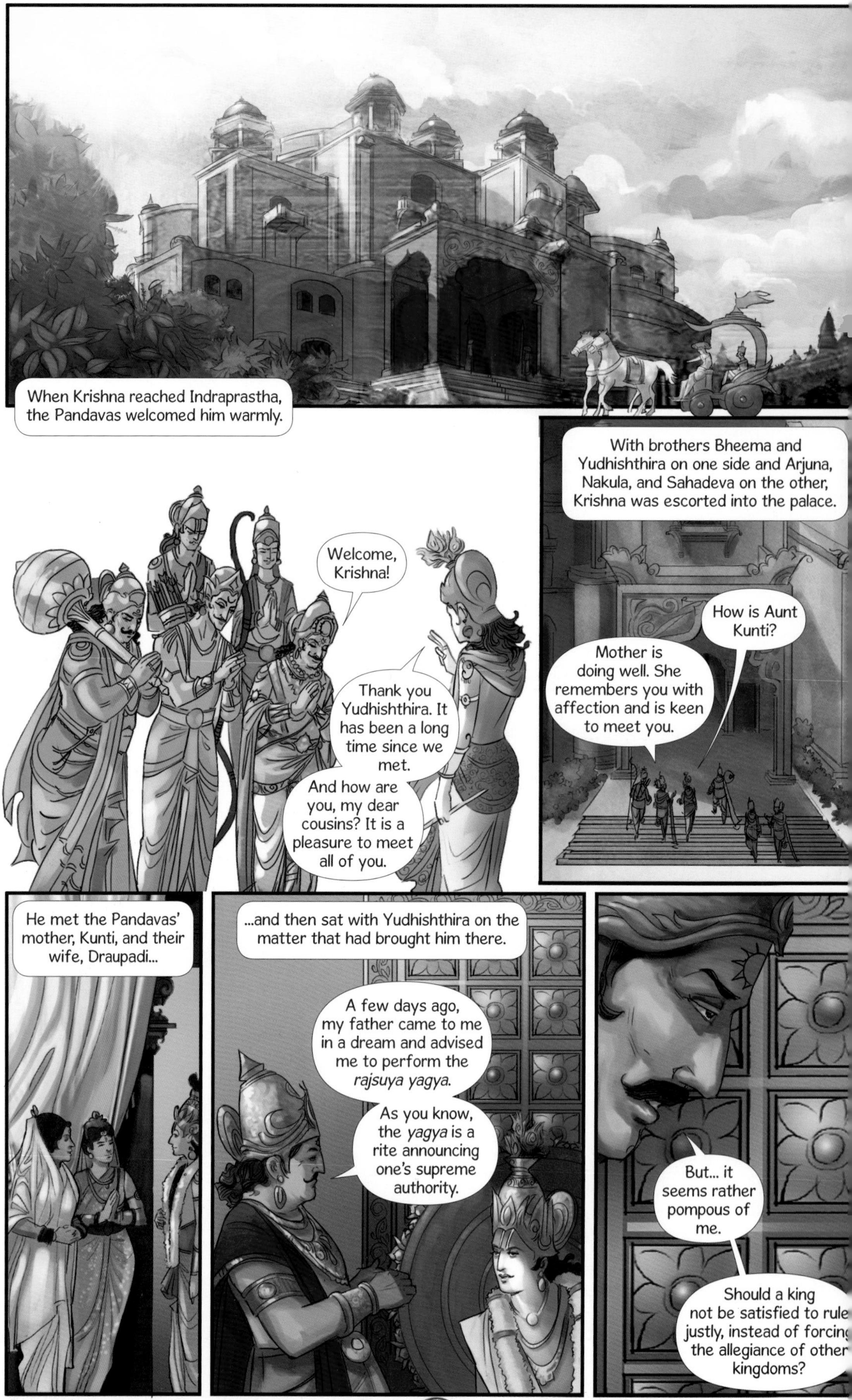
When Krishna reached Indraprastha, the Pandavas welcomed him warmly.
Welcome, Krishna!
Thank you Yudhishthira. It has been a long time since we met.
And how are you, my dear cousins? It is a pleasure to meet all of you.
With brothers Bheema and Yudhishthira on one side and Arjuna, Nakula, and Sahadeva on the other, Krishna was escorted into the palace.
How is Aunt Kunti?
Mother is doing well. She remembers you with affection and is keen to meet you.
He met the Pandavas' mother, Kunti, and their wife, Draupadi...
...and then sat with Yudhishthira on the matter that had brought him there.
A few days ago, my father came to me in a dream and advised me to perform the *rajsuya yagya*.
As you know, the *yagya* is a rite announcing one's supreme authority.
But... it seems rather pompous of me.
Should a king not be satisfied to rule justly, instead of forcing the allegiance of other kingdoms?

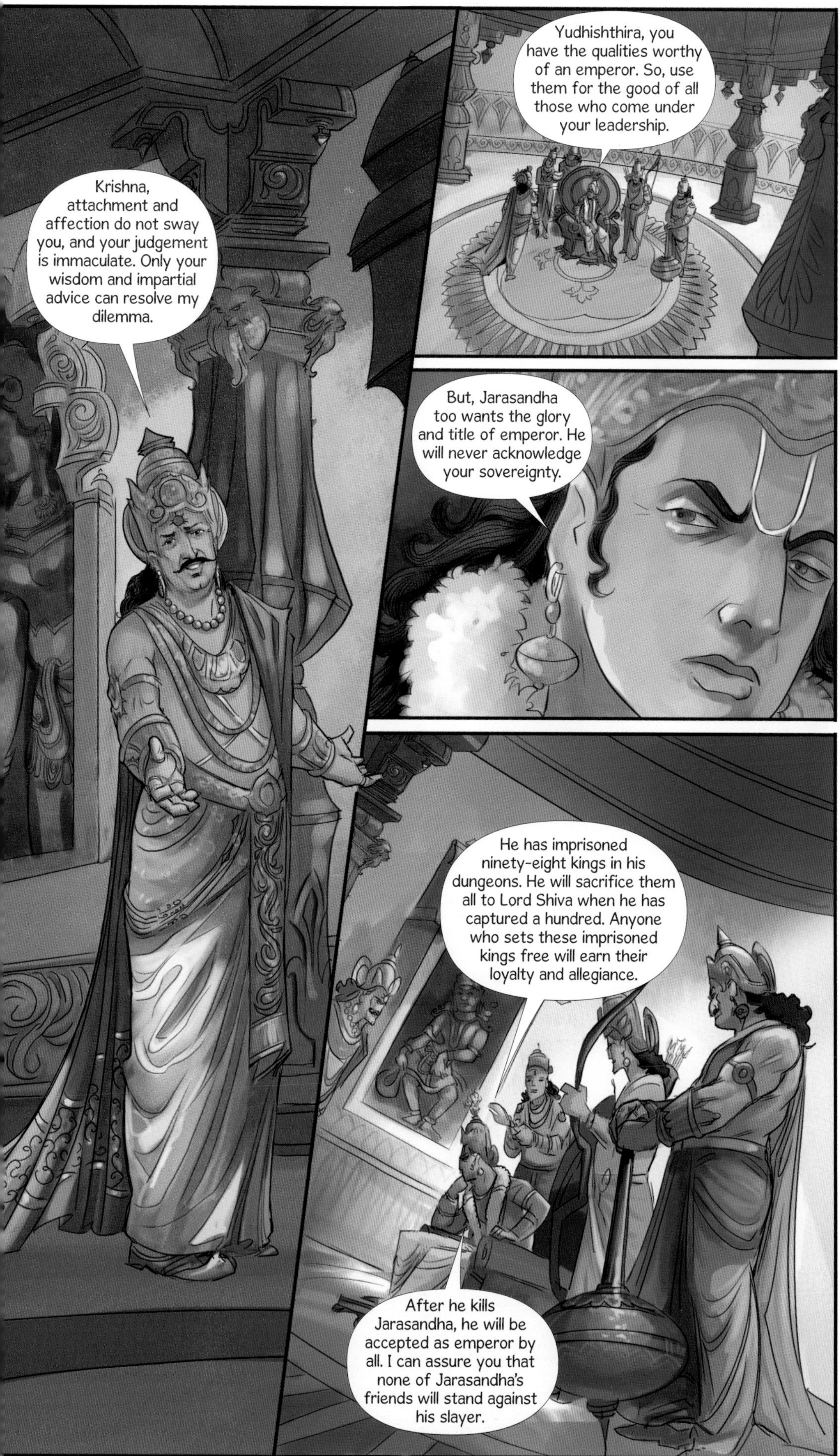
Krishna, attachment and affection do not sway you, and your judgement is immaculate. Only your wisdom and impartial advice can resolve my dilemma.
Yudhishthira, you have the qualities worthy of an emperor. So, use them for the good of all those who come under your leadership.
But, Jarasandha too wants the glory and title of emperor. He will never acknowledge your sovereignty.
He has imprisoned ninety-eight kings in his dungeons. He will sacrifice them all to Lord Shiva when he has captured a hundred. Anyone who sets these imprisoned kings free will earn their loyalty and allegiance.
After he kills Jarasandha, he will be accepted as emperor by all. I can assure you that none of Jarasandha's friends will stand against his slayer.

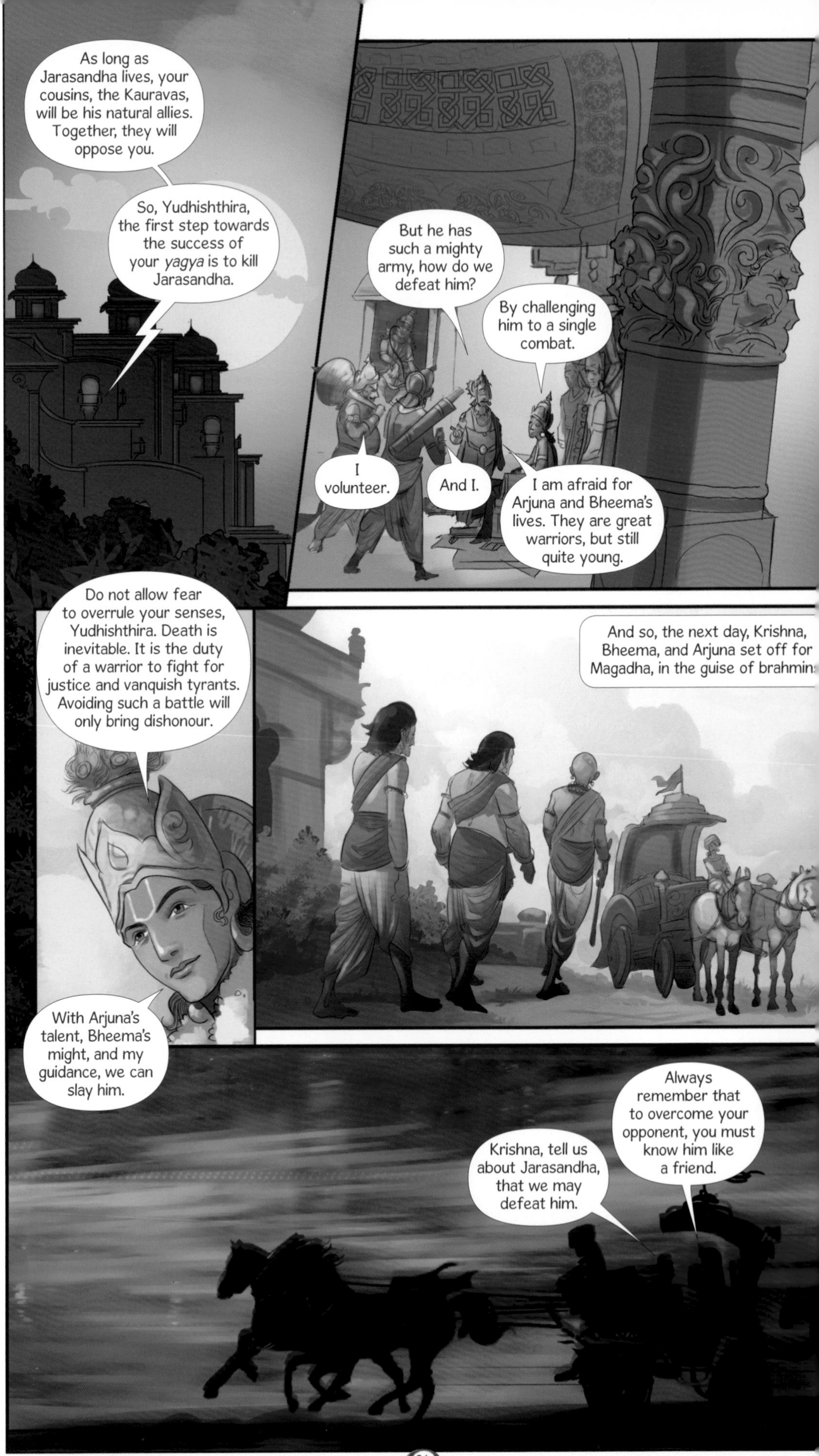

As long as Jarasandha lives, your cousins, the Kauravas, will be his natural allies. Together, they will oppose you.
So, Yudhishthira, the first step towards the success of your *yagya* is to kill Jarasandha.
But he has such a mighty army, how do we defeat him?
By challenging him to a single combat.
I volunteer.
And I.
I am afraid for Arjuna and Bheema's lives. They are great warriors, but still quite young.
Do not allow fear to overrule your senses, Yudhishthira. Death is inevitable. It is the duty of a warrior to fight for justice and vanquish tyrants. Avoiding such a battle will only bring dishonour.
With Arjuna's talent, Bheema's might, and my guidance, we can slay him.
And so, the next day, Krishna, Bheema, and Arjuna set off for Magadha, in the guise of brahmins
Krishna, tell us about Jarasandha, that we may defeat him.
Always remember that to overcome your opponent, you must know him like a friend.

Brihadrath, the ruler of Magadha, was married to the beautiful twin daughters of the king of Kasi. He had everything but an heir to his throne.

'Desperate for a son, he went to sage Kaushika.'

Give this mango to your wife. Ask her to eat it, and your wish shall come true.

'Since the king had promised both his wives equal love, he cut the fruit in two and fed one half to each.'

'To his delight, both were soon expecting a child.'

'In time, to his horror, both of them bore him half a child.'

O lord! What monster is this?

'They thought it was some demon's doing, and threw the two halves into the wild.'

'Jara, a female demon, discovered them and as she held the two halves, they came together miraculously. Since the baby was joined by Jara, it was named Jarasandha.'

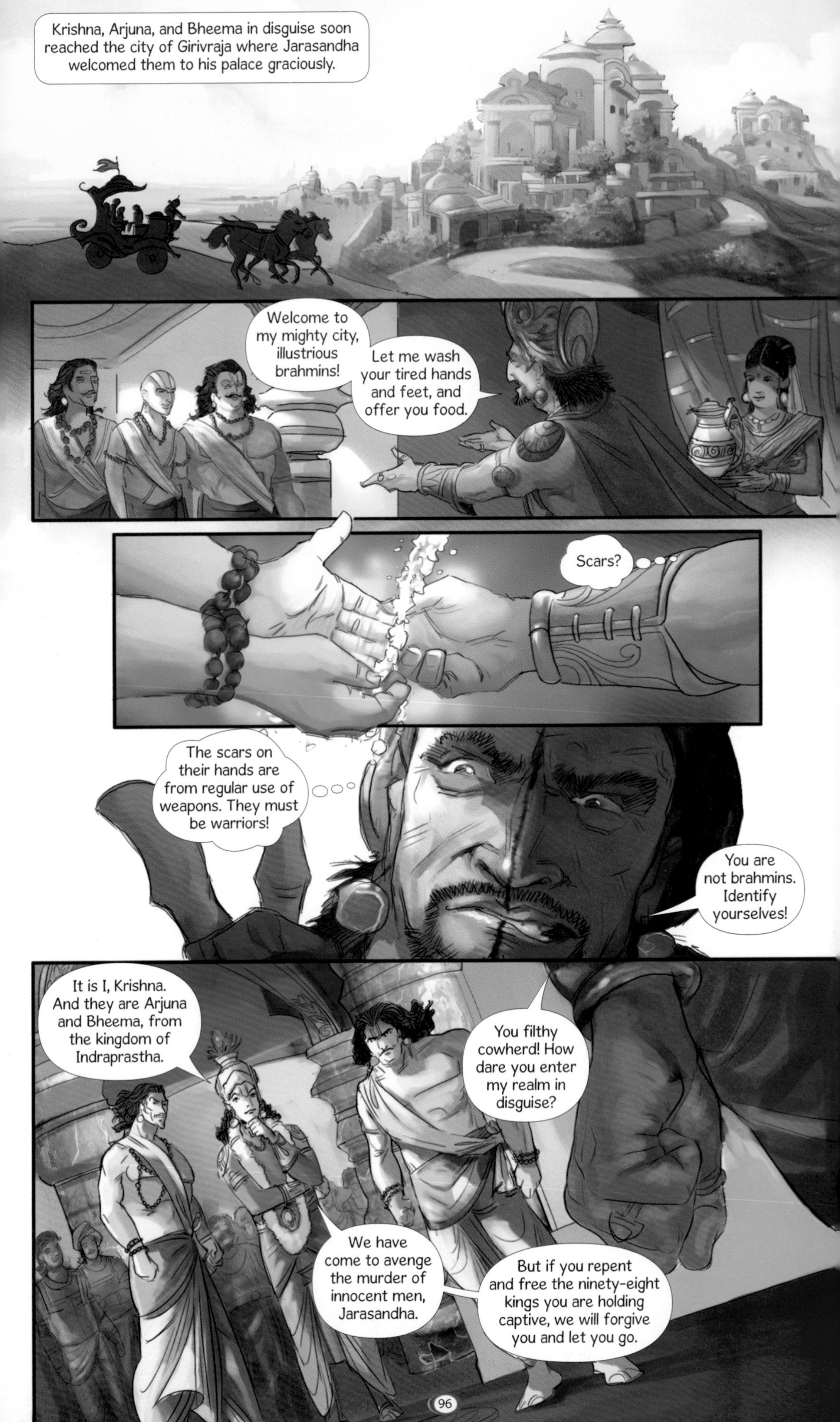

Krishna, Arjuna, and Bheema in disguise soon reached the city of Girivraja where Jarasandha welcomed them to his palace graciously.
Welcome to my mighty city, illustrious brahmins!
Let me wash your tired hands and feet, and offer you food.
Scars?
The scars on their hands are from regular use of weapons. They must be warriors!
You are not brahmins. Identify yourselves!
It is I, Krishna. And they are Arjuna and Bheema, from the kingdom of Indraprastha.
You filthy cowherd! How dare you enter my realm in disguise?
We have come to avenge the murder of innocent men, Jarasandha.
But if you repent and free the ninety-eight kings you are holding captive, we will forgive you and let you go.

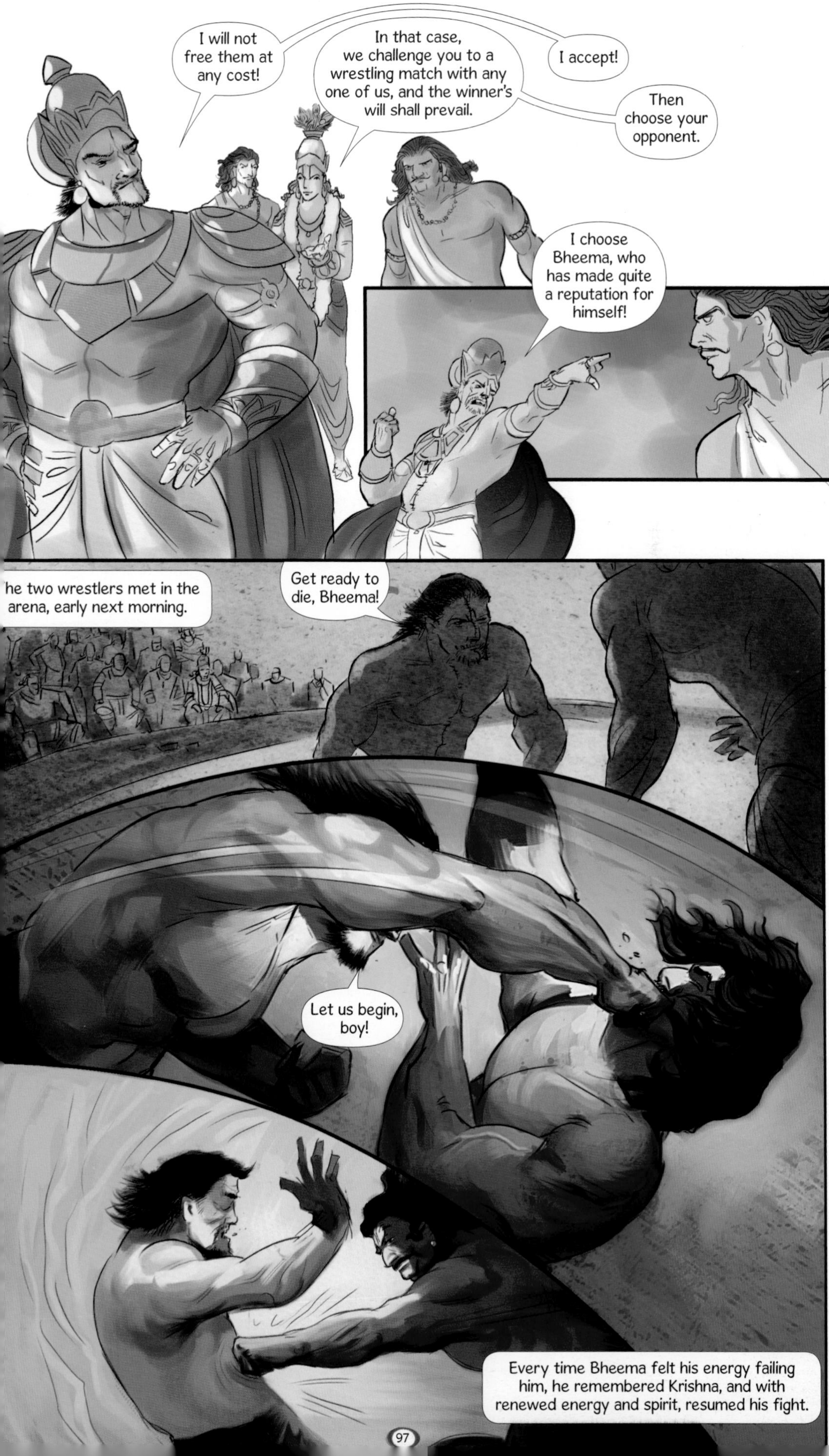
I will not free them at any cost!
In that case, we challenge you to a wrestling match with any one of us, and the winner's will shall prevail.
I accept!
Then choose your opponent.
I choose Bheema, who has made quite a reputation for himself!
he two wrestlers met in the arena, early next morning.
Get ready to die, Bheema!
Let us begin, boy!
Every time Bheema felt his energy failing him, he remembered Krishna, and with renewed energy and spirit, resumed his fight.

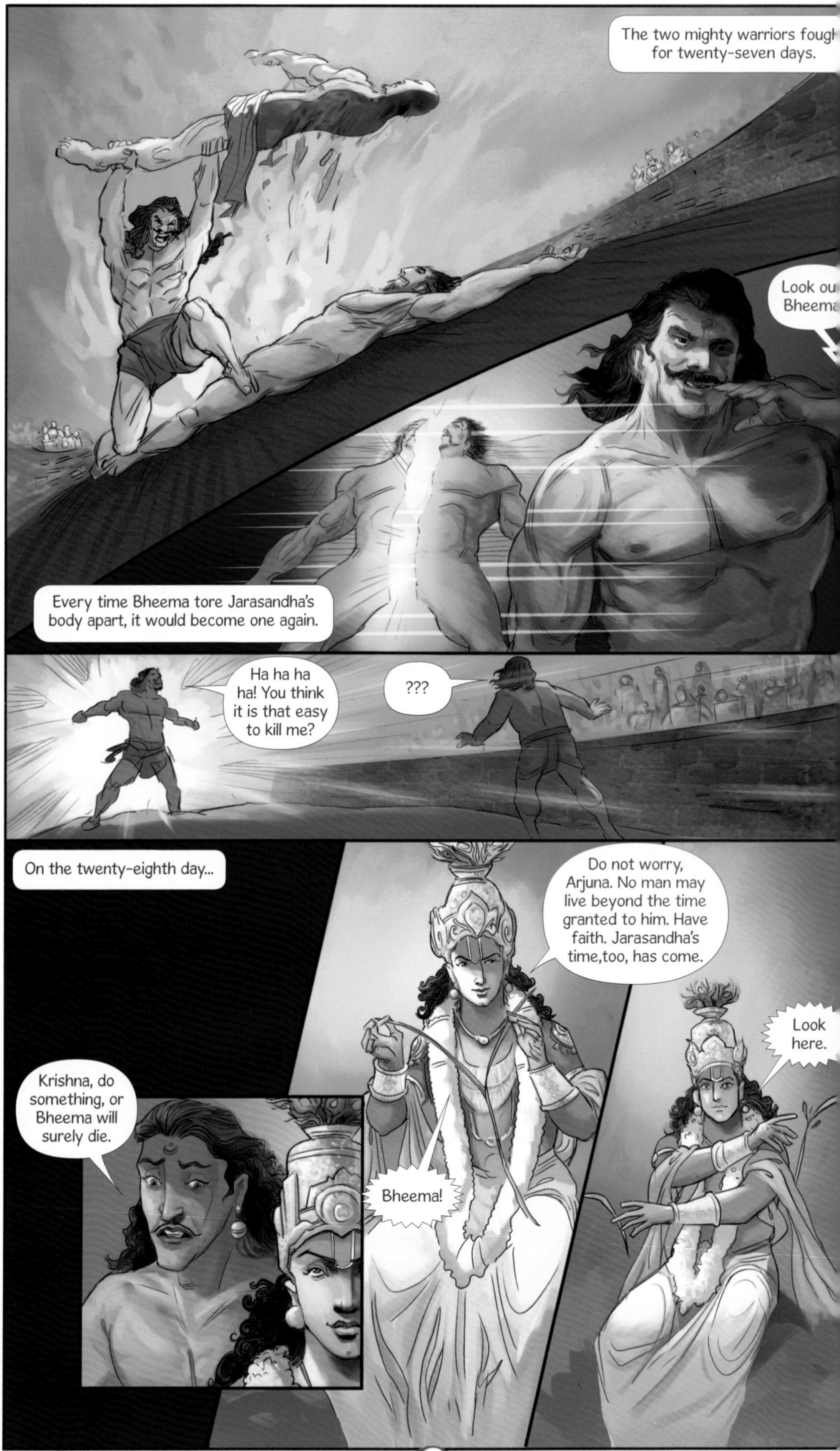
The two mighty warriors fough
for twenty-seven days.
Look ou
Bheema
Every time Bheema tore Jarasandha's body apart, it would become one again.
Ha ha ha ha! You think it is that easy to kill me?
???
On the twenty-eighth day...
Do not worry, Arjuna. No man may live beyond the time granted to him. Have faith. Jarasandha's time,too, has come.
Look here.
Krishna, do something, or Bheema will surely die.
Bheema!

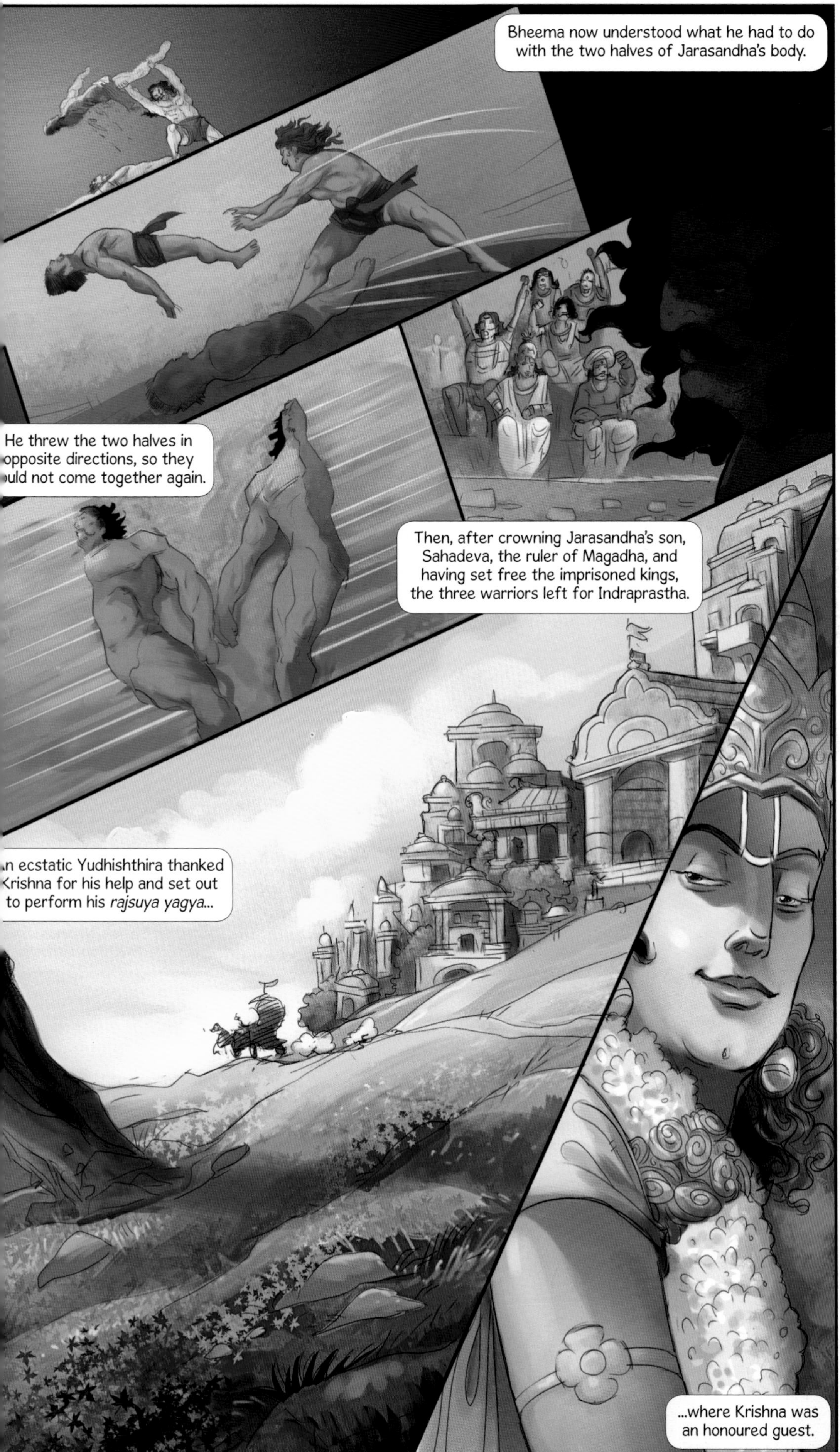
Bheema now understood what he had to do with the two halves of Jarasandha's body.
He threw the two halves in opposite directions, so they ould not come together again.
Then, after crowning Jarasandha's son, Sahadeva, the ruler of Magadha, and having set free the imprisoned kings, the three warriors left for Indraprastha.
n ecstatic Yudhishthira thanked Krishna for his help and set out to perform his *rajsuya yagya*...
...where Krishna was an honoured guest.

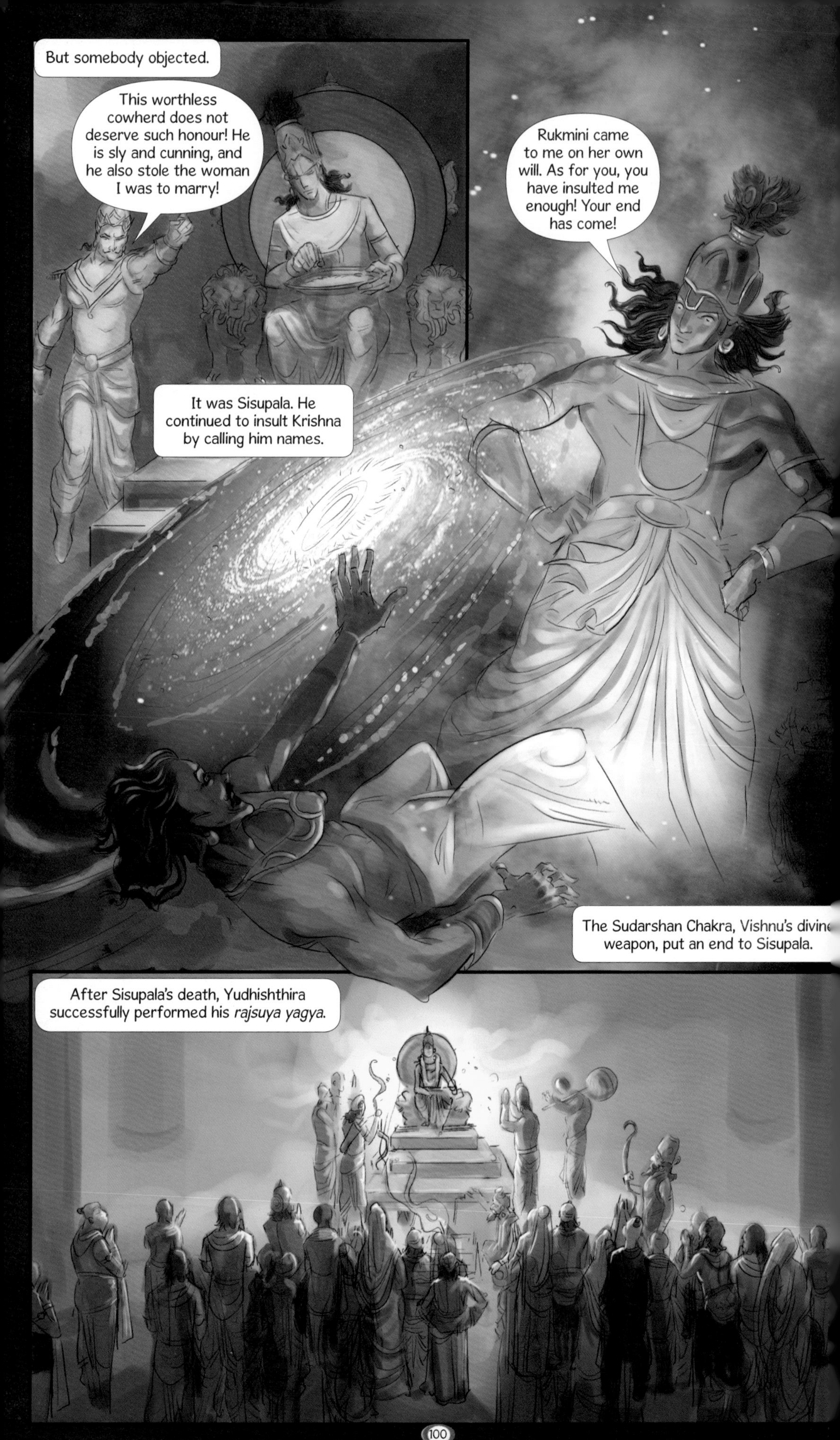

But somebody objected.
This worthless cowherd does not deserve such honour! He is sly and cunning, and he also stole the woman I was to marry!
It was Sisupala. He continued to insult Krishna by calling him names.
Rukmini came to me on her own will. As for you, you have insulted me enough! Your end has come!
The Sudarshan Chakra, Vishnu's divine weapon, put an end to Sisupala.
After Sisupala's death, Yudhishthira successfully performed his *rajsuya yagya*.

Kurukshetra

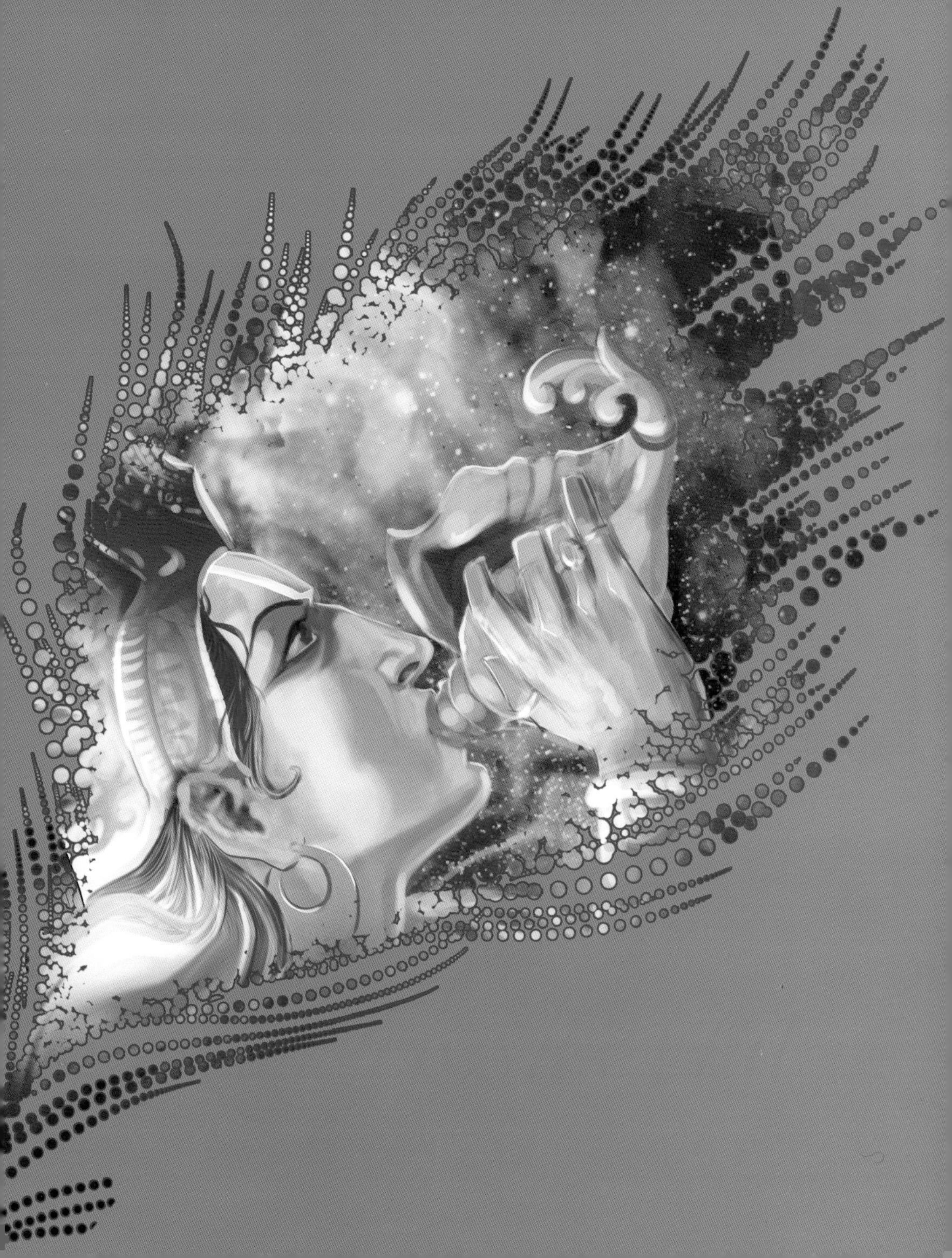

Kurukshetra

As fate would have it, Yudhishthira does not remain emperor for long. He loses his kingdom in an unfair game of dice to his cousins, the Kauravas. After a bitter humiliation of the Pandavas, which includes a public disrobing of their wife Draupadi, the eldest Kaurava, Duryodhana, becomes crown prince of the entire Kuru kingdom. All five Pandava brothers and their wife Draupadi are exiled into the forest for thirteen years. Their last year of exile is spent in hiding in the court of King Virat of the Matsya kingdom. As their exile draws to an end, it is time for Yudhishthira to regain his kingdom. The time has now come for Krishna to enforce the rule of righteousness and orchestrate a great war to fulfil his duty and to rid the earth of evil.

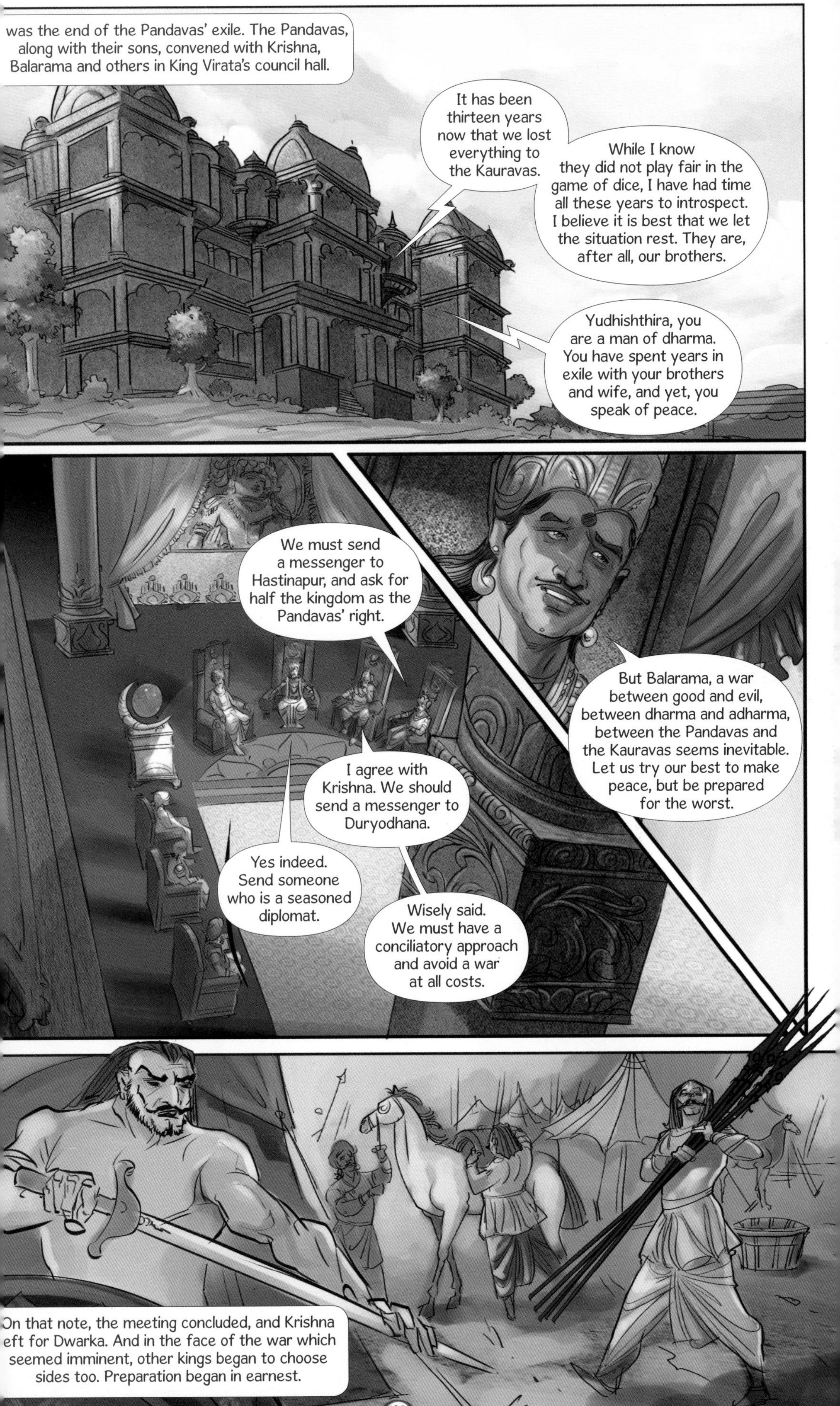
was the end of the Pandavas' exile. The Pandavas, along with their sons, convened with Krishna, Balarama and others in King Virata's council hall.
It has been thirteen years now that we lost everything to the Kauravas.
While I know they did not play fair in the game of dice, I have had time all these years to introspect. I believe it is best that we let the situation rest. They are, after all, our brothers.
Yudhishthira, you are a man of dharma. You have spent years in exile with your brothers and wife, and yet, you speak of peace.
We must send a messenger to Hastinapur, and ask for half the kingdom as the Pandavas' right.
But Balarama, a war between good and evil, between dharma and adharma, between the Pandavas and the Kauravas seems inevitable. Let us try our best to make peace, but be prepared for the worst.
I agree with Krishna. We should send a messenger to Duryodhana.
Yes indeed. Send someone who is a seasoned diplomat.
Wisely said. We must have a conciliatory approach and avoid a war at all costs.
On that note, the meeting concluded, and Krishna eft for Dwarka. And in the face of the war which seemed imminent, other kings began to choose sides too. Preparation began in earnest.

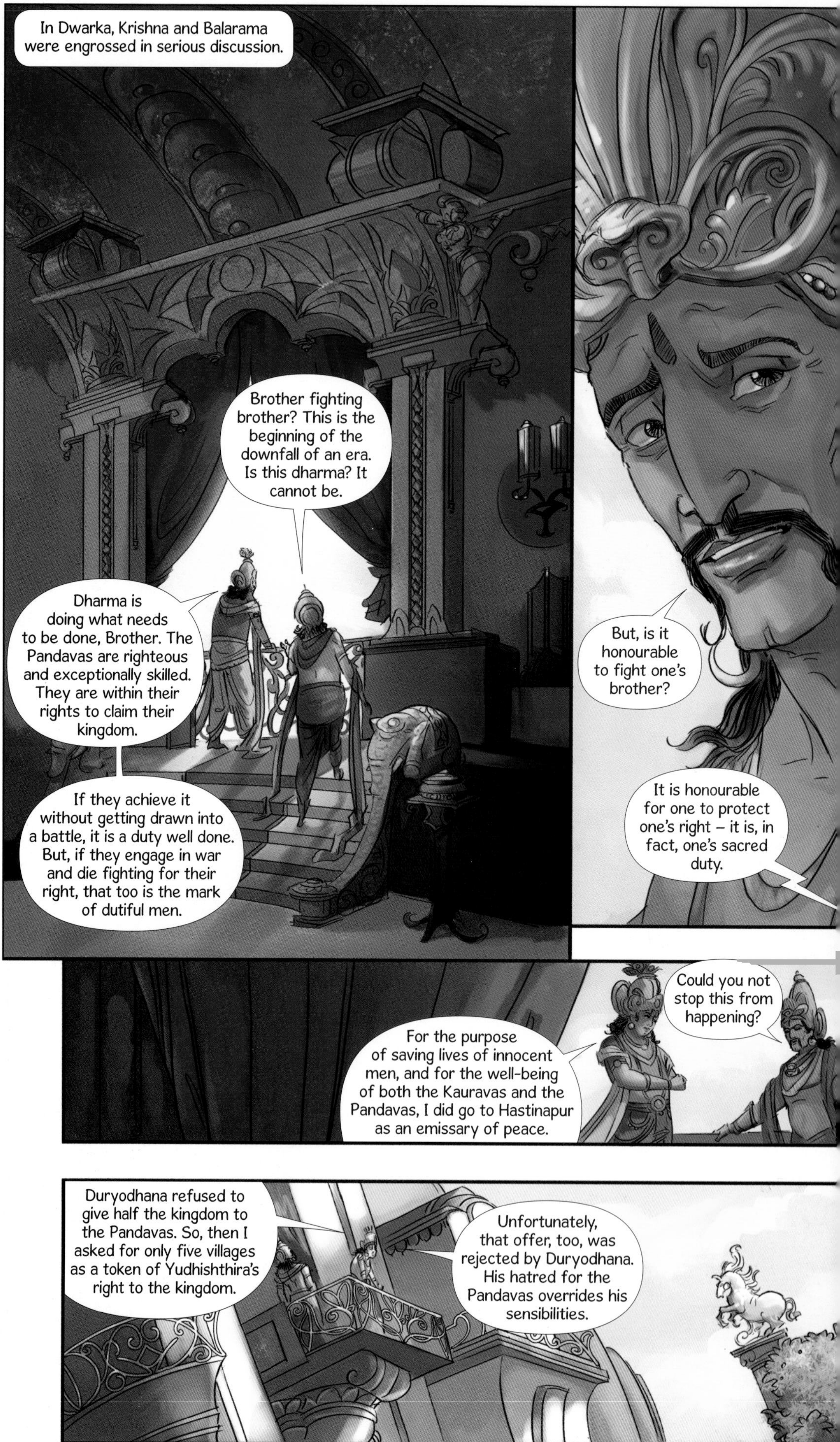
In Dwarka, Krishna and Balarama were engrossed in serious discussion.
Brother fighting brother? This is the beginning of the downfall of an era. Is this dharma? It cannot be.
Dharma is doing what needs to be done, Brother. The Pandavas are righteous and exceptionally skilled. They are within their rights to claim their kingdom.
If they achieve it without getting drawn into a battle, it is a duty well done. But, if they engage in war and die fighting for their right, that too is the mark of dutiful men.
But, is it honourable to fight one's brother?
It is honourable for one to protect one's right – it is, in fact, one's sacred duty.
Could you not stop this from happening?
For the purpose of saving lives of innocent men, and for the well-being of both the Kauravas and the Pandavas, I did go to Hastinapur as an emissary of peace.
Duryodhana refused to give half the kingdom to the Pandavas. So, then I asked for only five villages as a token of Yudhishthira's right to the kingdom.
Unfortunately, that offer, too, was rejected by Duryodhana. His hatred for the Pandavas overrides his sensibilities.

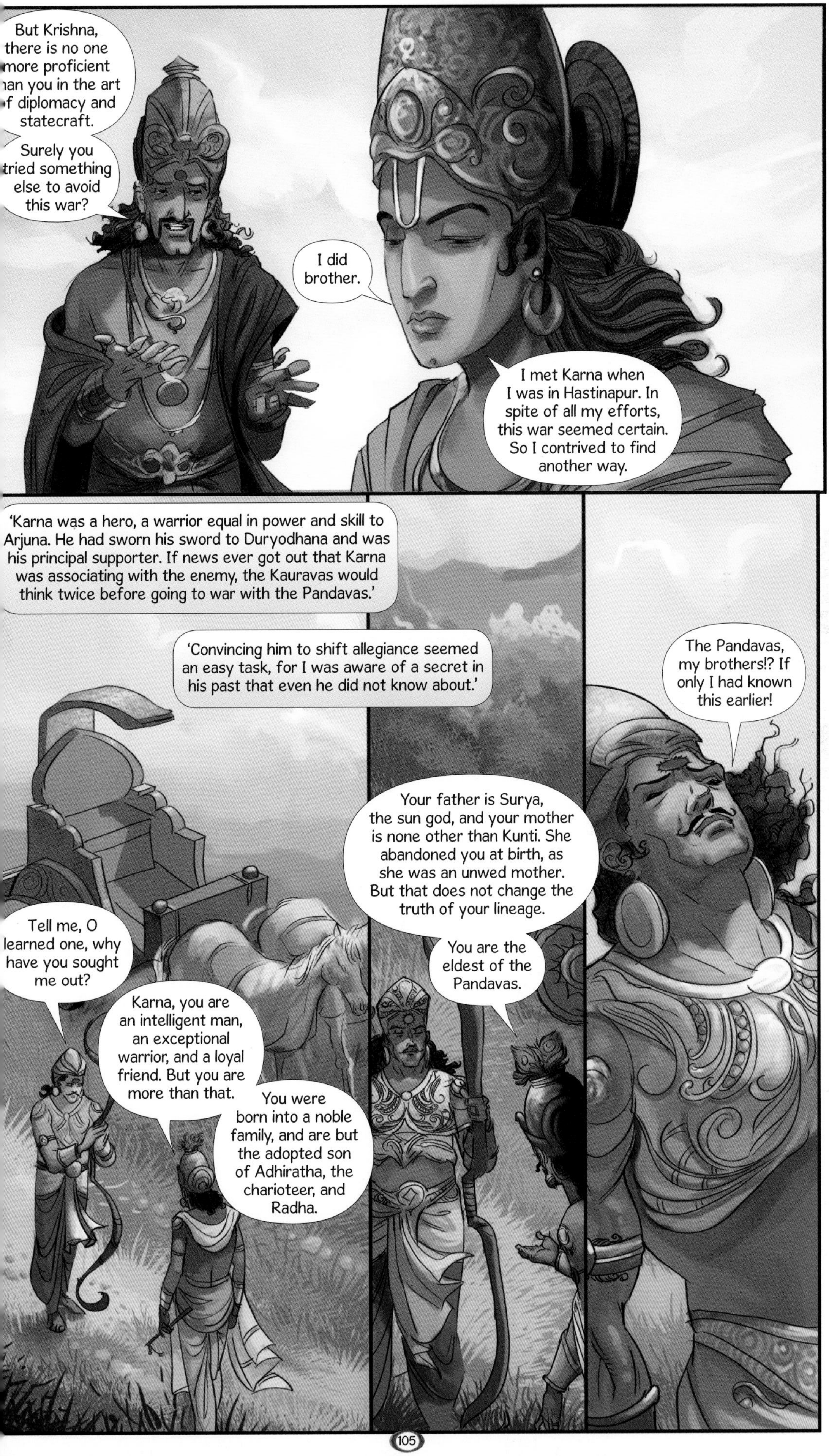

But Krishna, there is no one more proficient than you in the art of diplomacy and statecraft.
Surely you tried something else to avoid this war?
I did brother.
I met Karna when I was in Hastinapur. In spite of all my efforts, this war seemed certain. So I contrived to find another way.
'Karna was a hero, a warrior equal in power and skill to Arjuna. He had sworn his sword to Duryodhana and was his principal supporter. If news ever got out that Karna was associating with the enemy, the Kauravas would think twice before going to war with the Pandavas.'
'Convincing him to shift allegiance seemed an easy task, for I was aware of a secret in his past that even he did not know about.'
Tell me, O learned one, why have you sought me out?
Karna, you are an intelligent man, an exceptional warrior, and a loyal friend. But you are more than that.
You were born into a noble family, and are but the adopted son of Adhiratha, the charioteer, and Radha.
Your father is Surya, the sun god, and your mother is none other than Kunti. She abandoned you at birth, as she was an unwed mother. But that does not change the truth of your lineage.
You are the eldest of the Pandavas.
The Pandavas, my brothers!? If only I had known this earlier!

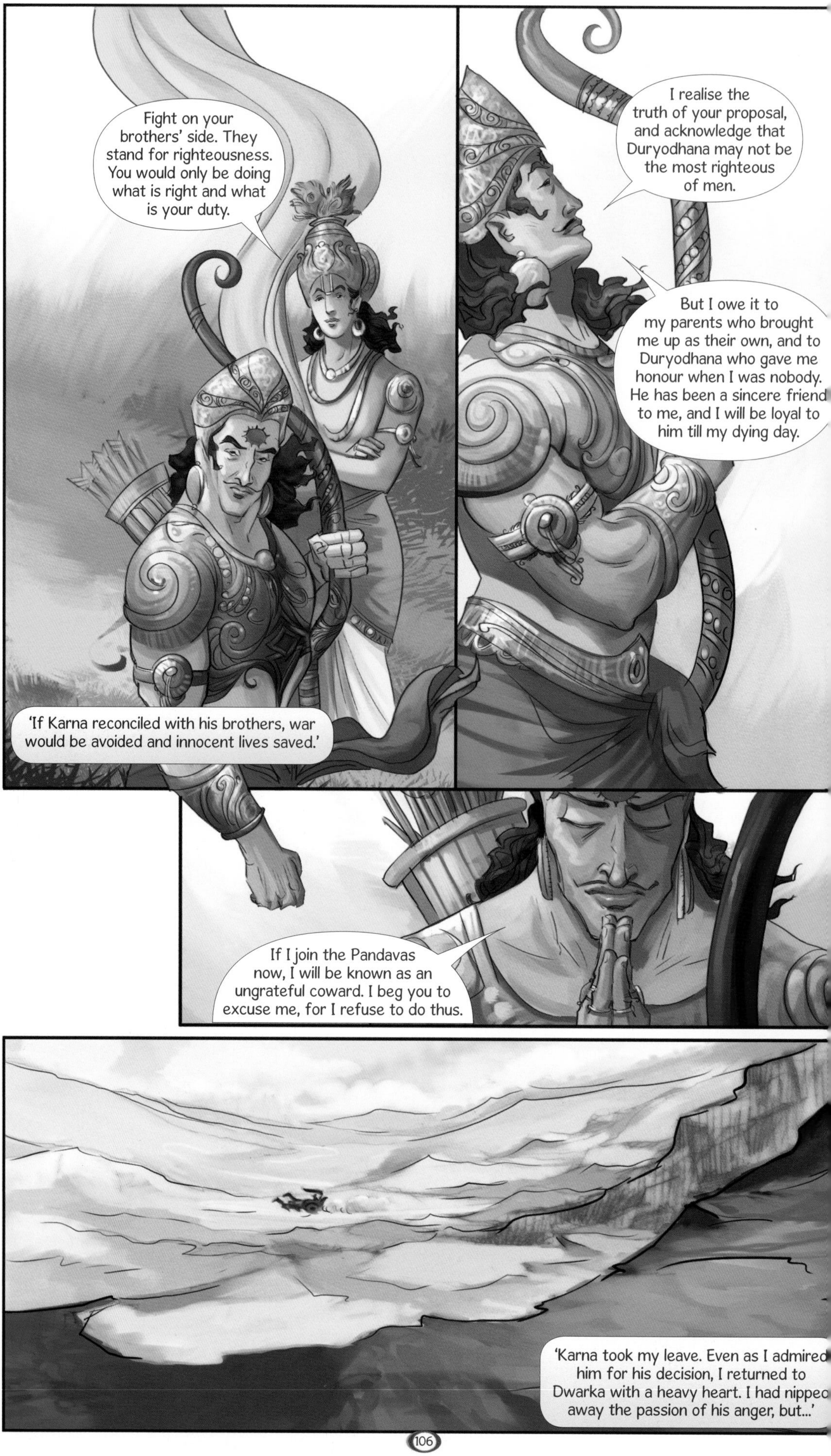
Fight on your brothers' side. They stand for righteousness. You would only be doing what is right and what is your duty.
'If Karna reconciled with his brothers, war would be avoided and innocent lives saved.'
I realise the truth of your proposal, and acknowledge that Duryodhana may not be the most righteous of men.
But I owe it to my parents who brought me up as their own, and to Duryodhana who gave me honour when I was nobody. He has been a sincere friend to me, and I will be loyal to him till my dying day.
If I join the Pandavas now, I will be known as an ungrateful coward. I beg you to excuse me, for I refuse to do thus.
'Karna took my leave. Even as I admired him for his decision, I returned to Dwarka with a heavy heart. I had nipped away the passion of his anger, but...'

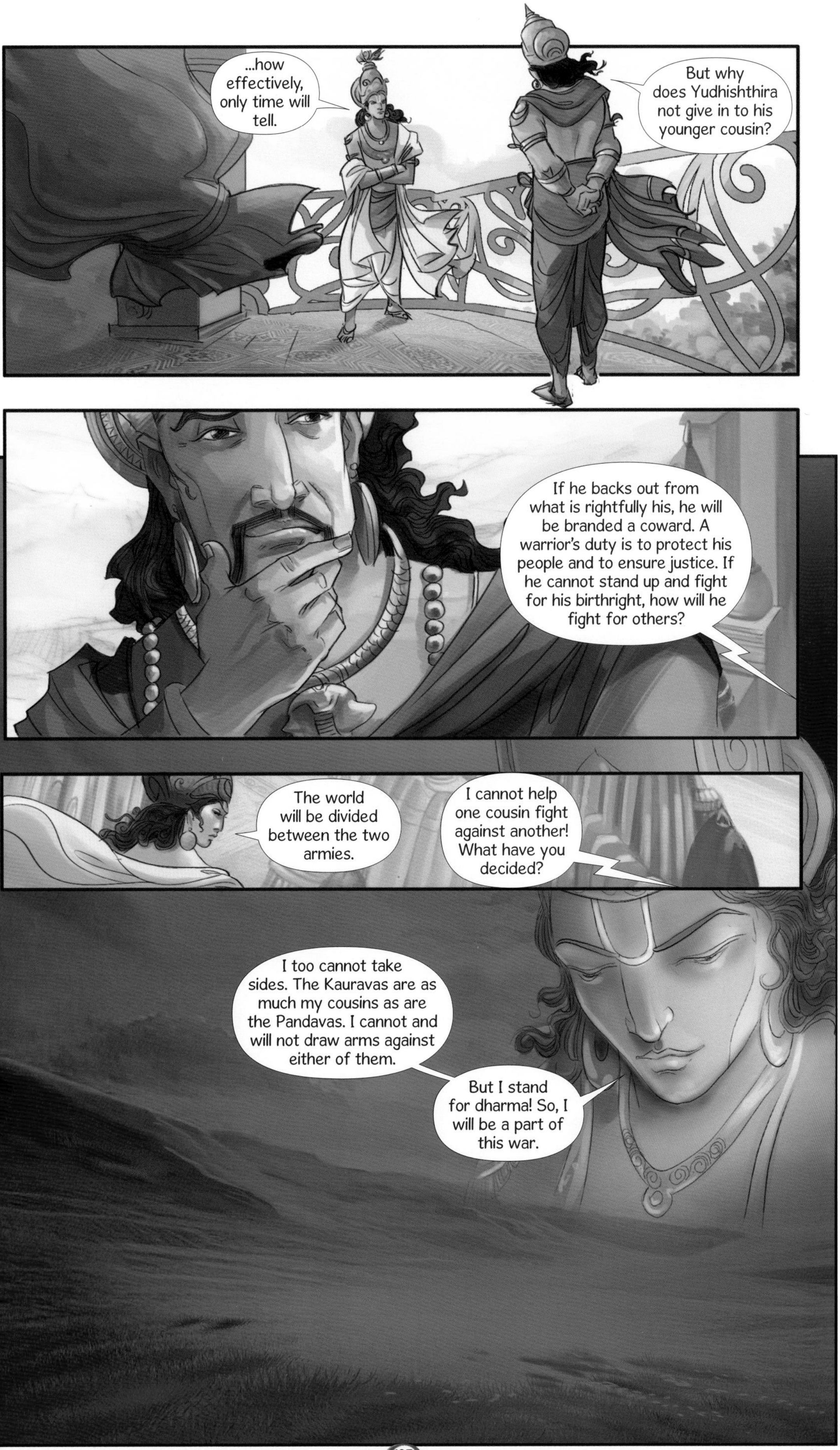
...how effectively, only time will tell.
But why does Yudhishthira not give in to his younger cousin?
If he backs out from what is rightfully his, he will be branded a coward. A warrior's duty is to protect his people and to ensure justice. If he cannot stand up and fight for his birthright, how will he fight for others?
The world will be divided between the two armies.
I cannot help one cousin fight against another! What have you decided?
I too cannot take sides. The Kauravas are as much my cousins as are the Pandavas. I cannot and will not draw arms against either of them.
But I stand for dharma! So, I will be a part of this war.

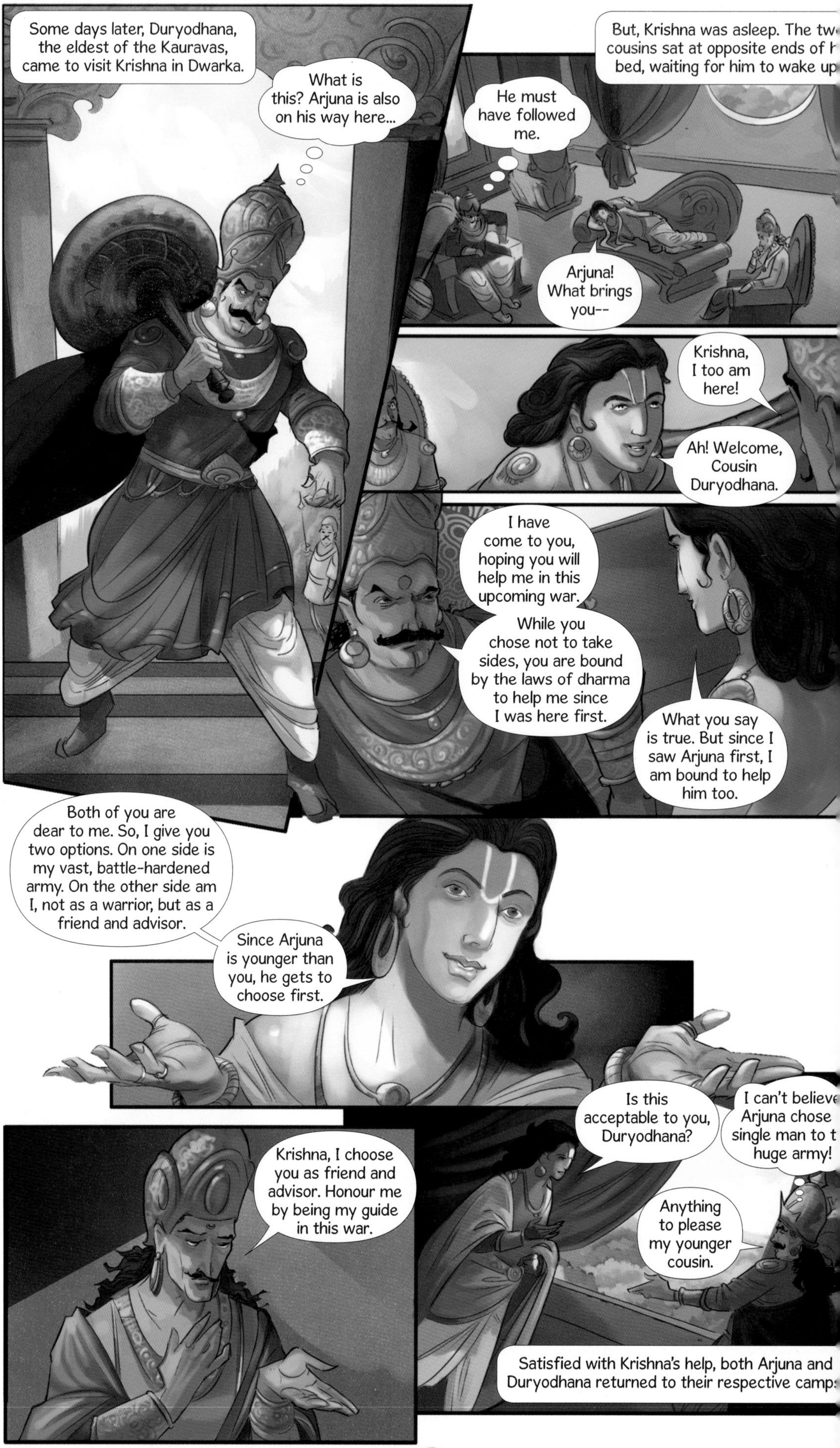

Some days later, Duryodhana, the eldest of the Kauravas, came to visit Krishna in Dwarka.
What is this? Arjuna is also on his way here...
But, Krishna was asleep. The tw cousins sat at opposite ends of h bed, waiting for him to wake up
He must have followed me.
Arjuna! What brings you--
Krishna, I too am here!
Ah! Welcome, Cousin Duryodhana.
I have come to you, hoping you will help me in this upcoming war.
While you chose not to take sides, you are bound by the laws of dharma to help me since I was here first.
What you say is true. But since I saw Arjuna first, I am bound to help him too.
Both of you are dear to me. So, I give you two options. On one side is my vast, battle-hardened army. On the other side am I, not as a warrior, but as a friend and advisor.
Since Arjuna is younger than you, he gets to choose first.
Krishna, I choose you as friend and advisor. Honour me by being my guide in this war.
Is this acceptable to you, Duryodhana?
I can't believe Arjuna chose single man to t huge army!
Anything to please my younger cousin.
Satisfied with Krishna's help, both Arjuna and Duryodhana returned to their respective camps

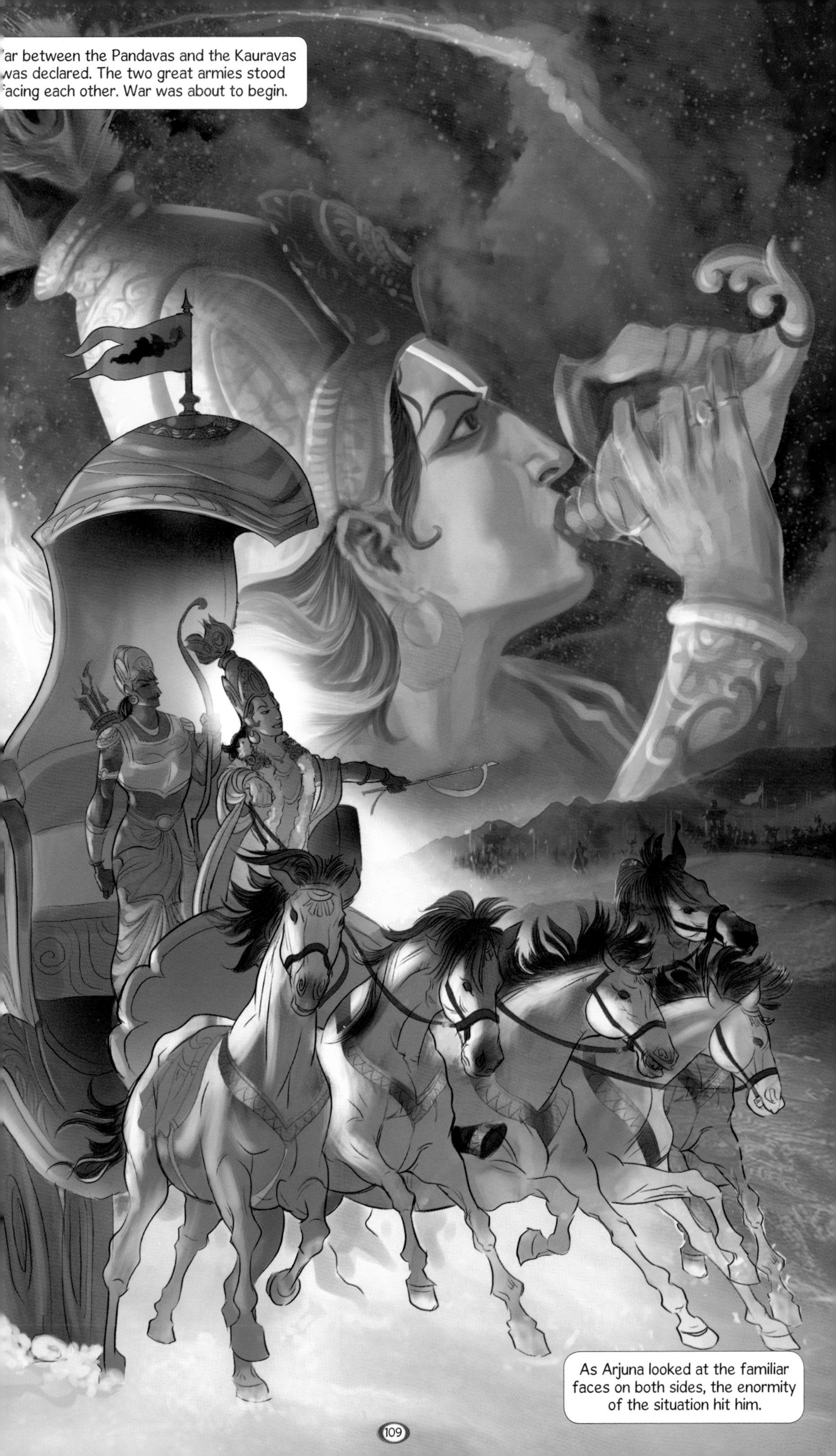
ar between the Pandavas and the Kauravas was declared. The two great armies stood acing each other. War was about to begin.
As Arjuna looked at the familiar faces on both sides, the enormity of the situation hit him.

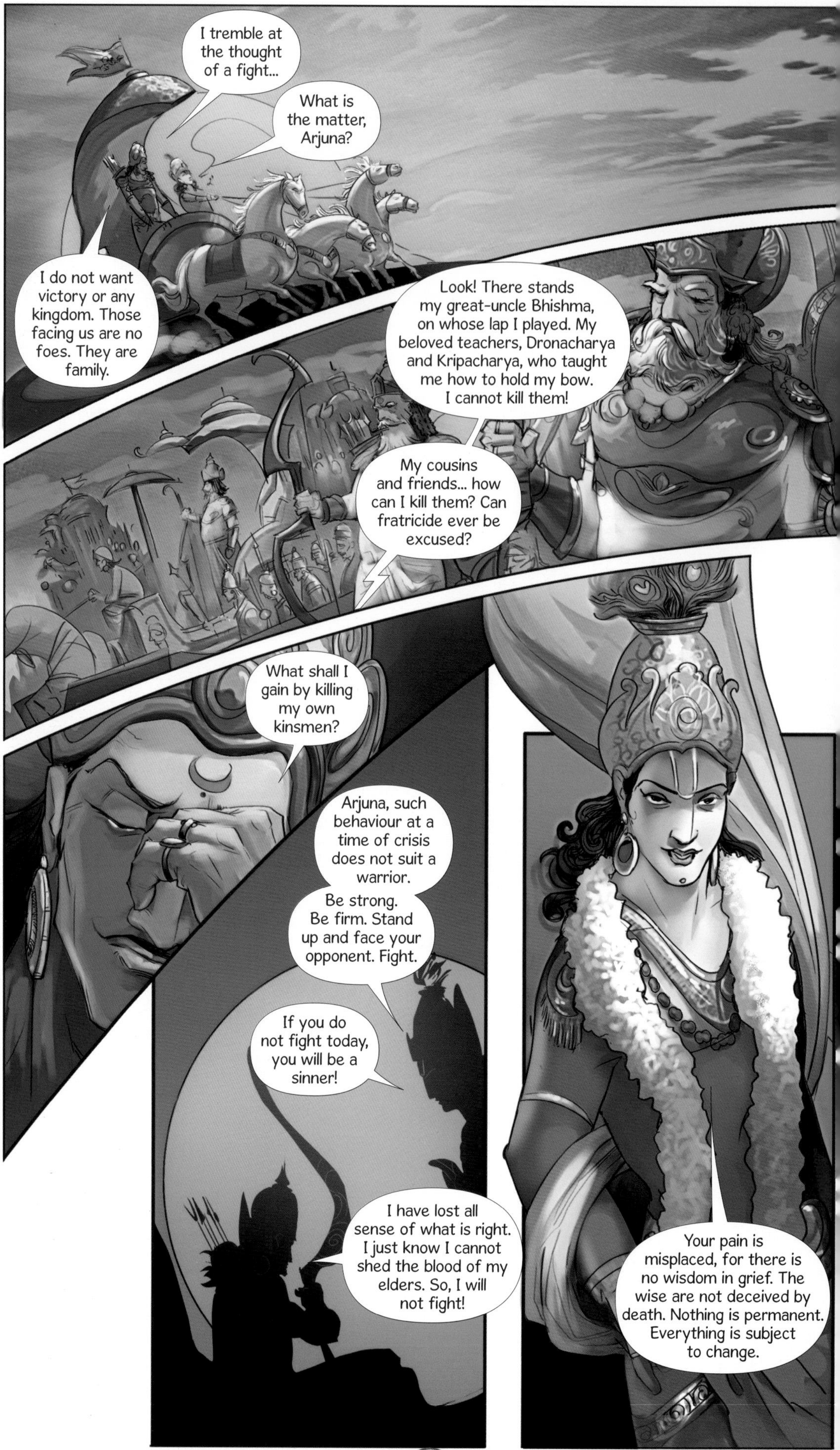

I tremble at the thought of a fight...
What is the matter, Arjuna?
I do not want victory or any kingdom. Those facing us are no foes. They are family.
Look! There stands my great-uncle Bhishma, on whose lap I played. My beloved teachers, Dronacharya and Kripacharya, who taught me how to hold my bow. I cannot kill them!
My cousins and friends... how can I kill them? Can fratricide ever be excused?
What shall I gain by killing my own kinsmen?
Arjuna, such behaviour at a time of crisis does not suit a warrior.
Be strong. Be firm. Stand up and face your opponent. Fight.
If you do not fight today, you will be a sinner!
I have lost all sense of what is right. I just know I cannot shed the blood of my elders. So, I will not fight!
Your pain is misplaced, for there is no wisdom in grief. The wise are not deceived by death. Nothing is permanent. Everything is subject to change.

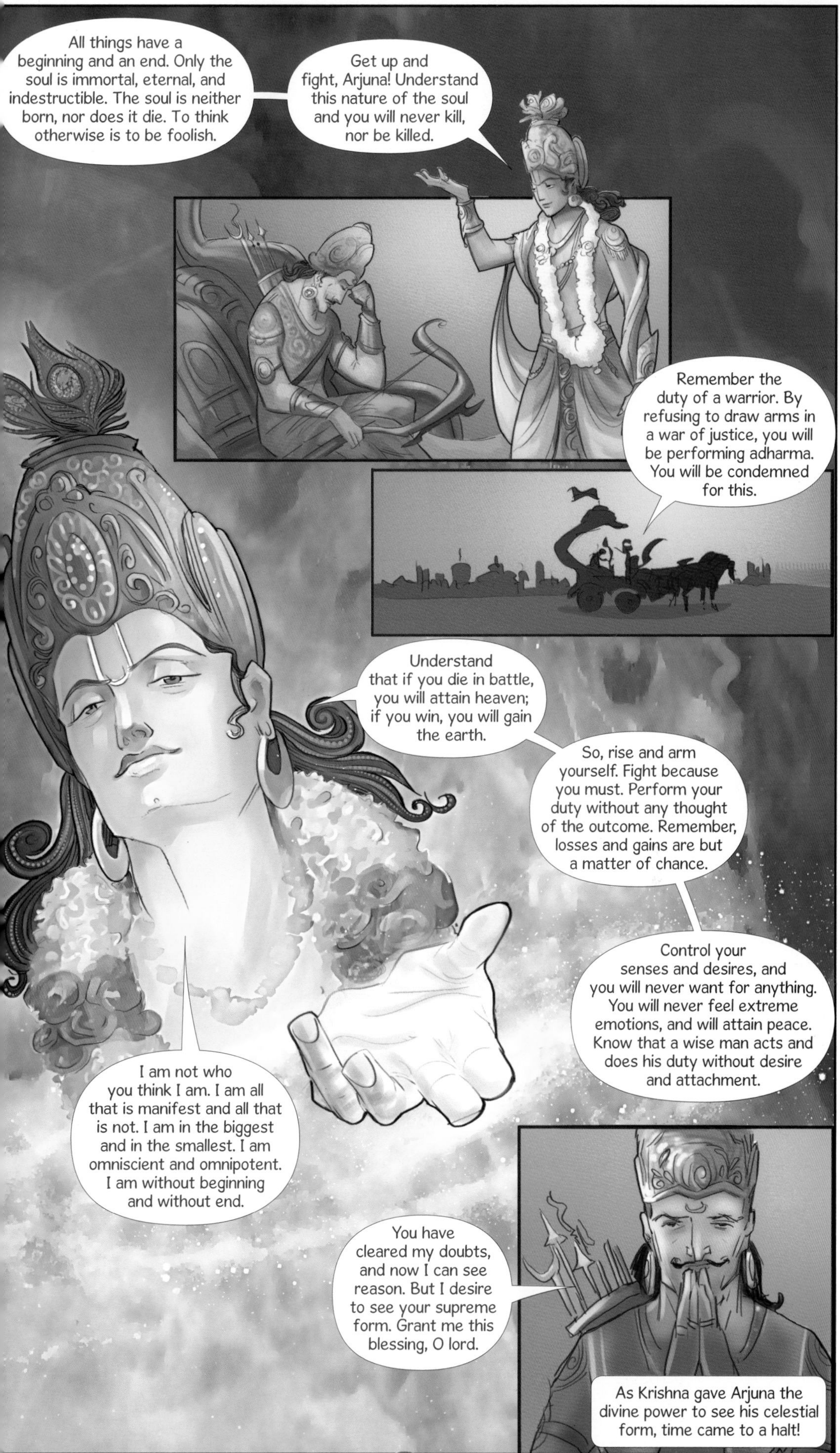
All things have a beginning and an end. Only the soul is immortal, eternal, and indestructible. The soul is neither born, nor does it die. To think otherwise is to be foolish.
Get up and fight, Arjuna! Understand this nature of the soul and you will never kill, nor be killed.
Remember the duty of a warrior. By refusing to draw arms in a war of justice, you will be performing adharma. You will be condemned for this.
Understand that if you die in battle, you will attain heaven; if you win, you will gain the earth.
So, rise and arm yourself. Fight because you must. Perform your duty without any thought of the outcome. Remember, losses and gains are but a matter of chance.
Control your senses and desires, and you will never want for anything. You will never feel extreme emotions, and will attain peace. Know that a wise man acts and does his duty without desire and attachment.
I am not who you think I am. I am all that is manifest and all that is not. I am in the biggest and in the smallest. I am omniscient and omnipotent. I am without beginning and without end.
You have cleared my doubts, and now I can see reason. But I desire to see your supreme form. Grant me this blessing, O lord.
As Krishna gave Arjuna the divine power to see his celestial form, time came to a halt!

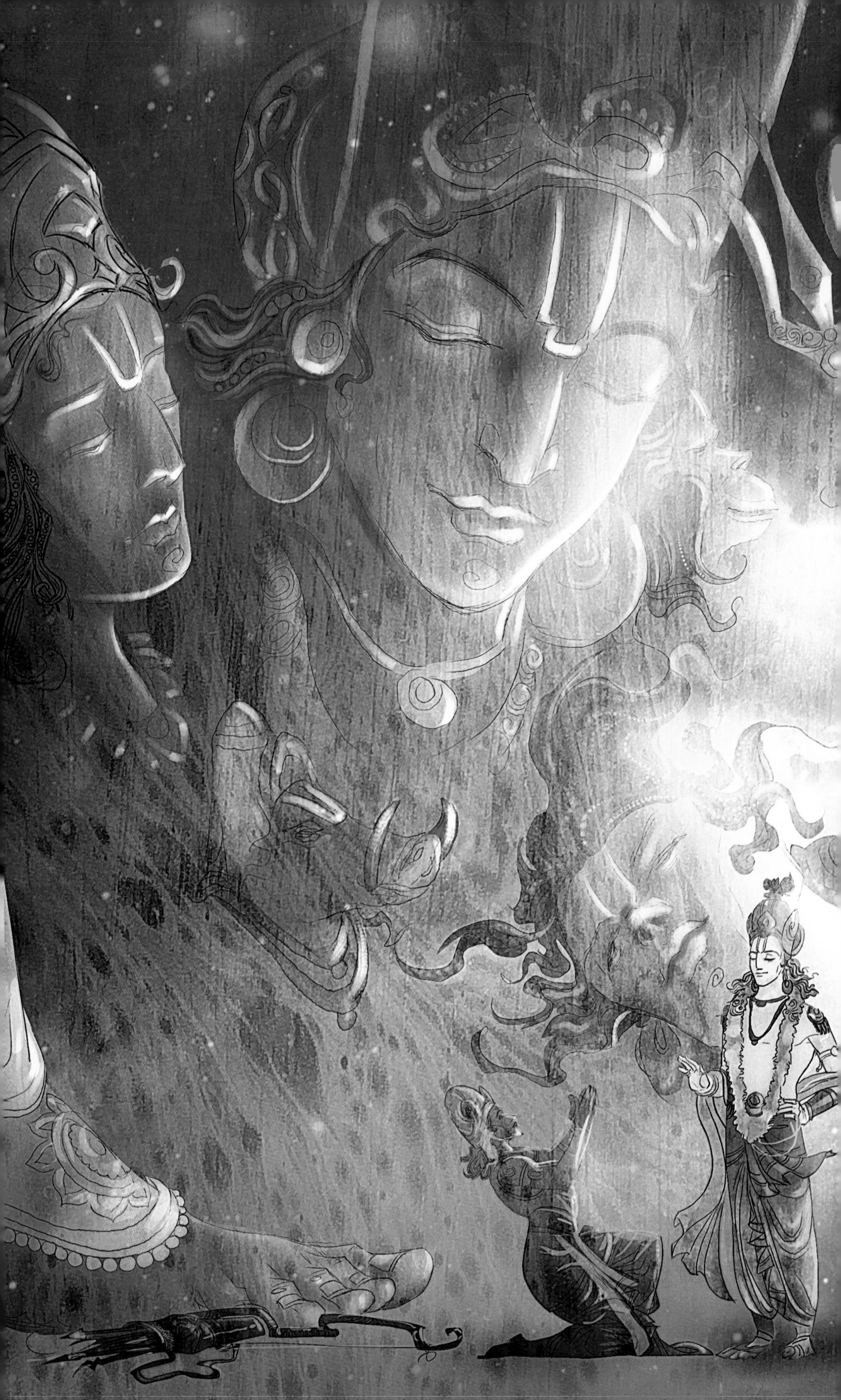

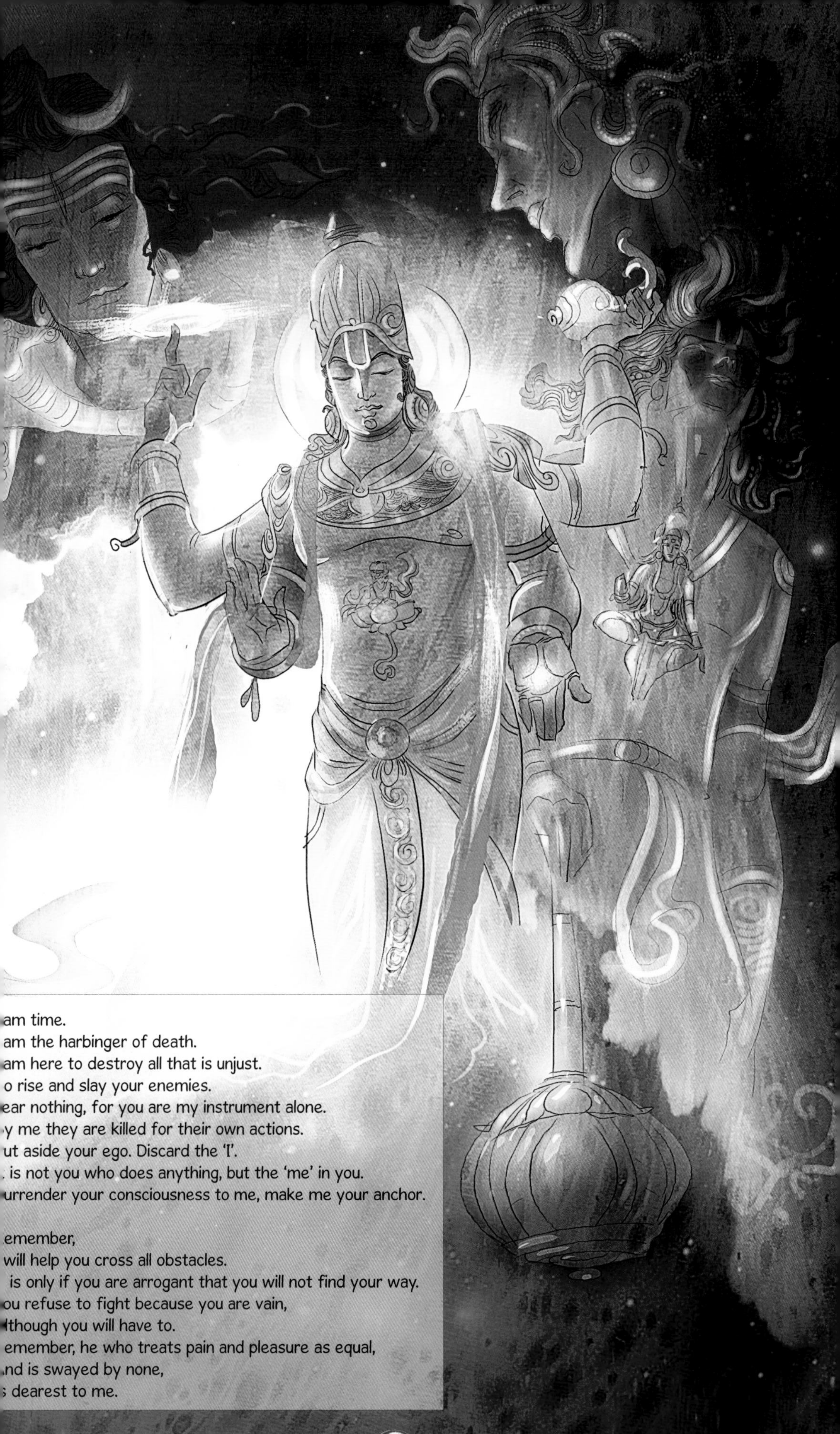
am time.
am the harbinger of death.
am here to destroy all that is unjust.
o rise and slay your enemies.
ear nothing, for you are my instrument alone.
y me they are killed for their own actions.
ut aside your ego. Discard the 'I'.
is not you who does anything, but the 'me' in you.
urrender your consciousness to me, make me your anchor.
emember,
will help you cross all obstacles.
is only if you are arrogant that you will not find your way.
ou refuse to fight because you are vain,
lthough you will have to.
emember, he who treats pain and pleasure as equal,
nd is swayed by none,
s dearest to me.

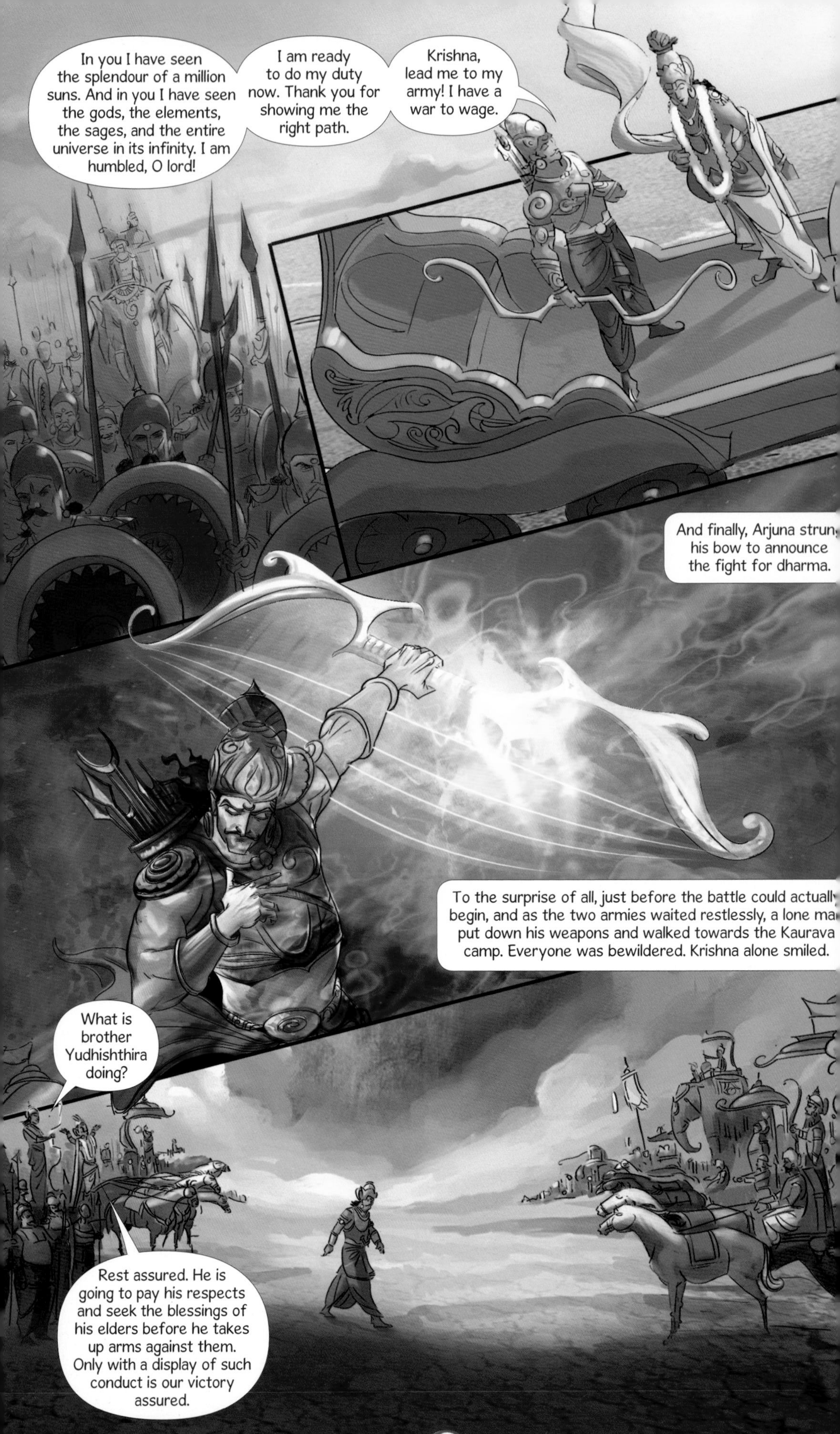
In you I have seen the splendour of a million suns. And in you I have seen the gods, the elements, the sages, and the entire universe in its infinity. I am humbled, O lord!
I am ready to do my duty now. Thank you for showing me the right path.
Krishna, lead me to my army! I have a war to wage.
And finally, Arjuna strun his bow to announce the fight for dharma.
To the surprise of all, just before the battle could actuall begin, and as the two armies waited restlessly, a lone ma put down his weapons and walked towards the Kaurava camp. Everyone was bewildered. Krishna alone smiled.
What is brother Yudhishthira doing?
Rest assured. He is going to pay his respects and seek the blessings of his elders before he takes up arms against them. Only with a display of such conduct is our victory assured.

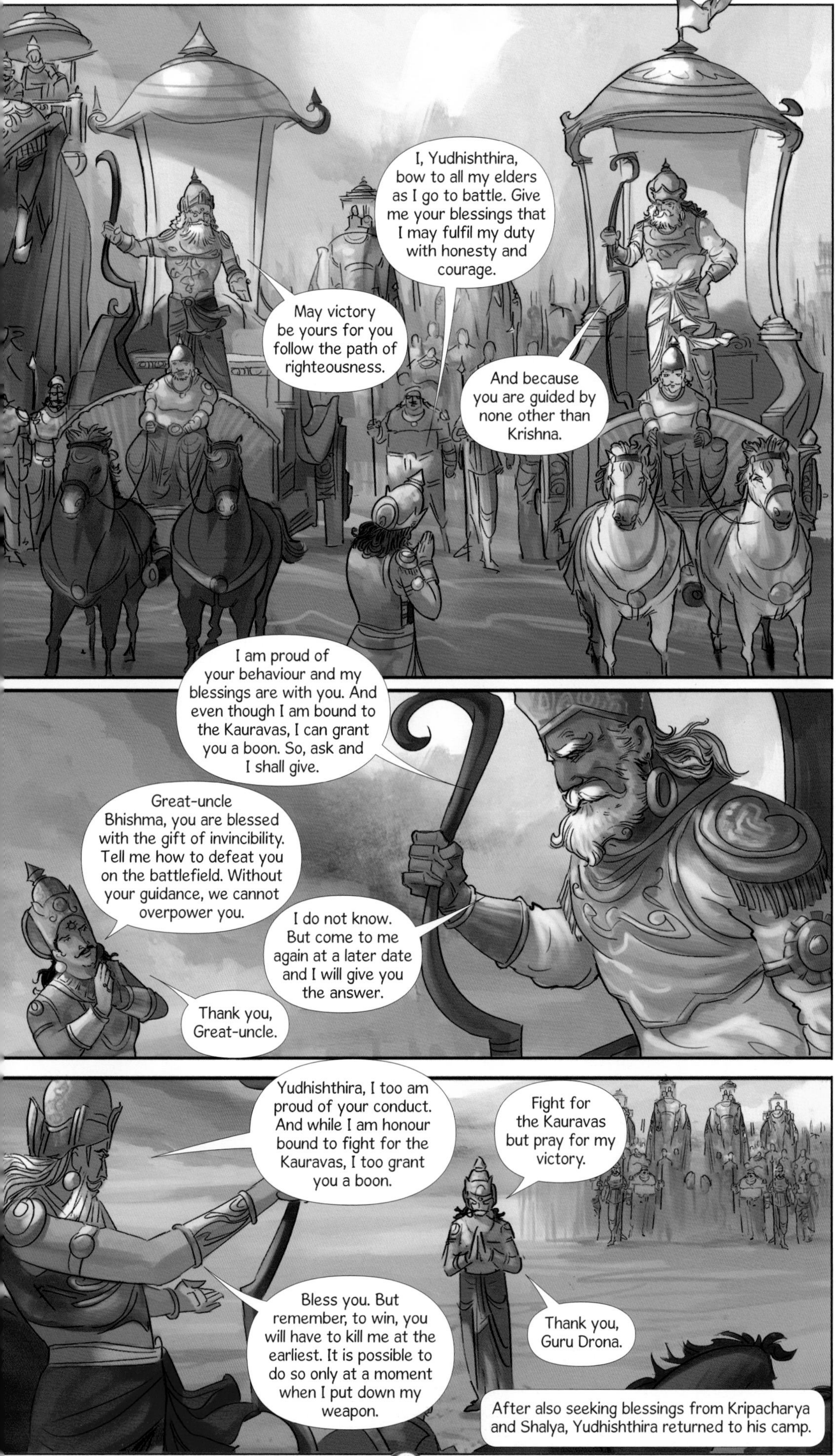
I, Yudhishthira, bow to all my elders as I go to battle. Give me your blessings that I may fulfil my duty with honesty and courage.
May victory be yours for you follow the path of righteousness.
And because you are guided by none other than Krishna.
I am proud of your behaviour and my blessings are with you. And even though I am bound to the Kauravas, I can grant you a boon. So, ask and I shall give.
Great-uncle Bhishma, you are blessed with the gift of invincibility. Tell me how to defeat you on the battlefield. Without your guidance, we cannot overpower you.
I do not know. But come to me again at a later date and I will give you the answer.
Thank you, Great-uncle.
Yudhishthira, I too am proud of your conduct. And while I am honour bound to fight for the Kauravas, I too grant you a boon.
Fight for the Kauravas but pray for my victory.
Bless you. But remember, to win, you will have to kill me at the earliest. It is possible to do so only at a moment when I put down my weapon.
Thank you, Guru Drona.
After also seeking blessings from Kripacharya and Shalya, Yudhishthira returned to his camp.

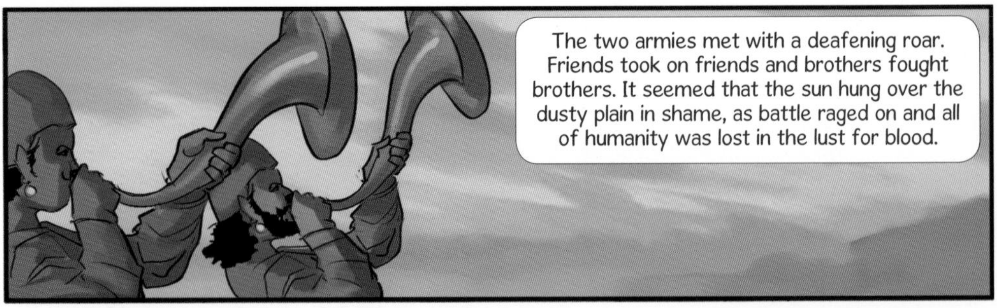
The two armies met with a deafening roar. Friends took on friends and brothers fought brothers. It seemed that the sun hung over the dusty plain in shame, as battle raged on and all of humanity was lost in the lust for blood.

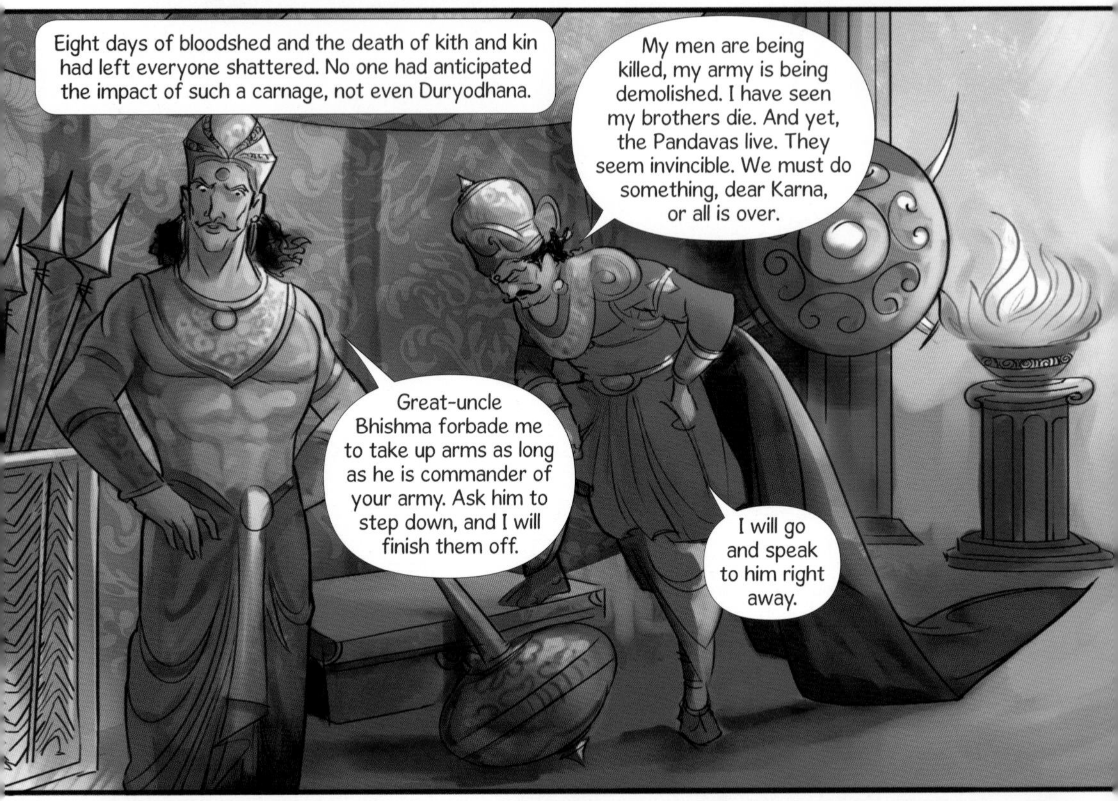
Eight days of bloodshed and the death of kith and kin had left everyone shattered. No one had anticipated the impact of such a carnage, not even Duryodhana.
My men are being killed, my army is being demolished. I have seen my brothers die. And yet, the Pandavas live. They seem invincible. We must do something, dear Karna, or all is over.
Great-uncle Bhishma forbade me to take up arms as long as he is commander of your army. Ask him to step down, and I will finish them off.
I will go and speak to him right away.

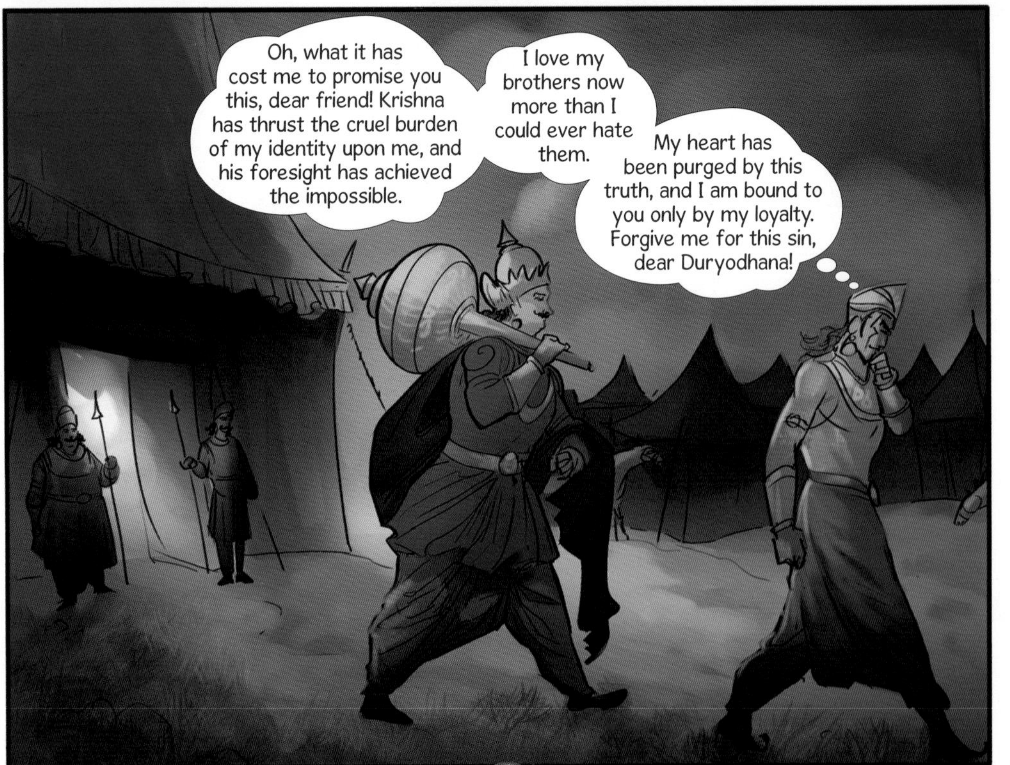
Oh, what it has cost me to promise you this, dear friend! Krishna has thrust the cruel burden of my identity upon me, and his foresight has achieved the impossible.
I love my brothers now more than I could ever hate them.
My heart has been purged by this truth, and I am bound to you only by my loyalty. Forgive me for this sin, dear Duryodhana!

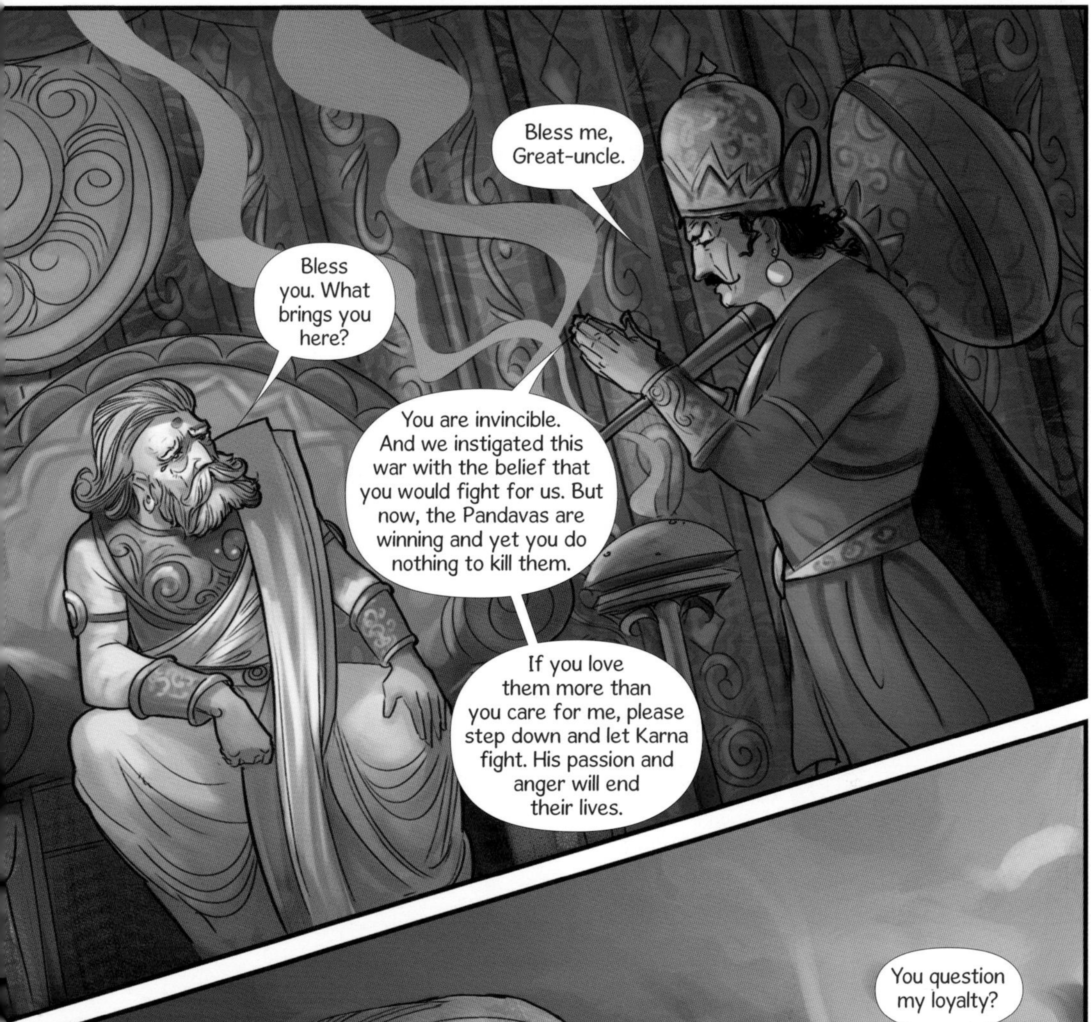
Bless me, Great-uncle.
Bless you. What brings you here?
You are invincible. And we instigated this war with the belief that you would fight for us. But now, the Pandavas are winning and yet you do nothing to kill them.
If you love them more than you care for me, please step down and let Karna fight. His passion and anger will end their lives.

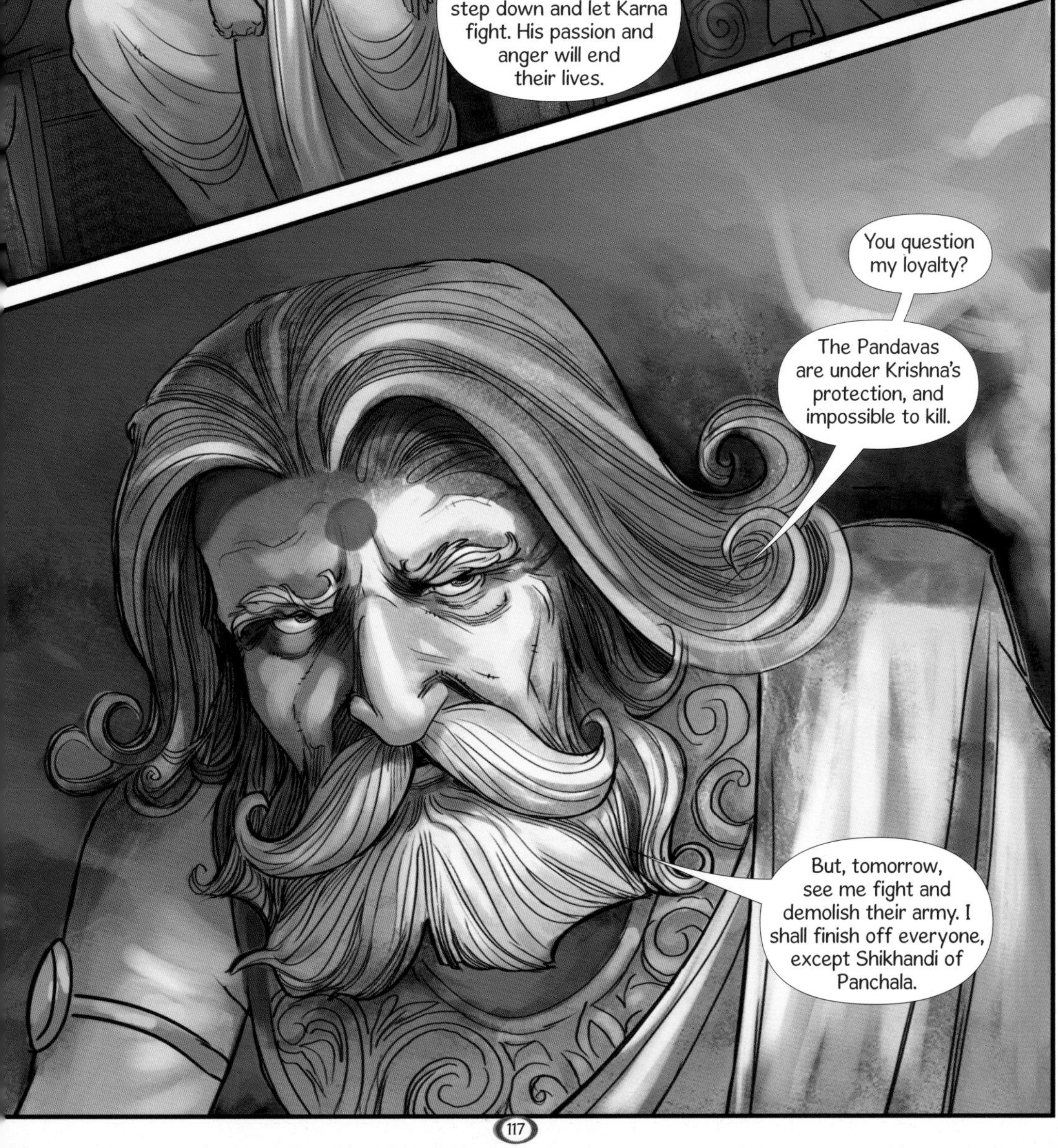
You question my loyalty?
The Pandavas are under Krishna's protection, and impossible to kill.
But, tomorrow, see me fight and demolish their army. I shall finish off everyone, except Shikhandi of Panchala.

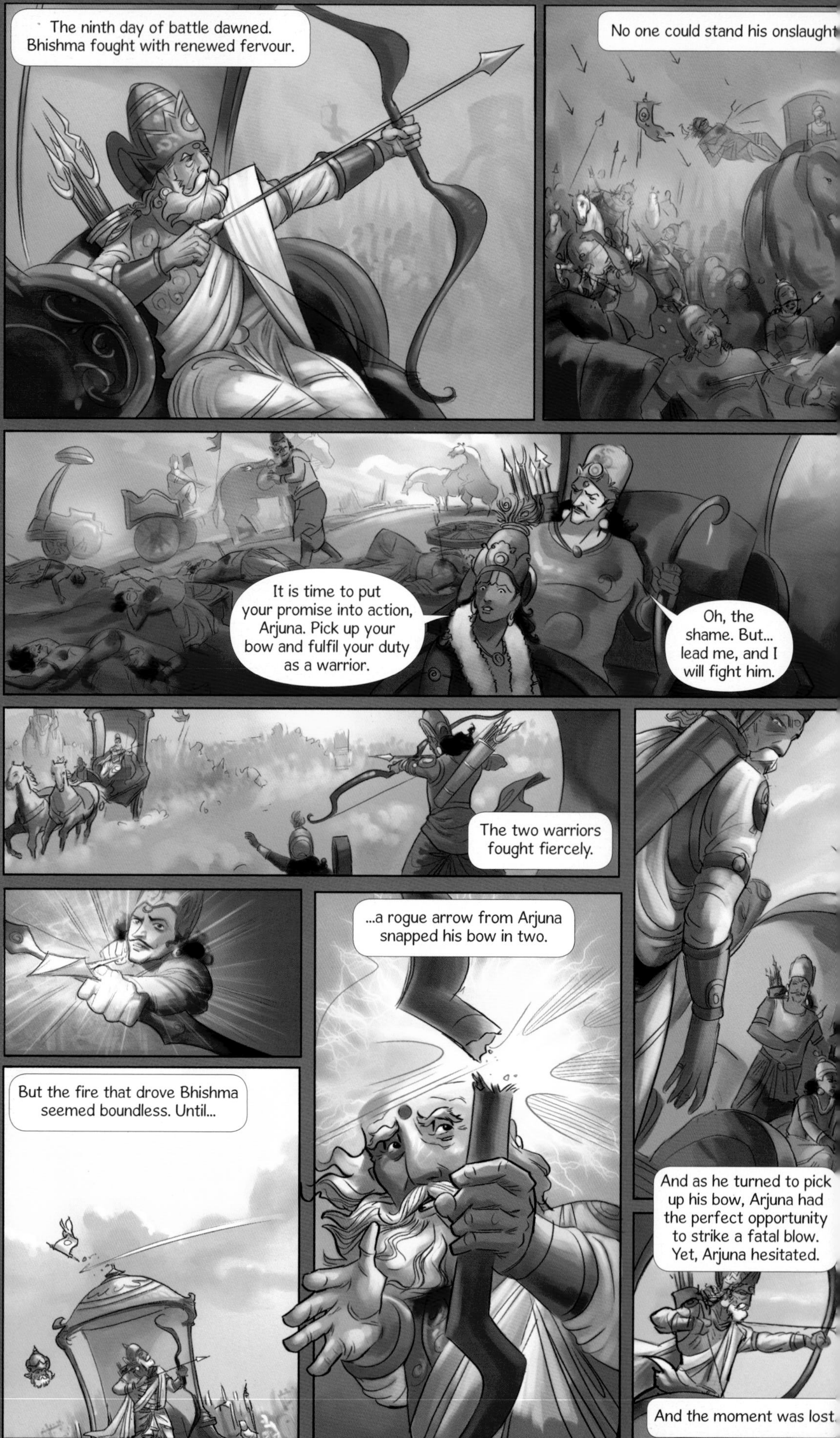
The ninth day of battle dawned. Bhishma fought with renewed fervour.
No one could stand his onslaught
It is time to put your promise into action, Arjuna. Pick up your bow and fulfil your duty as a warrior.
Oh, the shame. But... lead me, and I will fight him.
The two warriors fought fiercely.
But the fire that drove Bhishma seemed boundless. Until...
...a rogue arrow from Arjuna snapped his bow in two.
And as he turned to pick up his bow, Arjuna had the perfect opportunity to strike a fatal blow. Yet, Arjuna hesitated.
And the moment was lost.

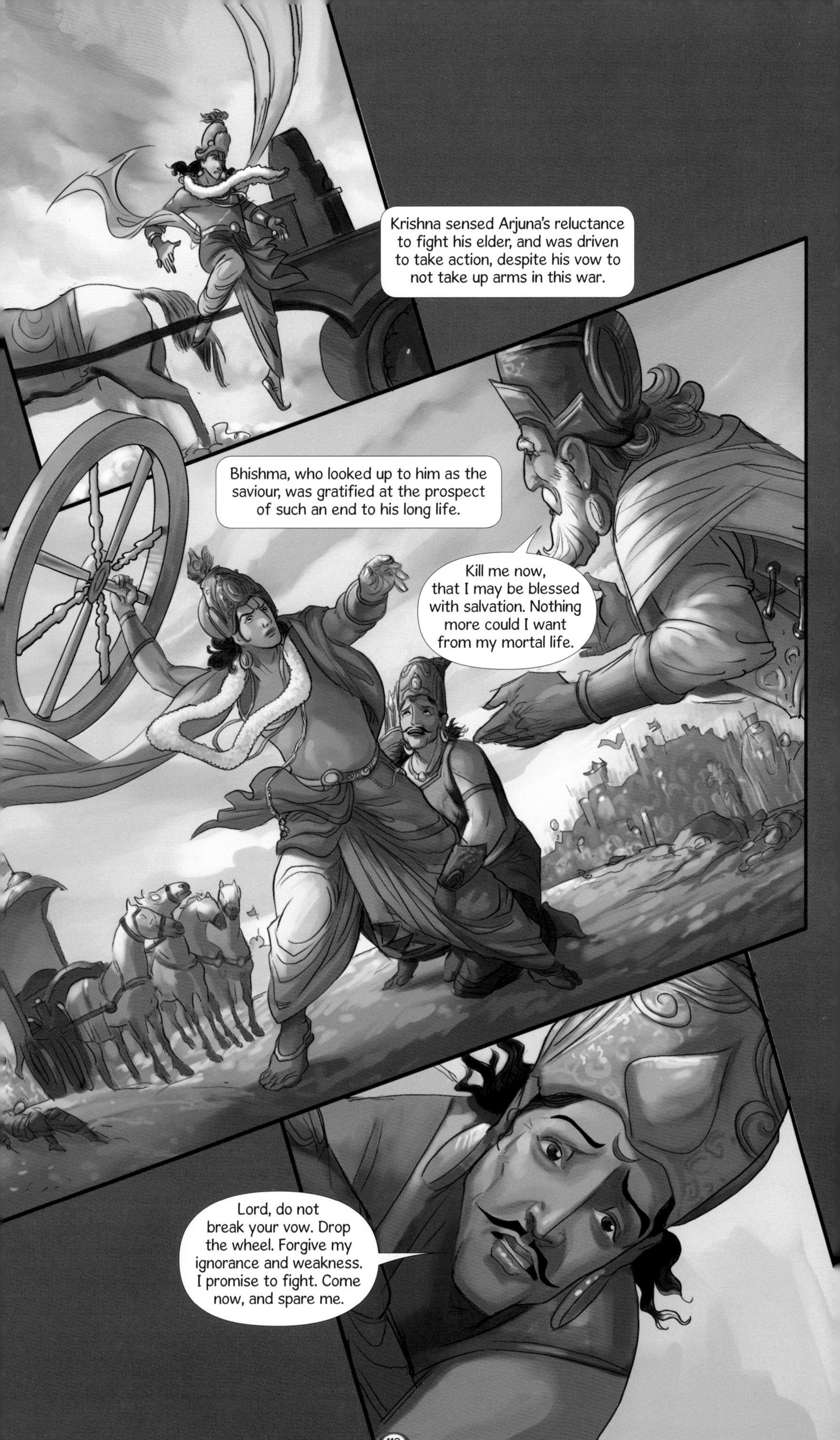
Krishna sensed Arjuna's reluctance to fight his elder, and was driven to take action, despite his vow to not take up arms in this war.
Bhishma, who looked up to him as the saviour, was gratified at the prospect of such an end to his long life.
Kill me now, that I may be blessed with salvation. Nothing more could I want from my mortal life.
Lord, do not break your vow. Drop the wheel. Forgive my ignorance and weakness. I promise to fight. Come now, and spare me.

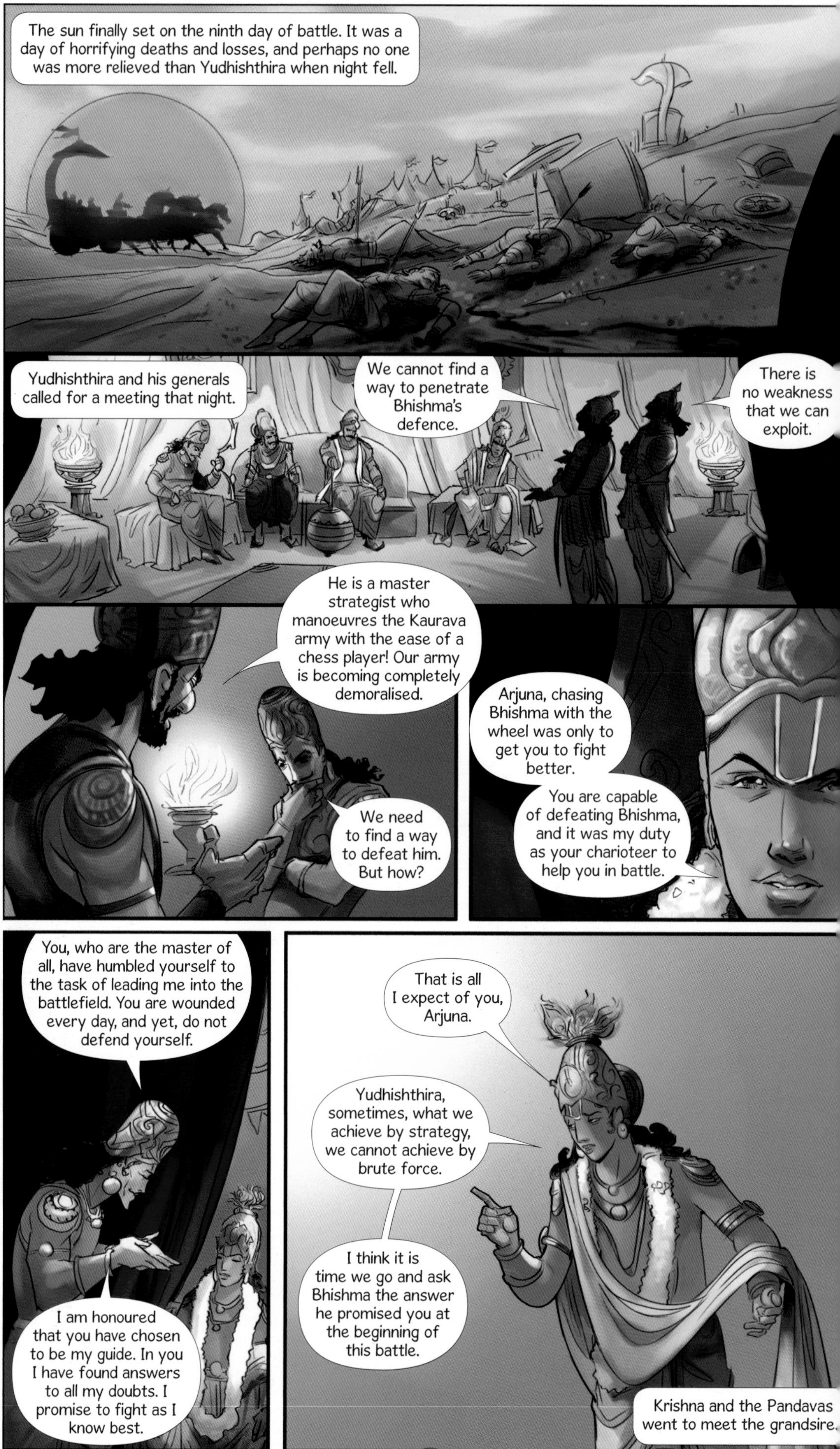
The sun finally set on the ninth day of battle. It was a day of horrifying deaths and losses, and perhaps no one was more relieved than Yudhishthira when night fell.
Yudhishthira and his generals called for a meeting that night.
We cannot find a way to penetrate Bhishma's defence.
There is no weakness that we can exploit.
He is a master strategist who manoeuvres the Kaurava army with the ease of a chess player! Our army is becoming completely demoralised.
We need to find a way to defeat him. But how?
Arjuna, chasing Bhishma with the wheel was only to get you to fight better.
You are capable of defeating Bhishma, and it was my duty as your charioteer to help you in battle.
You, who are the master of all, have humbled yourself to the task of leading me into the battlefield. You are wounded every day, and yet, do not defend yourself.
I am honoured that you have chosen to be my guide. In you I have found answers to all my doubts. I promise to fight as I know best.
That is all I expect of you, Arjuna.
Yudhishthira, sometimes, what we achieve by strategy, we cannot achieve by brute force.
I think it is time we go and ask Bhishma the answer he promised you at the beginning of this battle.
Krishna and the Pandavas went to meet the grandsire.

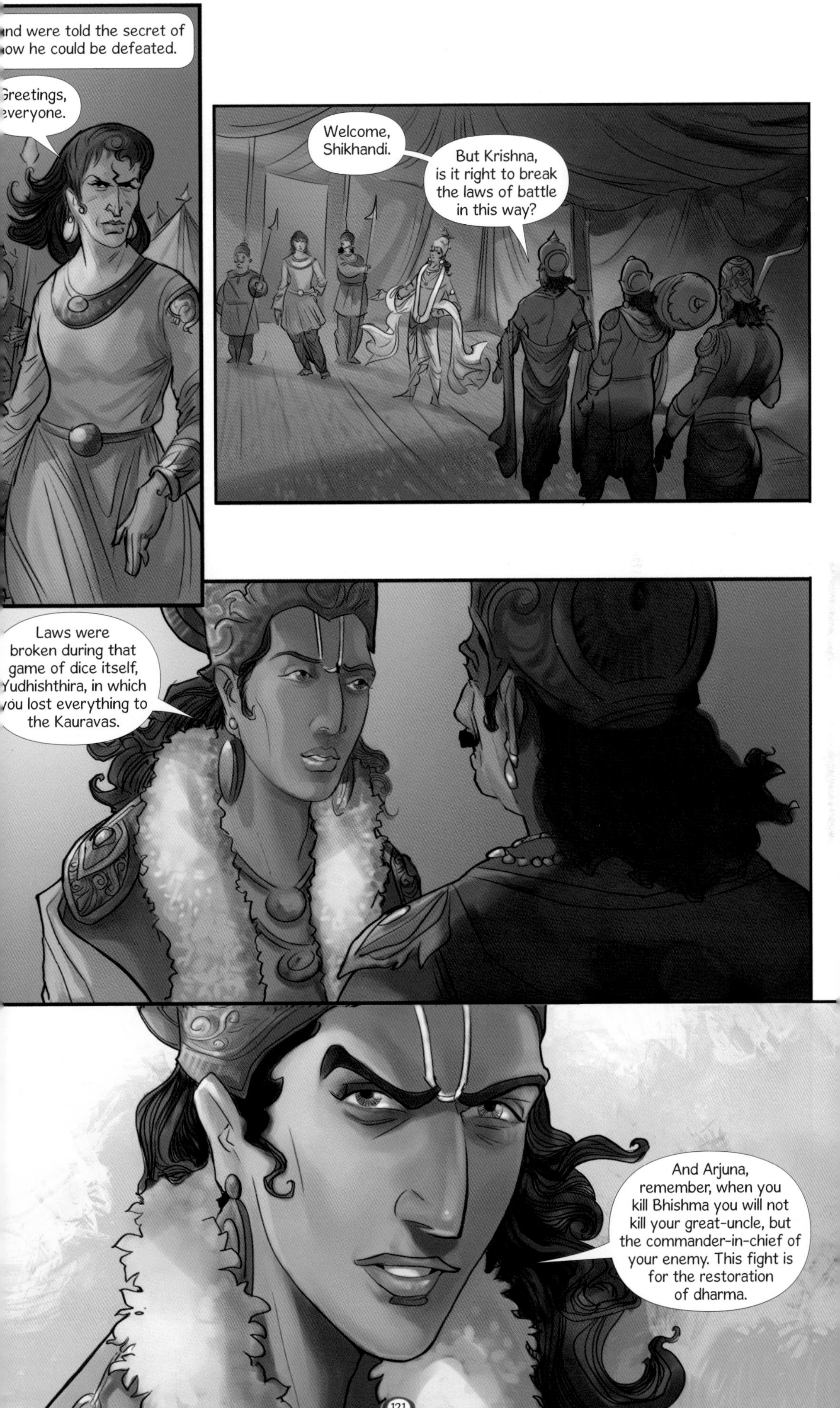

ınd were told the secret of ıow he could be defeated.
Greetings, everyone.
Welcome, Shikhandi.
But Krishna, is it right to break the laws of battle in this way?
Laws were broken during that game of dice itself, Yudhishthira, in which you lost everything to the Kauravas.
And Arjuna, remember, when you kill Bhishma you will not kill your great-uncle, but the commander-in-chief of your enemy. This fight is for the restoration of dharma.

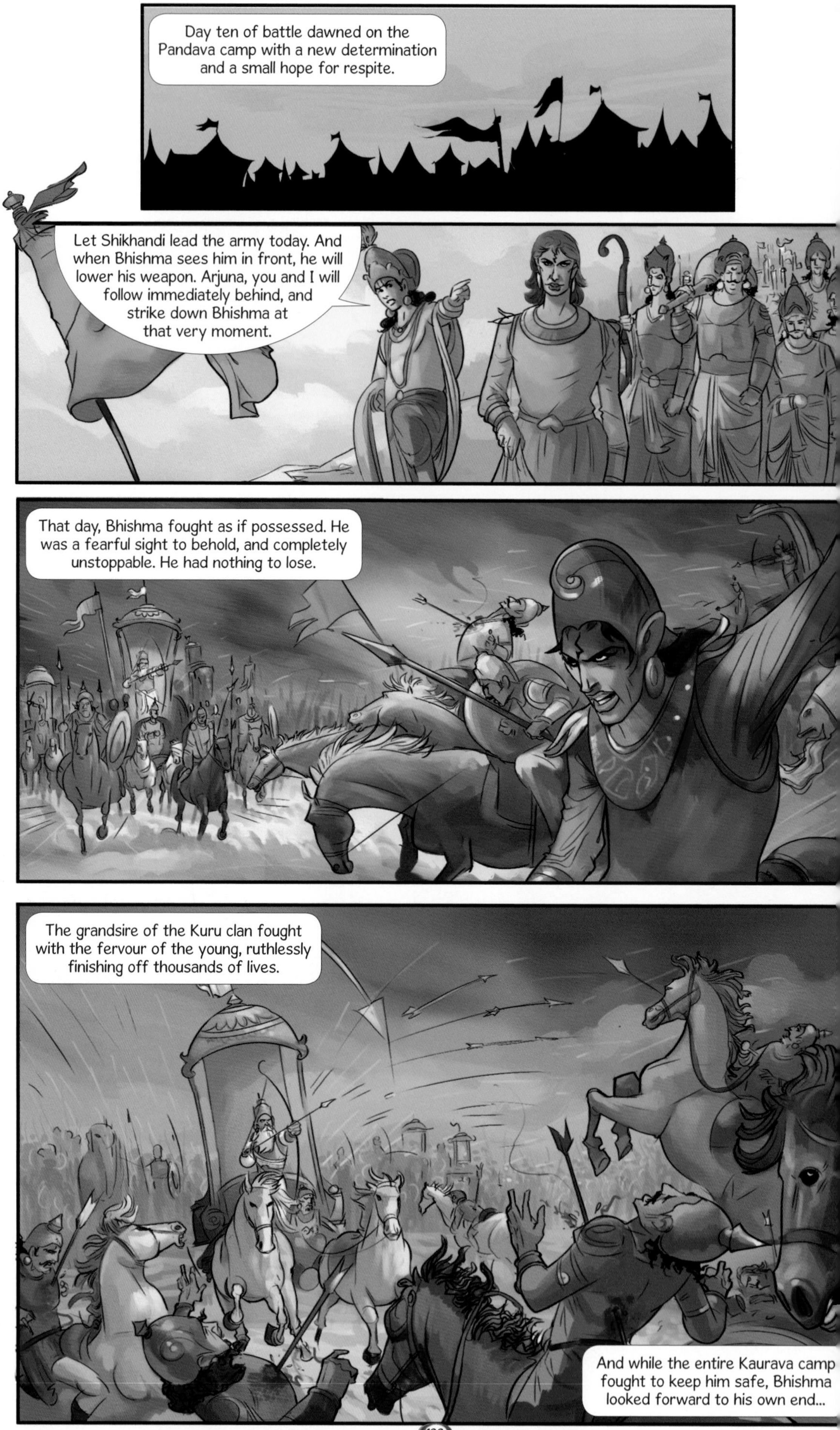

Day ten of battle dawned on the Pandava camp with a new determination and a small hope for respite.
Let Shikhandi lead the army today. And when Bhishma sees him in front, he will lower his weapon. Arjuna, you and I will follow immediately behind, and strike down Bhishma at that very moment.
That day, Bhishma fought as if possessed. He was a fearful sight to behold, and completely unstoppable. He had nothing to lose.
The grandsire of the Kuru clan fought with the fervour of the young, ruthlessly finishing off thousands of lives.
And while the entire Kaurava camp fought to keep him safe, Bhishma looked forward to his own end...

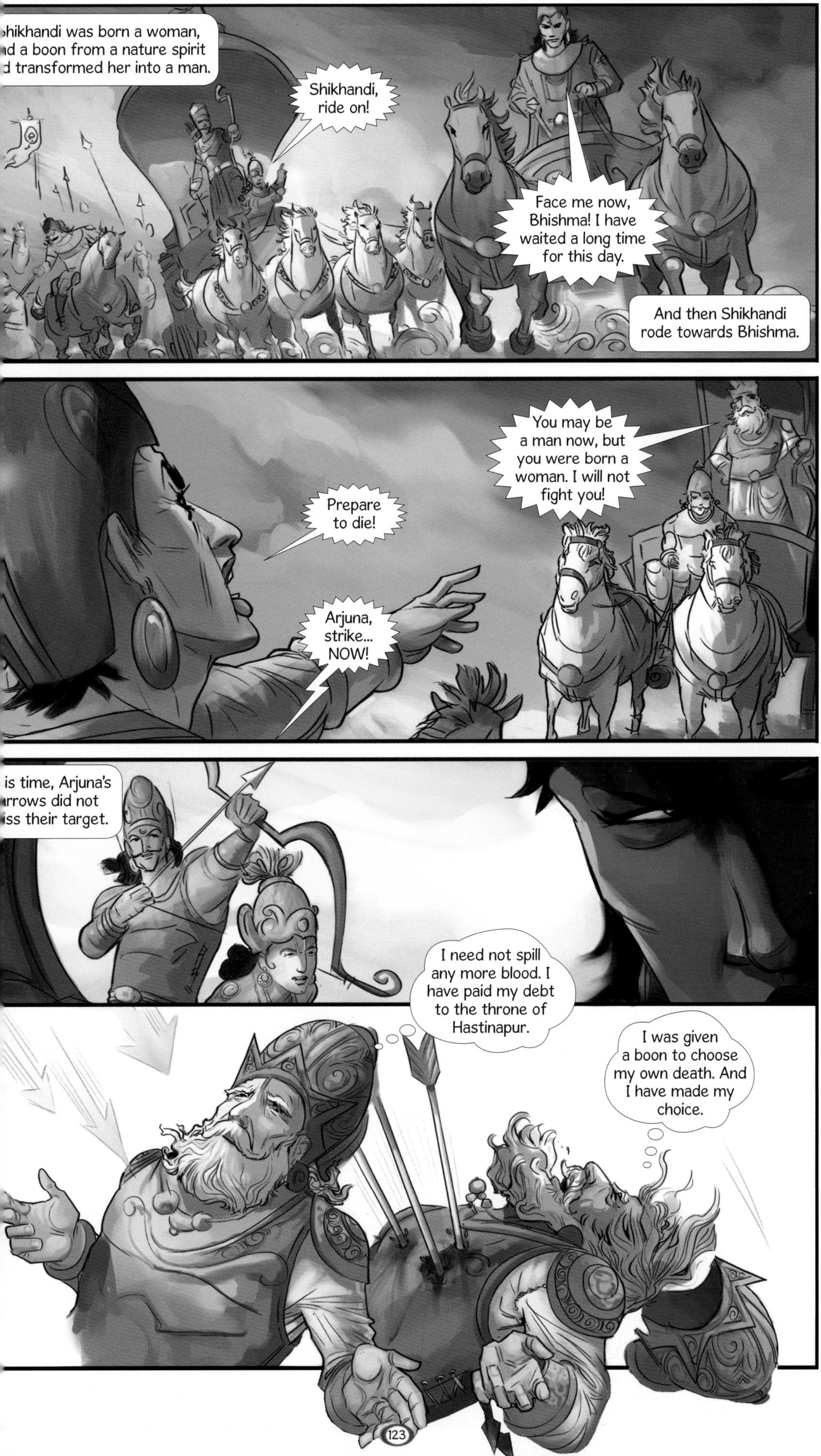
hikhandi was born a woman, d a boon from a nature spirit d transformed her into a man.
Shikhandi, ride on!
Face me now, Bhishma! I have waited a long time for this day.
And then Shikhandi rode towards Bhishma.
You may be a man now, but you were born a woman. I will not fight you!
Prepare to die!
Arjuna, strike... NOW!
is time, Arjuna's rrows did not iss their target.
I need not spill any more blood. I have paid my debt to the throne of Hastinapur.
I was given a boon to choose my own death. And I have made my choice.

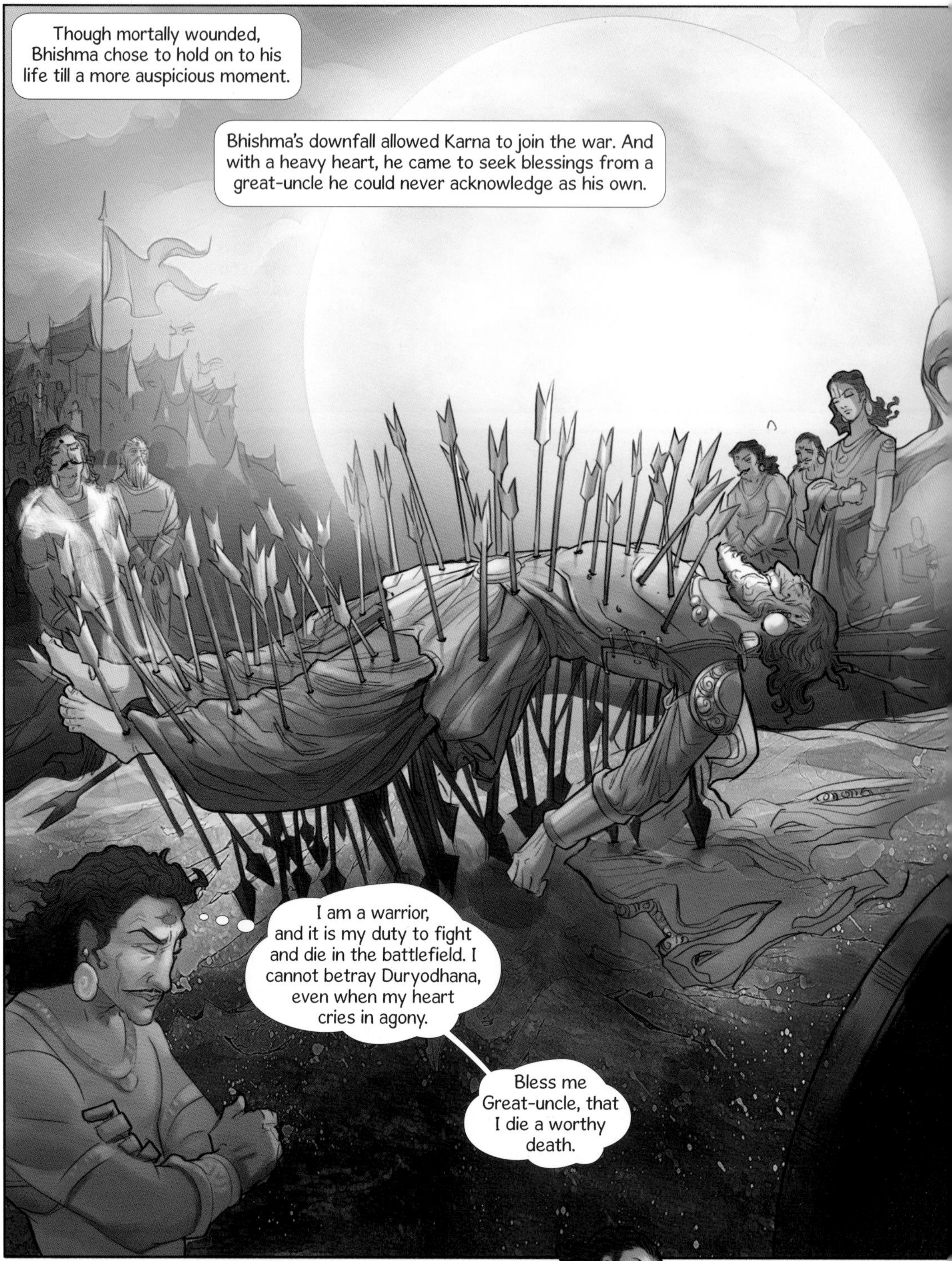
Though mortally wounded, Bhishma chose to hold on to his life till a more auspicious moment.
Bhishma's downfall allowed Karna to join the war. And with a heavy heart, he came to seek blessings from a great-uncle he could never acknowledge as his own.
I am a warrior, and it is my duty to fight and die in the battlefield. I cannot betray Duryodhana, even when my heart cries in agony.
Bless me Great-uncle, that I die a worthy death.

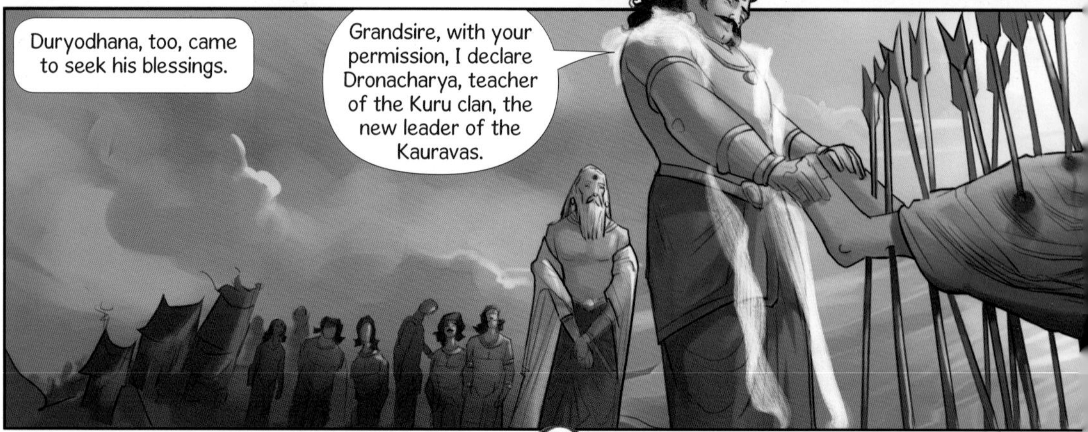
Duryodhana, too, came to seek his blessings.
Grandsire, with your permission, I declare Dronacharya, teacher of the Kuru clan, the new leader of the Kauravas.

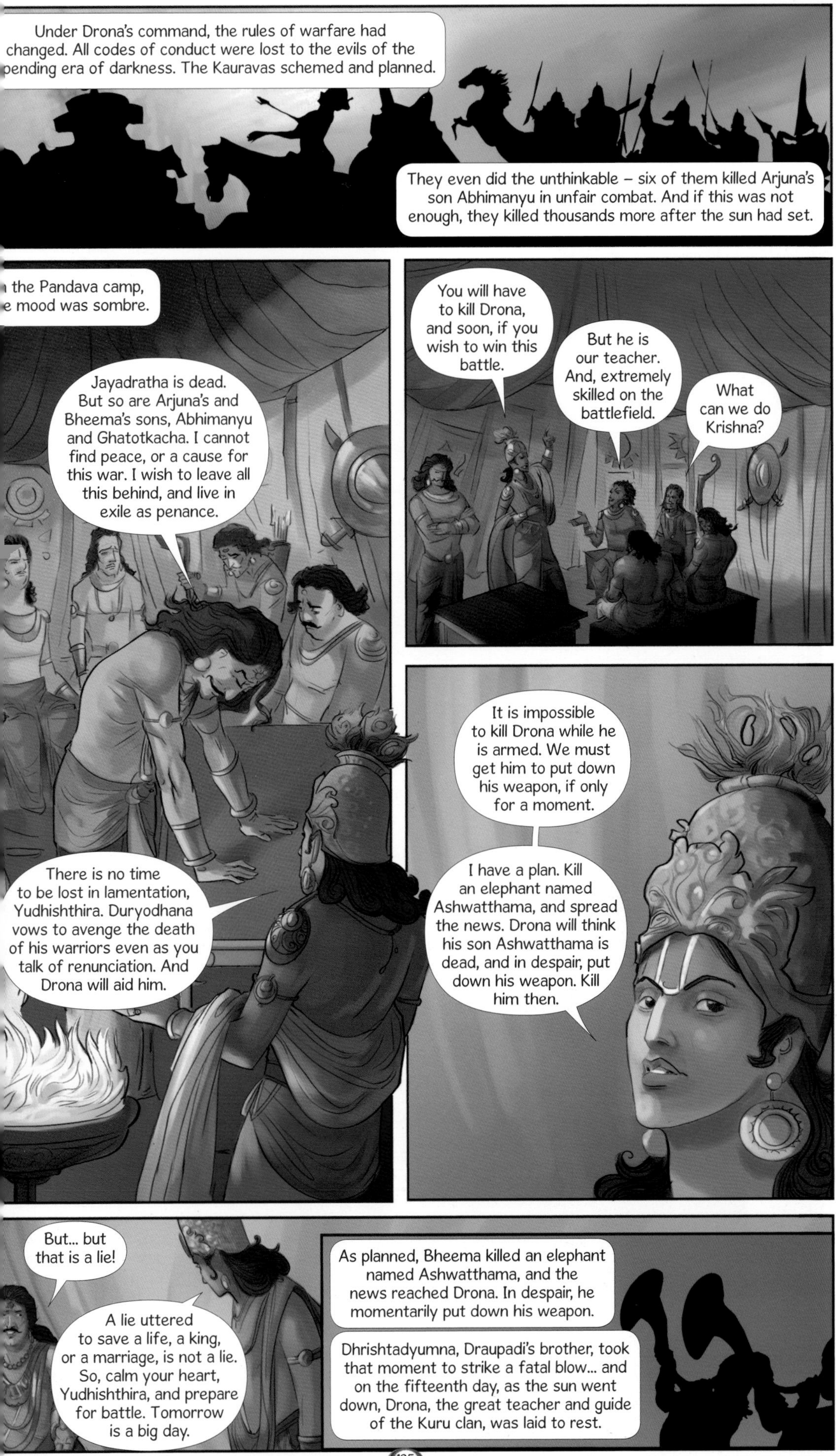
Under Drona's command, the rules of warfare had changed. All codes of conduct were lost to the evils of the pending era of darkness. The Kauravas schemed and planned.
They even did the unthinkable – six of them killed Arjuna's son Abhimanyu in unfair combat. And if this was not enough, they killed thousands more after the sun had set.
the Pandava camp, e mood was sombre.
Jayadratha is dead. But so are Arjuna's and Bheema's sons, Abhimanyu and Ghatotkacha. I cannot find peace, or a cause for this war. I wish to leave all this behind, and live in exile as penance.
There is no time to be lost in lamentation, Yudhishthira. Duryodhana vows to avenge the death of his warriors even as you talk of renunciation. And Drona will aid him.
You will have to kill Drona, and soon, if you wish to win this battle.
But he is our teacher. And, extremely skilled on the battlefield.
What can we do Krishna?
It is impossible to kill Drona while he is armed. We must get him to put down his weapon, if only for a moment.
I have a plan. Kill an elephant named Ashwatthama, and spread the news. Drona will think his son Ashwatthama is dead, and in despair, put down his weapon. Kill him then.
But... but that is a lie!
A lie uttered to save a life, a king, or a marriage, is not a lie. So, calm your heart, Yudhishthira, and prepare for battle. Tomorrow is a big day.
As planned, Bheema killed an elephant named Ashwatthama, and the news reached Drona. In despair, he momentarily put down his weapon.
Dhrishtadyumna, Draupadi's brother, took that moment to strike a fatal blow... and on the fifteenth day, as the sun went down, Drona, the great teacher and guide of the Kuru clan, was laid to rest.

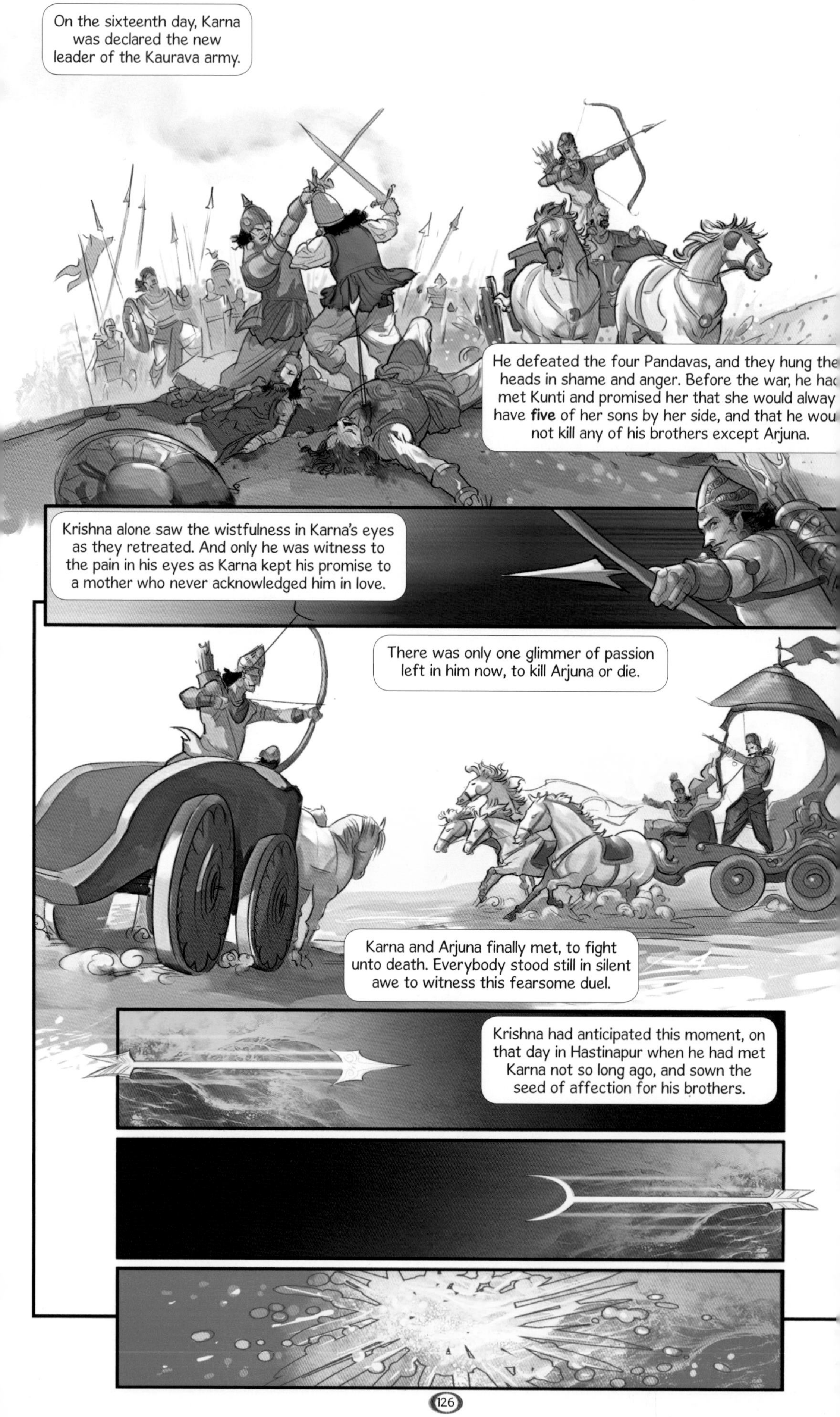
On the sixteenth day, Karna was declared the new leader of the Kaurava army.
He defeated the four Pandavas, and they hung the heads in shame and anger. Before the war, he ha met Kunti and promised her that she would alway have **five** of her sons by her side, and that he wou not kill any of his brothers except Arjuna.
Krishna alone saw the wistfulness in Karna's eyes as they retreated. And only he was witness to the pain in his eyes as Karna kept his promise to a mother who never acknowledged him in love.
There was only one glimmer of passion left in him now, to kill Arjuna or die.
Karna and Arjuna finally met, to fight unto death. Everybody stood still in silent awe to witness this fearsome duel.
Krishna had anticipated this moment, on that day in Hastinapur when he had met Karna not so long ago, and sown the seed of affection for his brothers.

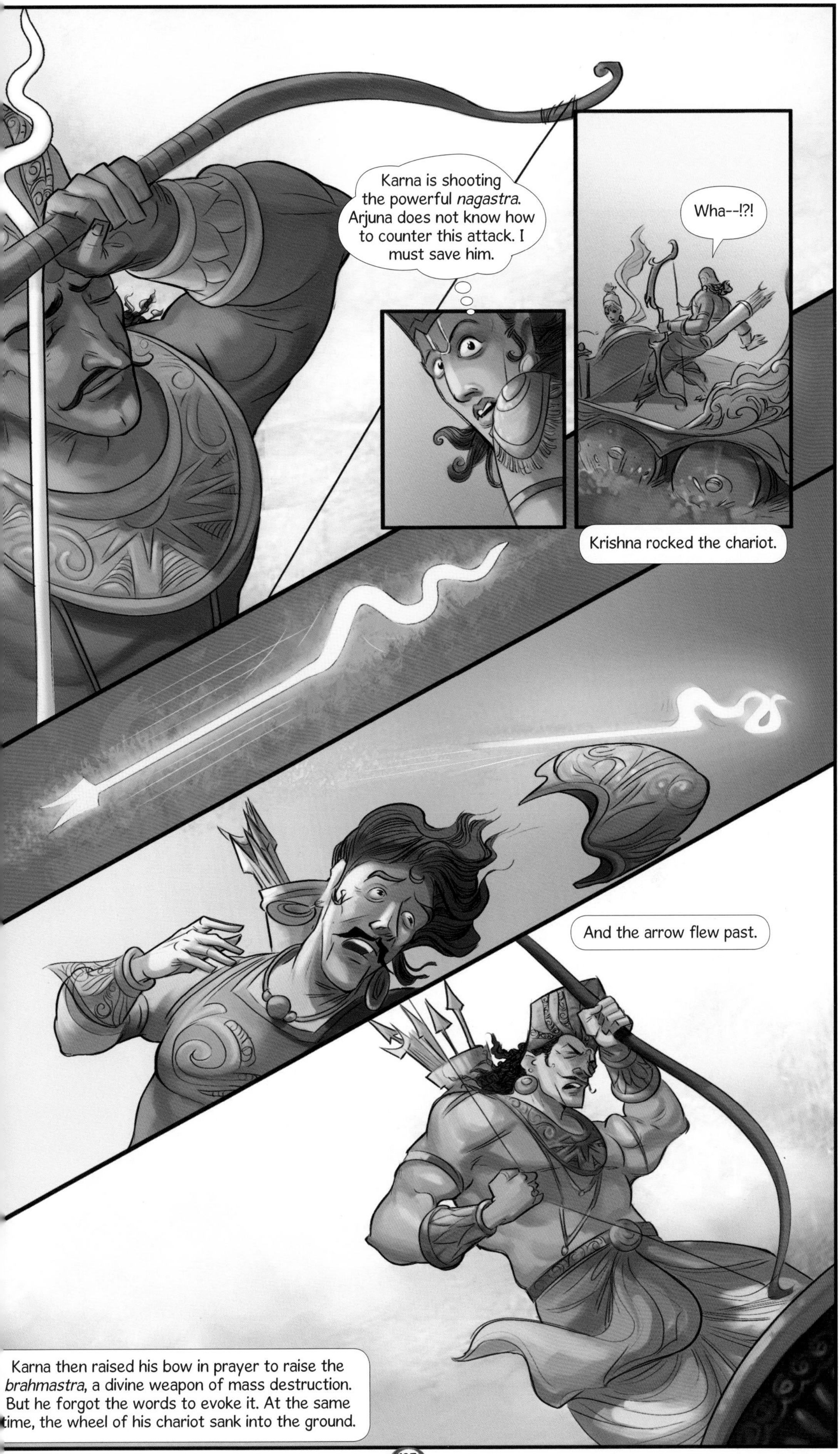
Karna is shooting the powerful *nagastra*. Arjuna does not know how to counter this attack. I must save him.
Wha--!?!
Krishna rocked the chariot.
And the arrow flew past.
Karna then raised his bow in prayer to raise the *brahmastra*, a divine weapon of mass destruction. But he forgot the words to evoke it. At the same time, the wheel of his chariot sank into the ground.

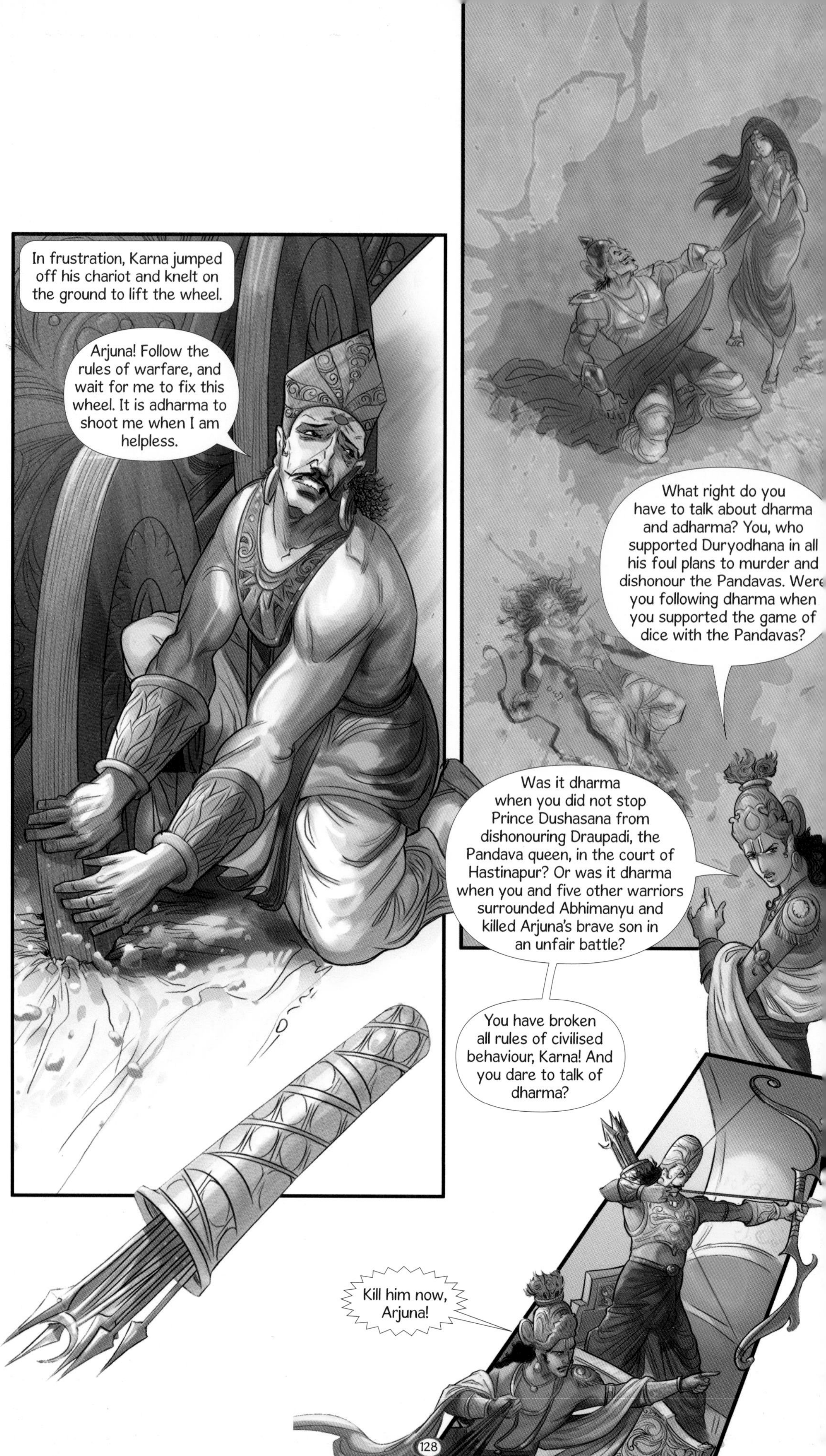
In frustration, Karna jumped off his chariot and knelt on the ground to lift the wheel.
Arjuna! Follow the rules of warfare, and wait for me to fix this wheel. It is adharma to shoot me when I am helpless.
What right do you have to talk about dharma and adharma? You, who supported Duryodhana in all his foul plans to murder and dishonour the Pandavas. Were you following dharma when you supported the game of dice with the Pandavas?
Was it dharma when you did not stop Prince Dushasana from dishonouring Draupadi, the Pandava queen, in the court of Hastinapur? Or was it dharma when you and five other warriors surrounded Abhimanyu and killed Arjuna's brave son in an unfair battle?
You have broken all rules of civilised behaviour, Karna! And you dare to talk of dharma?
Kill him now, Arjuna!

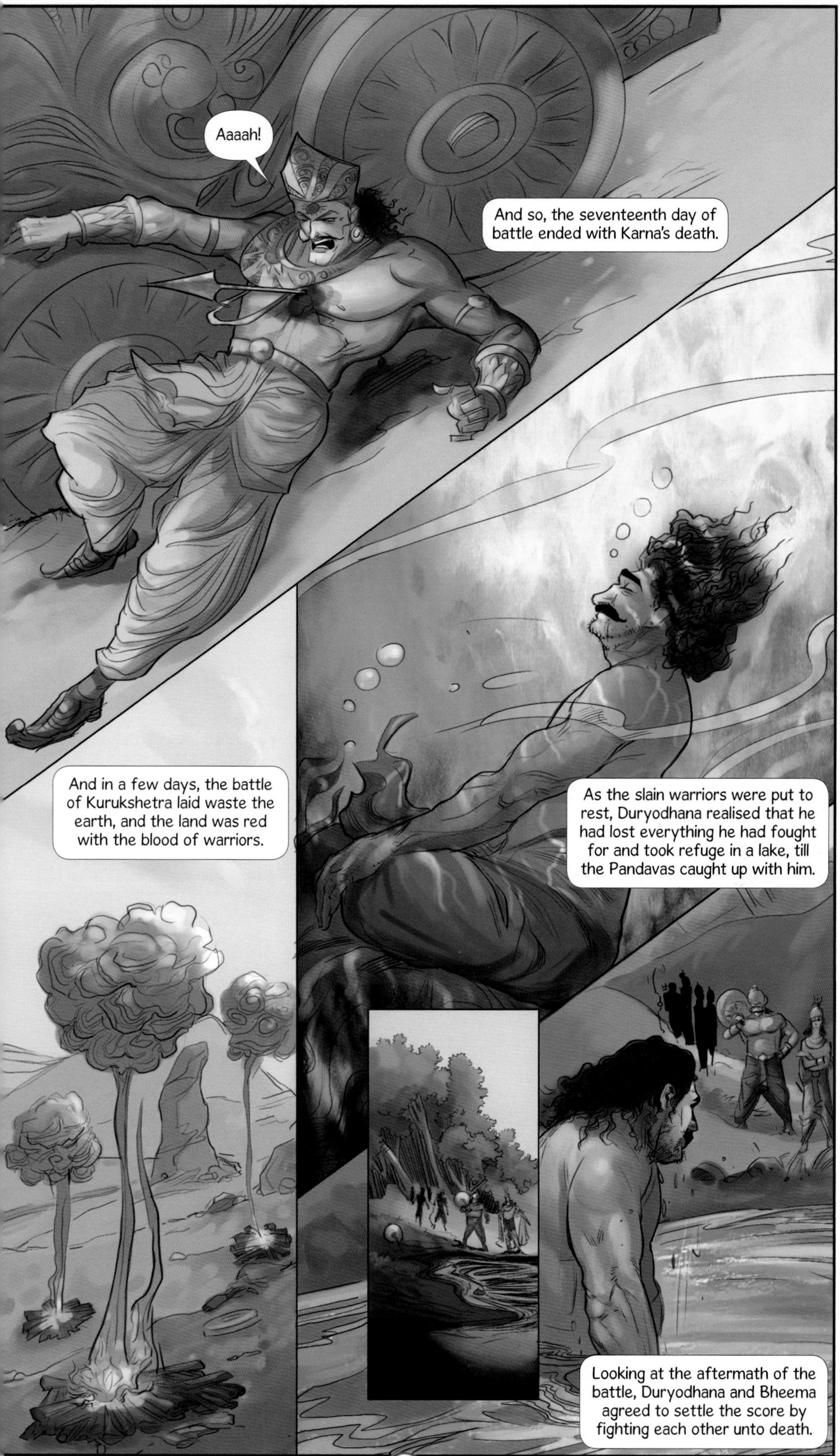
Aaaah!
And so, the seventeenth day of battle ended with Karna's death.
And in a few days, the battle of Kurukshetra laid waste the earth, and the land was red with the blood of warriors.
As the slain warriors were put to rest, Duryodhana realised that he had lost everything he had fought for and took refuge in a lake, till the Pandavas caught up with him.
Looking at the aftermath of the battle, Duryodhana and Bheema agreed to settle the score by fighting each other unto death.

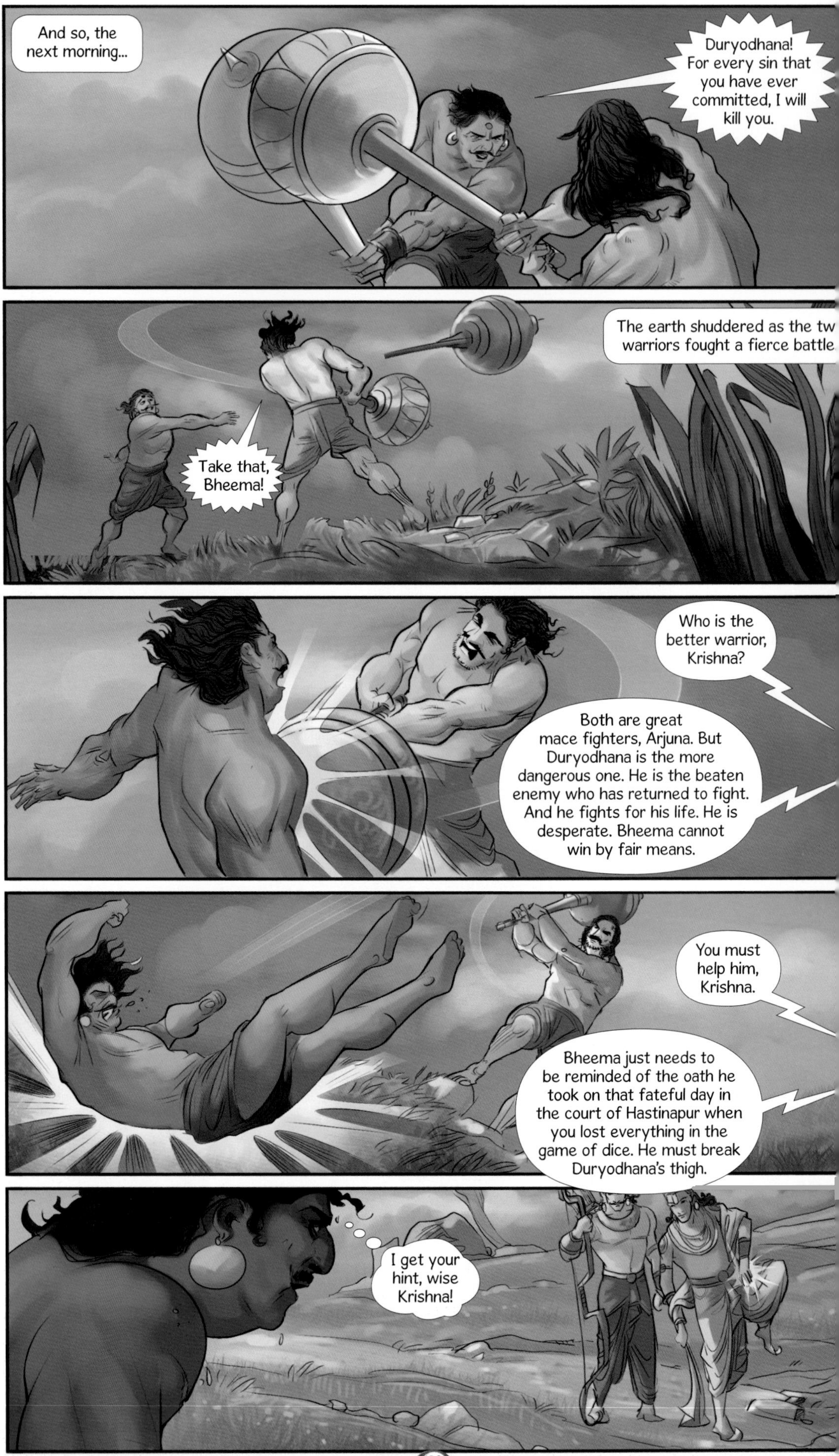
And so, the next morning...
Duryodhana! For every sin that you have ever committed, I will kill you.
The earth shuddered as the tw warriors fought a fierce battle.
Take that, Bheema!
Who is the better warrior, Krishna?
Both are great mace fighters, Arjuna. But Duryodhana is the more dangerous one. He is the beaten enemy who has returned to fight. And he fights for his life. He is desperate. Bheema cannot win by fair means.
You must help him, Krishna.
Bheema just needs to be reminded of the oath he took on that fateful day in the court of Hastinapur when you lost everything in the game of dice. He must break Duryodhana's thigh.
I get your hint, wise Krishna!

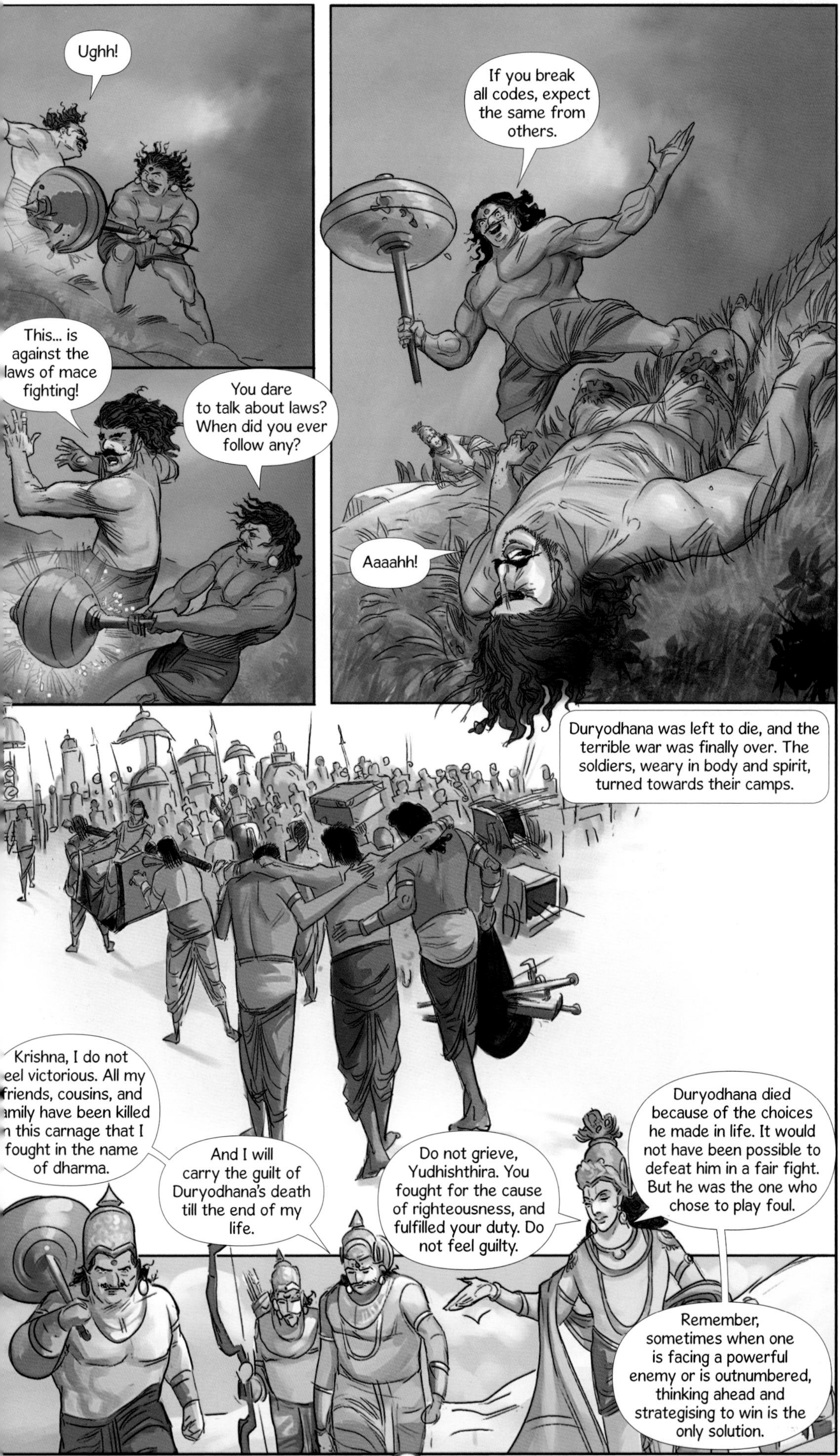
Ughh!
If you break all codes, expect the same from others.
This... is against the laws of mace fighting!
You dare to talk about laws? When did you ever follow any?
Aaaahh!
Duryodhana was left to die, and the terrible war was finally over. The soldiers, weary in body and spirit, turned towards their camps.
Krishna, I do not eel victorious. All my friends, cousins, and amily have been killed n this carnage that I fought in the name of dharma.
And I will carry the guilt of Duryodhana's death till the end of my life.
Do not grieve, Yudhishthira. You fought for the cause of righteousness, and fulfilled your duty. Do not feel guilty.
Duryodhana died because of the choices he made in life. It would not have been possible to defeat him in a fair fight. But he was the one who chose to play foul.
Remember, sometimes when one is facing a powerful enemy or is outnumbered, thinking ahead and strategising to win is the only solution.

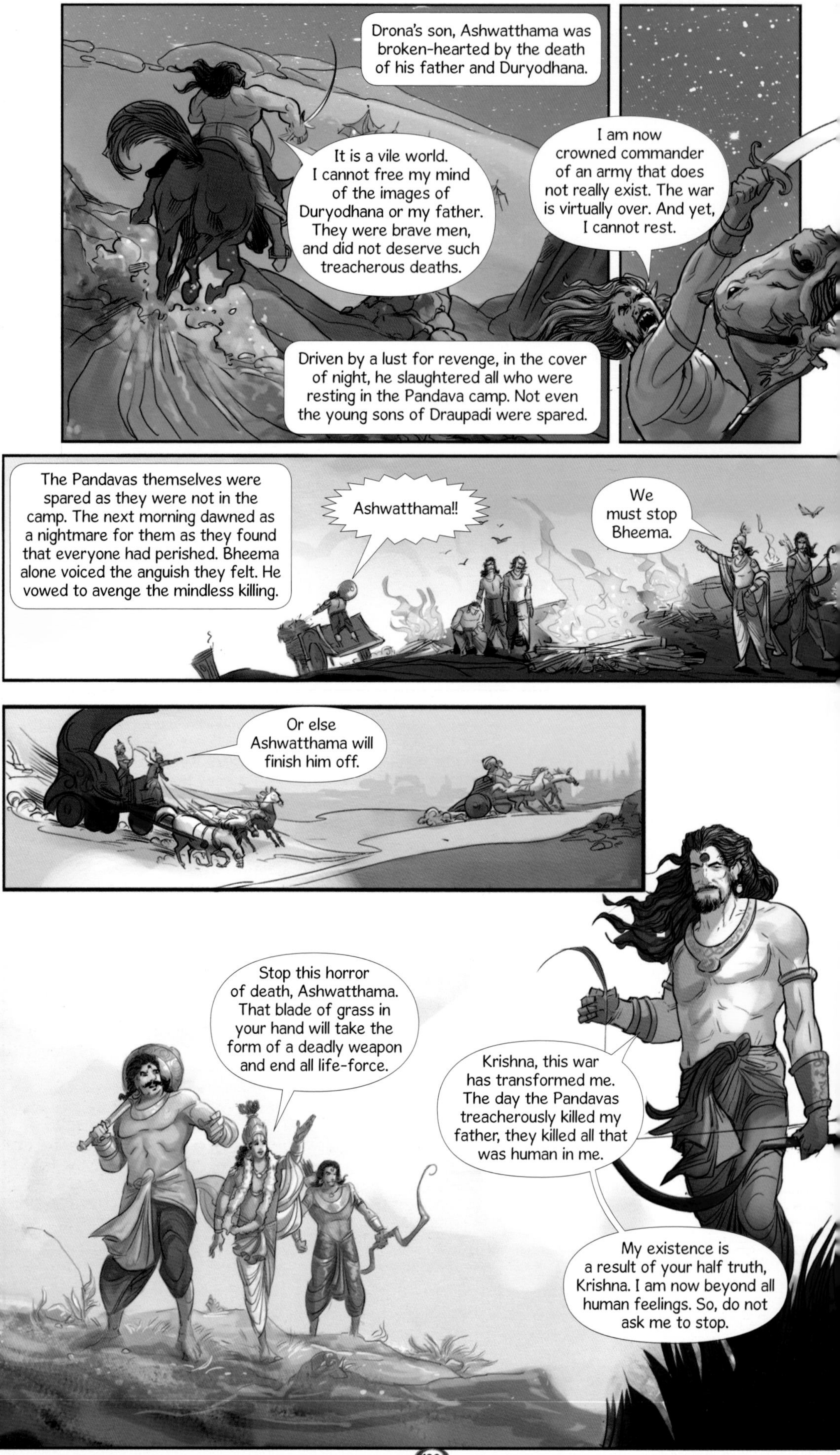
Drona's son, Ashwatthama was broken-hearted by the death of his father and Duryodhana.
It is a vile world. I cannot free my mind of the images of Duryodhana or my father. They were brave men, and did not deserve such treacherous deaths.
I am now crowned commander of an army that does not really exist. The war is virtually over. And yet, I cannot rest.
Driven by a lust for revenge, in the cover of night, he slaughtered all who were resting in the Pandava camp. Not even the young sons of Draupadi were spared.
The Pandavas themselves were spared as they were not in the camp. The next morning dawned as a nightmare for them as they found that everyone had perished. Bheema alone voiced the anguish they felt. He vowed to avenge the mindless killing.
Ashwatthama!!
We must stop Bheema.
Or else Ashwatthama will finish him off.
Stop this horror of death, Ashwatthama. That blade of grass in your hand will take the form of a deadly weapon and end all life-force.
Krishna, this war has transformed me. The day the Pandavas treacherously killed my father, they killed all that was human in me.
My existence is a result of your half truth, Krishna. I am now beyond all human feelings. So, do not ask me to stop.

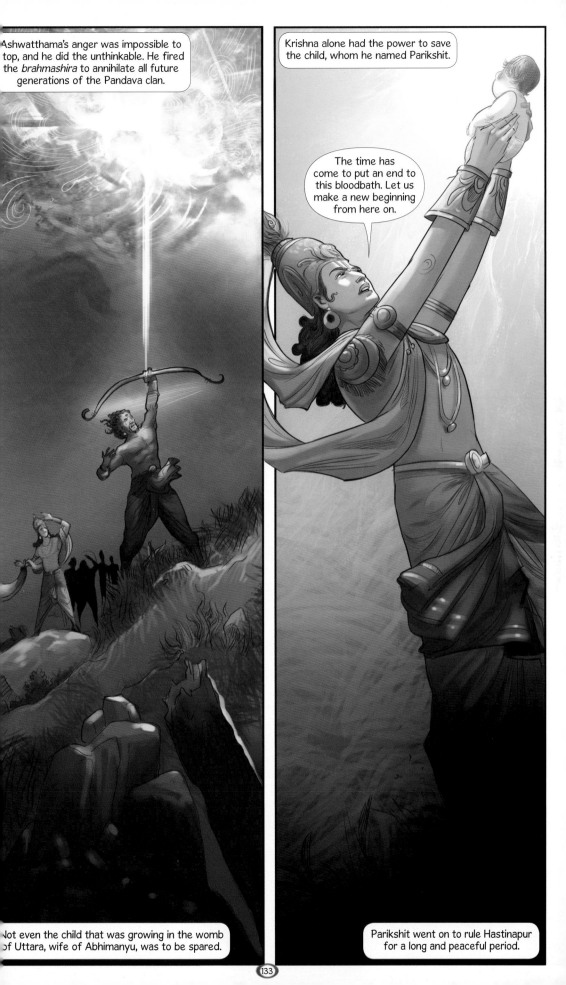

Ashwatthama's anger was impossible to top, and he did the unthinkable. He fired the *brahmashira* to annihilate all future generations of the Pandava clan.

Not even the child that was growing in the womb of Uttara, wife of Abhimanyu, was to be spared.

Krishna alone had the power to save the child, whom he named Parikshit.

The time has come to put an end to this bloodbath. Let us make a new beginning from here on.

Parikshit went on to rule Hastinapur for a long and peaceful period.

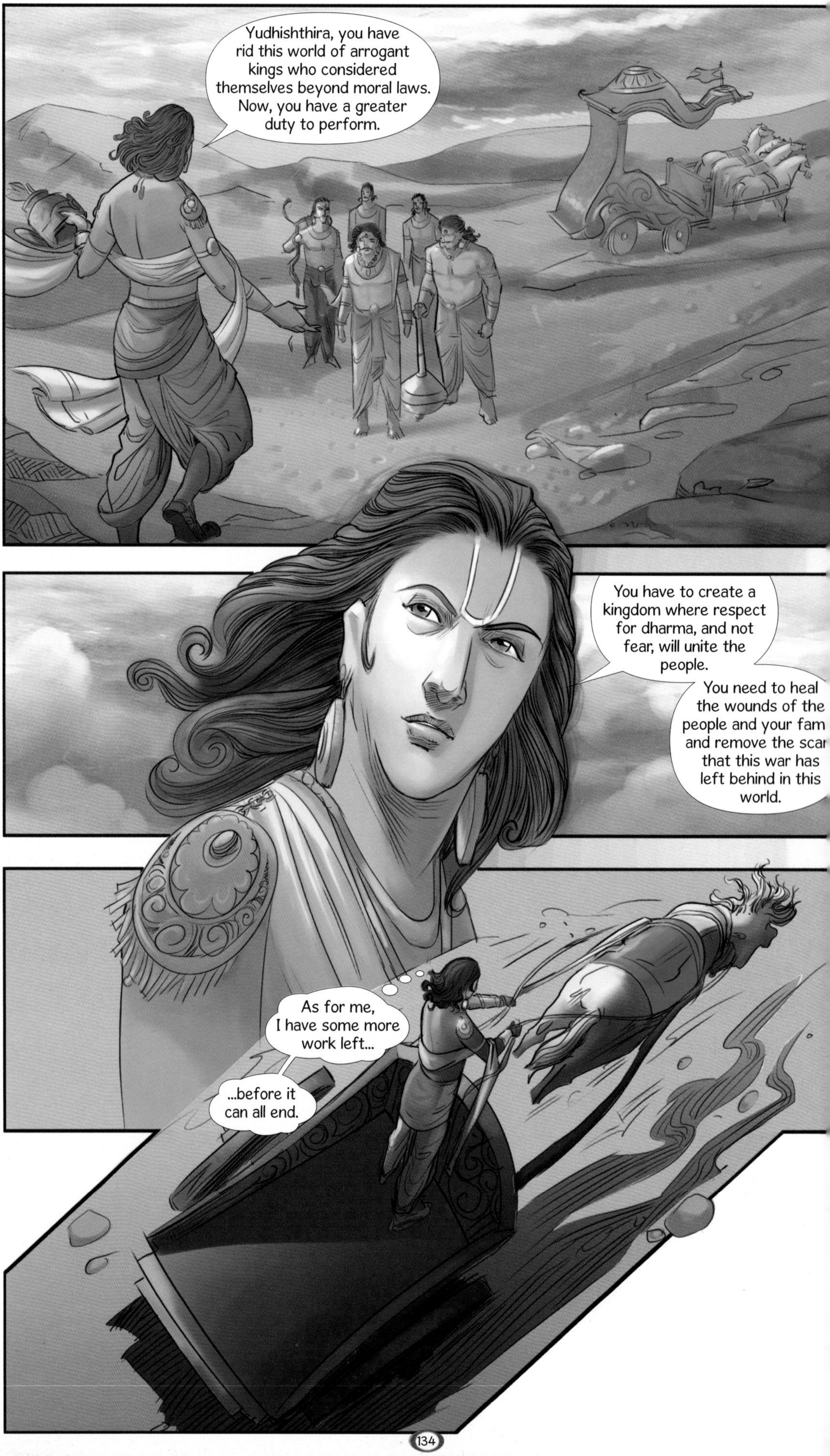
Yudhishthira, you have rid this world of arrogant kings who considered themselves beyond moral laws. Now, you have a greater duty to perform.
You have to create a kingdom where respect for dharma, and not fear, will unite the people.
You need to heal the wounds of the people and your fam and remove the scar that this war has left behind in this world.
As for me, I have some more work left...
...before it can all end.

Prabhasa

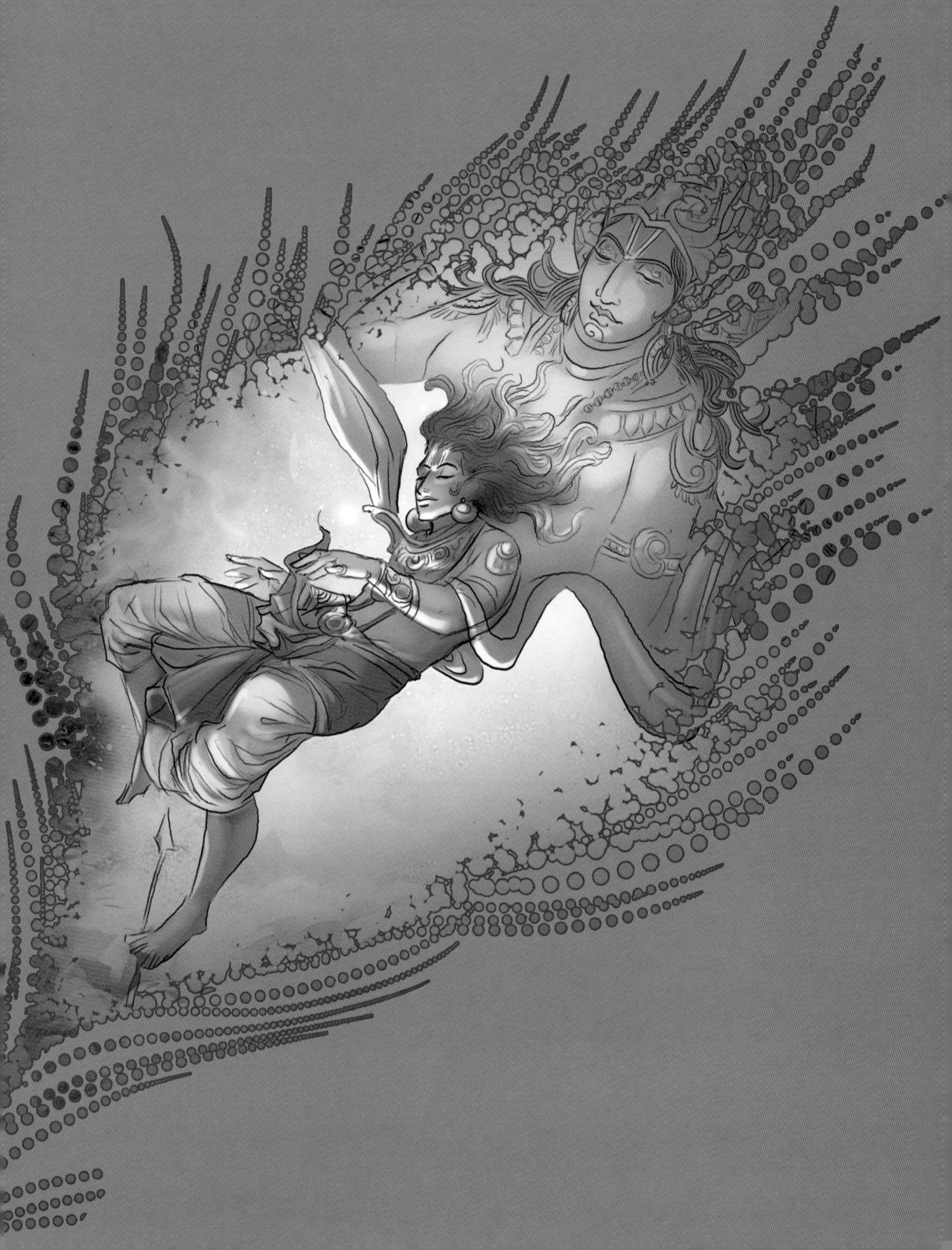

Prabhasa

The great war is over. Krishna returns to Dwarka. His duty as the defender of dharma is now nearly over. A new era of peace and prosperity has commenced. But the seed of discord and discontent has already been sown, and there is also another curse that remains to be fulfilled…

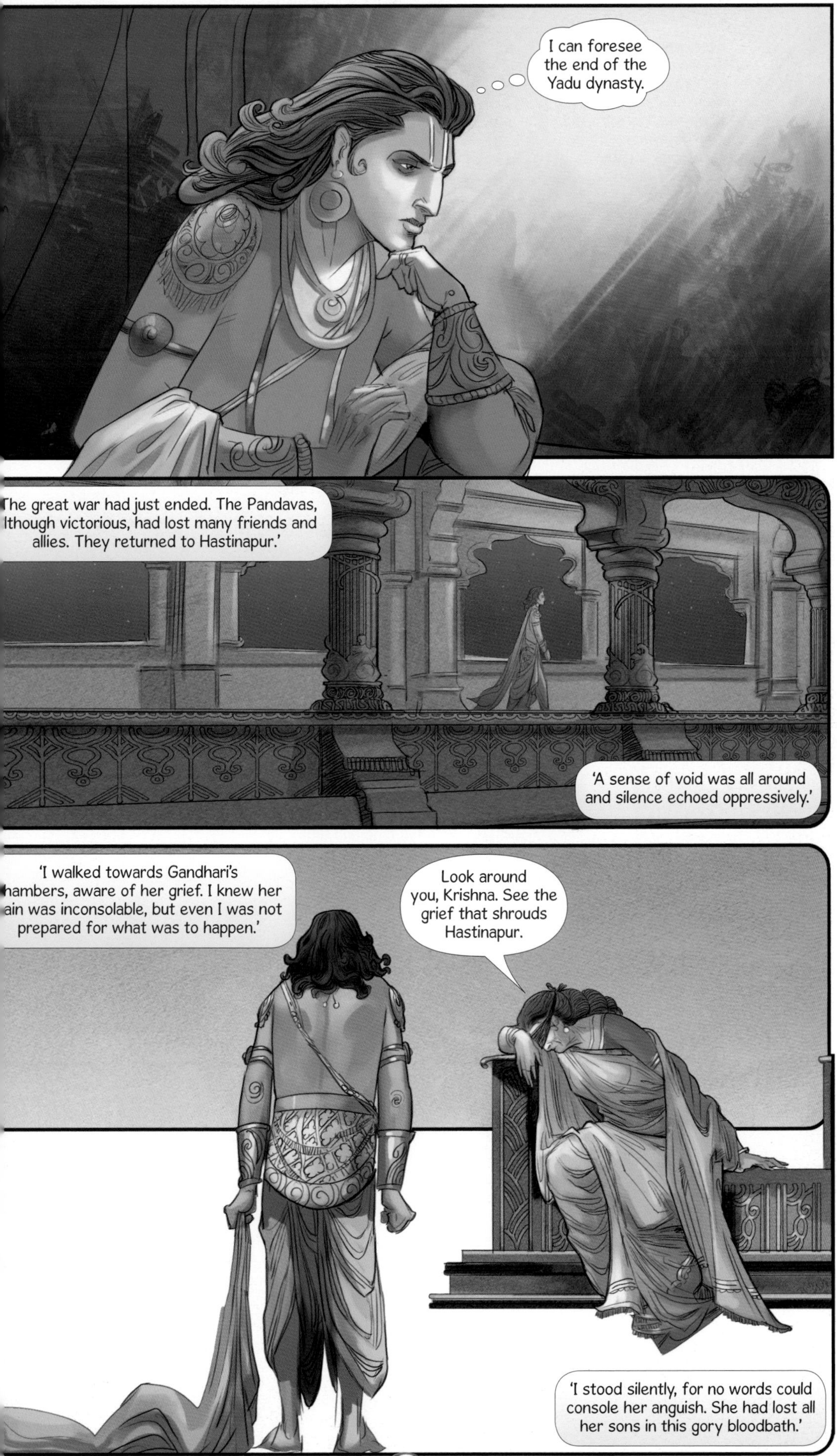
I can foresee the end of the Yadu dynasty.
The great war had just ended. The Pandavas, lthough victorious, had lost many friends and allies. They returned to Hastinapur.'
'A sense of void was all around and silence echoed oppressively.'
'I walked towards Gandhari's hambers, aware of her grief. I knew her ain was inconsolable, but even I was not prepared for what was to happen.'
Look around you, Krishna. See the grief that shrouds Hastinapur.
'I stood silently, for no words could console her anguish. She had lost all her sons in this gory bloodbath.'

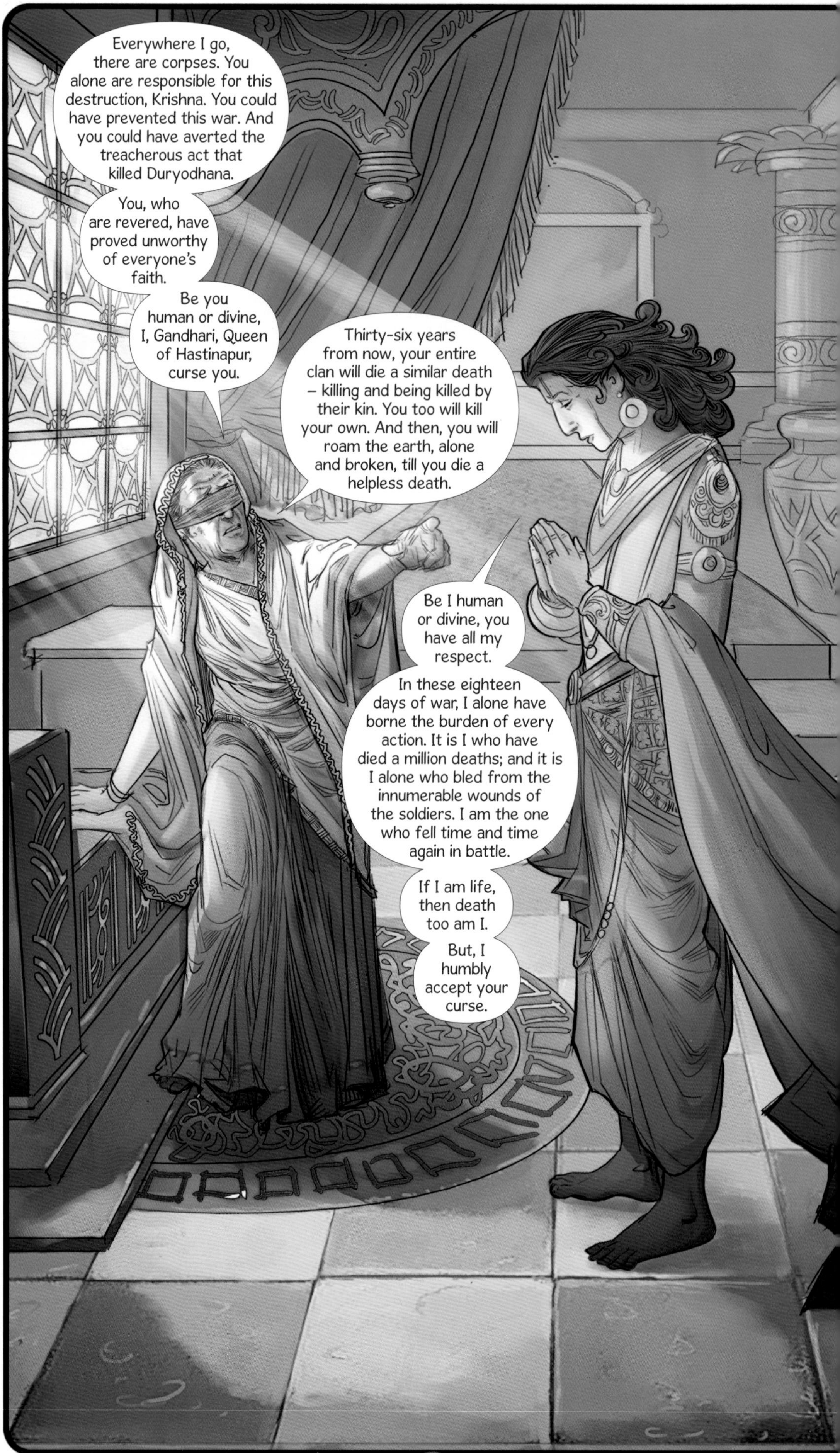
Everywhere I go, there are corpses. You alone are responsible for this destruction, Krishna. You could have prevented this war. And you could have averted the treacherous act that killed Duryodhana.
You, who are revered, have proved unworthy of everyone's faith.
Be you human or divine, I, Gandhari, Queen of Hastinapur, curse you.
Thirty-six years from now, your entire clan will die a similar death – killing and being killed by their kin. You too will kill your own. And then, you will roam the earth, alone and broken, till you die a helpless death.
Be I human or divine, you have all my respect.
In these eighteen days of war, I alone have borne the burden of every action. It is I who have died a million deaths; and it is I alone who bled from the innumerable wounds of the soldiers. I am the one who fell time and time again in battle.
If I am life, then death too am I.
But, I humbly accept your curse.

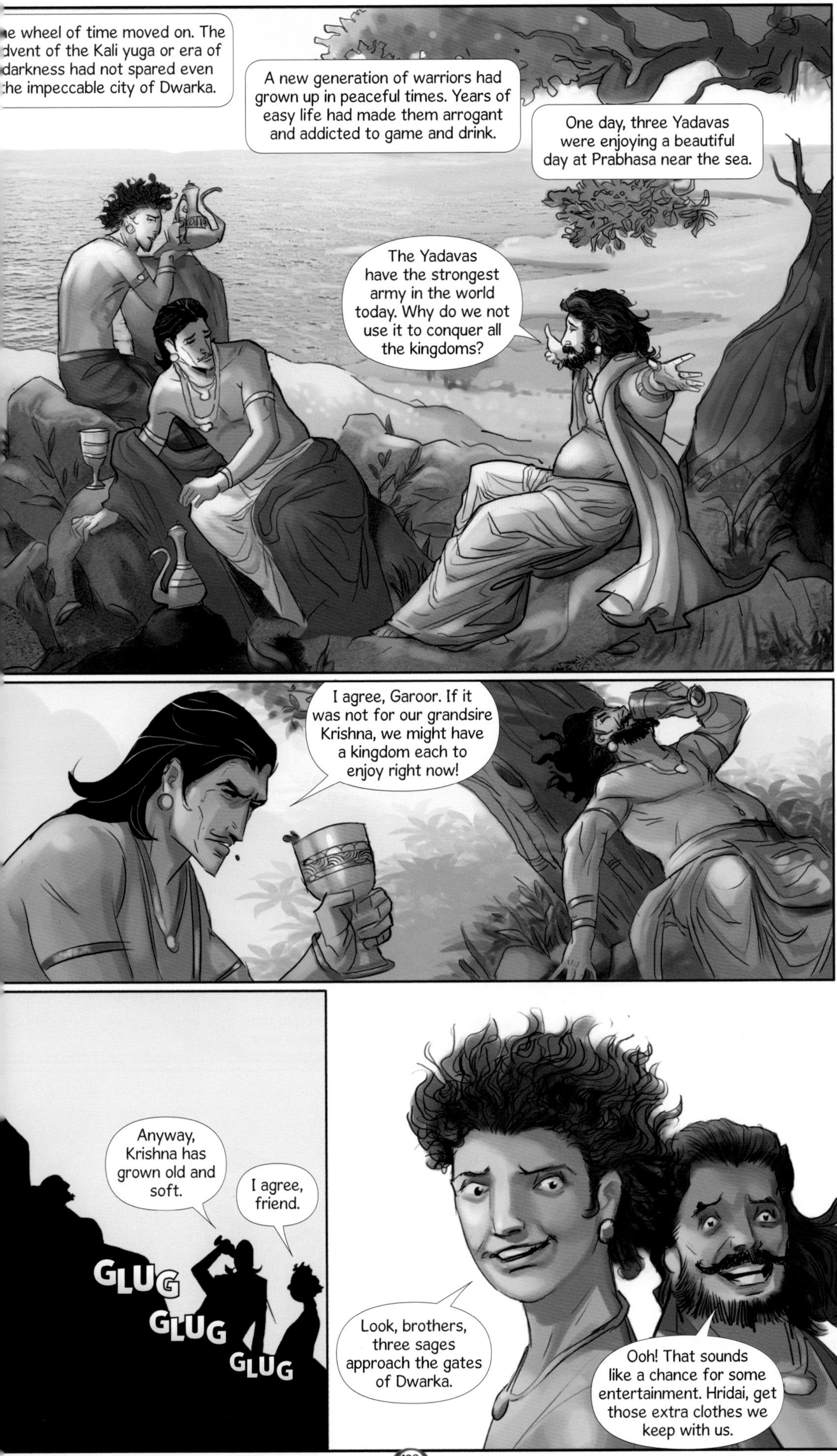

e wheel of time moved on. The dvent of the Kali yuga or era of darkness had not spared even the impeccable city of Dwarka.
A new generation of warriors had grown up in peaceful times. Years of easy life had made them arrogant and addicted to game and drink.
One day, three Yadavas were enjoying a beautiful day at Prabhasa near the sea.
The Yadavas have the strongest army in the world today. Why do we not use it to conquer all the kingdoms?
I agree, Garoor. If it was not for our grandsire Krishna, we might have a kingdom each to enjoy right now!
Anyway, Krishna has grown old and soft.
I agree, friend.
GLUG GLUG GLUG
Look, brothers, three sages approach the gates of Dwarka.
Ooh! That sounds like a chance for some entertainment. Hridai, get those extra clothes we keep with us.

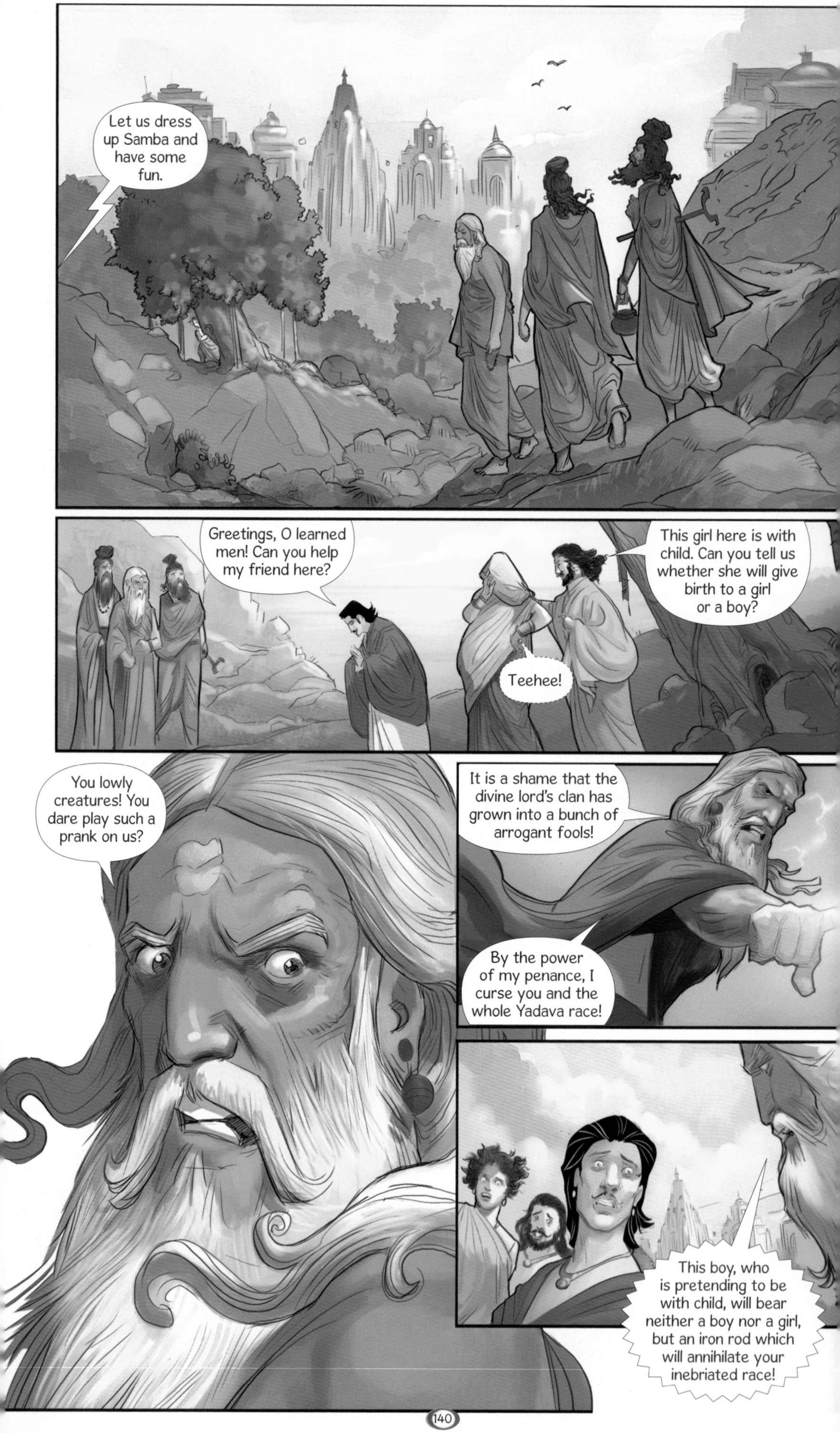

Let us dress up Samba and have some fun.
Greetings, O learned men! Can you help my friend here?
This girl here is with child. Can you tell us whether she will give birth to a girl or a boy?
Teehee!
You lowly creatures! You dare play such a prank on us?
It is a shame that the divine lord's clan has grown into a bunch of arrogant fools!
By the power of my penance, I curse you and the whole Yadava race!
This boy, who is pretending to be with child, will bear neither a boy nor a girl, but an iron rod which will annihilate your inebriated race!

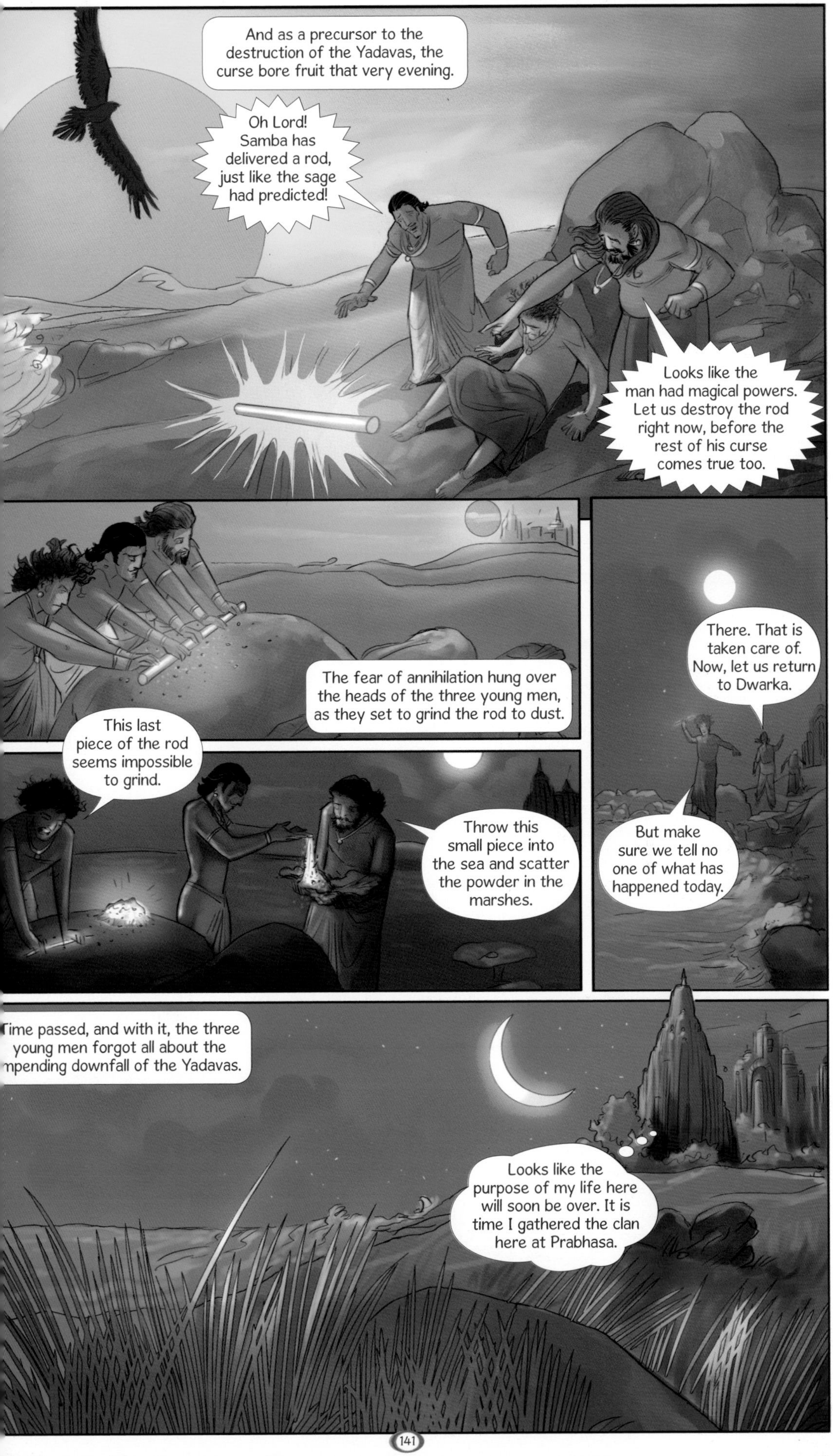

And as a precursor to the destruction of the Yadavas, the curse bore fruit that very evening.
Oh Lord! Samba has delivered a rod, just like the sage had predicted!
Looks like the man had magical powers. Let us destroy the rod right now, before the rest of his curse comes true too.
The fear of annihilation hung over the heads of the three young men, as they set to grind the rod to dust.
This last piece of the rod seems impossible to grind.
Throw this small piece into the sea and scatter the powder in the marshes.
There. That is taken care of. Now, let us return to Dwarka.
But make sure we tell no one of what has happened today.
Time passed, and with it, the three young men forgot all about the impending downfall of the Yadavas.
Looks like the purpose of my life here will soon be over. It is time I gathered the clan here at Prabhasa.

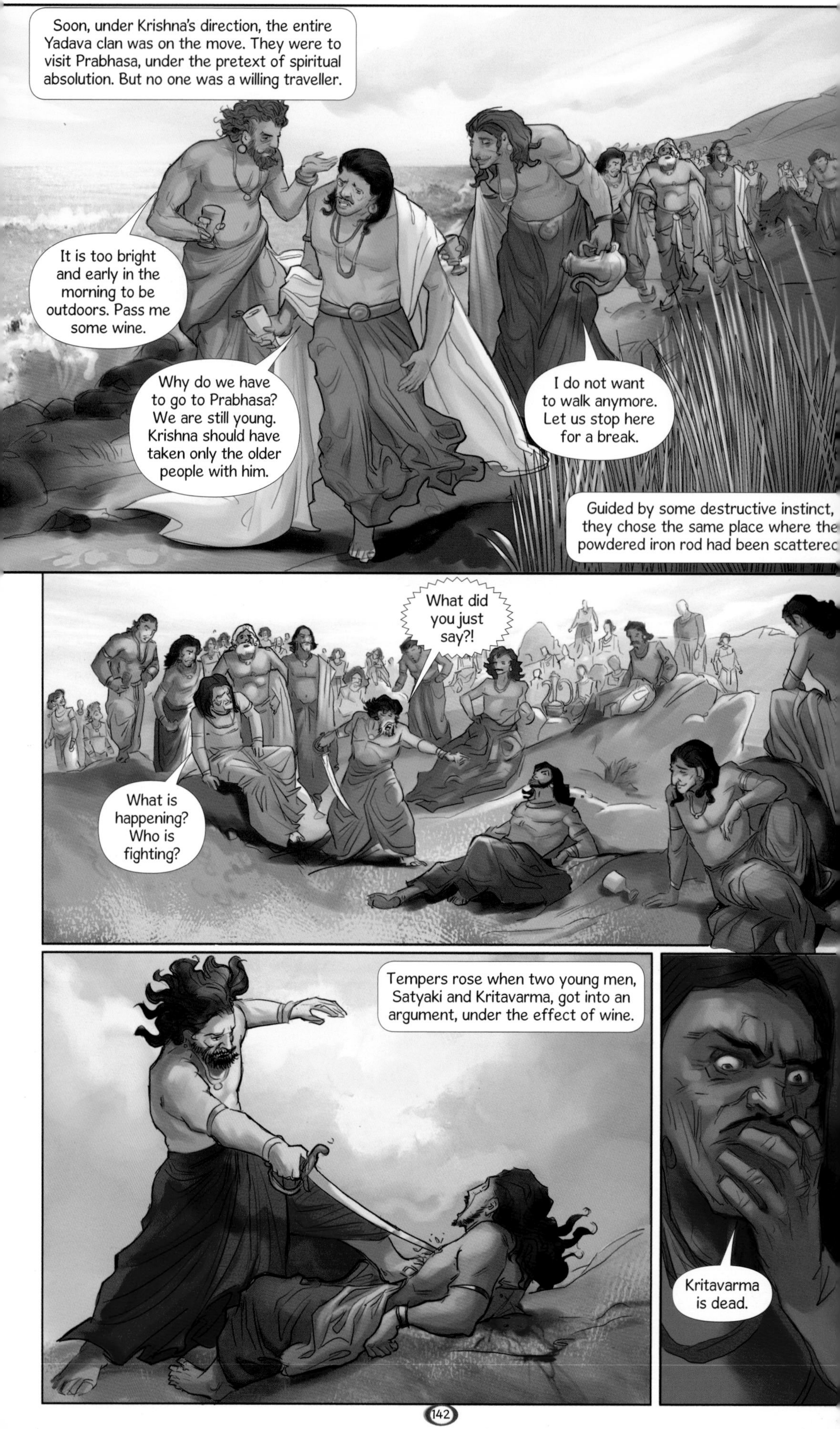
Soon, under Krishna's direction, the entire Yadava clan was on the move. They were to visit Prabhasa, under the pretext of spiritual absolution. But no one was a willing traveller.
It is too bright and early in the morning to be outdoors. Pass me some wine.
Why do we have to go to Prabhasa? We are still young. Krishna should have taken only the older people with him.
I do not want to walk anymore. Let us stop here for a break.
Guided by some destructive instinct, they chose the same place where the powdered iron rod had been scattered
What did you just say?!
What is happening? Who is fighting?
Tempers rose when two young men, Satyaki and Kritavarma, got into an argument, under the effect of wine.
Kritavarma is dead.

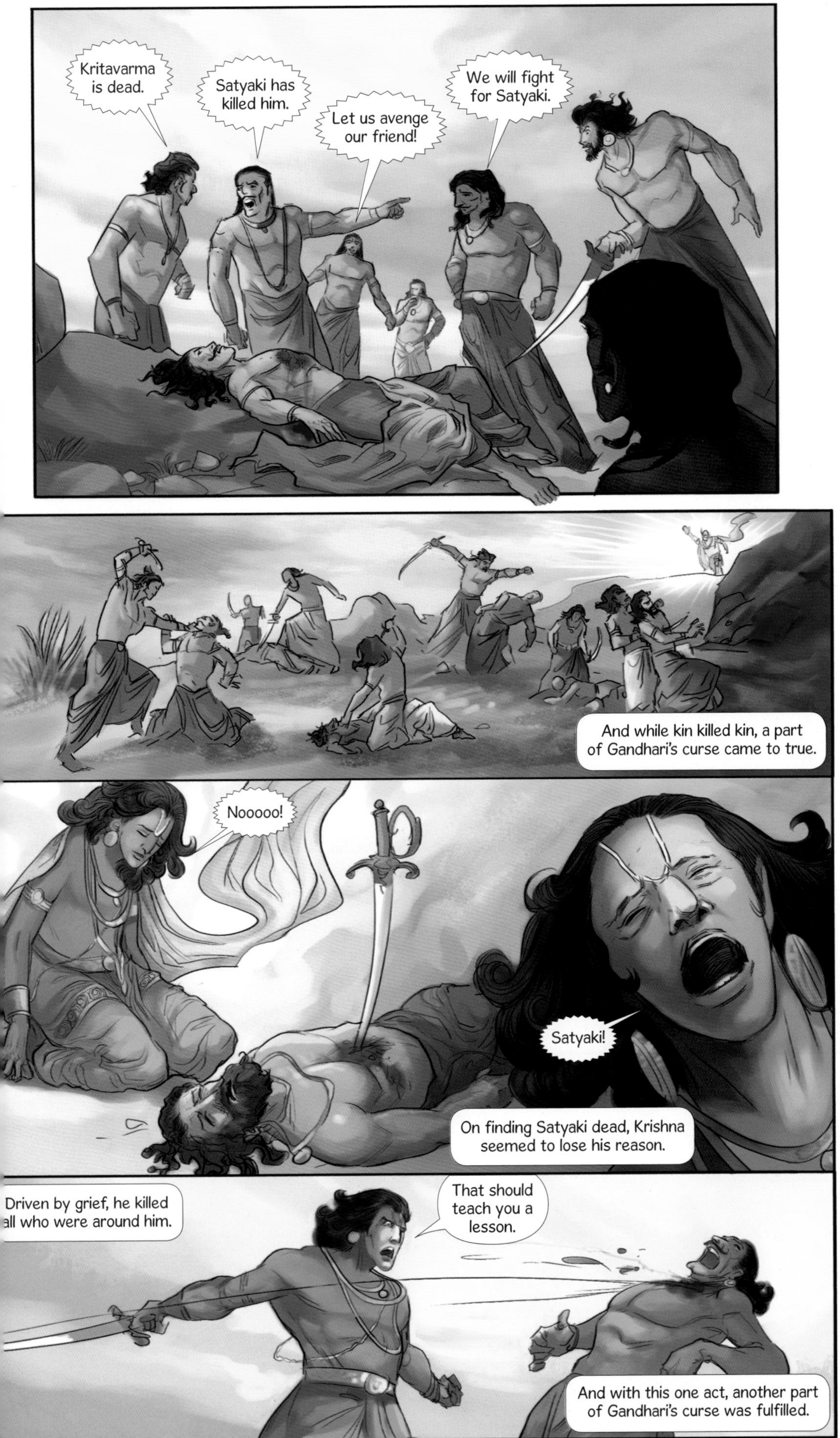
Kritavarma is dead.
Satyaki has killed him.
Let us avenge our friend!
We will fight for Satyaki.
And while kin killed kin, a part of Gandhari's curse came to true.
Nooooo!
Satyaki!
On finding Satyaki dead, Krishna seemed to lose his reason.
Driven by grief, he killed all who were around him.
That should teach you a lesson.
And with this one act, another part of Gandhari's curse was fulfilled.

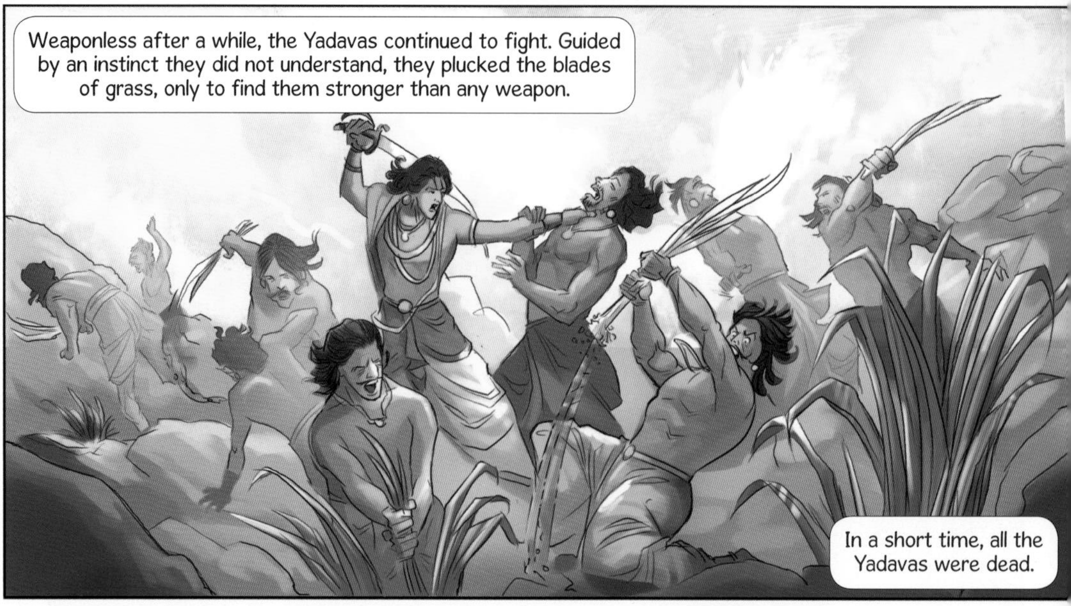
Weaponless after a while, the Yadavas continued to fight. Guided by an instinct they did not understand, they plucked the blades of grass, only to find them stronger than any weapon.
In a short time, all the Yadavas were dead.

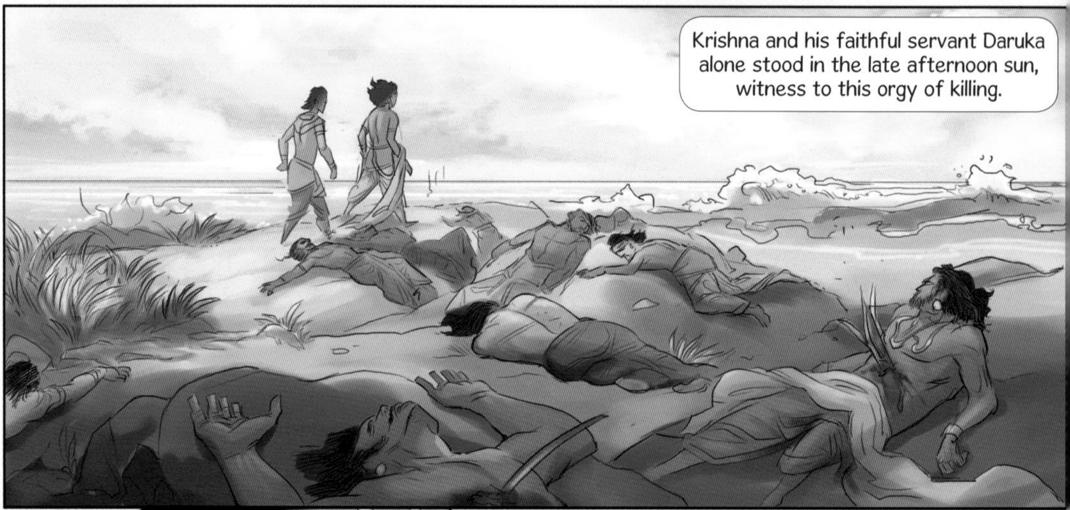
Krishna and his faithful servant Daruka alone stood in the late afternoon sun, witness to this orgy of killing.

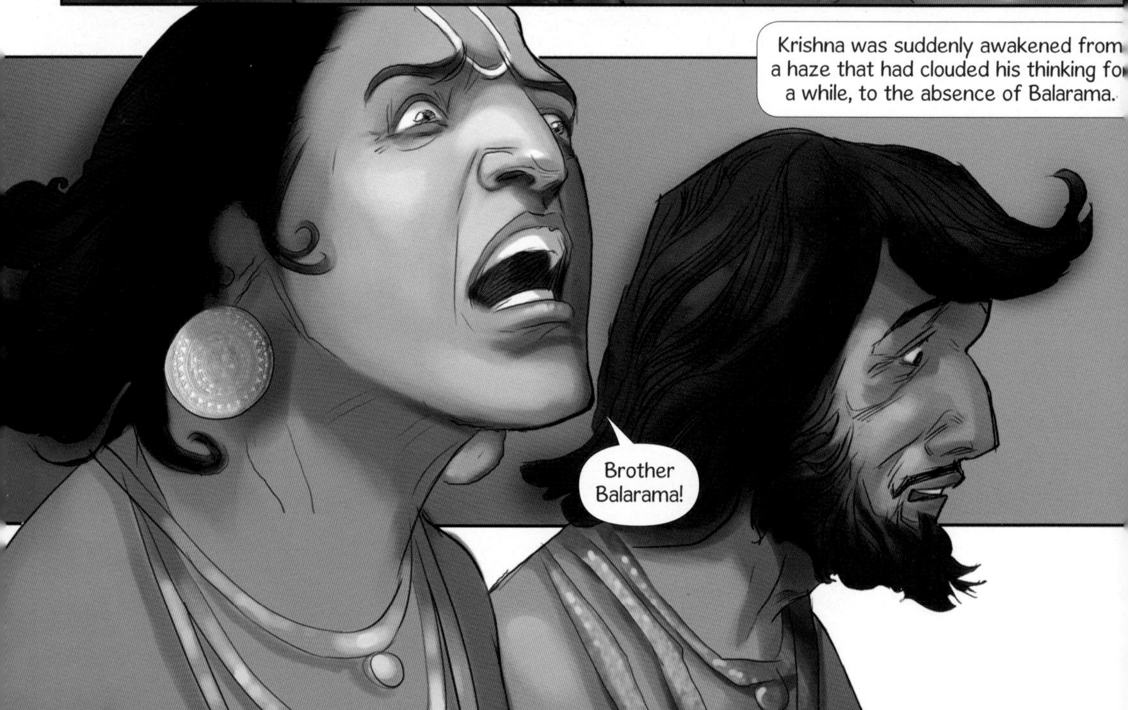
Krishna was suddenly awakened from a haze that had clouded his thinking fo a while, to the absence of Balarama.
Brother Balarama!

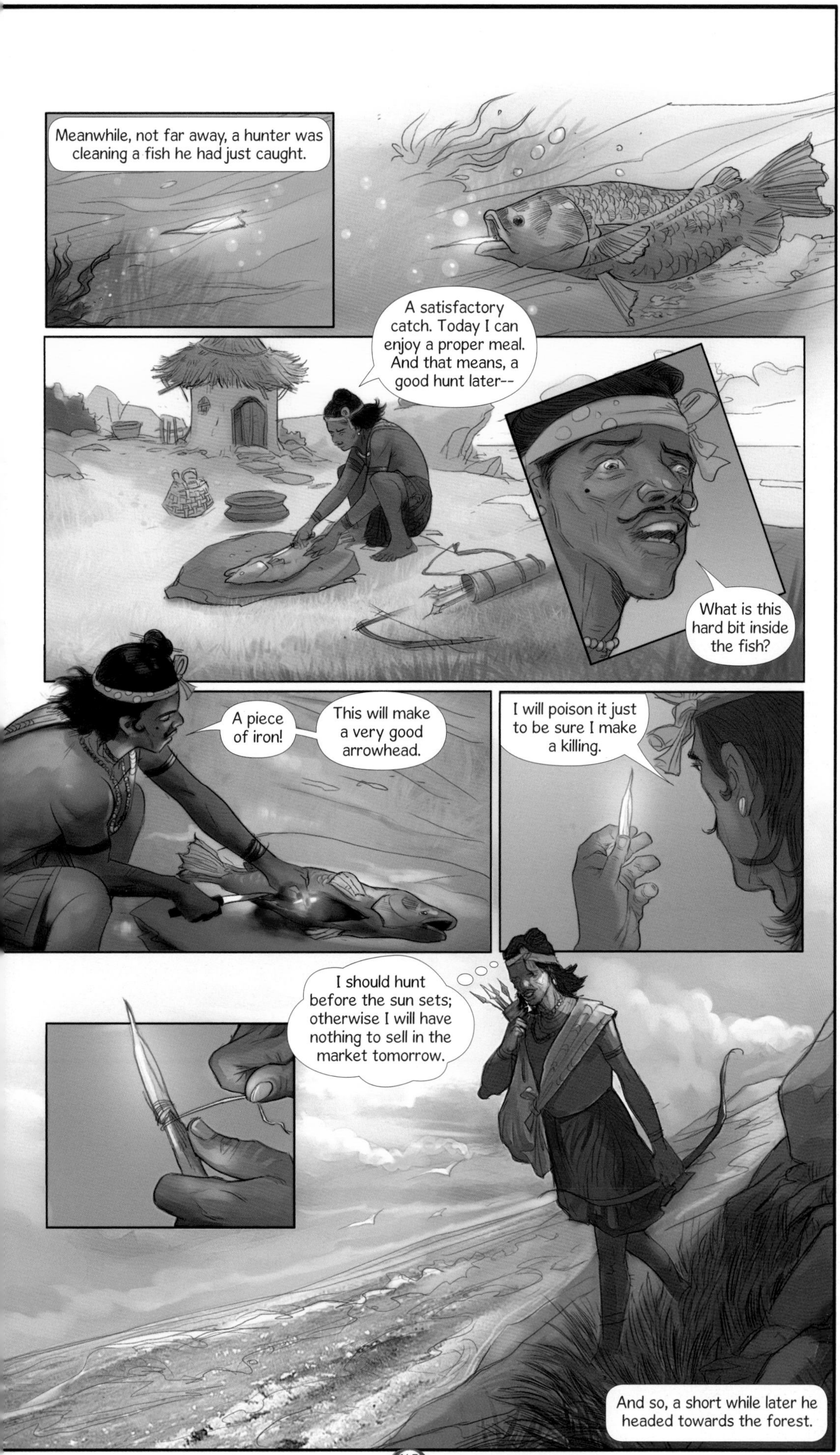
Meanwhile, not far away, a hunter was cleaning a fish he had just caught.
A satisfactory catch. Today I can enjoy a proper meal. And that means, a good hunt later--
What is this hard bit inside the fish?
A piece of iron!
This will make a very good arrowhead.
I will poison it just to be sure I make a killing.
I should hunt before the sun sets; otherwise I will have nothing to sell in the market tomorrow.
And so, a short while later he headed towards the forest.

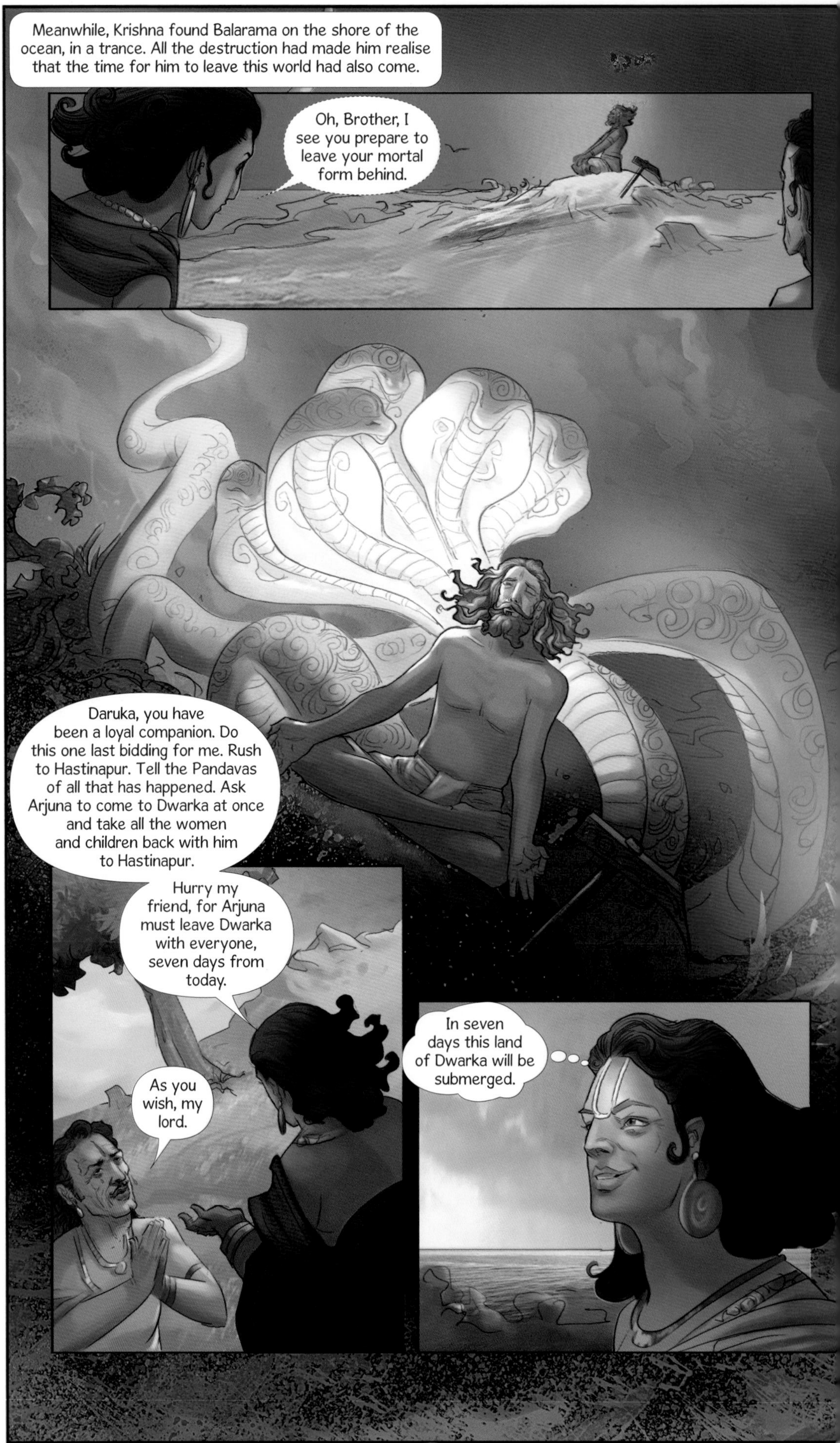
Meanwhile, Krishna found Balarama on the shore of the ocean, in a trance. All the destruction had made him realise that the time for him to leave this world had also come.
Oh, Brother, I see you prepare to leave your mortal form behind.
Daruka, you have been a loyal companion. Do this one last bidding for me. Rush to Hastinapur. Tell the Pandavas of all that has happened. Ask Arjuna to come to Dwarka at once and take all the women and children back with him to Hastinapur.
Hurry my friend, for Arjuna must leave Dwarka with everyone, seven days from today.
As you wish, my lord.
In seven days this land of Dwarka will be submerged.

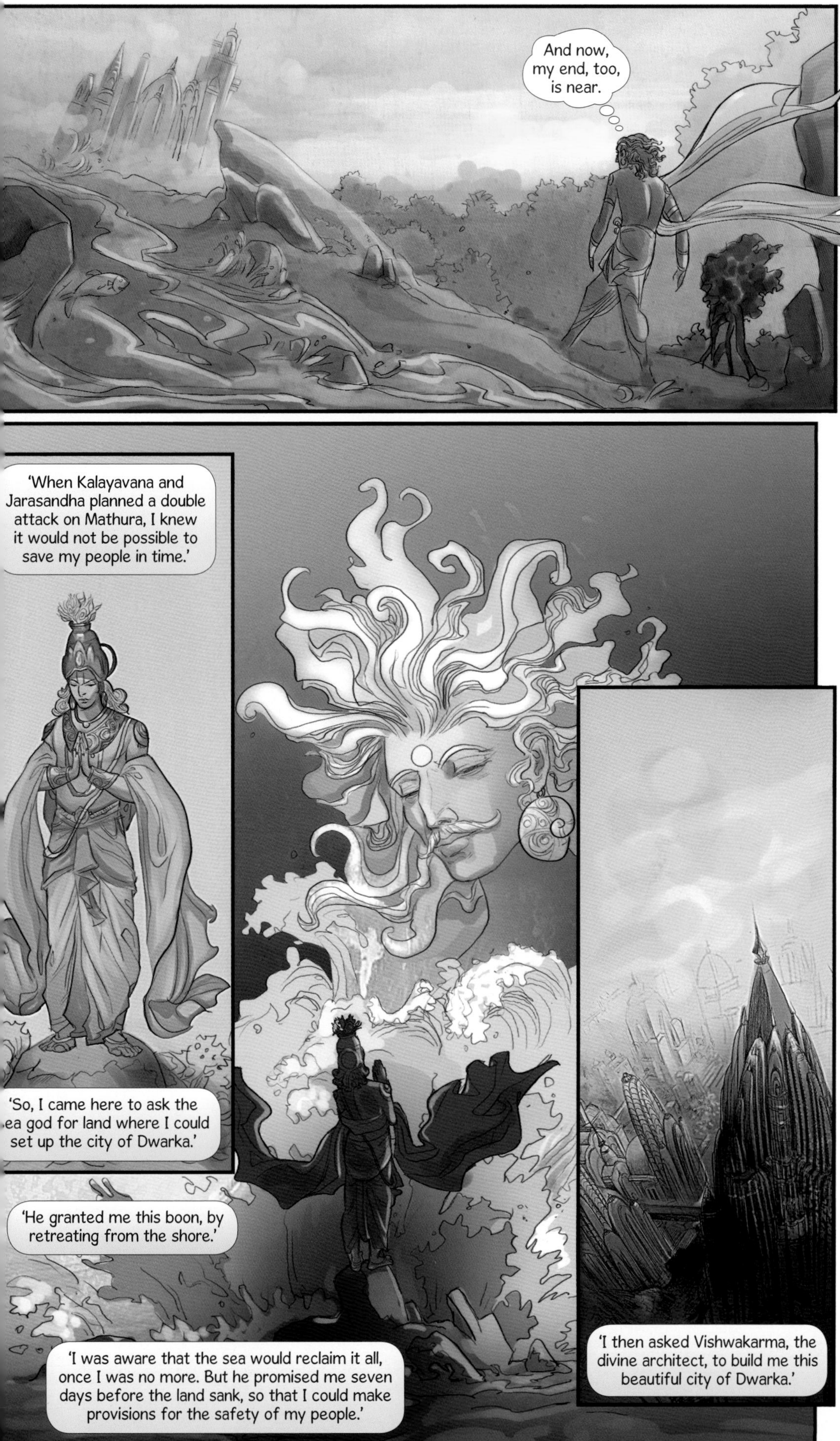
And now, my end, too, is near.
'When Kalayavana and Jarasandha planned a double attack on Mathura, I knew it would not be possible to save my people in time.'
'So, I came here to ask the sea god for land where I could set up the city of Dwarka.'
'He granted me this boon, by retreating from the shore.'
'I was aware that the sea would reclaim it all, once I was no more. But he promised me seven days before the land sank, so that I could make provisions for the safety of my people.'
'I then asked Vishwakarma, the divine architect, to build me this beautiful city of Dwarka.'

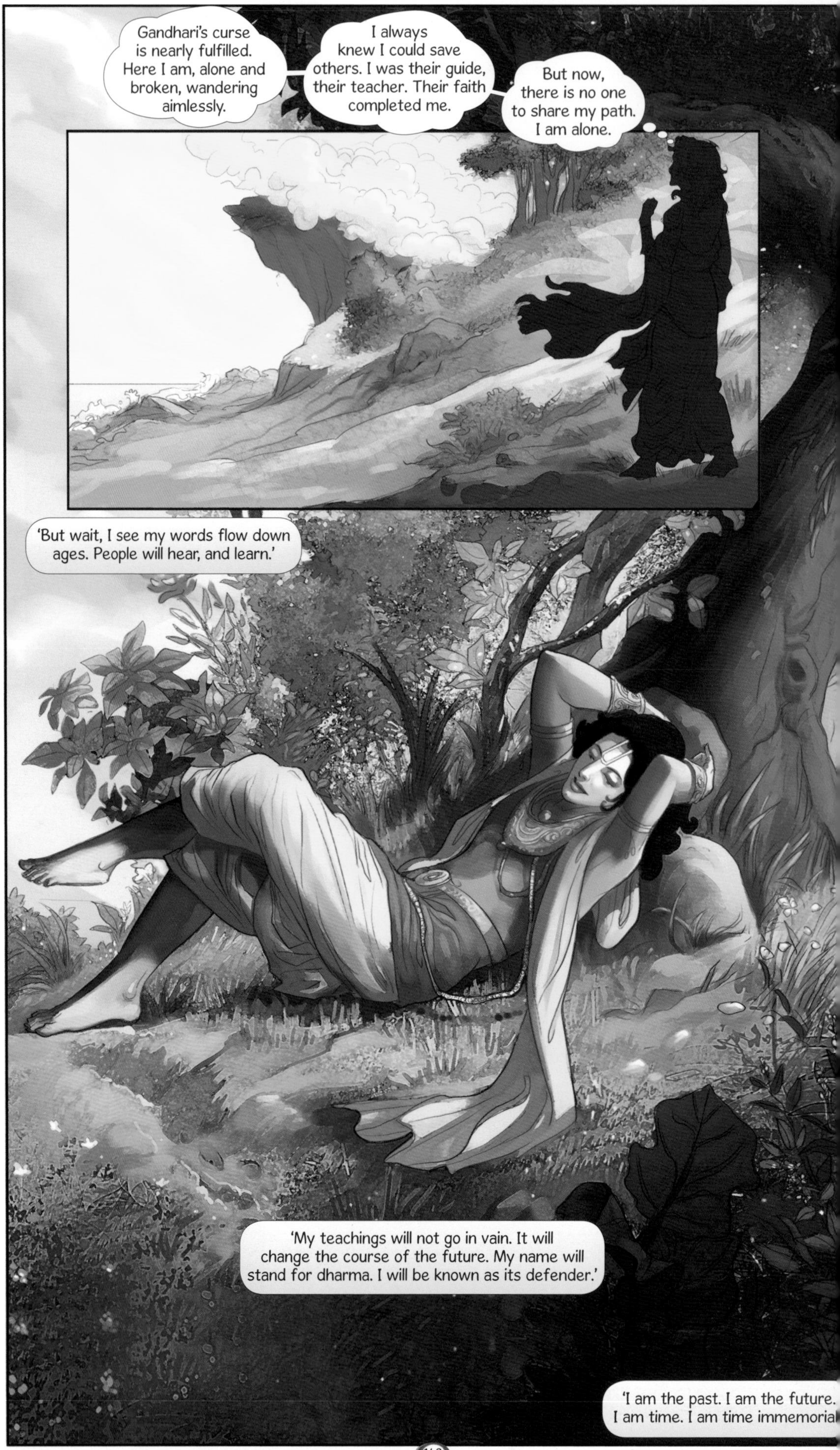
Gandhari's curse is nearly fulfilled. Here I am, alone and broken, wandering aimlessly.
I always knew I could save others. I was their guide, their teacher. Their faith completed me.
But now, there is no one to share my path. I am alone.
'But wait, I see my words flow down ages. People will hear, and learn.'
'My teachings will not go in vain. It will change the course of the future. My name will stand for dharma. I will be known as its defender.'
'I am the past. I am the future.
I am time. I am time immemorial

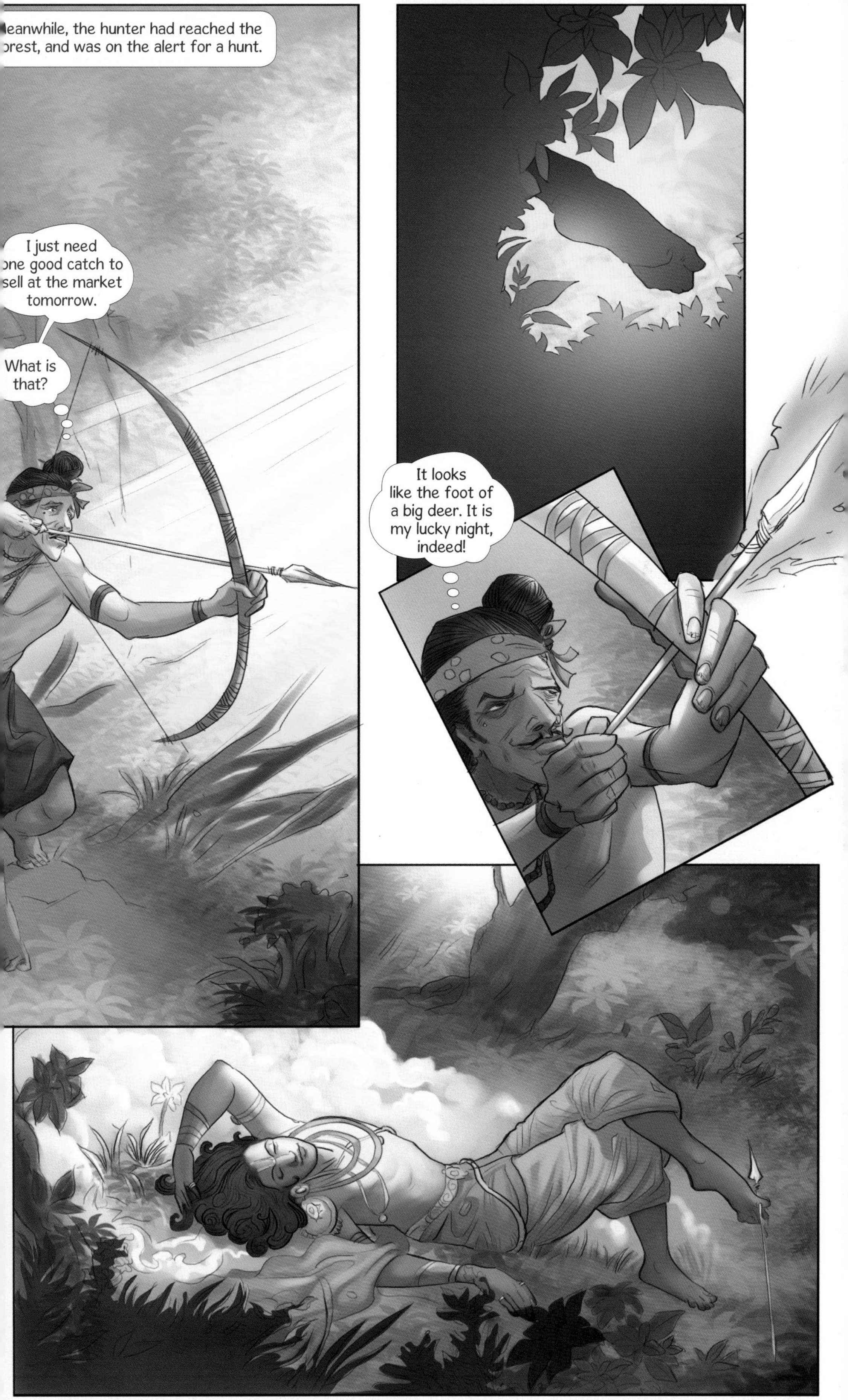
eanwhile, the hunter had reached the orest, and was on the alert for a hunt.
I just need one good catch to sell at the market tomorrow.
What is that?
It looks like the foot of a big deer. It is my lucky night, indeed!

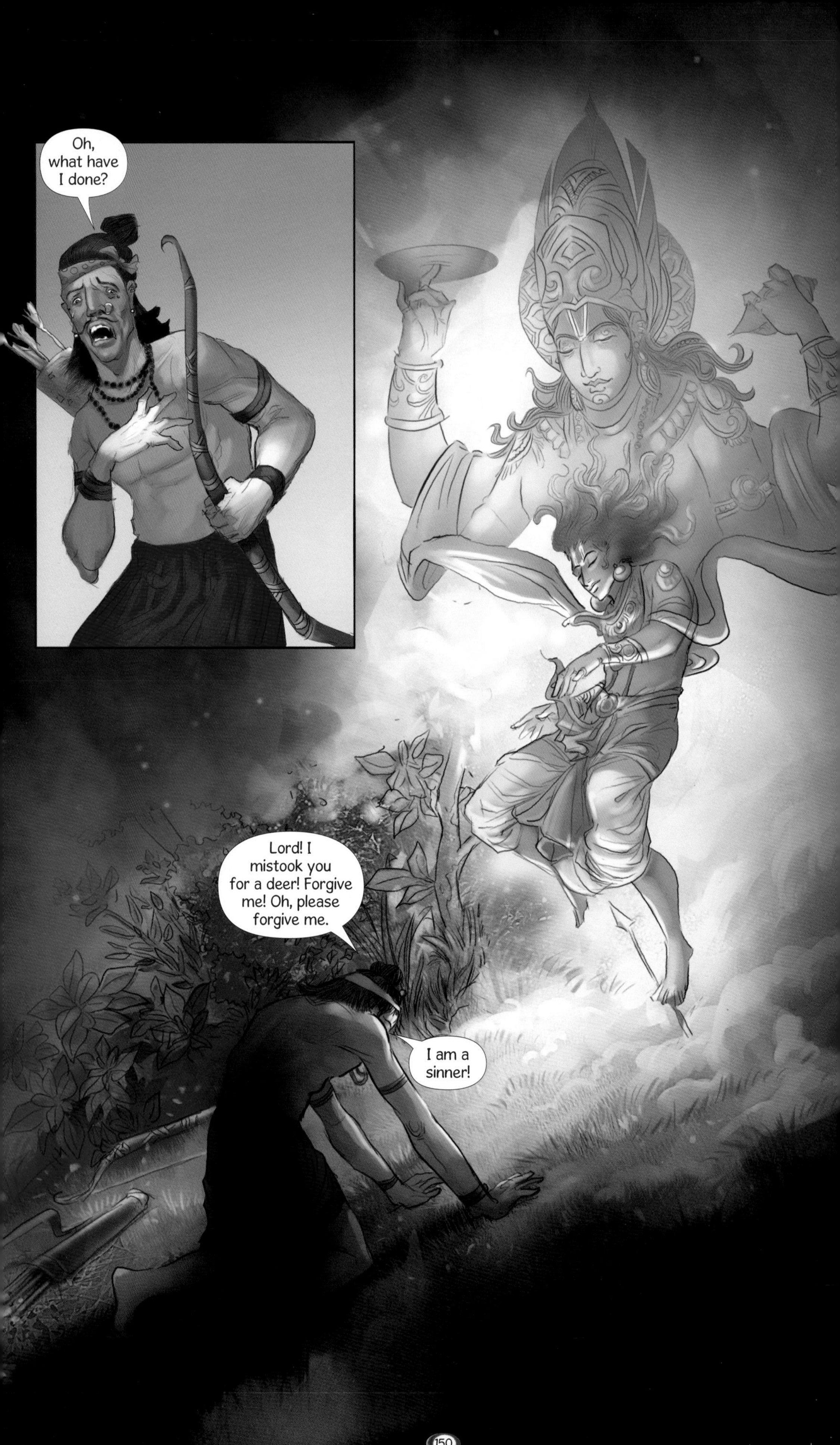
Oh, what have I done?
Lord! I mistook you for a deer! Forgive me! Oh, please forgive me.
I am a sinner!

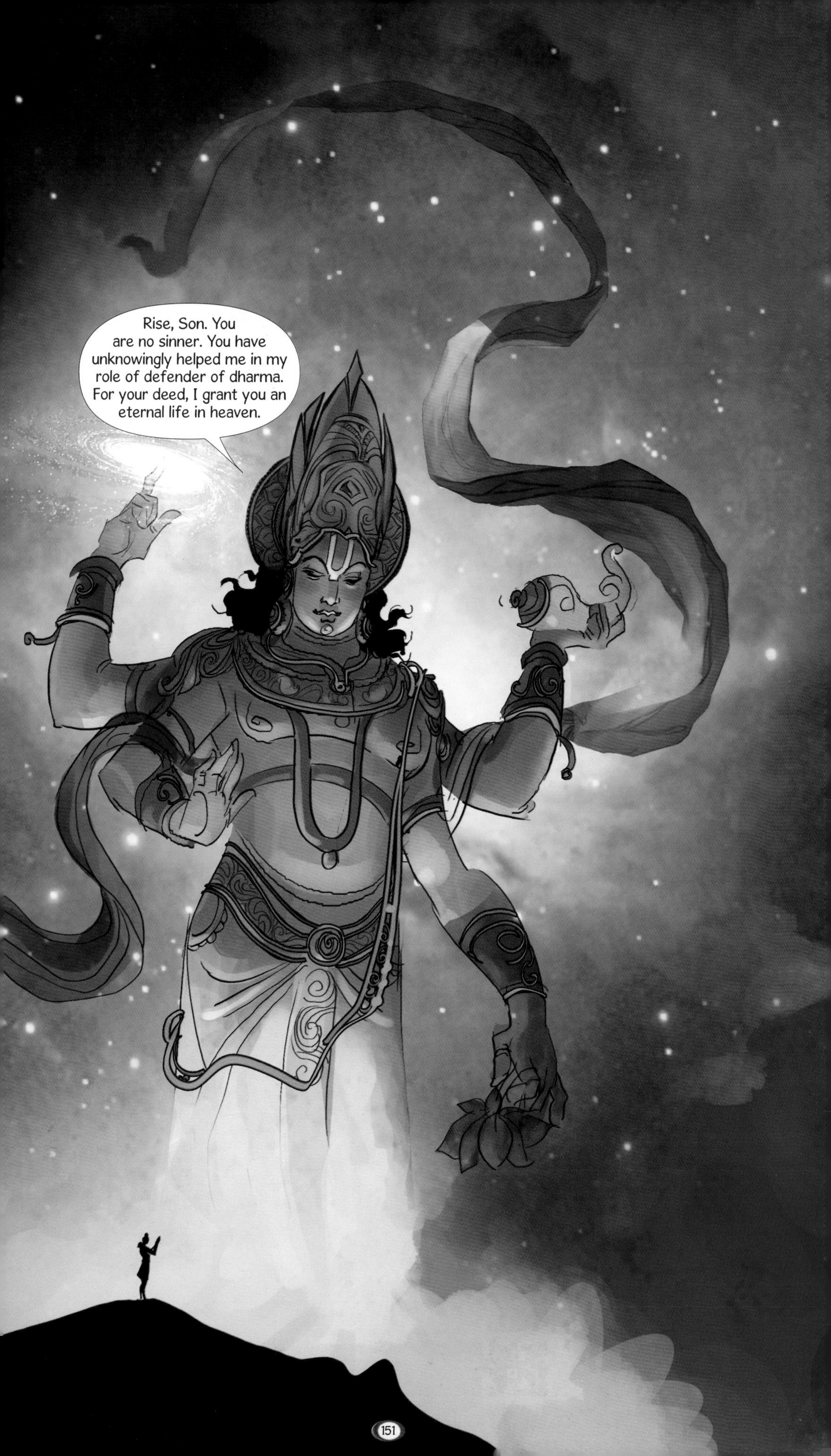
Rise, Son. You are no sinner. You have unknowingly helped me in my role of defender of dharma. For your deed, I grant you an eternal life in heaven.

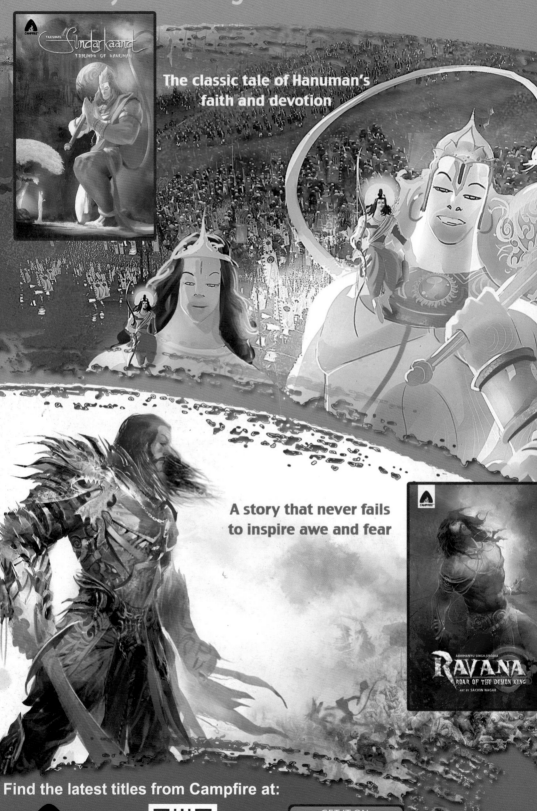